I0525508

A GLITTERING PERIL

Catrin Surovell Mysteries
Book Three

Angela Ranson

SAPERE
BOOKS

A GLITTERING PERIL

Published by Sapere Books.

24 Trafalgar Road, Ilkley, LS29 8HH

saperebooks.com

ISBN: 978-0-85495-631-9

Dedicated with love to:
Jean, Jeanice, Pearl, Stephen, Martha, Vance, Lenny, Hilda, Gloria,
Jeff and Liz

And in memory of three beloved uncles:
Albert, Sammy and Myles

ACKNOWLEDGEMENTS

I would like to thank my friends on the Board of Trustees for the York Literature Festival — Rob, Sally, Alex, Chloe, Shelby, Julia and Vybarr. They have all been very supportive and encouraging, and agreed that Catrin could make a guest appearance in this year's festival program.

Thanks also to Isla at Criminally Good Books and Kirstie at Fox Lane Books for making the Catrin Surovell series part of their fantastic stock of crime fiction.

Also, I would like to thank everyone who reads the blogs and the newsletters and visits my website. You make it all worth it.

CAST OF CHARACTERS

Members of the Queen Elizabeth's Court on Progress
Catrin Surovell, Countess of Ashbourne, Lady of the Queen's Bedchamber
Lucy Howard, Lady of the Queen's Bedchamber
Florie Genevois, her maid servant
Angharad Surovell, Dowager Baroness Aberavon, Catrin's mother
Pierrick de Bourbon, Comte de Soissons
Thibault and Symon, his body servants
Lord Robert Dudley, Knight of the Garter
Sir William Cecil, Secretary of State
Henry Carey, Baron Hunsdon, the queen's first cousin
Bartholemew Walsall, Viscount Walsall
Mistress Kat Ashley and Mistress Blanche Parry, ladies of the bedchamber
Finn, a page
Master Blacquier, a harbinger

Progress Hosts
Lord North, master of the Charterhouse
Griffin Petre, Lord Heatherleigh, master of Saintlow Hall
Master Ronald, his steward
Lord John Grey, master of Pyrgo Palace
Lady Mary Grey, his wife
Master Anthony Grey, his son
Sir William Petre, master of Ingatestone

Other

Alice, a lost maiden

Godfrey Breen, a baker's apprentice

Edrys Pedler, Lady Angharad's apprentice

.

CHAPTER ONE

July 1561

Catrin Surovell, Countess of Ashbourne, raised her arm and let her *stiletto* fly. She felt the tip of the blade leave her fingers, and then the knife vanished into the early morning mist that swirled around her. She closed her eyes and waited, until the silence was broken by a soft *whump* and she knew she had hit her target.

The mists before her thinned, clouds drifting lazily out of the way, and she could see the straw bale with its painted rings twenty paces in front of her. The *stiletto*'s hilt was protruding from the right side of the centre circle — a most acceptable result, in the current circumstances. And far more satisfying than the papers in her chamber, which she had abandoned despite their urgency.

She pushed them out of her mind and walked toward the bale, holding the skirt of her travelling costume up out of the sand of the tiltyard. In front of her loomed Greenwich Palace, currently in a state of chaos as every servant in every building worked frantically to prepare for the court to leave for Queen Elizabeth's annual journey around the kingdom. In contrast, the vast open space of Greenwich Park behind her was utterly serene. On that chill, damp morning, even the birds were quiet.

Perhaps that was why Catrin noticed the faint crunch of a footstep on the lane. She spun around, her silken hood fanning outward like the wings of a bird, and spotted a round-shouldered figure in plain doublet and hose in the distance. He was certainly not a hunter, for the constant restless movement of his feet and hands would have alerted any prey. Nor was he a courtier; if he were, he would not be approaching from the direction of the park. He was a stranger, and one with a distinct air of menace about him. She could almost feel the heat of his anger.

Catrin flipped the knife in her hand, ready to throw. "What-ho! State thy pleasure, or begone."

The figure did not respond, but he clenched his fists as if considering a means of attack. Catrin strode toward him, lifting her blade with its tip between her fingers, and the figure immediately retreated into the mist. She stopped, listening, and heard the faint squeak of leather shoes on wet grass. The man was retreating rapidly; already he was too far away for her *stiletto* to reach.

The chapel bells started ringing then, bright solemn notes calling everyone to the morning service. Catrin sheathed her knife and picked up her cloak, dismissing the man from her mind — at least until he had the courage to face her.

Catrin emerged from the palace with Mistress Kat Ashley, the queen's former governess, beside her, and the two of them fell into their place in the procession going down to the Thames. In the courtyard behind them, hundreds of carts sat piled high with household goods, guarded by the servants who were responsible for them. Men in the queen's livery darted between them with their hands full of scrolls, recording everything they saw. These were the harbingers, who kept lists of everyone on the progress who was entitled to meals and a place to sleep. They travelled constantly alongside the travelling court, telling people where to lodge and at what times they could gather to dine.

"Look at them all," Catrin murmured. "Going on progress seems to require as many supplies as going to war."

"More, I fear." Mistress Ashley gave a great sigh. "It turns the royal court into nothing more than a travelling village."

Catrin hid a smile. "I sense you are not so fond of the annual progress as the queen is."

"'Tis naught but trouble," Mistress Ashley said, and jumped when the blast of trumpets rent the air. It seemed to be a sign for the harbingers; they galloped off, and the dust of their departure had barely settled when a second trumpet-call gave the signal for the carts to follow. Wheels creaked into motion, horses shook their manes in mild protest at the weight they had to draw, and dozens of chamberers, cooks, maids and stableboys jumped onto the nearest cart so they did not have to find their own means of transport.

The rumble of wheels shook the ground under their feet as Catrin and Mistress Ashley joined the courtiers and ladies walking in solemn stateliness down to the water-door on the Thames. There they were sent to the queen's barge by the harbinger Master Blacquier, where they found that one man had already taken a place near the stern. He rose to his feet when they arrived and gave a somewhat stiff courtly bow. "My lady Ashbourne. Mistress Ashley."

Catrin curtsied in return. "My lord North. I did not know you were joining us for this royal visit to the mint. I thought we would first see you tonight, when we arrive at your home, the Charterhouse."

Lord North drew his lips inward, making his face look very flat. Even his nose seemed to retreat. It made for a strong contrast to his eyes, which bulged with barely restrained hostility. "I only intend to travel with you; once we are in the city, I will return to my home to ensure all is at the ready."

"I'm sure it will be lovely," Catrin said, and decided to pull aside the polite veil drawn over those protruding eyes, merely to see what would happen. "You must be very proud to be the first host for this year's progress."

He smothered a derisive snort, which intrigued Catrin all the more. "Of course, your ladyship. And *you* must be very proud to be travelling so closely with the queen. Others more experienced with the duties of the nobility on progress are usually given such a position."

Ah, so that was the source of his irritation. "Oh? Such as whom, my lord?"

Wisely, he did not answer, choosing instead to greet another lady of the bedchamber as she stepped cautiously onto the boat. Catrin turned away from him, and caught Mistress Ashley glaring at a woman with tight curls framing her face, who seemed to be considering boarding the queen's barge.

Mistress Ashley made an irritated sound. "Oh, she's a saucy creature, that one."

"What do you mean, mistress?"

Mistress Ashley jerked her chin toward the woman. "Lady Worcester," she spat. "She betrayed our queen's mother to her enemies, and then dares to show her face for a great event such as this."

"It does seem like a strange thing to do," Catrin said. "Surely she will not try to join us — ah, I see that Lord John Grey has spoken to her, and she is moving away."

Mistress Ashley gave a curt nod. "It is well that he was the one to speak to her; he is her kinsman. She is his wife's aunt, and knows that she ought to listen to him."

Lord John Grey watched his troublesome relative move safely out of sight, then boarded the queen's barge. Catrin watched idly as he shuffled slowly toward an empty seat. "The queen intends to lodge with him during this progress, does she not?"

"Yes, he is on the itinerary. However, I'm sure you remember from last year that our queen does not always follow the plan," Mistress Ashley said. "We can never truly say where we will lodge for the next few months."

Another flare of trumpets near the palace announced the arrival of the queen, and all around them men and women turned toward the sound, their eyes alive with excitement as Queen Elizabeth emerged from the crowd. She wore a light silken gown of Tudor green, embroidered with delicate birds and flowers in vivid colours and sewn with jewels at strategic points to dazzle the eye. She wore a smile that seemed to say she was enjoying every second of the day, and most people were probably fooled by it. Not Catrin. She saw that the queen's face was pale and taut, and her hands — with their famously long, white fingers — were fluttering like birds in a cage.

Still, she moved with her customary grace as she stepped onto the barge, and made people smile with her welcome. Catrin escorted her to a place in the bow while the rest of her guests boarded: first, Lord Robert Dudley, the queen's favourite. Then Sir William Cecil, her Secretary of State and closest advisor. Then Mistress Blanche Parry, one of the queen's favourite ladies of the bedchamber, who did not like to travel by water.

She looked ill as the barge rocked under her feet, and fell into the closest seat, landing rather too close to Lord North. He got up to give her room, and promptly tripped over another lady's skirt. The lady squealed, a sudden, shrill sound that cut through the air and startled them all. The queen jumped nearly out of her skin, and to Catrin's horror she lost her balance.

Time slowed to an agonising crawl as Catrin watched the queen's body tilt toward the water. She saw the horror on Lord Robert's face, the fear that filled Sir William's eyes, the lurking pleasure twisting Lord North's lip. She knew no one would move, for to touch the person of the monarch was strictly forbidden — even when failing to do so could mean losing said monarch to the powerful currents of the Thames.

Catrin threw out an arm and grabbed the railing, and the queen latched on just in time. For a horrible second she teetered over the edge, and then her grip tightened on Catrin's arm and she pulled herself upward.

"Fools! Cowards and traitors!" she roared. "Did none of you think to help me?"

"We dared not, Your Majesty," Lord North gasped. "Out of — of — respect for your person."

"*Respect* for my *person*?" the queen spluttered. "Did you not think to hold any respect for my *life*?"

"It happened very quickly, Your Majesty," Lord North said smoothly. "No one had the chance to react."

"Except Lady Catrin," the queen snapped. "And for her quick thinking, I give her hearty thanks."

Catrin put on a smile, her heart still racing. "I am happy to give you the use of my arm, Your Majesty — but I confess that I did not want to go for a swim with you."

A nervous chuckle swept the barge, but the queen did not laugh. "Remember this, all of you: there are times when inaction will subject you to greater punishment than action."

Lord Robert bowed low. "Our humblest apologies, Your Majesty. We beg your forgiveness."

The queen took her seat with an angry huff of breath, showing she was not yet ready to give it. "If I were an ordinary woman, would you then have shown your chivalry?"

"To a lady of such beauty, nobility and grace? Of course, Your Majesty," Lord North said. "It is only the long-held tradition that restrains us."

"Then I must find a gentleman who either knows nothing of this tradition, or nothing of me. Only then will I truly be treated with the proper esteem," the queen retorted. No one dared respond. Every eye lowered, and every shoulder slumped. She lifted her chin, quite satisfied with that reaction, and waved a regal hand. "Let us depart."

The queen insisted on visiting every workshop in the mint, dragging them all amongst the furnaces while she kept a scented handkerchief against her nose to filter out the smell of smoke, sweat and molten metal. Catrin was glad to attend her; she found it fascinating to watch as gold, silver and bronze was melted in crucibles and poured, red-hot and bubbling, onto stone slabs. Men with thick muscled arms watched each pool with eagle eyes, and when it had cooled just enough they used flat shovels to scoop it onto an anvil. Other men then started beating the molten metals into a thin plate using colossal hammers, and the ring of metal against metal seemed to bounce off the walls until it was like the sound was all around them. Catrin was glad that her dear companion Lucy was still travelling with her new husband Lord Pierrick; the noise and heat would have been very distressing for her.

Finally the queen emerged into the quietest of the workshops, where men placed blank circles of the soft hammered metal between iron stamps and struck them with mallets, thus imprinting the coins with the queen's profile. The gentle thud of the mallets and the tinkle of falling coins was a great contrast to the noise and heat of the other workshops, and seemed to calm the queen. She quietly watched the creation of her image several times, and then lifted her chin, as if a thought had just occurred. "Lady Catrin."

Catrin immediately moved closer to her and curtsied. "Yes, Your Majesty?"

"Is Baroness Aberavon joining the court on progress?"

Catrin blinked. Baroness Aberavon was part of the queen's court by reason of her status, but she attended only on the greatest of occasions. Her age did not allow for more. "She did not plan to come, Your Majesty, but I am sure she would attend you if you so wish."

The queen picked up a gold coin and brushed her thumb over the pristine lines of the fresh engraving. "I wish to see her today," she said thoughtfully. "Prithee go now to her home and request that she join us at Lord North's Charterhouse for the evening meal."

Immediately Catrin wondered why, but knew better than to ask. "Yes, Your Majesty."

"Take one of the yeomen as an escort, if your own servants are still in Ashbourne."

"They are; thank you, Your Majesty." Catrin curtsied. "We will meet you at the Charterhouse this afternoon."

The queen let the coin fall and it landed amongst its fellows with a faint but cheerful jingle. "Until then, my talisman."

CHAPTER TWO

Catrin and her escort travelled through the city on horseback, and soon arrived at the tall, narrow house squeezed in between the Queen's Wardrobe building and a bustling inn. The door opened before Catrin could knock, revealing a woman wearing a simple gown of grey, with a wimple over her hair that covered part of the scar that stretched down over her cheek from her right temple. It was the baroness herself — a woman known as Niada to the poor women and children who came to her for help with their troubles and pains, and as Angharad Surovell, Baroness Aberavon, to the nobility. Most called her Lady Angharad, but to Catrin, she was simply "My lady mother."

Lady Angharad's compelling blue eyes sparkled and she flung her arms wide. "Never mind the formality, my kitten. Enter freely; you are welcome here."

Catrin gave her mother a hug. "It's so good to see you," she said, and followed her into the house. The kitchen smelled fresh and fragrant, for bunches of dried herbs hung from the rafters, and a cauldron was bubbling on a low fire. "What are you making?"

"I must temper the juice of southystel in hot water. The fairies have told me that we will soon have a spate of fevers; it will be best to have a supply of the cure prepared."

Lady Angharad always attributed her own wisdom to the fairies, which greatly enhanced her reputation as a wisewoman and healer. It amused Catrin to pretend to believe it too. "Can you leave it for an evening?" she asked. "The queen wishes you to join us at the Charterhouse for tonight's grand feast."

Her mother pursed her lips. "Feast?"

"Tonight the annual progress begins. The queen intends to spend three days with Lord North at the Charterhouse before we travel to Wanstead and the home of Lord Richard Rich. As the first host, I am sure Lord North has planned something extraordinary for the first night."

"If the queen wishes it, I will certainly attend." Her mother rubbed her forefinger over a scar on her wrist. "However, I do not find anything to celebrate in this progress."

Catrin chuckled. "Nor does Sir William Cecil, or Lord Robert Dudley. Gathering all the supplies and horses — and the servants needed to take care of them — has nearly driven them both mad."

Her mother crossed to the fire and stirred the mixture in the cauldron. "And they are aware of the danger, no doubt."

"Very much so," Catrin said. "You need not fret, Mother. The queen is travelling with a reduced court — fewer ladies-in-waiting, for example, and none of the maids of honour — but she will be surrounded by a full complement of yeoman of the guard."

"And still it is dangerous. She shall travel on the lanes and byways, leaving herself vulnerable to lurking vagrants. She shall sojourn in homes where the chambers are not designed to keep naysayers away from her. And, worst of all, she has deliberately chosen to visit men who are hostile to her person and her reign."

Catrin could not disagree. "Including the first host, Lord North."

"Yes; he firmly supported Queen Mary, our queen's poor misguided sister." Lady Angharad glanced at the door to make sure it was firmly closed against prying ears. "I have been told that he once tried to secure a prince for Queen Mary, by offering to purchase a poor woman's newborn son."

Catrin shivered at the thought. "Thank God he did not succeed."

"Aye, thank God indeed." Her mother shook her head. "Verily, my kitten, it seems a foolish risk for our current queen to stay at his home."

"The queen knows that, I think, for she seems as nervous as she is excited."

"Then why go?"

"As she has told Lord Robert several times, she considers the progress worth the risk, for she longs to form strong bonds with her nobles and the local people." Catrin quirked her lip. "And there are other advantages."

"Such as?"

"She is about to spend weeks enjoying endless pageantry and revels. There will be plays, tableaux, poetry, dancing, music and singing, performances of every kind. Last year she met most of the Roman gods and a fair few Greek maidens, not to mention a dozen nymphs and fairies, who all pledged undying love in beautiful blank verse."

Her mother chuckled. "I can see why that would be a welcome change from everyday life — if the players know their craft."

"Fortunately, even terrible ones offer amusement of sorts." Catrin glanced out the window, noticing the sharpening slant of the summer sunshine coming in. "We should leave as soon as possible, if we are to meet the queen at the proper hour."

"So we should. I will go and find a gown fine enough for court." She stirred the cauldron once more, then handed the wooden spoon to Catrin. "You take care that it does not boil dry; if I lose the batch, the fairies will be displeased."

"Alas." Catrin hid a smile. "How terrible that would be."

Behind them receded the peaked roofs of London, with their thin columns of smoke rising steadily to join the haze that hovered over the city. Before them, the fields faded into a dark green smudge against the delicate blue of a late afternoon sky. The air smelled of freshly turned earth warmed under a summer sun, and Catrin breathed it in with a sense of deep contentment. Her mother, too, lifted her face to the breeze with a smile as they approached Fynsburie Field. "I should stop to gather some linden leaves," she said. "They must be gathered in July, and such a day as this would be ideal. Is there time enough, do you think?"

Catrin drew the reins of her horse, Ariadne, between her fingers, considering. "The ground is not much disturbed, so I wager that the court has not yet passed. We may be ahead of the queen, and could safely stop for a few minutes."

"Hold, my lady, if you will," their escort said. "I see a gathering of men; it may be best to put some distance between us before we stop."

Catrin peered ahead, and could soon confirm that there were men on the path before them. Several were walking around in a sort of circle, looking down at the ground. One was astride a massive black stallion, and wore a breastplate that gleamed dull silver. "Why, 'tis no threat, goodman. Lord Robert Dudley is amongst them. He too must be travelling ahead of the queen."

Lord Robert himself saw them then, and raised a hand in a weary greeting. "Stay back, my ladies — there is trouble here."

"What is it?" Lady Angharad asked. "Is someone ill? Can I help?"

"I fear not, my lady, " Lord Robert said. "He is beyond help."

Catrin slid from her horse and drew close enough to see the limp figure lying on the path. It was a man, dressed simply in a rust-coloured doublet. His shirt had lace at the wrists and collar, suggesting he was a man of some repute, but it was dirty and torn. "He is not a courtier, is he? I do not recognize him."

"No, he is certainly not a courtier. He has a pack on him, but no coins, and no letters or emblems that would tell us his name." Lord Robert scowled. "I wonder if he was left here deliberately, to taint the queen's progress from its infancy."

Catrin reached out a finger to flick the dead man's collar away from his neck. The skin was mottled and discoloured, so it was difficult to see if there was a pattern there. "He may have been strangled, but he may have died naturally. It is difficult to tell."

"I take him for a vagrant," Lord Robert said. "On his way to the church for alms, no doubt."

Catrin's mother urged her own horse closer and looked down at the man with sorrow on her face. "Poor man … no family to take care of him," she said. "Send him to my home; my apprentice will alert the coroner's clerk."

"Thank you, my lady," Lord Robert said, and nodded to two of his men. They began to prepare the body for removal, but Catrin suspected they would not be fast enough.

"Do you hear that?" she asked Lord Robert. He listened for a moment, then raised his fist to get his men's attention.

"The queen and her court approaches," he said. "Get him out of sight — now. Go behind that copse of trees until she has passed."

The men jumped into action, and Catrin resumed her seat on her horse. The three of them moved off the path just in time, for moments later a great cloud of dust arose on the horizon. A dozen horses galloped into view, with men in gleaming satin doublets astride them. Behind them rode the gentlemen and pensioners, wearing an assortment of livery and court clothing. Then the knights on powerful horses, glittering in polished armour or resplendent in brightly patterned ornamental cloth coverings. A company of men followed in tight formation, their scarlet robes marking them as aldermen. Then came the serjeants of arms and the heralds of arms, in full armour polished so bright as to be blinding.

The Lord Mayor of London followed, weighted down with his golden chain of office and carrying the queen's sceptre. After him came Lord Hunsdon, as was his feudal right, carrying the queen's sword. And then, finally, the queen herself, on a horse of purest white. Her red-gold hair shone amongst the darker colours around her, and even the mask she wore to protect her complexion did not cast doubt on who she was. This was the Queen of England, by divine right and the will of Henry VIII, and all were expected to acknowledge her.

The queen beckoned to the three of them with a regal hand, and they urged their horses forward to join her. It felt like becoming one with a powerful force as they moved together at a steady pace over the fields, one which drew people from their work in cottages and fields so they could watch in awe as they passed. It made Catrin feel proud and humbled at the same time.

They entered the city at Aldgate, and found the way lined with the craftsmen of London, each wearing the livery and badge of their trade. The streets, normally so muddy, were freshly gravelled with sand, and the houses were draped with patterned fabric, thick arras cloth and ribbons of silk and satin. People leaned out of windows, waving flags and handkerchiefs as they cheered and shouted for their queen. The queen waved back, calling down blessings upon them that could barely be heard in the din.

The noise kept growing, bouncing off the high stone walls of the Charterhouse that rose up before them. Then it suddenly dropped, as the Lord Mayor and aldermen split off from the greater company to return to their homes and the harbingers set to work, diverting some of the queen's court to their lodgings outside. Meanwhile, the queen and a select group were ushered through the gates and into a large courtyard.

The gates closed, and the sounds of the city were abruptly silenced. The queen led the way to the doors, where a dozen stableboys stood ready to take the horses, and they all dismounted. Lord Robert moved to help the queen, but Lord Hunsdon stepped in ahead of him. Lord Robert's mouth thinned with displeasure, but he simply turned to help Catrin's mother instead, and then Catrin herself.

They fell in behind the queen as she approached the door, which was set neatly inside an archway of yellow stone. Lord North himself emerged on cue, carrying a small domed coffer in his hands, and sank down to his knees. "Your Majesty the queen," he said, loudly enough for his voice to carry despite the clattering and chatter all around them. "I humbly offer my home to you, and pray that you will allow me to abide with you as long as it suits your pleasure."

The queen removed her mask, revealing a flushed and happy face and sparkling dark eyes. "We receive your grant with pleasure, my lord."

He held up the coffer. "Allow me to give you this gift, as a symbol of my delight and devotion."

"We thank you," the queen said, and Catrin moved forward to take the coffer. As she had been instructed, she opened it toward the queen, turning herself in a half-circle so the queen could fully see the gift inside.

Resting on a bed of red velvet was a golden ouche, with a table-cut diamond at the centre surrounded by a swirl of turquoise and sapphires. Catrin knew of such jewellery, designed to be worn either as a pendant or a brooch, but this was a piece far richer than she had ever seen. Indeed, far richer than most people had ever seen. Even Lord Robert's eyebrow quirked in surprise, and the queen herself was momentarily silenced. "What a beautiful piece," she said at last. "My hearty thanks to you, Lord North."

"You are most welcome, Your Majesty," Lord North said, and then rose to his feet to indicate that the queen should enter the house ahead of him. It was then that his eyes fell on the ouche, and he gave a little start of dismay.

"Did you — where did —" He stepped forward, crowding Catrin away from the doorway. "Lady Catrin, what have you done?"

"Nothing, I assure you," Catrin said coolly. "Of what do you accuse me?"

"Deception." Lord North pointed a shaking finger at the ouche. "That is not my gift. I have never seen it before."

Catrin glanced at the queen's retreating back. "Speak softly, my lord, we do not need any further trouble this day. What was your gift?"

"An alabaster cup. It was worth a great deal, though not as much as that thing. Are you sure you did not put it there?"

"I did not, nor do I have reason to make such an exchange." Catrin closed the coffer and held it up so she could examine the lock. "Where was this coffer kept until now?"

"When I returned from travelling with the queen to the mint, I placed it on a table in the Great Hall. I thought it safe enough there, for it was locked and secured to the table with a chain."

"Who had the key?"

"Only myself and my steward, and he has been with the harbingers all afternoon."

"I wager that it was not your steward who opened it. I see scratches, and something is rattling loose inside, so I would guess that the person who made the exchange broke the lock."

"But why? Why would anyone break into a coffer not to steal a gift, but to exchange it?"

"I do not know, my lord." Lord Robert's voice rose in Catrin's mind, suggesting that someone was trying to taint the queen's progress by leaving a corpse along her path. Could this have the same purpose? Surely not … but the possibility did exist. And that made Catrin long for Lucy, with her innocent insight and clever mind. She was returning to London soon, to take her rest before joining the queen's court on progress. Perhaps she could be persuaded to come and help. "But I will do my best to find out."

CHAPTER THREE

Rich hangings of satin in many shades of blue covered the stone walls of Lord North's Great Chamber, creating the illusion that the feast was taking place within the petals of a flower. More flowers, all blue and purple and surrounded by fronds of green, spilled out of vases all along the tables that had been pushed back against the walls once the feast was over. They left a large open space for dancing, which soon filled up as the musicians took up their places at the back of the room.

"Lady Catrin, attend upon me. And Lady Angharad, I wish to ask you a question."

The queen's voice cut through the chatter and the first tentative notes of lutes and tambors. Catrin and Lady Angharad immediately wove through the crowd and joined her on her dais at the front of the room, where she was resting in a cushioned chair under a woven canopy of state.

Catrin curtsied with a smile. "Do you intend to ask my mother for a game of triumph, Your Majesty?" she asked. "If so, I warn you that she becomes strangely fierce when playing cards."

Lady Angharad sank down beside her. "No, my kitten, it is about Queen Anne," she said gently. "The queen wishes to ask about her lady mother."

Catrin felt herself freeze, her breath coming fast. No one talked about Queen Anne; it was a sure way to incur the queen's anger. "Your Majesty — I'm sorry — she didn't know —"

"Fret not, Lady Catrin; she is correct," the queen said, and tilted her head. "How did you know, Lady Angharad?"

"I could think of no other reason for your invitation tonight." A certain sorrowful tenderness filled Lady Angharad's eyes. "As ever, I am your willing servant, Your Majesty. Ask whatever you wish."

The queen glanced cautiously around but had no cause to worry; Lord Robert was ensuring no one came too close. "Do you remember much of your time as her lady-in-waiting?"

Lady Angharad tilted her chin, gazing over the queen's shoulder as if looking into the past. "Aye, I do. I remember the day she married your father the king... I remember her interest in religious reform... I remember her love for you." She chuckled. "But mostly I remember the sewing. Your mother kept her ladies busy, Your Majesty. We sewed for the poor every day, so she would have alms to give whenever we were out of the palace. Always it was a set of bedsheets and two shillings for pregnant women, and shirts or skirts for the poor with one shilling."

"That was very kind," Catrin murmured, and the queen took a deep breath.

"My mother *was* kind — not many people remember that. But I do. I have been thinking about our last time together at Hatfield... It must have been less than a month before she was imprisoned." The queen looked up, her gaze defiant. "She played with me and sang me to sleep, and we spent hours dressing in different kirtles and trying on velvet caps."

"A lovely memory," Lady Angharad said. "I am not surprised you remember that, Your Majesty. You were always so clever; far in advance of other children of a similar age."

"You flatter, my lady, but I will still accept the compliment." The queen laughed, but a note of urgency dulled the humour in it. "I will also accept your company, should you find it possible to attend us for the first leg of our progress."

Lady Angharad abruptly pressed her fingertips to the scars on her right hand; a sign of surprise that only Catrin recognized. "I would be happy to attend you, Your Majesty, if you would find me useful."

"I believe I will. I would like to speak about this again — though not tonight," the queen said. "Now, it is time to dance."

After a light, fast galliard or two, Lord North's dancing-master taught them all a new version of the pavane. It was a slow dance with intense and intricate footwork, and Catrin loved the graceful movements and sweeping turns. It was followed by La Volta — a delightful whirl that quite exhausted her. She simply had to step away when that dance was done, catching her breath with a wander along the length of the gallery outside the Great Chamber. It was decorated with the emblems of all the great houses — the bear and ragged staff of Lord Robert, the roses and bull's heads of Lord Hunsdon, the strange dragon-like creatures on Lord North's own shield.

"I apologise that the Ashbourne emblem is not there, Lady Catrin."

Catrin turned toward the voice and kept her face carefully neutral. "I had not noticed its absence, my lord North."

Lord North came closer, his soft dancing slippers shuffling on the flagstone floor. "We thought it best not to use the old earl's emblem. It was a battle axe, and that would be most inappropriate for you."

Catrin turned back to the dragon-like creatures, letting her gaze trace the path of the golden chains that wound around their necks. "You think so?"

"Of course! After all, you will not be taking up weapons in the queen's defence, will you?" He clicked his tongue. "One of the greatest responsibilities of nobility, and you cannot fulfil it."

She chose not to comment. "I have intended to choose my own emblem for some time now," she said instead. "Something that truly reflects my service to the queen over these past few years."

Lord North made a sound that might have been intended as a laugh, but was closer to a snort. "What would that be — a sewing needle? A singing bird?"

Icy anger slid down Catrin's spine, but she kept her voice calm and even. "A talisman of some sort, perhaps, since that is how the queen refers to me."

"A talisman is just a good-luck charm," he said. "That is not appropriate; no other emblem has such a figure."

"No? Then I shall have to consider further, but do not worry. I'm sure the queen and I will think of something." She dropped a curtsy, but did not smile. "Good night, my lord."

"Good night," he said sullenly, and went back into the Great Chamber. Catrin decided it was time to retire to the ladies' chamber, and that meant walking along the gallery that lay parallel to the entrance courtyard.

She was just passing the front door when it swung open, forcing her to jump out of the way. A man in a green cloak hurried in, and she recognized his long, thin frame with a distinct lack of enthusiasm. It was Griffin Petre, the Viscount Heatherleigh. "My lord Heatherleigh, I was not aware that you were joining us."

"'Twas a near thing," Lord Heatherleigh said breathlessly, and shook his cloak free of dust. "We are building new kitchens at my home, Saintlow Hall, and there were some difficulties with the mortar. I had to tarry there until its quality matched my expectations."

"Could your steward not take charge of such things?"

He paused, and Catrin suddenly had the distinct impression that he had to search for an answer. Was he attempting to deceive her once again? Surely not... It was just a few weeks since his alliance with religious reformers had nearly cost him everything. Surely he knew that the queen would not stand for dishonesty a second time.

"Yes, but I prefer to ensure that all is well before I leave it to him," he said at last, and tugged on his cap to restore it to a pleasing angle. "Am I too late to dance with you, my lady?"

"I fear so; I am about to retire."

"Alas. May I escort you to your chamber, then?"

Only if she could not prevent it. "My lord, surely you are hungry and thirsty from your journey. I fear that if you take the time to escort me to my chamber, all the food in the Great Chamber will be cleared away before you arrive."

"I appreciate your air of concern, my lady, but it is not convincing me. There is another reason that you do not wish me to accompany you." He drew in a deep breath through his teeth. "Is it because you are afraid of me?"

Afraid? Of *him*? The notion was nothing short of amusing. "Why would I be, my lord?"

"I thought perhaps you heard that my first wife died. It was childbed fever — no fault of mine — and I mourned her sincerely. But some have spread false rumours." He heaved a sigh. "And I wondered if that was why you have been avoiding me of late."

"Not at all." Catrin smoothed a hand over her hood. "There has been much to do to prepare for the progress, my lord."

"But now that the progress has begun, others will take the greatest burden." He reached out and rested his hand on her arm. "You will have the leisure to consider my suit."

She pulled away, irritated by both the touch and the words. "I have already considered it, my lord, and I have already given you my answer. You must accept it."

"I cannot, my lady." He took off his cap and crushed it between his hands. "We have been through so much together —"

"Aye, but by your own fault."

"Verily so, my lady." He dropped his gaze to the velvet between his fingers. "If you marry me, I will do my utmost to mend the damage."

"I cannot marry you," Catrin said, and turned away. "And the damage is done."

Lucy felt like her every bone had rattled loose during the long ride from Dover, and she longed for the comfort of a cool bed and a warm meal. The rest of the party seemed equally as tired: her husband Pierrick's riding-seat had lost its grace and his eyes were closed as often as open. His two body servants, Thibaut and Symon, were also slumped in their saddles. Only Lucy's French maidservant, Florie Genevois, had any spirit left. She was looking around at everything as they travelled through the city, her wild red hair sticking out in every direction and both her eyes and her mouth round with awe. "What a beautiful city," she said. "St Paul's Cathedral! So majestic."

Lucy chuckled. "Florie, it's covered in scaffolding."

"That is what is so majestic. Rebuilding after such a terrible fire is such a noble project!" She beamed at Lucy, and then wrinkled her nose with concern. "Oh, my lady, you look weary."

"I fear I am."

"I know, I know." Florie tapped the side of her nose in a show of wisdom. "The last mile is the longest. But we will arrive soon, won't we, my lord?"

"Any moment now," Pierrick said, and reached out to rest his hand on Lucy's. "Hold fast, my love. Once we have arrived at Lady Angharad's home, we will be nicely taken care of."

Lucy found a smile for him. "Just like the days we spent on your home estates in France. Everyone was so kind."

"They were all so pleased to meet you, my lady," Florie said.

Thibaut nodded agreement. "And it did much good for your people to see you, my lord."

"Perhaps so," Pierrick said, and perked up when Lady Angharad's house came into view. "Ah, we have arrived at last."

"Thank God," Lucy murmured, and gratefully accepted his help to get down from her horse. All this travel had certainly improved her riding, but had not made her any more fond of the activity.

The front door swung open, but to Lucy's surprise it was not Lady Angharad who stood there but her companion and apprentice, Mistress Edrys Pedler, with her hands folded tightly beneath her apron.

"Welcome, my lord. Welcome, my lady," she said shyly. "I fear my lady mistress was called to attend the queen this afternoon, but she has left me to care for you."

Lucy felt a quiver of disappointment so intense that her knees went weak. She had to lean rather heavily on Pierrick. "Why did Her Majesty ask for the baroness? Is she unwell?"

"I do not know, my lady — but I do have a letter." She held out a folded piece of parchment with a familiar seal. "It is from—"

"The Countess of Ashbourne," Lucy said, and took it with pleasure. "Thank you, mistress."

"Prithee come in and rest yourself before you open it," Mistress Edrys said. "I will bring you food and drink."

"Thank you," Pierrick said, and slid an arm around Lucy's waist to help her in as she broke the seal and unfolded the parchment.

Dearest Lucy,

I am truly sorry to take away your hostess, as I imagine you were looking forward to this time together. My mother is very skilled at soothing the sorrows of travel. She is equally disappointed, but the queen requested her presence specifically, and I suspect that she has a reason for it. Forsooth, the queen has been strangely quiet and pensive of late, and I wonder if my mother's presence will encourage her to finally reveal what is weighing so heavily on her mind.

Selfishly, I hope that this loss of a hostess means that you will join us at the Charterhouse sooner than expected. We all miss you, little Lucy — and I miss you most of all. Please do come to us soon.

Your affectionate friend,
Catrin, Lady Ashbourne

"Hmm … this is interesting," Lucy said, and handed the letter to Pierrick. "It seems that something is disturbing our queen."

He read it quickly, and his brow wrinkled in the way that it did when he was thoughtful. "And I suspect that Catrin's hope is more of a plea," he said. "Do you think she is truly worried?"

"If she was, she would never say so more openly than that." Lucy buried her face in her hands. "But I confess, I do not wish to join them right away. I would prefer to rest here for a few days."

"As would I," Pierrick said softly. "Though I fear it is not to be."

"No, it is not," she agreed wearily. "Let us leave for the Charterhouse tomorrow."

CHAPTER FOUR

"Lady Catrin?"

It was a whisper amongst many whispers, for the ladies' chamber was never truly silent, but something in the tone woke Catrin at once. She sat up in her bed and found herself surrounded by ladies in white nightgowns, each one holding a candle in front of them so that their faces were merely flickering patches of light and shadow. They all had wide, frightened eyes.

Catrin swept a hand over her face, forcing herself awake. "What is it?"

"We heard something in the corridor," one of the ladies whispered, and her candle wavered in her trembling fingers.

"We peeked out, and saw a man in a ragged cloak walk down the corridor and turn right," another said. "He was a stranger, my lady — he shouldn't be here."

"*Especially* near the ladies' chamber," a third lady said, in a tone of righteous outrage. She was tiny and very young, and obviously trying hard to fit in. She also had a dangerous tendency to wave her candle about to emphasise her words.

Catrin yawned. "Then I suggest you call for the gentleman usher assigned to us. He will deal with the situation."

"We did!" The tiny lady swung her candle toward the door and nearly set another lady's nightgown on fire. "He never returned."

That piqued Catrin's interest. She started to rise from her bed, but her mother's hand reached out and delicately wrapped around her wrist. "I don't think you should go," she murmured sleepily, and rose gracefully upright. "There are guards a-plenty to deal with this stranger."

"But no one to help the usher," Catrin said. "Come with me, Mother; he may need you."

Lady Angharad immediately forgot her protest in the face of such a possibility and rose to collect her bag of supplies. Then both of them wrapped up in dressing gowns and slippers and left the room. They told the ladies to stay behind but took two of the candles, and so crept down the darkened silent corridor with an arch of light travelling above them.

They reached the end of the corridor and turned right, and Catrin felt her first real niggle of unease when she saw that the door to Lord North's chamber was unguarded. "Perhaps the usher sent this guard to investigate," she whispered. "And he hasn't returned, either."

Lady Angharad slid her arm around Catrin's waist. "Then we should go and find Lord Robert instead of blindly —" She broke off at the sound of groaning. "What was that?"

"Let's find out," Catrin said, and quickened her pace down the corridor and around the corner. They ended up in the wide-open space outside the Great Chamber, where the heraldic emblems hung like tapestries on all the walls. A man was lying on the ground, his legs splayed out and his hand pressed weakly against a bleeding gash on his forehead. "It's the usher," Catrin said, and dropped to her knees beside him. "What happened, goodman?"

"I was set upon," the man moaned. Lady Angharad bent down and took a cloth from her bag, wetting it with rose oil. "It was a big bearded man, but I couldn't see his face."

"Where did he go?"

"Toward the chapel, I think. I had one of the yeomen here with me and he ran in that direction when I fell."

Catrin frowned. "Was he chasing the man with the beard?"

"I hope so," the man said, and gave a hiss of pain when Lady Angharad dabbed gently at his wound. "If not, he's nothing but a blackguard and a coward."

Catrin got up and started searching the flagstones for a set of footprints she could follow. There were scratches and smudges of dirt a-plenty from the hundreds of people who had filled the chamber just a few hours before, but it was difficult to see any pattern.

She paused near the door of the Great Chamber, turning her back on Lord North's banner. A scent was coming from beyond the darkened doorway… What was it? It was like mushrooms, or moss, or —

A figure darted out from the black space, and a pair of hands landed hard against her chest, shoving her backward with such ferocity that Catrin tumbled backward and cracked her head hard on the stone wall.

Her mother dropped the cloth and stumbled across the floor, heedless of the damage it did to her dressing gown. "Catrin! Kitten — are you hurt?"

Lady Angharad's frantic fingers slid over the back of Catrin's head, and a sharp pain made her wince.

"I hit my head, Mother, that is all," Catrin said, and pushed herself upright with difficulty, for her arms and legs did not want to obey. "That was the man in the ragged cloak — the man with the beard. He's running away; he's going to escape."

"Let him go, and stay right where you are," Lady Angharad said sharply. "I'm going to get some help for this man here, and then I am taking you straight back to bed. Do you hear?"

"Yes, Mother," Catrin said, and decided it was best to lie down.

The morning was already warm by the time Lucy, Pierrick and their party left the city. They travelled through the markets and emerged near Whitechapel field, where the fresh green crops seemed to be bursting with delight as they stretched toward the sun. The haze of the city hovered just to their left, but the horizon was bright and clear.

A bit too bright, actually. Lucy would have been quite happy to hide under her blankets, and leave the sunshine to others for a little while. But she felt her mood lightening when Florie started singing a sweet French *chanson*, and eventually she felt awake enough to join in.

That is, until a dog's sudden snarl made her horse shy backwards. She stopped abruptly to get her under control, and Florie choked on a high note. "What was that?"

"Just wild dogs," Symon said, and pointed ahead of them. "I think they've got a sheep."

"Bad tidings for the shepherd," Lucy said. "The loss of one sheep can mean a great loss of —"

Pierrick swore, drowning out the rest of her sentence. "That's not a sheep," he said, and urged his horse into a gallop. Lucy swallowed hard and seriously considered riding away, but she knew she had to be brave. She had to help, if she could.

She urged her horse onward, and drew close enough to see what the dogs were worrying at. It was a man's naked body — a man so hairy he could almost have been an animal himself. From the claw-marks on the earth and the bites on his arms, she could guess that he had once been buried, but the dogs had dug him up.

Pierrick and his servants charged at the pack, yelling and swinging their swords, and the dogs retreated with growls and snarls. Their muzzles were caked in blood, their eyes wild with the lust of the kill, and they hovered just out of range as

Pierrick jumped down to look at the poor creature on the ground.

"It is difficult to say what killed him," he said grimly. "But he was stripped — there is no purse, no satchel. I doubt we will be able to find out who he is."

Lucy jumped down from her horse and strode away, her stomach heaving. Florie ran after her, and wrapped her plump arms around Lucy's shoulders, holding her upright. "Oh, my lady," she murmured, and stroked Lucy's hair back from her forehead. "How terrible a sight this is for you."

"It's more than that," Lucy said. "It's — it's just that I can't help but think that this is a horrible way to end one's life … lost and abandoned … left to the dogs, without family or friends to mourn you."

A tear trickled down Florie's cheek. She flicked it away and straightened. "We will mourn him, then," she said stoutly.

"Yes, we will," Lucy said, and made herself return to the body. Florie stayed close beside her, and they arrived just as Symon bent over it. His eyes were full of curiosity, but devoid of compassion.

"What should we do with him, my lord?"

"Go and fetch the coroner," Pierrick said. "Thibaut, stand guard and keep the dogs away. My wife and I shall continue on our way."

"But what about the person who k-killed him?" Lucy said, and her voice wobbled, though she tried to keep it steady. "What if he is waiting out there somewhere?"

"'Tis unlikely," Pierrick said, but his moss-green eyes were soft with concern. "But would you prefer to return to London until we have a full escort, my lady?"

"I'd rather stay together," Lucy said, and blinked back more tears. "And I think we should do our best to make sure the poor man finds a resting place."

"Very well, my lady." Pierrick sheathed his sword and urged his horse back to her side. "So we shall do."

Catrin woke up early and reluctantly, her head pounding. For a few minutes she stayed in bed, drinking a herbal concoction that her mother brought for her, which smelled like rue and sage. Once the cup was empty, though, she forced herself to get up and dressed. There was work to be done before the day's activities began: the papers she had been avoiding had become so urgent that she could delay no longer. She now had no less than three letters from her steward, Ned, each one begging for a response. He wanted her to approve the summer's expenditure, consider a dispute over a will, and grant permission for him to divert some funds to the village church. The last was easy; she was always willing to help the people of the village. The other two…

She was trying to determine whether the expected cost of repairs to the smithy was reasonable when running footsteps approached her door. She stood up as the footsteps slid to a stop, and drew her shawl more tightly around her before she opened the door.

The pageboy on the other side jumped back, his hand still raised to knock. "My lady!"

She smiled at him. "Did I frighten you, Finn?"

"No, my lady," he said stoutly, but his sheepish eyes told a different story. And then he remembered his duty, and his whole frame stiffened into formality. "I've come from the queen, my lady. Lord North is very angry, and she asks that you come at once."

"Of course," Catrin said, and followed him to the Great Chamber once she had locked her papers away. There the servants were setting out food for the midmorning meal, and the queen was sitting under her canopy of state at the far end. Lord North was kneeling before her, his lips drawn in so that his face looked unnaturally flat once again.

"Your Majesty," Catrin said, and sunk down into a curtsy. "Finn said that you asked for me. Are you well?"

"Well, and yet not well," the queen said. "Our gracious host made an unpleasant discovery this morning."

"Gone," Lord North said grimly. "My grandmother's brooch, the trio of roses set in gold, my own ring —"

"Are you saying that someone has robbed you?" Catrin asked.

Lord North flushed red. "A member of the queen's company, I wager. It is no coincidence that these thefts took place after you all arrived."

"My people are honest, Lord North," the queen said coolly. "They would not steal."

"If I may be so bold, that is a matter of belief, not of fact, Your Majesty," Lord North said. "Have you any proof of their honesty?"

"No more than you have any proof of perfidy," the queen responded tartly. "Beware of questioning the word of a prince, Lord North."

Lord North bowed stiffly. "I am not questioning you, Your Highness, but your servants."

"My loyal servants, who serve me well and cleverly." The queen folded her hands together gracefully. "So cleverly, indeed, that if they did turn to thievery, they would do a better job of it."

"What do you mean, Your Majesty?" Catrin asked.

"They took only the diamonds," Lord North said. "Any piece of jewellery or plate with a diamond is gone. But they left a sapphire ring, two pearl pendants, gold and silver plate, my wife's emeralds…"

"How strange," Catrin murmured. "Where were these items?"

"Scattered about the house, in various locked cupboards and chests." He scowled. "Bar my ring, which was on my finger."

"A bold theft indeed," Catrin said. "If you wish, Your Majesty, I will look into the matter."

"Prithee look thoroughly," Lord North said. "Cast about every room, and question every person."

"As I said, the villain is not one of my people," the queen said. "And I will not allow them to be treated as thieves."

"There is no need to treat them as thieves, Your Majesty." Catrin brushed her fingers over the sore spot on her head. "I myself saw someone in the house last night who did not belong; I suspect he is the thief. I will question the guards and the servants, and find out if anyone knows where he went. Also, I will look for the jewels themselves. Perhaps the thief hid them here and intends to return for them."

"A goodly plan indeed, my lady," the queen said, and turned to Lord North. "Come, my lord. Let us break our fast."

In a sprawling place such as the Charterhouse, doors abounded and there were hiding places a-plenty. Catrin started her search in the chapel, searching through chests and coffers while a disapproving chaplain looked on. "Was the chapel door locked last night?" Catrin asked him, and bent to look under a row of chairs.

"Yes; I did it myself, once evening prayer was complete and before I went to have my supper," the chaplain said in an injured tone. "And I can assure you that I did not steal any diamonds."

"I did not say you did," Catrin said patiently. "Can you tell me why the two bedchambers outside are empty, when the house is so full?"

"The roof leaks," the chaplain said. "One of them used to be mine, so I know full well how bad it is. Lord North is having the roof repaired next week."

"I see," Catrin murmured, and moved out of the chapel into the first of the chambers. The musty smell of damp caught in her nose as soon as she opened the door, and the floorboards beneath her feet were unpleasantly spongy as she went in. None were loose, though, and there was nothing hidden in the —

The back of her neck prickled and she spun at once to face the door. A figure darted away a second too late, so she saw that he wore livery and had a crumpled ear. "Who are you? Stand your ground, man. Surely you are not afraid of a mere woman."

Her voice rang and echoed in the almost empty room, and she heard him stop short a few feet away. Slowly he returned, and stood in the doorway with his hands clasped behind him. "I am not afraid of you, but of what I have done."

She rested her fingers on the hilt of her *stiletto*, just to be sure. "And what have you done, goodman?"

"I ran," he said bitterly. "And proved myself a coward."

"Ah," Catrin said. "You were the yeoman guard who failed to help the usher last night."

"Yes, God forgive me." He covered his crumpled ear with his hand, as if trying to hide it. "I wish to — to — make amends."

"Then you must help me find the thief," Catrin said briskly.

His eyes brightened. "Yes — that is why I'm here. I wanted to show you something."

"Very well," Catrin said, and kept her hand on her *stiletto* as the man led her past the great chamber and around the outer courtyard to the kitchens. It was hideously warm in those rooms, for every fire was burning and water bubbled in a dozen massive cauldrons. But the smell was pleasant — sage and fresh bread and a hint of wild garlic.

One tall, plump maid stood stock-still against the wall of the largest room, a dripping cloth in her hand and her eyes as round as the plate she was washing. "All is well," the yeoman said to her. "Just tell the lady what you saw."

The plump maid curtsied, her eyes twinkling. "It was just the cat."

The yeoman stared at her in disbelief. "But you told me there were items disturbed in here, as if someone went through."

"There was." The maid flicked her head so that her long plait fell down her back. "But Cook just told me that it was the cat."

"How does *she* know?"

The maid giggled. "She and the cat are courting."

The yeoman, it seemed, was too literal to understand that answer, and Catrin did not bother to explain. There was something far more interesting by the door, so she left them to their wordplay and moved closer.

The latch was hanging loose, showing raw, rough wood against the weathering. It looked as if someone had put a piece of steel between the door and the jamb and forced it upward, throwing the latch out of its socket and nearly destroying them both.

"Your cat has powerful claws," Catrin said, and the argument behind her abruptly stopped. The maid came over to examine the door, and her round, dull eyes grew rounder still.

"Oh, the cat didn't do that, my lady," she said, and mischief gleamed in her eyes once again. "He didn't need to — Cook lets him in whenever he lets out his mating-cry."

"If that is the case, mistress, then your first thought was the right one," Catrin said. "Someone came through here."

CHAPTER FIVE

Catrin went out to the cloister at the back of the Charterhouse to meet the queen as she returned from hunting, and found most of the servants already there. Evidently something was about to happen; they were all gathered around a large pavilion with white silk walls that seemed to glow in the afternoon sunlight. Branches, leaves and trailing ivy were draped all over the ground, hiding the flagstones, and in the centre was a large pool. A woman reclined next to it, dressed in the style of ancient Greece, with a belt of gold and her hair caught up in silver bands. Around her sat several young maids in short tunics, with wings of thinnest silk that suggested they were meant to be fairies.

The maids jumped up when the queen rode into view, and ran toward her crying out her name. "Your Majesty! Our queen! Please come, please come! Our goddess wants to welcome you!"

"Forsooth, it would not be seemly for a queen to refuse a goddess," the queen said wryly, and allowed Lord North to help her down from her horse. She looked weary and somewhat dishevelled from the ride and the heat, but she approached the tent with a gracious smile — one which widened somewhat when she saw the goddess.

The berobed woman rose up onto her knees, and somewhere a harp began to play. "Great queen, I beg thee hear me," the goddess said. "For I have words of great import."

The queen's smile held fast. "Then speak, fair goddess."

The woman spread her hands wide, palms cupped and facing upward. She raised her gaze to heaven, drew in a deep breath, and spoke.

"From ancient wisdom and the truth of faith
Strong counsel comes to light the way ahead
As countless others of our sex doth know
Our comfort lies within the marriage-bed."

Catrin winced. Lord North had chosen the worst possible message to give the queen — and worse, he had thrust it at her with all the grace and subtlety of a bull in a cathedral. It was inevitable that the queen would be furious, and it wasn't over yet. Verse after verse hammered home the same theme, until the tension in the air shimmered like a heat-haze before a storm. There was an audible sigh of relief from the entire audience when the goddess' words finally came to an end.

"Such rejoicing from peers and peasants both
Has not been beheld before nor since
When comes a gift to bear as well as be
A sovereign new, a great and gloried prince."

The woman bent gracefully from the waist with the last line, so she did not see the queen's smile slide from her lips.

"Thank you, fair goddess," the queen said tightly. "I wager such eloquence took much effort and design. Do you not agree, my talisman?"

Catrin stepped forward at once. She knew a call for aid when she heard one. "Of course, Your Majesty, but I fear you must be weary. Such a stirring performance makes one tired."

"It does indeed, much to my chagrin," the queen said. "Lord North, pray excuse me. I must rest until our evening meal."

Lord North was not fooled, or so Catrin assumed from the way his eyes bulged. "Of course, Your Majesty. And after supper, we have another surprise for you — a beautiful, colourful surprise."

"I look forward to it," the queen said. "Please attend me, Catrin."

"Yes, Your Majesty," Catrin said, and took her place at the queen's side. They left the cloister together, moving rather more quickly than the queen's claim to weariness might have allowed.

"The marriage-bed, indeed," the queen muttered. "I am much kindled and wax warm. How *dare* he?"

"I wager he dares because he does not care if he draws out your wrath, so long as you take his advice and marry," Catrin said wryly.

"The insolence of the man! By my troth, Catrin, if you have found the thief who took his diamonds, I will give him a knighthood instead of a noose."

Catrin hid a smile. "I have not found him yet, Your Majesty, but I am further ahead than I was this morning. I am sure our thief is not one of those in the house, for the door to the kitchens was forced."

"As I suspected; my people would not be so clumsy. Did anyone see the thief leave again?"

"No, but the cowardly guard who ran away from danger last night is eager to redeem himself, so he is searching the surrounding houses for any sign of the man."

"An excellent beginning, my talisman."

"Thank you, Your Majesty," Catrin said, and pushed open the door of the queen's chamber. A pleasant scent floated out, the freshness of mint and lavender mingling with musk.

The queen stopped short. "Is someone in there?"

Catrin leaned in and found only a tidy chamber with a freshly swept flagstone floor, and diamond-paned windows glittering in the afternoon sun. "No one, Your Majesty. I imagine Mistress Blanche is fetching your washing-water, and Mistress Ashley —"

"Open the windows." The queen strode in and did it herself, swinging every pane as wide as it would go. "And light the fire."

It was already warm in there, but Catrin obeyed. "Are you well, Your Majesty?"

"Of course," she said, and clenched her fingers into a tight white-knuckled knot. "Now leave me be; I need to rest."

Catrin rose to her feet and sent the queen a considering glance. "Shall I —"

"Go, and stand not upon the order of thy going."

The sudden formality was mystifying, but this was no time to question it. Instead, Catrin bowed low and backed away. "As you wish, Your Majesty."

The queen was deliberately merry during the evening meal, applauding the antics of the jugglers and complimenting the musicians. She made a great show of anticipating the 'beautiful, colourful surprise' Lord North had promised, and only her ladies could tell that she was still angry. Lord North may have suspected it, when he saw how little she ate, but Lord Robert wisely prevented him from saying anything.

The meal ended with fruit and marchpane shaped like a chessboard, with pieces that were gilded in gold. Marchpane, made from almonds and sugar and flavoured with rosewater, was one of the queen's favourites, so it was a wise choice. Then Lord North offered her both queens, along with a passionate declaration of love and loyalty, and that proved a masterful move. Much of the queen's anger faded away as she nibbled on them.

When the marchpane had all disappeared, Lord North asked them to join him in the courtyard, and the company moved as one outside. The moon was waxing, the air was warm, and the stars peeked out between thin, drifting clouds. There was a cushioned chair available for the queen, and Lord North chose a position on her right while Catrin and Mistress Ashley took their places at her left.

And then ... nothing happened. Anticipatory silence in the crowd around them turned to awkward giggles as time stretched on, and Lord North's face turned deep red. "Prithee excuse me, Your Majesty; I will go and see what the difficulty is."

"Of course, my lord," the queen said graciously, but her eyes glittered with fresh irritation. Lord North strode away, pushing into the restless crowd. People started whispering and shifting about, and several courtiers sat down on the low wall surrounding the courtyard and called for wine.

Lord Heatherleigh, meanwhile, was speaking to Mistress Blanche. He had hold of her arm, and kept talking even though she kept shaking her head and trying to leave. Catrin glanced at the queen in a silent question. She nodded her approval at once, and Catrin left her side to approach the pair.

Then a man stepped in front of her — a young man with a thin beard and heavy-lidded eyes. She did not know him, but there was something familiar about his round-shouldered shape. After a moment, she recognized him from that misty morning at Greenwich. "You are not a courtier."

"No," he agreed, in a voice that was strangely devoid of any inflection. "But I should be."

"You will have to leave."

The man smirked. "You don't want me to leave."

"On the contrary." Catrin raised her hand, and one of the yeomen of the guard started marching in their direction. "As you will soon see."

"You will want to hear what I have to say."

Catrin glanced over at Mistress Blanche, who was starting to look very distressed. "I do not have the leisure for that, I'm afraid."

The yeoman arrived at Catrin's side and immediately took the man's arm in a tight grip. Anger suffused the man's dull eyes, but he did not resist. "You will regret this," he hissed. "There will come a day when you will wish you had listened to me."

"Perhaps," Catrin said, and resumed her journey toward Lord Heatherleigh as the guard pulled the man out of the courtyard. Mistress Blanche saw her coming and relief washed over her face, but Lord Heatherleigh did not notice her until she spoke. "Good evening, my lord."

Lord Heatherleigh let go of Mistress Blanche's arm at once. "Good evening, my lady."

Catrin folded her hands in front of her and gazed at him limpidly. "Are you both well?"

Lord Heatherleigh nodded dumbly, but tears welled in Mistress Blanche's eyes. "I must attend the queen," she said, and walked away without another word.

Catrin kept her eyes on Lord Heatherleigh. He shifted his feet, glanced up at the sky and down at the flagstones, and finally met Catrin's gaze.

"I had some questions, that is all," he said. "I did not mean to upset her."

"What sort of questions?" Catrin asked coolly. "Perhaps I can answer them."

"No, you were not born then," he said absently, and then abruptly lifted his chin so he could see over the crowd. "But your mother — Lady Angharad — she might be able to —"

"I fear she has retired," Catrin said. "And I would prefer you did not treat her thus."

Lord Heatherleigh scowled. "This is not the time for delicacy," he said. "I have urgent questions, and naturally become annoyed when I am blocked from getting answers."

"Perhaps it would be best to ask Sir William Cecil, then," Catrin said. "If he does not know the answer, I am sure he could find someone who does."

"No, he would mention it to the queen," Lord Heatherleigh said, and then tugged sharply on his beard. "Not that she cannot know — it is nothing against her or her reign. It is just — just too small to bother her with."

Catrin stared at him for a long moment. "The queen forgave you once, Lord Heatherleigh, and at a cost. Many people thought you should have been fined or imprisoned for your association with the so-called brethren who wanted to reform the queen's church, but she defended you. I hope you are not rewarding her mercy with further … plotting."

"No, certainly not. Her mercy surprised me as much as it did everyone else, and I am grateful," Lord Heatherleigh said with a hearty conviction that seemed sincere. Then he paused, and drew in a long breath through his teeth. "But I have long wondered if … anyone … knows the reasoning behind her decision."

Catrin's eyes narrowed. "Is that what you were asking Mistress Blanche?"

"Among other things."

"It is an easy answer, then. No. No one does."

Disappointment washed over his thin face. "Thank you, my lady," he said, and bowed. "Prithee pardon me; I must retire."

"Good night," Catrin said, but her words disappeared in a sudden loud crackling sound that made several of the ladies scream in surprise. Above her head, blue sparkles streaked through the air and exploded into a green halo.

Fireworks. That was the 'beautiful, colourful surprise'. And it certainly pleased the queen; she clapped her hands in delight when a second roar resulted in a plume of red and white that formed a single Tudor rose. Lord North returned to her side in time to see her reaction, and beamed with pompous pride.

Then came musicians, dozens of them, strumming lutes and tapping drums as more explosions overhead bathed them all in coloured light. One man wandered near the queen and gave a great courtly bow. He had a receding hairline and a strange square beard, but his smile was charming and his fingers were nimble on the lute strings.

"Western wind, when wilt thou blow? The small rain down can rain, can rain," he sang, in a clear, pure voice that sounded far more youthful than he looked. "Oh! If my love were in my arms, and I in my bed again." He winked roguishly at the queen, who giggled girlishly.

"How scandalous," she said. "Away with you, sirrah, before the rumours start."

CHAPTER SIX

"If it be so that I forsake thee
As banished from thy company,
Yet my heart, my mind, and mine affection
Shall still remain in thy perfection,
And right as thou list so order me."

The musician's voice trailed after the queen and her ladies into the entrance court, into the house, and along the corridor that led to the queen's chamber. Some of the ladies thought it sweet that he was following them, reciting poetry to the strains of his lute, but to Catrin it was rapidly growing irritating.

Finally she lost her patience and strode back to the man. She took two coins out of the purse at her belt, held them out and let them go. It forced the man to stop playing so he could catch them. "Thank you," she said. "You have been most delightful. Now good night."

The man took a half-step backward, more from surprise than inclination. "Does the queen not wish to —"

"The queen wishes to sleep," Catrin said, and indicated the path to the door with a wave of her hand. "Good night."

"Good night," he said reluctantly, but did not leave. He remained where he was until Catrin returned to her place by the queen's side.

"One never knows what perils will arise while on progress," the queen said with a quirk of her lip. "Let us hope it never grows worse than a poet with too much to say."

Mistress Ashley chuckled. "How lovely that would be."

"Indeed," the queen said, and let Catrin enter her chamber first. It was quite cool inside, for the windows were still open and the fire had long since died. Mistress Blanche started shutting the windows, while Mistress Ashley and Catrin began getting the queen ready for bed.

The queen submitted to their attentions absently, her long white fingers tracing the pattern of the lace on her wrist. "Yes, it would be lovely … but it will never be," she murmured. "We know little about the future, but this I dare to predict: worse things will come."

Catrin removed the jewelled pins from the queen's hair one by one, releasing red-gold tendrils that slowly uncurled down her back. "As will better things, Your Majesty. Perhaps on this very progress."

"One can hope, but there are constant dangers to face when on progress. One is always vulnerable." The queen gave a long sigh. "But then, a queen is always vulnerable, whether she is on progress or not. One needs only look to my mother for proof of that."

Catrin exchanged a glance with Mistress Ashley, surprised by a second open reference to Queen Anne in as many days. "She lived in a dangerous, unsettled time, Your Majesty."

"Yes, and she paid the price. Condemned for treason — a crime she was far too clever to commit — and executed despite her innocence."

Mistress Blanche quickly shut the door, blocking out the sights and sounds of the people in the corridor beyond. Catrin hesitated, but simply had to ask. "How do you know she was innocent, Your Majesty?"

The queen arched one eyebrow. "What an impertinent question."

Catrin curtsied. "My apologies, Your Majesty. You need not speak of it if —"

"I have a letter," the queen said abruptly. "She wrote a letter to my father the king from the Tower. It explained how she was falsely accused of betraying him and taking lovers, and asked that he treat me well."

Mistress Ashley sighed. "Some say that letter was forged, Your Majesty. Please, do not hold it so dear."

"It was not forged," the queen said. "In my heart, I know it was not forged."

Catrin set down the jewels on a table near the bed. "How did you find it, Your Majesty?"

"I did not find it; it was given to me by Sir William Cecil. He found it amongst the papers of one of my father's chief ministers." The queen turned her coronation ring round and round on her finger. "I have always wondered if my father ever saw it."

"That is an unanswerable question," Mistress Blanche said gently. "Please, Your Majesty…"

"I know, I know," the queen said impatiently. "It is not seemly to dwell on a wrong that cannot be righted."

Catrin started to agree, but broke off as a voice rose from just outside the window. The words were somewhat muffled, but she caught most of it. "A hind … graven with diamonds … written her fair neck round about…"

The queen's impatience transformed into amusement. "It is our poet," she said with a smile. "Quite persistent, is he not?"

"Quite annoying," Mistress Ashley grumbled, and opened the chamber door so she could speak to one of the yeomen outside. Catrin crossed to the window and saw the man in his black doublet and green hose striding about below. The lace on his wrists fluttered white in the darkness as he waved his hands in the air to punctuate each syllable.

"…*noli me tangere*, for Caesar's I am," he cried. "And wild, wild … though I seem tame."

Four guards approached him at a run, and he let out a yelp like a startled puppy and took to his heels, evading them by no more than a handsbreadth. They gave chase, shouting for him to stop, which he did not do.

Catrin watched them out of sight, greatly amused. "Methinks your poet's ardour has been thoroughly cooled, Your Majesty."

The queen chuckled. "What a shame."

Catrin sat down next to her mother at the morning meal, at the table next to the queen's. The queen herself was busy with attendants and courtiers, including Lord North and Lord Heatherleigh, so she felt safe enough to relinquish her duties and enjoy her mother's company for a little while.

"Good morrow, my kitten," Lady Angharad said, and passed her a basket of fresh white bread. "Break your fast well, for I hear that today we are back on the hunt."

Catrin took a piece of bread. "Is that what Lord North has planned?"

"I don't know what he has planned," she said solemnly, and poured some small ale into Catrin's cup. "I know only that the fairies came to me early this morning, and warned me that there will be more jewels for which to search."

"Forsooth, I very much hope to meet these fairies someday," Catrin murmured, and smiled at her mother's reproachful look. "Chastise me not, Mother — I only wish to thank them for all the wisdom they impart."

"Do not question them, or they will leave us to our ignorance," Lady Angharad said, and filled a bowl with pottage. "Now eat your breakfast."

Catrin hid a smile. "Yes, Mother," she said dutifully. Her mother often seemed to forget that she was no longer a child, but Catrin did not mind. Lady Angharad had been missing, presumed dead, for a long time. It was a blessing to hear her voice again — even when she was fussing.

The queen's voice rang out from the next table. "Lord Robert, where shall we next travel in our progress?"

Catrin looked across and saw Lord Robert consult a scroll. Lines of strain were clearly marked around his eyes. "We are due to visit Sir William Cecil at his house on the Strand tomorrow, and then return here. The following day we will visit Sir Richard Rich at Wanstead, and the day after that we will go to your royal estate in Havering."

"No," the queen said in a clear voice that carried easily through the Great Chamber. "Instead of Wanstead and Havering, I wish to go to Saintlow Hall."

Lord Heatherleigh fumbled with his cup and it landed on the table with a thump, splashing liquid in all directions. "To my home, Your Majesty?"

"Yes, to your home. I have never been there," the queen said, and spread her hands wide. "Do you not wish for me to visit, Heatherleigh?"

"Oh — I — we — of course I wish for you to visit, Your Majesty," Lord Heatherleigh said. "I would be most happy for you to come. Most happy."

The queen's eyes narrowed. "Would you?"

"Certainly, certainly." Lord Heatherleigh looked at Lord Robert in obvious dismay. "But I am not prepared for such a great — illustrious — visitor. Nor such a large ... company."

The queen waved a hand. "Lord Robert and Sir William Cecil can aid you in that. And you may leave my presence now, to begin your preparations."

"Thank you, Your Majesty," Lord Heatherleigh said breathlessly, and rose to his feet. Lord Robert left with him, both men looking somewhat wild-eyed.

The queen turned to Lord North with a smile. "And now, Lord North, do tell me. What have you planned for us today?"

"Hawking, Your Majesty, if it pleases you."

"It does indeed." The queen rose to her feet. "I shall go and prepare."

"Lady Catrin! *Catrin*!"

The queen's shrill cry cut across the corridor to the chamber where her ladies were all getting dressed for riding. Catrin dropped her boots and ran across on stockinged feet, followed by Mistress Blanche. "Your Majesty! What is wrong?"

The queen held out a small wooden box in trembling hands. "It's gone, Catrin — it's gone!"

Catrin looked into the box and saw a large emerald, a piece of parchment and a painted miniature portrait of Lord Robert Dudley. She had seen that collection of items before, and so she knew what was missing: a string of pearls with a golden 'B' pendant, from which hung three teardrop pearls. A costly piece, but it was valuable to the queen for an entirely different reason. "Alas! Your mother's necklace is gone."

"It was in this box when we left London," the queen said. "I checked just before it was packed."

Catrin's heart sank. They had travelled for miles since then, and the carts were not guarded as the queen was. "Was the box stored on one of the wagons?"

"No, I ensured that it was hidden with my personal items and carried on my litter."

"Then it was most likely stolen from here in the Charterhouse." Catrin took the box and lifted out the emerald. "It is interesting that this was left behind."

"In the other thefts, they took the diamonds, but left the other jewels behind." The queen wrung her hands. "Why then did they take this necklace, made of only gold and pearls? Why? Why couldn't they have taken something — anything — else?"

"I will do my best to find out, Your Majesty," Catrin said, and wished she dared give her better assurances. But what could she do? They did not know when the necklace had been taken, so they could not determine who had been with the court at the relevant time. Nor did they know why or how it was taken, so that would not provide any aid. All they knew was that it was gone.

Catrin's eye was suddenly caught by something glinting at the bottom of the box. She reached in and pushed the miniature aside, revealing a bent golden hoop. "Do you recognize this, Your Majesty?"

"No, I have never seen it before."

Catrin returned the box to the queen and carried the hoop to the window so she could examine it in better light. "Mistress Blanche, could you bring me the ouche that the queen just received?"

Mistress Blanche went straight to a chest with a large padlock that sat near the queen's bed. She took a key from a chain around her neck and unlocked it, then withdrew a bundle wrapped in a length of linen. Catrin took it from her, unwrapped it, and cupped it in her hands. Turquoise and sapphires, swirling around a table-cut diamond like waves on the sea. "I see that this diamond survived."

"Perhaps the thief could not get it out. It is an unusually well-made piece," Mistress Blanche said nervously.

Catrin nodded. "I would wager it was made more than thirty years ago, based on the design, but still all the parts are well-anchored."

"The choice of stones is significant too. Sapphires and turquoise are said to protect the wearer," Mistress Blanche said. "Turquoise, especially, is said to turn pale when the wearer is in danger."

"So Lord North wanted to protect me," the queen said listlessly, and sank down into a chair. "If only he had protected this chamber instead."

"It wasn't Lord North," Catrin said. "He told me that this was not the gift he planned to give you. Someone else gave you this."

The queen straightened in her chair. "What? *Who*?"

"Whoever stole your necklace — and the other jewels too, I wager." Carefully, Catrin fitted the gold hoop into the back of the ouche, where a small slot had been made for it. "See? This means that the same person handled both your wooden box and Lord North's coffer, when they placed the ouche there."

"I see that, but how does that help us?"

"It doesn't." Catrin returned the ouche to Mistress Blanche with the hoop still attached. "Not until we find an alabaster cup."

CHAPTER SEVEN

Catrin sat down on a worn wooden bench in the chapel courtyard and idly watched a child kicking a ball while she waited for Finn. Part of her did not want to involve him, for he had already risked his life once before helping her find a dangerous magician. Another part of her knew, however, that his unique childhood spent as a pickpocket and errand-boy on the streets of London made him ideal for this task.

She was thinking of the day she'd first seen him, playing the urchin for coins beside London Stone, when he arrived. As always, he moved silently, and his eyes held the wary wisdom of a much older boy. "My lady? You called for me?"

The ball bounced across the courtyard and Catrin watched it go without really seeing it. "Have you ever seen a portrait of Queen Anne Boleyn, Finn?"

Finn scratched his temple. "I thought they were all destroyed, my lady."

"Destroyed or hidden, yes. I have never seen one myself. And there aren't many people still alive who remember what she looked like." Catrin slid her fingers along the weathered arm of the bench. "But everyone remembers her necklace."

"Oh yes — my grandmother told me about the shining gold and giant pearls." Finn drew the letter 'B' on the centre of his chest, then tilted his head to the side. "She thought King Henry took it and melted it down, and put the pearls on his own crown."

"That may have been his intention, but in truth the necklace was saved for Queen Elizabeth. She has had it for years, and treasured it as one of the few items left that belonged to her mother." Catrin sighed. "And the thief who took Lord North's diamonds stole it from her."

Finn scowled. "What a heartless thing to do."

"And strange," Catrin said. "I found evidence that the person who stole the necklace was the same person who put a valuable ouche in a coffer that was presented to the queen. But the ouche was not supposed to be in the coffer; it was supposed to be an alabaster cup."

"So what happened to the cup?"

"It has not been found, and I suspect it is not here. I think our thief knew that being found with the cup would prove his guilt, so he sold it."

"The best place to do that would be London," Finn said. "And I know every place where a body could make such a bargain."

Catrin smiled. "I thought you might. So, if you are willing, I would like you to go to London and look for it."

"I be willing, my lady. And I'll bring the blackguard back in chains if I can."

This fierce vow from a half-grown boy with the smooth freckled cheeks of a child was both endearing and amusing, but Catrin hid her smile so she did not quench his fervour. "No need for that, my lad. Just find the cup, and get the name of the seller. The queen's guard can find the man himself."

He looked disappointed, but agreed. "Is there anything else I can do for ye, my lady?"

"A small task only," Catrin said. "Before you leave, please ask my mother to speak to the servants about the issues we have discussed, and then meet me in the chapel in an hour's time."

Finn bowed, then bounced up on the balls of his feet, eager to go. "Yes, my lady."

Catrin was gazing up at an image of St Paul in stained glass when she heard her mother's step behind her. "What did you learn from the servants?"

Lady Angharad spread her hands. "They know nothing, but are quite afraid that they will be blamed nonetheless. Did anything turn up in your search?"

"No, and nor did I think anything would. I wager the necklace was stolen at the same time as Lord North's diamonds, so we would have found it with them in our first search, if it was here."

"Did you speak to the queen's other ladies? Did they have any insights?"

"None of them even knew the necklace existed." Catrin sighed. "The queen kept it carefully hidden, as she does most things relating to her mother. She avoids taking it out for fear someone hostile to her will see it, and thus she had not opened that box since she showed me the necklace last September. Even when they were packing, she only glanced at it to ensure it was there; she did not take it out."

Lady Angharad turned a thoughtful gaze toward the chapel ceiling. "Tell me, kitten, who was there when she showed it to you?"

Catrin had to think about it. "Sir William Cecil and his clerks."

"Sir William's clerks have been in and out of the Charterhouse constantly since we arrived, trying to convince the queen to do the business of the realm," Lady Angharad said. "Perhaps I should write and ask him to inquire."

"Yes, please do." Catrin contemplated her for a moment, freshly aware of all the troubles her mother had lived through before she herself was born. "Do you remember Queen Anne wearing that necklace?"

Faint sorrow crossed Lady Angharad's face. "Aye, I do; it looked lovely on her white throat, with her black hair for contrast. I think I first saw it in the early days of the king's courtship, but I don't think the king himself sent it. It did not come with a note or letter, as his gifts usually did."

"Who gave it to her, then?"

"She never said. But tears would well in her eyes when she put it on, and often she would sigh."

"Did all the king's gifts make her do the same?"

"No, not at all. The king gave her so many jewels — mostly diamonds, for they represented constancy — and she would dance with delight at each one."

"So maybe she was troubled by the necklace because it referred to the Boleyn family, and she wanted to marry and leave that side of her behind."

"Perhaps, yes." Lady Angharad shook her head. "Poor Queen Anne."

"Our current queen is sure that her mother was too clever to commit treason and adultery." Catrin tilted her head. "What do you think?"

"She was clever, and cunning. Her ambition was great, and I doubt very much that she would risk her status with the king for mere love-play."

"I find it hard to believe as well."

"And there is another reason: Anne loved Henry, at least in the beginning, and she loved Elizabeth. I think she would have sacrificed any other relationship if it would have kept Elizabeth safe." Lady Angharad pressed a hand to her heart. "But then again, desperation makes fools of us all. And in the end … Queen Anne was desperate. Desperate for a child, for the return of her influence, and for stability and peace. She had learned the limits of her own will: she could push her way into the queenship, but she could not make people love her."

"Yes, I have seen the truth of that many times." Catrin thought of Lord North's dismissal of her emblem, and of all the small snubs and prickles she received from her peers. "You cannot force people to change their minds."

Lord North had planned a very formal dinner for that evening. The heralds called people into the Great Chamber by order of precedence, under the direction of a sour-faced man who had the distinction of being the marshal of the hall.

Catrin paid little attention to it all at first, but she soon picked up on the heralds' unease. They had moved smoothly through the first names, but then hesitated when calling out the Earl of Huntingdon. Catrin just had time to wonder whether it was due to the earl's near-disgrace the month before when the herald called out the next name with indecent haste. "Edward, Viscount Walsall."

That was not right; as a countess, she should have been called next. Several pairs of eyes turned her way, including that of Viscount Walsall himself. Catrin glanced at Lord North, saw him smirking, and knew it was a deliberate slight. By ignoring her, Lord North was making it very clear that he did not acknowledge her status.

She curtsied to Viscount Walsall. "Fret not, my lord. It is a perfectly understandable mistake."

He scratched his nose in puzzlement. "Do you think so, my lady?"

"Most certainly," Catrin said with her most charming smile. "To Lord North's aged eyes, we must look remarkably alike."

Since Walsall was a very tall, very large man with a huge red nose and an even redder beard, this caused a chorus of laughter. Walsall himself shook from head to toe. "I would not wish this visage on anyone, much less a lady," he chortled, and sent the herald a pointed look before he raised his voice. "And a *countess*."

The herald glanced at Lord North, but he really had little choice. "Catrin, Countess of Ashbourne," he called out.

Catrin thanked the viscount and moved into the Great Chamber, where the tables had been set up in a giant U shape and set with silver plate. Another herald indicated that she should go to the left, so she made her way along the table to her place, only to find another obstacle.

The man with the dull eyes stood flat-footed beside her chair. "You have returned, I see," Catrin said. "You seem very skilled at gaining admittance to places where you should not be."

"There are those willing to help me," the man said. "They know you need to hear what I have to say."

Catrin deliberately stepped around him. "Speak, then," she said, taking her seat. "And begin with your name."

"Godfrey Breen," the man said, and paused as if expecting her to know it. When she didn't react, he hurried on. "Roger Surovell, your stepfather, was my father."

Catrin felt her heart skip a beat. "Was he?"

"Yes. And that means I should have your title." Godfrey Breen folded his arms and planted his feet wide. "I should be the Earl of Ashbourne."

CHAPTER EIGHT

Lucy was walking in the kitchen garden behind Lady Angharad's home, enjoying the cooling breeze of the approaching evening, when she heard a knock at the front door. A few minutes later Florie appeared in the doorway, her face suffused with suspicion and her hand firmly clamped on the shoulder of a small, thin figure. "A boy is here, my lady. He's looking for a bed, and thinks you would grant him one."

"A boy?" Lucy said. "We don't know any — why, it's Finn! I thought you had joined the queen on progress!"

Finn bowed low. "I had, but Lady Catrin had a task for me here in the city. As it is growing too late to return tonight, I had hoped to stay here."

"You are always welcome," Lucy said. "Florie will find you a blanket and a pallet."

Florie curtsied and trotted off, and Lucy led Finn into the Little Chamber, a small room off the large hall that was the centre of the house. It was cosy there, with wood panelling covering the brick walls and a set of cushions on the floor by the fire. Lucy took a seat in one of the large chairs, and indicated that Finn could sit on the cushions.

"Oh, no, your ladyship, I couldn't sit while in your presence," Finn said.

"We will waive that rule this once," Lucy said. "You look thoroughly exhausted, Finn, and if you do not sit you may fall down."

"There is truth in that," Finn said, and lowered himself to the floor. "There has been much upset at the Charterhouse, my lady."

Lucy frowned. "Is the queen well?"

"Well in body, but somewhat disturbed in mind. There was a strange theft," Finn said, and told Lucy all about the missing alabaster cup and stolen diamonds. "Worst of all, the queen's mother's necklace has been stolen."

"Oh, woe. That must be most distressing for her," Lucy said. "Why have they sent you here?"

"To see if I can find where the thief took the cup," he said. "No one has heard of it so far, and I have worn my shoes through visiting shops that would sell such goods. However, I'm pleased to say that there haven't been any floods of diamonds for sale, either."

"Why does that please you?" Lucy knew the answer as soon as she asked the question. "Oh, yes. If they are not yet for sale, the thief may still have them."

Finn nodded in agreement, and leapt to his feet when the sound of footsteps heralded the arrival of Pierrick. He bowed low, clutching his cap in both hands. "Good evening, my lord."

"Finn," Pierrick said, and sent Lucy an enquiring look.

"He has brought news from court, my lord," Lucy said. "Prithee explain, Finn."

Finn bowed and re-told his tale, while Pierrick paced restlessly from one end of the room to the other. He stopped only when Finn fell silent, and clasped his hands behind his back. "My lady, the time has come," he said gravely. "We must return to our duties."

Lucy held in a sigh. "I must agree. That poor vagrant found on the path by Lord Robert is in the care of the coroner, so there is nothing further to do here."

"*Bien.* Then we will leave tomorrow." He paused and glanced at Florie as she carried in a bundle of bed linens. "Florie, I have an important task for you."

Florie gave an eager little hop, much to the detriment of her burden. "What is it, my lord?"

"Find a good hiding place for her ladyship's jewels." Pierrick tugged on the hem of his doublet. "It no longer seems wise to carry them with us."

Catrin retired when her mother did, because there was no dancing and she had had her fill of games. They walked together down the corridor, while her mother hummed a Welsh ballad Catrin knew well. It made her heart ache with gratitude that she could hear her mother sing it once again.

They entered the ladies' chamber and found it dark and quiet. Catrin stirred up the fire and chose a taper to hold to the embers. It flared alight at once, and she lit several of the thick, stubby candles that lined the mantel.

"You seem troubled," Lady Angharad said, and pulled off her veil so that her silver hair could flow free. "Does it bother you, what Lord North did this evening?"

"Not at all; I am accustomed to such pettiness," Catrin said. "But I do have a question I hesitate to ask."

"That sounds terribly grave." Lady Angharad retrieved a comb from her chest at the end of the bed. "Come and sit."

Catrin sat down on the other end of the bed and watched as her mother drew the comb through her hair. She remembered when it had been as black as her own, but time and trial had taken its colour if not its gloss. "Was my stepfather married before you and he wed?"

Lady Angharad pushed her hair over her shoulder and began to comb the other side. "I believe there was a woman, but I doubt they were married."

"When was this?" Catrin brought Godfrey Breen's face to mind and made a guess at his age. "Nineteen years ago?"

"Yes, at about that time. Her name was…" Her mother's face took on a tinge of sorrow. "It started with a J… Was it Joan? July? I don't remember. I never met her, but I am sure Roger treated her no better than he treated me."

"Did she bear him children?"

"None that he acknowledged." Her mother let her hand fall from her hair. "These are odd questions to ask at this time, when you should be occupied with the queen's great loss. Is there a connection?"

"Not to me," Catrin said thoughtfully. "That is the difficulty."

The morning meal was just ending when the cherubs ran into the chamber: three children, dressed in loincloths, with goose-feather wings strapped to their backs and harps in their hands. They leapt about as if they were flying, and then a curly-haired blond boy stopped before the queen and bowed low. "We angels three, come to thee, in honest faith and charity," he said, with a dramatic swirl of his hand.

A little girl with a crooked front tooth followed him. "To give to you, best wishes true, and the great love we have for you."

The third angel had a spark in his eyes that reminded Catrin of Finn at his most mischievous. "Sad we are to see you go," he said, and pulled a comical face that made the queen laugh out loud. "But of your return we doth know, so until then our love will grow."

"For thou art our sovereign queen," they chanted together. "A greater prince has never been, nor will greater e'er be seen!"

They shouted the last, and then fluttered and ran and leapt their way out of the hall to a great round of applause.

The queen clapped her hands in delight. "A fair way to begin the day!" she cried. "It makes even a grey sky such as this seem brighter. Come, let us to horse."

Most of the court remained at the Charterhouse, for the queen's sojourn at Sir William Cecil's city home on the Strand was meant to be for only one evening. The queen chose just a few ladies — Catrin and her mother amongst them — and only ten or so courtiers. There were still quite a contingent of yeoman of the guard and servants, but most of those would be left to find their supper in the city before they escorted the queen back to the Charterhouse.

They travelled through the city again, along freshly gravelled roads lined with people cheering and waving handkerchiefs. The queen waved graciously at them all from her litter and accepted bouquets of flowers and little gifts from the children brave enough to approach. Catrin and the other ladies were charged with distributing alms, so they spent the entire journey surrounded by grubby hands reaching out in anxious hope.

Once the queen's coins ran out, Catrin gave away her own, until they arrived in the entrance courtyard of the Strand and the pressing crowds were kept back by brick walls. Once they were all inside and the gates were shut, two manservants set a pair of steps by the queen's litter, and then held the horses to ensure that they didn't move while she descended.

Sir William Cecil came out of his house holding a golden bowl that shone like the sun itself, and bowed low as the queen approached him. "Great queen, beloved sovereign," he said. "I owe all that I am to you, and thus I give you all I have. In this bowl are the keys to my humble home: prithee take ownership of this house as you have of my heart."

The queen accepted the bowl, and her dark eyes shone with tears for a brief moment. A blink and they were gone. "Good my lord, and my hearty and well-beloved friend," she said, and her voice echoed off the brick that surrounded them. "I accept your gift, and return your home to you with my thanks."

Sir William bowed again and accepted the keys, but the bowl was discreetly handed over to Catrin. She took it, surprised at its weight and fascinated by the fine polish. She could nearly see her face in it.

She held it before her as they all entered the house with stately dignity and moved together into the Great Chamber. It was at the back of the building, just like at the Charterhouse, and faced over the gardens. The tables were laid with wine and ale for those thirsty from the ride, and several courtiers took immediate advantage.

The queen, however, moved closer to Sir William and dropped her voice. "Did you receive Lady Angharad's letter?"

"I did, but it will not do to discuss it here," Sir William murmured. Then he looked around at the milling crowd and pasted on a smile. "Allow me to show you how we have improved the garden, Your Majesty."

"That would be most welcome," the queen said with easy cheer, and glanced at Mistress Blanche. It was a cue they all knew well; Mistress Blanche started chasing everyone away, taking the golden bowl with her so Catrin was free to follow the queen outside.

They travelled along a path bordered with fresh green herbs until they were a safe distance from the house, and only then did Sir William answer the queen's question. "I have questioned my clerks very closely — about the necklace itself, and anything they may have seen that day."

"Did you search your home?" the queen asked. "Was there any sign of my necklace — or Lord North's diamonds?"

"I did, Your Majesty, and there was not," Sir William said. "Nor did my clerks know of any such theft. However, I must tell you that I could not question one of them, for he is not here."

Annoyed, the queen snapped a branch from a plant that had caught on her gown. The scent of mint rose around them, but it did not soothe her. "Where is he?"

"I sent him to Greenwich two days ago — the same day you left London. He was due to return to the Charterhouse, and has not yet arrived." Sir William clasped his hands behind his back. "In truth, Your Majesty, I am somewhat concerned."

"What is his name?" the queen asked sharply. "How would our searchers recognize him?"

"His name is John, but he is better known as Ursus."

"The bear, my lord? Why?" Catrin asked.

Sir William rocked back on his heels and did not smile. "He is remarkably hairy. Despite his youth, his beard begins at his cheekbones."

"I see." The queen pressed her lips together, whether from disapproval or humour Catrin could not tell. "Send two of my yeomen to find him and bring him to me."

Sir William bowed. "Yes, Your Majesty."

CHAPTER NINE

The Great Chamber was transformed for Sir William's feast. Exquisite tapestries lined the walls, depicting the queen as the goddess Athena, accepting a golden apple from Paris. All along the polished oak table, silver dishes and glass bowls and cups made a glittering display under tri-branched candlesticks. Catrin had never seen so much glass in all her life, nor had she ever seen wine glasses with such delicate stems. She said as much to the queen, who lifted her own glass up so that the light reflected in the pale wine. "It is true, Sir Spirit," she said, using her nickname for Sir William. "The glass is so thin and clear it almost seems as if the wine is floating on its own."

Sir William smiled at her with sincere affection. "Do you like the effect, Your Majesty?"

"I do. It is remarkable."

"Then the glass is yours." He raised his voice so that the whole table could hear. "Everyone may keep their wine glass, so that we can all remember this beautiful evening with our queen."

Catrin met her mother's gaze and knew they both felt the same. This was an enormous gift; the glasses must have cost him many pounds. "You are very kind, Sir William," Catrin said. "That is a very noble gesture."

"It is the least I can do for my queen," Sir William said, and inclined his head toward her. "And the loyal servants who have brought her through another year."

Catrin lifted her glass. "Here is to many more."

"Many more indeed," Sir William agreed, and took a sip from his glass. His grey eyes remained fixed on her, however.

And once the queen turned to speak to the table companion on her far side, he leaned in close. "I sense that something is troubling you, my lady."

Catrin set down her glass. She had known Sir William for a number of years and trusted him implicitly as a confidante. "It has not yet progressed so far as to be a trouble, my lord, but I would like to ask you a question."

"You are welcome to ask, and I will do my best to give or find an answer."

"It regards inheritance law," Catrin said, and the back of her neck tingled as if someone was watching. She glanced back over her shoulder, toward the large windows that lined the chamber, but there was no one there. "Am I correct in thinking that a bastard child cannot inherit a title and estate, even if he is older than the legitimate sibling?"

Sir William steepled his fingers together, resting his elbows on the table. "Yes, that is correct."

"And if one sibling was a bastard and the other adopted rather than related by blood, which one would be considered legitimate?"

"Whichever of the two the father acknowledged as his own in the will," Sir William said. "However, there may be some complications if the adopted sibling was female. It would depend on the letters patent."

Catrin tilted her head. "I was given letters patent when my title was granted to me, outlining my privileges and responsibilities. Are those what you mean?"

"Yes. When a title and estate are under dispute, it is very important to consider the original letters patent that transferred the title to its first owner. Some declare that females cannot inherit; others allow it. Some force the title to revert back to the Crown; others allow the owner of the title to choose his successor. Each one is different."

"I see," Catrin murmured, and wondered if Godfrey Breen could possibly have seen her letters patent. It was a question for Ned, her steward at Ashbourne Manor, and that gave her an additional task to complete that evening. "Thank you, my lord. You have been very helpful."

Lucy and her husband left London late in the afternoon, and knew at once that they should have left earlier. The sky was growing thick with clouds, making the green grass take on a tinge of grey. Worse, in the distance they could see what looked like a bank of thunderclouds moving along the ground.

"Heavy fog approaches, I fear," Pierrick said.

Lucy nodded. "Have we brought lanterns?"

"We have, your ladyship," Florie said cheerfully. "And I'm sure we'll be nearly at the Charterhouse before that fog bank catches up to us."

"Yes, I'm sure you're right," Lucy said, but she knew from Pierrick's face that this was a comforting lie. A rush of wind made the fog roll quickly toward them, like a wave speeding over the sand on the shore, and they were immediately swallowed by it. It blotted out the trees around them, the hills on the horizon, and even the sky itself.

"Slow down," Pierrick said. "It would not do to run into anything."

They reined in and proceeded at a walk, and for many minutes no one spoke. The wind blew, the fog swirled and somewhere the leaves rustled. There was no other sound — no birds sang, no running water splashed, not even the howl of wild dogs could be heard.

And then, a faint scream. Lucy reined in, bringing her horse to a stop. "What was that?"

"I didn't hear anything," Pierrick said. "Perhaps you are just nervous, *mon amour*."

"I heard something," Lucy insisted, and then the cry came again. "There it is — did you hear? Someone is in pain."

"I heard it too, my lady," Thibaut said. "I believe it came from that direction."

He pointed at the dark forest to their right and Lucy urged her horse forward. They travelled for no more than five minutes before the ground dipped, forming a bowl at the base of which grew several pine trees. And in the centre of the bowl, a young woman lay in a pool of red and white. She was panting, her hands pressed to the mound of her belly, and even as they approached she threw her head back and cried out in pain.

Pierrick stopped short. "She is … she is…"

Lucy cleared her throat. "Giving birth."

Pierrick looked wildly from side to side, and it was somewhat amusing that he was so much more disturbed by this sight than by the body they had found the day before. "There is no one here — what should we do?"

"I will go to her, my lord," Florie said. "Perhaps you should find some towels or sheets amongst the bags, and send the men to look for water. We will need plenty of clean water."

He blinked at her in astonishment. "You know what to do?"

"I have helped two of my cousins and at least a dozen sheep give birth," Florie said, and hid a grin behind her hand. "But of course, if you would rather take care of it, my lord, I will —"

"I will fetch the towels and water," he said, and hastily retreated. Florie jumped down from her horse, tied the reins to a nearby tree and walked down into the earthen bowl, and after a moment Lucy forced herself to follow.

Immediately, compassion erased her discomfort. The young woman would have been pretty, with her black hair, high forehead and small pointed nose, but for the pain that flushed her skin and distorted her features. Pain — and fear, terrible fear. As Florie approached her, the young woman rose up with a startled cry. She wanted to run, but could not get her feet under her. Another wave of pain made her collapse with a wail.

"Do not fret," Florie soothed, and gently rearranged the blankets and bedsheets around the young woman so that they better protected her body from the earth. "My name is Florie Genevois, and I am here to help."

"This is not supposed to happen yet," the young woman said, and tears leaked from her dark, swollen eyes. "I should have more time to — to —" The words were swallowed in another cry. "Oh, it hurts so much more than I thought it would!"

"That is what I am told," Florie said, and pressed her hands gently to the mound of the young woman's stomach. An odd expression crossed her face. "How long have you been labouring?"

"All this day," the young woman whimpered. "Oh, my poor wee babe. What is to become of him?"

"All will be well," Lucy said with a confidence she did not feel. "What is your name?"

"Alice. Alice K—" She broke off and wiped sweat from her forehead. "Just Alice."

Florie rose to her feet. "My lady, may I speak to you?"

"Certainly," Lucy said, and they both retreated from the labouring woman. Florie leaned in close and dropped her voice to a whisper. "The babe is awkwardly placed, my lady. I think it might be a breech birth. And she is bleeding heavily — far more than she should."

"Then we need help," Lucy said, and Florie nodded. "I will send my lord Pierrick and return anon."

Florie's eyes darted in Alice's direction. "Quickly, please," she murmured.

Despite the low tone, Lucy caught the underlying urgency. She climbed the edge of the bowl again and rushed to Pierrick's side. "Pierrick, the girl is not doing well," she said. "We could well lose both mother and child if we don't get help."

His cheeks, already pale, turned a clammy grey. "What should I do?"

"I think the Charterhouse is the closest. Ride there as fast as you can and find Lady Angharad. She should be there with the court, and she will know what to do."

"I do not wish to leave you here alone. Thibaut will stay."

Another cry behind them made Lucy wince. "All right, but please go quickly. There is no time to lose."

Pierrick handed over a pile of towels with a trembling hand. "As you wish, my lady."

CHAPTER TEN

The weather forced the queen to cut the evening short. Fog rolled in while they were eating, so thick that even the streets of the city were blurred. Sir William and Lord Robert declared it safer not to stay at the Strand for the revels, but return as quickly as possible to the Charterhouse.

The queen chose to ride back rather than use her horse-drawn litter, so she and her ladies set off at the front of the procession, surrounded by a dozen yeomen of the guard. Sir William, Sir Robert, Catrin and Lady Angharad formed a pocket around the queen, and behind them rode Mistress Blanche and Mistress Ashley. The rest of the ladies and courtiers fell into place behind them, and all were merry as they rode out into the evening.

It was refreshingly cool outside, and the fog that bathed Catrin's face smelled of summer rain. The horses were well-rested and eager to go, making it a lively procession as they all tried to maintain the proper order through the streets. Lord Robert's black stallion was especially frisky; he danced sideways, reared up, and finally stretched his long, powerful neck and snatched the cap from a yeoman's head with his teeth.

It was amidst the chorus of laughter that the first haunting notes of the music began. First a recorder, fluttering through a series of gentle, calling tones. Then a voice, singing long, low notes in a tone of sweet sorrow. *"Quant je sui mis au retour de veoir ma dame…"*

The queen turned salt-white. "Tush, all of you," she said sharply. "What is that?"

Everyone went silent, so that the only sound that could be heard was the clop-clop of horses' hooves and the jingling of the reins. And that disembodied voice, drifting on the misty air. *"Il n'est peine ne dolour que j'aie, par m'ame."*

"Was this you, Sir Spirit?" the queen demanded. She was obviously unsettled, but she attempted to moderate her tone and smiled an uncertain smile. "Have you provided a musician to entertain us with the songs of France as we go?"

"I fear not, Your Majesty," Sir William said, and deliberately pitched his voice to drown out the song. But Catrin could still hear it and twisted about in her saddle, trying to determine where it was coming from. She could see nothing — not even shadows. It was eerie, how empty the streets had become.

"Dieus! c'est drois que je l'aime, sans blame … de loial amour."

The music had the soothing, serene beauty of a French ballad, but the words were sad, telling the tale of a woman who had given up someone who was deeply loved. The queen obviously did not like it; her dark eyes were wide in her pale face, like a deer facing a bowman.

Lord Robert drew his hand down his dark pointed beard. "If it bothers you, Your Majesty, I will find the singer and chase him away."

"No need," the queen said with another false smile. "The song surprises me, that is all. I have not heard it since I was a child."

"Very well, Your Majesty," Lord Robert said, but he was not convinced. He called for the yeomen to step up the pace, and they soon left the music behind. For a moment there was peace, and then — suddenly — they were swaddled in fog. The city dissolved behind them. The landscape blurred into featureless grey and black shapes, and even the stars disappeared.

It made Catrin's skin crawl, and she checked often that her mother was still by her side. She too seemed agitated, looking about and listening hard as if something was calling her. And then she spoke, so suddenly that the queen jumped. "Someone comes," she said. "Your Majesty, someone is riding toward us. I think he is in distress."

"Hold!" Lord Robert said sharply, and all along the procession the word was repeated, echoing through the fog.

"Hold, hold! Hold, hold!"

They all reined in, so all could hear the approach of a single rider. "Beware!" Lord Robert shouted. "We are armed!"

A distant voice wafted toward them on a swirl of mist. "I come in peace!"

Catrin went rigid in her saddle. "That's Lord Pierrick," she said, just as Lord Pierrick himself burst into view with his servant by his side, both of them sweating and breathing hard.

"'Tis I, my lords and ladies. I have long been searching for someone to help me, but no one is travelling in this mist."

"Where is Lucy?" Catrin asked sharply. "Is she well?"

"*Oui, oui, bien,*" Lord Pierrick assured her. "We came across a woman in trouble. My lady Lucy fears for both mother and babe. We need help, and quickly."

"I will go," Lady Angharad said at once. "Catrin, I will need your help."

"Take my litter, and bring them to the Charterhouse," the queen said. "We will meet you there."

"Thank you, Your Majesty," Lord Pierrick said, and plunged back into the mist. Catrin and her mother followed, and in seconds the queen's procession was out of sight. She could hear horses and voices for a few seconds more, but soon the sounds, too, grew muffled and faded away. For a few moments, all was silent.

And then, a scream tore through the air. Lord Pierrick let out an oath and urged them on faster — not that they needed urging. They all but flew to the edge of a bowl of earth, where a man in Pierrick's livery paced back and forth, waiting. He took charge of the horses and litter, while Catrin and Lady Angharad scrambled together down the sloping ground to the three women settled at the bottom.

Lucy was kneeling in the dirt, with the labouring woman's head in her lap. The young woman herself lay on a linen sheet that was folded so it lay partially over her. Another woman, a stranger with plump, pale cheeks, sat by the young woman's feet.

The earth beneath them was dark with blood.

Catrin's mother drew a large bottle of oil from her bag, then knelt beside the labouring woman. "What is your name, petal?"

The young woman just whimpered; it was left to Lucy to answer. "Alice."

Lady Angharad poured oil over her hands. The scent of lilies rose up around them, mingling with the smell of sweat and blood. "How long labouring?"

"Since early this morning," the stranger said wearily. She looked completely worn out, and her hands were bloodstained. Beside her, a bowl of bloodied water showed the meagre results of her efforts. "Her pains come one on top of the other."

Lady Angharad looked at the stranger curiously, and Lucy answered the unspoken question. "This is my maidservant, Florie," she said. "She has experience with birthing, but this one is … different."

"So it seems." Lady Angharad reached out for the sheet that covered young Alice, when something made her hesitate. She looked more carefully at Alice, and seemed about to speak when the young woman let out an agonised cry. Lady Angharad tensed her jaw and folded back the sheet. "Shh, shh, little one. Let us see what we shall see."

Catrin moved away from her mother and toward Lucy, settling down next to her so Lucy could lean against her side. "Dearest friend," Lucy murmured. "I knew you would come."

Catrin put her arm around her friend's shoulders, in part to help her stay upright. "All will be well, dearling. My mother has done this many times before."

"The baby is not in the proper position." Lucy buried her face in Catrin's shoulder. "Florie could not move him."

"All is not lost," Lady Angharad said briskly. "Alice, you must get up."

Tears poured down the young woman's cheeks. "I cannot … I cannot…"

"You must. Squat down as if you are about to sit on a chair — Catrin, Florie, help hold her upright." Lady Angharad wrapped the sheet around the young woman's waist, though not before she had trailed her finger over the stitching on the hem. It seemed to distract her for a moment, and then she bent over Alice again, her hands busy. "The cord is wrapped around his neck — there, it is free. Now push, Alice. You must push."

"I have no strength left," Alice whimpered. "It has been so long —"

"And that is why you must push now," Lady Angharad said. "For your baby, Alice. For this little one who needs you. Find the strength to push."

Alice found the strength, somehow. Her fingers clenched around Catrin's with the force of ten men, and she screamed as if she was being torn in two, but she pushed. Lady Angharad anointed her forehead and temples with oil, wiped her sweating face with a cloth that smelled of fresh herbs, and used gentle fingers to move the babe within her. And finally … finally … the baby came, and Lady Angharad caught him.

"It's a boy," Lucy said, and a trace of colour returned to her cheeks. "A handsome boy."

Alice fell backward, so suddenly that Catrin had to move quickly to catch her. "Is he alive?"

"He is well," Catrin said, just as the baby's cry rose up to the heavens. "Hear that? It is the sound of a good strong babe."

"Thank God," Alice murmured, and went completely limp.

Lady Angharad cradled Alice in the litter the whole way to the Charterhouse, worried that the jostling would start the bleeding again. Lord North's steward was waiting for them in the stable yard, and agreed somewhat begrudgingly to find a bed for Alice and a wet nurse for the babe. Alice herself was too weak to feed her son; she kept fading in and out of consciousness.

Lord Pierrick carried Alice to a small chamber and laid her down on the straw mattress prepared for her, and her eyes fluttered open for a brief second. "His name … the baby … he is Lufian."

"A fine name," Lady Angharad murmured, and settled the baby in the crook of his mother's arm.

"An ancient one, from before the time of the Conqueror," Lucy said. "It means love."

"His father chose it." A tear leaked from Alice's eye. "He will come. Once he knows, he will come."

"I'm sure he will." Lady Angharad smoothed a blanket over the young woman and turned to face Lucy and Pierrick. "I will stay with her until the wet nurse arrives; you must go and get some rest."

"Very well. But if you grow weary, send word and I will come," Lucy murmured, but she looked nearly as weak as Alice herself. Lord Pierrick had to help her as they left the room. "Good night, all."

"Good night," Catrin said, and turned to face her mother. She was gazing strangely at Alice, as if trying to remember something — or understand something. "Have you had a message from the fairies, Mother?"

The question seemed to startle her. "Why would you say that?"

"You seemed indecisive in the forest." Catrin linked her fingers together. "Did you consider leaving her to her fate?"

Lady Angharad gasped. "Of course not!"

"Then what gave you pause?"

Her mother closed her eyes, as if she did not wish to see what was before her. "I made the sheets she lay on."

"*What?*"

"I recognized the stitching, and the fabric. They are without doubt one of the sets I made for poor women during my time with Queen Anne."

Catrin stared at the sleeping woman — so small, so young. Far too young to have received alms from Anne Boleyn. "We will have to ask her where she got them."

"No, no. It does not matter — I am sure she simply inherited them from her own mother."

"But how can you be certain?"

"I cannot be certain, but..." Lady Angharad moved silently toward Alice and brushed her hair back from her forehead. "She does look familiar somehow. The dark eyes, the high forehead, the long fingers. Perhaps I knew her mother."

"But you will not know until you ask."

"And I will not ask," Lady Angharad said sternly. "It does not matter, Catrin, and the poor child has enough to worry about without answering questions that are merely idle curiosity. So you will think of it no more."

Catrin sighed. "As you wish, Mother."

"Very good." She came over and kissed her on the forehead. "Now go to bed."

Catrin considered protesting, but she was weary, and there was no real purpose in staying. "Send a page if you need me for anything."

"I will," Lady Angharad said, and settled into a chair near the bed.

Catrin left the room and started down the corridor toward the ladies' chamber. A yeoman with a crumpled ear appeared at the end, approaching with a somewhat unsteady gait. He looked, in truth, drunk with exhaustion. "My lady."

"Good e'en, goodman." Catrin glanced out the window at the dark sky and drifting mist. "You are on duty late, are you not?"

"I have just returned." He bowed low and then brushed sweat from his brow. "I was unable to find the stranger-thief."

Catrin blinked. She had all but forgotten about the dilemma of the jewels and the queen's missing necklace while occupied with the more urgent troubles of a labouring woman, but it soon came rushing back, and she recognized the man as the yeoman who had run away from the thief at the Charterhouse. "There was no sign of him at all in the buildings round about?"

The yeoman made a faint sound of irritation. "Very little," he said. "Only an old woman who saw a man in a ragged cloak like the one you described to me. He was riding away at speed late in the night."

"So he is gone, and Lord North's diamonds with him."

"I fear so, my lady."

Catrin sighed. "I am sorry to hear that, but thank you for your effort."

"I am happy to serve, my lady," he said, and bowed again before he retreated down the hall. Catrin resumed her journey, but the encounter had brought her mind back to her tasks for the queen, and raised fresh questions in her mind.

It was fortunate, then, that she found just the person who could answer them in the ladies' chamber. She was sitting on her bed in her nightgown, carefully removing dust from her skirt with a stiff brush.

Catrin closed the door. "May I ask you something, Mistress Blanche?"

"If you are quick; I am very weary."

"Do you remember anything about the queen's mother and the 'B' necklace?"

Mistress Blanche shook out the skirt and the fabric snapped like a whip. "By the time I took a position with the child Elizabeth, Queen Anne had had the necklace for some years."

"Yes, but I'm sure you noticed when she wore it and whether she liked it," Catrin said, and sat down on her bed. "You are, after all, an expert on royal jewels."

Mistress Blanche smiled, pleased at the compliment. "Aye, I remember Queen Anne wearing it when Her Majesty was a baby. The child Elizabeth reached for it and Queen Anne refused her. She said it was very precious to her so no one could play with it." She paused, remembering. "It was unique, that necklace. Many such pieces are remade from old ones, but no one had ever seen those pearls before. Three perfect teardrops."

"Do you know who gave it to her?"

"I am not sure —" Mistress Blanche folded the skirt and stored it in the chest at the end of her bed — "but I know the king gave Queen Anne money to redeem a jewel from her sister Mary. I have always wondered if it was that necklace. The 'B' could apply to either of them, after all."

"So it could," Catrin murmured. It was an intriguing notion, not least because it finally provided Catrin with an idea of who would want to steal that particular necklace. Henry Carey, Lord Hunsdon, was Mary Boleyn's son, and he was present at the Charterhouse. Could he have decided to reclaim his mother's property from his cousin, the queen? "Thank you, Mistress Blanche."

CHAPTER ELEVEN

Catrin started her day early, in search of Lord Hunsdon. She found him in the Great Chamber, sitting at a table while all around him servants set out the morning meal: cauldrons full of pottage, platters of boiled mutton and baskets of bread.

Lord Hunsdon did not seem to notice them; he was busy scowling over documents. He had a quill in his hand and periodically scratched at the parchment in sharp, angry slashes.

Catrin poured herself some small ale before she sat down across from him. "Something vexes thee, my lord?"

Lord Hunsdon dropped the quill and picked up his tankard. "'Tis nothing but estate business."

"I understand how frustrating that can be." She glanced down at the parchments and noticed that the numbers listed did not appear positive. "I often wonder if I will have to sell my jewels to pay wages."

It wasn't true, and a quirk of his eyebrow told her he did not believe it. "Is that so?"

Catrin put on her sweetest smile. "Perhaps it is my own fault; I do not understand ledgers and numbers as well as you do, I'm sure."

Lord Hunsdon gave a half-laugh and took a long drink. "Lady Catrin, I know you to be both wise and clever; you need not dissemble with me. Just ask the question you are trying to trick me into answering."

His bluntness surprised her into a laugh. "Why, Lord Hunsdon, how could you accuse me of such deception?"

"You forget, I am related to the Boleyns," he said dryly. "Never has there been such a collection of clever and dangerous women. I learned early that it is simplest to meet them on their own ground, and I will pay you the compliment of treating you the same as they."

"A compliment indeed," Catrin said. "And, as it happens, it is about a Boleyn woman that I wish to ask. Your mother, Mary."

He stiffened, and drank again from his cup. "What of her?"

Catrin watched idly as people started trickling into the Great Chamber, drawn to the scent of hot meat and fresh bread. "Do you know anything about a jewel that her sister redeemed from her?"

He paused, considering. "No such jewel has been mentioned to me," he said, but his gaze drifted away from hers as if he did not want her to see his thoughts. "But I wager my mother owned some jewels which others did not wish her to have."

She knew what he meant. Rumours abounded that Mary Boleyn had been King Henry's mistress, before he set her aside in favour of her younger sister, Anne. Indeed, there were some who thought that Lord Hunsdon himself was not the queen's cousin, but her half-brother. "Did she keep them?"

"She may have, but we do not have them now," Lord Hunsdon said. "Her second husband, Lord Stafford, sold many of her possessions after she died."

Lucy entered the Great Chamber, and settled at the table near the queen's chair. Catrin acknowledged her with a smile and then returned her attention to Lord Hunsdon. "Was there a necklace among them?"

"Not that I know of." His gaze lifted to the ceiling, and this time she could see regret in his eyes. "But I was not present at the sale, so I would not have known."

"I understand." Catrin rose to her feet, her cup in hand. "That has helped me greatly; thank you."

He inclined his head in response and picked up his quill again. "I am at your service, my lady."

Catrin acknowledged that with a curtsy and moved over to sit next to Lucy. "Good morrow, dearling."

"Good morrow," Lucy said, and squeezed Catrin's hand as she sat down. "Did you sleep well?"

"Well enough," Catrin said. "And you?"

"Very well indeed." She blushed a little, and changed the subject. "I saw Alice this morning. She is already growing stronger, but her milk has not yet come."

"She had a difficult time of it."

"Aye, she did indeed." Lucy took a piece of bread from the basket in front of her and then promptly dropped it into a steaming bowl of pottage when Lord North barked out her name and made her jump.

"Lady Lucy!"

Lucy pressed a hand to the fluttering pulse at the base of her neck. "Yes, my lord?"

Catrin heard Lord North's footsteps approach behind her and did not deign to turn around. If he could so easily forget his manners, so could she. And he seemed to have other things on his mind. "That girl with the baby — I hope you have planned for her to travel with the court," he said. "I do not want her bastard staying here."

"Yes, my lord, I have," Lucy said. "She wants to travel with us to Saintlow Hall; she said it will bring her closer to her father's house."

Lord North tapped his whip against the side of his riding boot. "Her father, or the child's father?"

Lucy looked uneasily at Catrin, as if wondering what she should say. "I am not sure. She would not tell me who her father is, nor would she name the father of the babe."

Lord North's lip curled. "If she wants to go to Saintlow, perhaps Lord Heatherleigh is the child's father."

"If that is true, I hope Lord Heatherleigh acknowledges him," Lucy said. "He is a sweet babe — such long eyelashes and deep blue eyes!"

"All babies have blue eyes; it makes him no less a bastard," Lord North snapped, and Catrin felt her stomach grow cold with anger. "Have you told the harbingers that there will be two more to travel with you?"

"Aye; I spoke to Master Blacquier," Lucy said. "He agreed to find space on a cart both for Alice and the wet nurse."

"Very well." Lord North looked around the room, a fresh scowl darkening his face. "It is not right that this useless wench has birthed a healthy son, while our queen is still barren."

At this, Catrin's irritation broke free. "Perhaps you should try to buy the babe, then," she said coolly. "A bastard prince is better than none, no?"

Lord North went white. "What did you say?"

"I said it was a problem you could solve." Catrin turned to face him squarely. "I have heard that you are skilled in finding sons for barren queens."

Lord North stumbled backward, his mouth working silently as if he was trying to find something to say. And then he turned abruptly on his heel and left them alone.

"Thank God," Lucy said fervently. "I do not think I could have borne him a moment more."

"Nor I," Catrin said grimly.

Lucy's blue eyes went round. "Did he really try to find our queen a son?"

"Not our queen, no. But there are rumours that he tried to find Queen Mary a son," Catrin said, and leaned back in her chair. "And rumours are useful weapons sometimes."

"Weapons?" Lucy giggled uneasily. "You make the court sound like a battleground."

Catrin sipped some ale. "For so it is."

Lord Pierrick was assigned a place in the procession with the high-ranking courtiers that flanked the queen, leaving Lucy to take a place with Catrin and the other ladies-in-waiting. They settled into a place a few paces behind the queen, who had Sir William Cecil on one side and Lord Robert on the other. It was warm, so many people removed their cloaks, draping them over their horses' necks as they cantered out of the city.

They were soon riding free on a dusty weatherbeaten track, and Catrin could enjoy watching sheep graze in green rolling fields. Lucy, however, shifted uncomfortably in the saddle. "How long is the journey today?"

"If we were just riders, a mere three hours," Catrin said. "However, such a long trail of carts behind us slows us down. Also, the queen often stops where people gather, so we may not arrive at Saintlow until late in the evening."

Lucy sighed. "There has been too much travel lately; I am saddle-sore. Distract me, dearling."

"Very well," Catrin said. "Did you see the emblems hanging outside Sir William's Great Chamber? I noticed that your husband's lions and fleur-de-lis were included."

Lucy sent her a knowing glance. "But not yours."

Catrin squeezed the smooth leather reins between her fingertips. "I do not have an emblem as yet."

"A problem we can easily fix. We can choose one this very moment." Lucy set her finger against her lips. "What about a sparrow? They represent someone ready to serve, and that certainly suits you."

Catrin hid a smile. "What others do you think suit me?"

Lucy knitted her brow. "An owl, because you are wise and quick-witted. Or a key, to celebrate how you guard the queen's secrets."

"That could be construed as threatening."

"True. Perhaps not that, then. Ooh, what about a sunflower? Sunflowers turn toward the light, just as you turn toward the queen in loyalty and service."

A flower? That did not suit her at all. "All good ideas, dear one. And I am not surprised that you know so many possibilities."

"Lord Pierrick and I have been discussing them of late. He is considering changing his emblem to a wolf —"

The queen's voice drowned her words. "Lady Catrin, attend me please."

"Of course, Your Majesty," Catrin said, and urged Ariadne forward. Several ladies gave way for her, so she arrived at the queen's side without causing more than a ripple of disturbance in the procession.

The queen leaned from her horse, moving close enough to whisper, "I wish for you to investigate Lord Heatherleigh while we sojourn at Saintlow Hall."

Catrin tilted her head. "What should I be looking for?"

"Anything suspicious."

"Do you suspect that he has resumed his former activities pushing radical religious reform?"

"My spies have seen no evidence of that. They cannot find him doing anything particularly dubious. And yet I do not trust him. He does not seem truly…" She paused, searching for the word. "Honest."

"Do you think he may have taken the necklace?"

The queen hesitated before she answered. "Not directly, no. But I wonder if he might know why it was taken."

"I did not think he even knew it was in your possession."

"He should not have known ... no, he should not have known. Sometimes I think he *cannot* have known, and I am chasing a flight of fancy..." The queen seemed to be speaking to herself as much as to Catrin. "But I must know for certain."

It was Catrin's turn to hesitate. "You have protected him until now. Has something changed?"

The queen sent her a cutting glance. "That is what I hope you will discover. But know this, Catrin: he is still under my protection, and I have my reasons for it."

"Very well, Your Majesty, I will do all I can." Catrin adjusted the mask she wore to protect her complexion; its ribbons seemed too tight over her ears. "May I ask you something about the necklace?"

The queen nodded. "Anything to help find it."

"Do you know who gave it to your mother?"

"Archbishop Parker told me it was a gift to my mother from her father, Thomas Boleyn." The queen's hands clenched on the reins. "I have always doubted that; Thomas Boleyn was not the sort to think of others in that way. I have always thought it was a gift from my mother's brother George, to remind her of their childhood bond."

"What a lovely idea; I hope that is the truth of it."

"As do I, but I have not yet found any proof — and there are those who would say that none of the Boleyns were so generous."

Catrin smiled at her. "Perhaps not, until you broke the mould, Your Majesty."

The queen laughed merrily. "Do not tell anyone else you think so, or I will be besieged by petitioners."

"Never fear, I will hold the secret fast," Catrin said, and then a sound caught her ear and she tensed. "A rider approaches."

"Fall in," Lord Robert said sharply, and all around them the yeomen slowed their pace so that they drew closer to the queen. Catrin was looking out through a forest of caps, feathers and horses' manes when a horse appeared to their right, riding fast. She recognized the round-shouldered figure on its back as Godfrey Breen, and her fingers went at once to the *stiletto* in her sleeve.

"Thief! Wanton whore! Lady Catrin is no lady! She takes the jewels of another's crown!" Breen cried, and swung his horse in a wide arc, away from the procession. "She steals the wine from another's cup!"

"Impertinence!" the queen cried. "How dare he disturb our progressing with such slander!"

"Lady Catrin is no better than a peasant!" Breen circled the front of the procession and drew close on the left side. "She has taken what is not hers, and I vow to take it back! Thief, thief!"

"What is he talking about?" the queen asked. "What have you supposedly taken, Lady Catrin?"

"A title," Catrin said, and chose not to explain further. It was, quite frankly, embarrassing. "He has challenged my possession of an earldom in my own name before."

"He dares question my decision? I will not have him in my presence. Chase him away," the queen ordered, and three yeomen took up the task with good will, letting out cries that made their horses leap into action. They aimed for Godfrey Breen with grim intent, and he bent over his horse's neck, retreating with all speed.

Lord Robert chuckled. "See him flee! Forsooth, he does not have the courage of his convictions, does he?"

"Good riddance to him," the queen said hotly. "And we will not be so merciful if he appears again."

"Of course not, Your Majesty," Catrin said with all outward semblance of calm. Inside, though, she felt distinctly uneasy. Would the queen support her if others more powerful than Breen took up his cause? Would she be forced to give up all she had?

Perhaps it was not the time to choose an emblem after all. Suddenly, it seemed rather like tempting fate.

CHAPTER TWELVE

Saintlow Hall was surrounded by a high wall made of stone. At the entrance, the wall curved inward, forming a deep U shape. At its base was an ancient square fortress, with later additions on either side that made the house resemble a giant owl with wings unfurled.

The queen's procession swept past the empty gatehouse into the courtyard, following a harbinger into a great arc as they divided into two groups. The queen and her favourites stopped right at the front doors, while the rest of the procession flowed past them and through an ancient archway to the stables beyond. They were gone ere the queen removed her travelling-mask.

The two arched doors at the main entrance swung open, revealing Lord Heatherleigh himself wearing a silver doublet stitched with black. He stepped out and bowed, and immediately dozens of musicians arose from every nook and cranny — behind the wall, under the archways, on the roof of the gatehouse, even between the bushes in the garden. Recorders, lutes, pipes, drums and the rumbling whine of a hurdy-gurdy accompanied the queen as she glided up the centre steps to the house.

"Your Majesty, you are most welcome," Lord Heatherleigh said, and held out a ring of iron keys. "I give you my humble home; let it be yours, as I am."

"My hearty thanks, my lord," the queen said, and took the keys from his hand. Some rust rubbed off on her fingers, which displeased her. "I return them to you, for you are a good and loyal subject."

He accepted the keys, and then stopped as if anticipating something. Nothing happened, and he sent a sharp glance behind him. "I have a gift for you, Your Majesty," he said awkwardly. "It may have been slightly — ah. Here we are."

A servant girl ran on bare feet toward them, bearing a golden cup half-filled with coins. "For you, Your Majesty," she said, and lifted the cup up in her hands. "To show our love and ded-def-defecation."

Lord Heatherleigh closed his eyes in embarrassment, but the queen chuckled. "Thank you, child. It is very beautiful and very kind," she said, and passed a hand over the girl's hair before she accepted the cup. There was another awkward pause, and Sir William Cecil stepped into the breach.

"Shall we go in?" he asked.

Lord Heatherleigh let out a breath of relief. "Yes, please do," he said, and led the way into a grand hall, complete with vaulted ceiling and wood-panelled walls. Several tables filled the space, covering the rush-strewn floor, and a high table faced them all, placed on a dais so obviously new that the raw wood still oozed sap.

In front of that table was a frozen tableau, with a man dressed in royal robes sitting on a throne. At his feet sat a woman wearing a crown, with a baby made of cloth nestled in her arms, and above them stood two children dressed as angels. They held a scroll that read: *From a reformed queen came a reformed faith, and a reign of untold bliss.*

Lord Robert buried his face in his hand. Every other eye turned to the queen, whose face was blank of all expression. "That is beautiful; my hearty thanks to the performers," she said, and turned her back on it. "But it reminds me that we have a babe in our company, my lord Heatherleigh. He and his mother both need aid."

"My steward, Ronald, will attend to it at once," Lord Heatherleigh said, and to his credit did not ask for an explanation. "Would you like time to rest before we dine?"

"Yes," the queen said coolly, and swept out of the room.

The evening meal was fast approaching, but no one was ready. Supplies were still being unloaded, people were still finding their assigned rooms, and the tents were still lying flat in the fields. All the queen's ladies were tasked to help, and Catrin took up a place in the ladies' chamber just as servants carrying chests started arriving one after the other. Catrin directed each one to leave the chest at the end of the bed where its owner would sleep, making sure that ladies who did not get along were placed far apart. Lady Angharad's chest was the last to arrive, and Catrin noticed when it was set in place that her own had not come.

She went out to the corridor in search of it, just in time to see a man far older than the other servants carrying her chest through a door several rooms away from the ladies' chamber. "Prithee, hold. That does not belong there," she said, but the man continued as if she had not spoken.

Lord Heatherleigh himself stepped out of the room next to where the servant had disappeared. "Fear not, my lady, that is my steward, and he is right to take it there. I have given you a room of your own for your visit here."

Catrin folded her arms and regarded him through narrowed eyes. "That is kind of you, Lord Heatherleigh, but why?"

He spread his hands wide. "I know you have had a difficult few days, and thought some peace and solitude would soothe you."

Catrin stepped out of the way of a maidservant carrying a gown and nearly ran into a chamberer with a basin of washing water. "No matter where we are, there is no peace on progress."

"I feared as much."

"And I would like my mother to sleep in my chamber."

"Very well; I will have her chest brought in." He sucked in air through his teeth. "The queen's welcome was not up to standard, was it?"

Not even close, but she did not want to add to his distress. "It was adequate, considering the short amount of time you had to prepare." She hesitated, and then decided it must be said. "But I would suggest, in future, that you avoid all mention of the queen's mother. It is a sensitive topic for her."

Lord Heatherleigh winced. "As well it might be. Hopefully she will be more pleased with the evening's entertainment — the musicians have agreed to return, so there will be dancing."

"A wise choice; she loves to dance," Catrin said, and took a step back as a page flew past with a stack of books in his arms. "I must return to my duties."

"Yes, of course. Please do tell the queen that I have given Alice and her bonny lad a room of their own, so they can rest."

"She will be pleased at that; thank you."

"Do you know what will happen to the babe?"

"Once we find out who Alice's family are, we will send mother and child to them," Catrin said, and tilted her head back so she could look directly into his eyes. "Unless the father of the baby comes forward and takes responsibility."

Lord Heatherleigh blinked at her in blank incomprehension. "Who is the father?"

"We do not know." Catrin paused. "Do you?"

He blinked at her again, and then understanding dawned and he chuckled. "I do not, I assure you. Why do you suspect me, my lady?"

"Because Alice wanted to come here."

"Then the nearby village of Ilford may well be her home, and I will find out if I can," he said. "But please remember, I bear no responsibility for the existence of this child."

"Very well," Catrin said, and was inclined to believe him. "Thank you for your help, Lord Heatherleigh."

Catrin knew she was dreaming as she rose up from her bed, because she floated out of her chamber without opening the door and drifted down to the Great Hall. It was empty, the tables devoid of clutter, benches all properly aligned, the torches in their iron holders along the wall black and cold.

But there was a circle of light on the platform, and inside it stood the three people who had posed for the queen that day. The king, the queen, and the infant Elizabeth.

But no — they were not the same people. The king had been replaced by a figure she knew well. It was her own father who gazed out at her, eyes twinkling with mischief as if he thought this a fine jest.

She had not dreamt of her father for months ... not since she had found her mother. And before then, her dreams had always centred around that day when he had been executed for treason. She had seen the blade fall a hundred times, and each time it hurt as badly as if it had landed on her own neck.

Anger rushed from Catrin's heart to her fingers, making them tingle as if with winter frost. "Why did you leave us, when you did not have to go?" she asked. "Why did you protect that evil man, when you should have protected us?"

The light around the platform blinked out so suddenly that it frightened her, and Catrin awoke with a gasp. She pushed herself upright slowly, trying not to wake her mother, but she was too late. Her mother was already awake, and gazing at her with understanding.

"You dreamt of your father."

Catrin made herself smile, although her heart was still beating fast. "Did the fairies tell you that?"

"No … you said his name." Lady Angharad drew Catrin into her arms and held on tight. "I did not realise that you still miss him."

"I do," Catrin said. "But mostly I think of that day we … we saw him die."

"I should have insisted that we go nowhere near the Tower that day," Lady Angharad said, and her voice was raw with grief and regret. "I should have protected you from that."

"Lord Roger would not have allowed you to protect me," Catrin said. It was a hard truth she had accepted long ago. "He wanted me to be ashamed of my father, so that he would be elevated in comparison."

"Yes, that is true," Lady Angharad muttered. "That vile man."

"Vile he was, to gloat at my father's execution when he knew that my father was taking the place on the block that rightfully should have been his."

"Some would say that they both deserved to die." Tears shimmered on Lady Angharad's lashes. "They both fought against Queen Mary in Wyatt's rebellion, after all. My Dafydd simply did not manage to escape. He got Roger to safety before he considered his own, and left his flight too late."

Catrin was really not sure what to think about that. Was she ashamed of her father for fighting against the Catholic Mary? Did she consider him a traitor?

No, she did not. "I think," she said slowly, "I would have fought for Wyatt too, had I been a man."

Lady Angharad rested her head against Catrin's. "As would I, my kitten."

CHAPTER THIRTEEN

A woman approached the queen as they wandered through the gardens the next morning, petitioning her for help. Everyone else paused to listen to the woman's plea, but Catrin hung back. She had noticed Finn arrive at the garden gate, and so she waited for him to join her.

"My lady." He bowed, but popped upright so quickly he reminded her of a bird drinking water from a puddle. "I have news."

"So I guessed; you are almost shaking with excitement," Catrin said. "Did you find the cup?"

"I did," he said, and drew a bundle of cloth from the pouch at his side. He unwrapped it carefully, and Catrin caught her breath at the sight of the pure pearly gleam he revealed. The cup was white with faint veins of cream and golden brown, and carved with elegant delicacy.

"Beautiful," she murmured. "So beautiful that I hate to return it to Lord North. How did you find it?"

"By chance alone, my lady. I had given up the search, and stopped at an inn on the way back for some food. The landlord had it up on a shelf in the common-room."

"You did well to notice it, then. Did you ask where he found it?"

"Yes; the landlord said a man exchanged it for a horse," Finn said. "He said the man was very common-looking, except that he never blinked."

"Strange indeed," Catrin said, and lifted the alabaster cup to enjoy its glow in the sunlight. "When was it sold?"

"On the same day the queen began her progress. Five days ago."

"Let me think… Who was with us then, and who could have been at this inn?" Catrin murmured. "Godfrey Breen had not yet shown himself when the ouche was discovered, and nor had Lord Heatherleigh. He arrived late that evening, and said he had been delayed leaving his manor."

Finn's brow wrinkled. "So they could have been in London to sell the cup, but could not have been at the Charterhouse to take it."

"Aye, it seems so. I must look elsewhere to find the thief." Catrin wrapped up the cup again. "Did anyone in the city speak of diamonds?"

"No one at all, and I asked everyone who may have made such a trade."

"That is interesting," Catrin said, and handed him the cup. "Thank you, Finn. You have done very well."

The boy blushed with pleasure. "Thank ye, my lady," he said, and then squinted toward the manor when an impatient voice cut through the air from that direction.

"My lady, prithee wait for me."

It was Lord Heatherleigh himself striding toward them, and he looked irritated. Catrin hastily asked Finn to hide the cup in her chamber, then turned to face him. "As you wish, my lord."

"My hearty thanks." He sent Finn a sideways look. "Are you well, my lady?"

"Very well. Why do you ask?"

"I thought it odd that you are not with the queen."

"I am about to join her." Catrin folded her hands demurely in front of her. "Would you like to come along?"

"I would," Lord Heatherleigh said, and fell into place at her side. Finn discreetly melted away, and they started off at a measured pace to catch up with the rest of the court, circling the house on the same side as the stables and progressing toward the park. "I had intended to join you from the beginning, but … estate business made it difficult."

"Ah, yes, estate business. I sympathise with those sort of troubles."

He made a sound in his throat that was less than polite. "Those sapphires along your neckline suggest that you do not."

"I beg your pardon?"

His mouth twisted to one side. "Ashbourne, I hear, has been remarkably prosperous since you became countess."

"I place responsibility for that squarely on my steward," Catrin said. "He is a very clever and capable man."

"Perhaps I will try to steal him, then," Lord Heatherleigh said. "Though I doubt even that would help, after this visit from the queen."

They emerged from the shade of the house into an area where the grass was rough and torn. To their left, an area had been laid bare, and a course of stones laid as a foundation, marking off several rooms where the new kitchens were to be constructed. The walls were almost at waist height, clearly showing the outline of windows, and wooden scaffolding had been erected all around the site. However, there were no materials lying about, and no men at work. Catrin suspected that the funds had been forcibly diverted. "I am sorry this visit has forced you to alter your plans for building."

"As am I," Lord Heatherleigh said quietly. "However, my sorrow is the greater that I commented on your clothing, my lady. That was vulgar and unmannerly."

"Yes, it was, but I understand," Catrin said. "I know what it is like to see wealth all around me and know I have little in comparison. It makes one … indiscreet."

"I fear that is too true. It comes out particularly when I behold a precious jewel." His eyes took on a certain dreamlike quality. "They have beauty as well as power... They are dangerous, but give one safety. So alluring."

Catrin narrowed her eyes, wondering if she might have found her thief. "Aye, they do hold a certain fascination. My personal favourite is sapphires."

"I prefer diamonds. That sharp glitter ... the clarity of them..." He shook his head as if to bring himself back to the present. "I do apologise, my lady. What were you saying?"

She sent him her sweetest smile. "Nothing of any importance, my lord."

"No matter, then. I am taking the queen hawking later today; will you join us?"

"I fear not." Catrin glanced back at the great edifice of the house. "The queen has given me a different task to complete."

It was not difficult for Catrin to lure Lucy and Lady Angharad away from the hawking; neither were particularly fond of such sport, and both were happy to help her fulfil the queen's request to investigate Lord Heatherleigh.

Once the majority of the court had left, they met in the Great Hall. "What are we looking for?" Lucy asked, and her voice echoed among the massive hammer-beams above them.

"The queen was not specific. She seems to suspect Lord Heatherleigh of something, but would not explain what," Catrin said. "As for me, I suspect that he may have stolen the jewels, purely out of desperation."

"How sad that would be," Lucy said, and spread her hands wide. "I don't think anything could be hidden in this room, though. It's too empty of hiding-places and, usually, too full of people."

"Let us try his chamber, then," Catrin said, and led the way past the winding staircase that led to servants' rooms above. Lord Heatherleigh's chamber was across from Lucy's and next to Catrin's, and fortunately the door was ajar, so they could slip inside without disturbing anything.

Lucy set to searching under and around the bed and its hangings. Lady Angharad began with a domed chest in the corner, and Catrin went to a cupboard that stood near the window. She found a very old and very large Bible that looked like it belonged on display in a church, a rounded ceramic demijohn containing wine, and no less than three quill-and-ink sets. But no jewels, and no hidden drawers or corners where they could be found.

Then Lady Angharad let out a gasp and staggered backward, both hands clenched at her sides. Catrin ran to her, throwing her arms around her shoulders so she didn't fall. "What is it? Mother, are you ill?"

"I found — I found —" She drew in a deep breath and opened one shaking hand, revealing the glitter of diamonds.

Diamonds.

Lucy pressed her fingers to her lips. "Surely those can't be the diamonds we're looking for." She glanced up at Catrin, her blue eyes pools of distress. "Can they?"

"No, they're not," Catrin said, and plucked the jewels from her mother's hand. "These diamonds are set into a brooch, shaped like a ship with a lady inside. Very pretty, but nothing that would draw the queen's suspicion."

"Oh, my kitten, I'm afraid you're wrong," Lady Angharad said numbly. "I have seen that piece before, and thought never to see it again."

"Truly? Where?"

"In Queen Anne's hand," Lady Angharad whispered. "She sent it to King Henry as a token of her affection. It was after he received it that their … relationship began."

"Oh, I see. It's symbolic," Lucy said. "She is the lady, safe in the ship of his constancy."

"Yes, that is what she meant by it." Lady Angharad brushed her hand over her eyes. "How sad, that her faith was misplaced."

"Yes, very sad," Catrin said absently, but her mind was on a greater problem. "How did Lord Heatherleigh come to have it?"

"I can't imagine the king wanted to keep it, after Queen Anne was executed," Lucy said. "He must have given it away. To Lord Heatherleigh's father, perhaps?"

"Perhaps," Catrin said, "but not likely. I do not think that the elder Lord Heatherleigh ranked so high in the king's estimation."

"Nor did I." Lady Angharad took the brooch back and hid it in the purse that hung at her side. "I will talk to Lord Heatherleigh about it."

"I'll come with you," Lucy said.

Catrin brushed her fingers free of dust. "And I will speak to the queen."

"No!"

Her mother's vehemence surprised Catrin into taking a step back. "No? Why not?"

"This will upset her greatly, and we do not know why Lord Heatherleigh has it," Lady Angharad said. "We must tread carefully, my kitten. I am very sure of that."

"And there might be more to find," Lucy said. "Perhaps we should finish the search before we speak to the queen."

"Very well," Catrin said reluctantly. "Let us continue."

CHAPTER FOURTEEN

Lucy followed Lady Angharad into the ancient chapel that nestled next to Saintlow, and along a side aisle into the private chapel that faced the Holy Table. Lord Heatherleigh was already there, kneeling at a prayer-desk, but he rose to his feet when he saw them. "My ladies," he said. "You look like you have something on your minds."

"Indeed we do," Lady Angharad said, and pulled the diamond brooch from the purse at her belt. Instantly, Lord Heatherleigh's face turned to stone.

"By God's wounds, my lady. Where did you find that?"

Lady Angharad lifted her chin, and froze him in place with the intense blue gaze that Catrin had inherited. "Hidden in your chamber, of course."

"How *dare* you —"

"We were acting on the queen's instructions, my lord," Lucy said. "Otherwise we would never have gone into your chamber."

"The queen?" A vein in his forehead started to throb. "Does she know about this?"

"Not yet," Lady Angharad said with a faint curve to her lip. "Now tell us who gave you this piece."

Lord Heatherleigh closed his eyes. "You would know her as Mary Shelton."

Lady Angharad glanced at Lucy with mingled sorrow and fear. "I feared as much. When?"

"She sent it to here to Saintlow while I was with the court in the Charterhouse. It was here when I returned."

"And why did she send it?"

Lord Heatherleigh looked away from her, focusing instead on a brass candelabra. "She is a kind lady, and quite lonely. I paid her a visit a few days ago, on my way to the Charterhouse, and she was grateful to be remembered."

"I don't believe that she is lonely," Lucy said. "She has four children and a husband to care for."

"Her children are grown," Lord Heatherleigh said defensively. "And being so far from court does not suit her."

"Aye, a courtier she was," Lady Angharad said. "A lady-in-waiting, no less. She must have much information about life at court in days past."

"I am sure she does," Lord Heatherleigh said bitterly. "But she would tell me none of it. Like Mistress Blanche, she says it is best not to speak of those days."

"Mayhap that is true," Lucy said. "Why would you want to talk about those days? You weren't even there."

"No, I was not, but I am bound by them nonetheless," Lord Heatherleigh muttered, and held out his hand. "My brooch, if you please."

To Lucy's surprise, Lady Angharad dropped it into his palm. "Best none of us are seen with that, my lord," she said. "It is more deadly than a vial of poison."

Lord Heatherleigh laughed and tucked it into his doublet. "And worth more than a milk-cow, so I will take the risk."

Lady Angharad put her arm around Lucy's shoulders and turned them both away. "So be it, my lord."

Catrin paced from one side of the double-arched chapel doorway to the other, offering smiles she did not feel to the people who streamed past her. Her place by the queen would be lost if she did not go in soon, and it would be her own fault. How could she have forgotten her prayer book? Forsooth, she did not need it — she knew the service by heart. But attending chapel without a prayer book was sometimes read as hostility to the new Church, and would give her enemies fodder against her.

Finn burst through the door at the back of the Great Hall and sprinted toward her, book in hand. He skidded to a stop in front of her and bowed before he handed it to her. "I am so sorry, my lady," he gasped. "I was coming to ye, and Mistress Alice called me to her. She would not let me leave — she kept asking where we be headed next."

"I understand, Finn. Thank you," Catrin said, and turned to go into the chapel. Something made her pause. "What did you tell her?"

"I said the queen next intends to visit Lord John Grey at Pyrgo Palace, but that the whole court would not follow, as it was for an evening only. After that, Ingatestone Hall. And then I started to tell her the next part of the journey, but she stopped me. She said she was tired and wanted to be left alone." Finn scowled. "Is she a lady? She certainly acts like one sometimes."

"I don't think she is a lady, no, but we do need to find out who she truly is. I am going to speak to her after the service, and Lord Heatherleigh is inquiring around the village to find out if anyone knows her."

Finn nodded. "Yes — I heard he is offering a reward. Five guineas!"

Catrin's fingers tightened on the prayer book. "Truly?"

"Yes, I heard him telling Mistress Alice so. She tried to convince him not to, but he said that she and her son should have every chance to live in a home all their own. He vowed to help them both in any way he could."

That seemed like an enormous amount for someone with the money troubles Lord Heatherleigh had claimed. "I am surprised, I must admit. I thought he would consider a stray girl and her newborn nothing but a burden."

"He's not treating them as a burden. I even saw him holding the baby." Finn shrugged. "Mayhap he feels a kinship to the poor wee thing."

"No, he swore to me he was not the father."

"Not that kind of kinship, my lady," Finn said. "I meant that he began life without a home, too. He was abandoned as a baby."

"He was?" Catrin had to take a moment to digest that information. "That is … unexpected. How do you know?"

"His steward told me. Talkative fellow, Master Ronald, once he's into his cups. He said that old Lord Heatherleigh's wife died of fever, and old Lord Heatherleigh refused to marry again. It seemed that his brother would inherit, but — two years later — a babe was left here. Old Lord Heatherleigh adopted him and named him his heir." Finn chuckled. "That annoyed his brother greatly, if I may be so bold to say."

"I wager it did," Catrin said thoughtfully. "Where is the brother now?"

"He was killed for preaching reform in the reign of Queen Mary."

"Does Lord Heatherleigh know who his true parents are?"

"The steward didn't say. I can ask, if it would please ye, my lady."

"Prithee do, Finn." Catrin turned again to enter the chapel. "Discreetly."

Finn flashed her a grin. "Of course, my lady."

"The Lord be with you."

"And also with you," Catrin murmured, her voice blending in with all the others in a soft, soothing rumble. It was a common refrain; the words came to mind without the need to think about it or refer to the prayer book. But, just to show that she had it, she kept it open before her and kept her gaze on the pages — until something outside the window distracted her.

Lord Heatherleigh was walking with Alice, who held her baby tight against her chest. Her gait was hesitant at best, and Catrin could not help but wonder what Lord Heatherleigh was thinking of, to ask a woman to leave her childbed for a walk in the gardens. He certainly seemed to have something on his mind; he was showing signs of agitation and annoyance. With Alice, it seemed. She kept shaking her head and holding the baby closer.

Finally, Lord Heatherleigh stopped and rested a hand on her arm. She jumped back, her face a study in fear, and a wave of hurt crossed his face. He turned abruptly and walked away, and immediately a man emerged from the woods. He wore a hooded cloak, drawn up over his face despite the summer heat, and he was easily four times the size of poor Alice.

Catrin tensed, wondering if she should intervene. But perhaps this was the baby's father — the man Alice most wanted to see, and most wanted to hide. She did seem to know him; she watched him cross the garden to her with astonishment on her face, but she did not seem concerned.

The man took her arm, bending low to speak in her ear. She shook her head and he spoke again, then reached out a hand for Lufian. Alice let out a cry of fear and tried to pull away, and Catrin immediately jumped to her feet, letting her prayer book tumble to the floor. She was ready to run to the rescue, but stopped when Florie appeared, her red curls springing loose from her cap as she flew across the garden. She shouted something Catrin couldn't hear, and the man jumped, losing his grip on Alice.

Florie threw her arms around Alice and shouted again, and the man stumbled backward, nearly losing his hood before he turned and fled. Alice burst into tears, and Florie held her close as she helped her back inside.

Catrin lowered herself slowly back into her seat, suddenly aware of all the whispers and sidelong glances her movement had caused. Across the aisle, Lucy's blue eyes were wide. Mistress Ashley's lips were pressed together in disapproval, and Lord Robert was looking at Catrin with open curiosity. "Is there trouble, my lady?"

Catrin hastily retrieved her prayer book and settled it on her lap. "No more than usual, my lord."

Lucy hastened to Catrin's side after the service, as they all emerged into the heat of noonday sun. "What happened, Catrin?"

Catrin told her what she had seen, and Lucy's rosebud lips slowly formed an astonished 'O'. "I am going to ask both of them for an explanation right now," Catrin told her. "Will you come? I suspect Florie is more likely to speak to you than to me."

"Certainly," Lucy said, and they both turned toward the door that would lead directly to Alice's chamber. Their plan was thwarted, though, when a yeoman approached them, looking weary and travel-worn. Catrin recognized him at once; he was one of the two yeomen sent to find Sir William Cecil's clerk.

Suddenly she was aware of the heat prickling across her forehead. "I suspect you do not come with happy news, goodman."

The yeoman bowed low. "No, my lady. We have still not been able to find the clerk."

"The clerk?" Lucy asked.

"A young man serving the queen under Sir William Cecil," Catrin said. "He went missing between the Strand and Greenwich."

Lucy bit her lip. "What did he look like?"

"We are told that he was very hairy," Catrin said, "like a bear."

Lucy gasped and burst into tears. "Oh, Catrin. H-h-he is dead."

"What do you mean? How do you know?"

Lucy started burbling about a body they had found, each phrase so punctuated with sobs it was hard to decipher. Catrin was trying to calm her when Sir William Cecil himself approached them. "By God's heart, my lady — is Lady Lucy ill?"

"Just upset," Catrin said, and patted Lucy's back in soothing circles. "I fear she may have seen your missing clerk, John, my lord."

"Where?"

"He was found by wild dogs in a shallow grave outside the city. Lord Pierrick and Lady Lucy took the remains to the coroner in London."

Sir William's nostrils flared. "I will go at once to confirm that it is he, if you will explain my absence to the queen."

"Of course, my lord." Catrin slid her hand over the silk of Lucy's hood and wondered who would want to kill a clerk. A man without influence or wealth … but with special access to the travelling court, and the queen at its centre. "I wish you Godspeed."

There was laughter coming from Alice's chamber when Catrin finally managed to get there. Alice was in bed, and Florie was dancing with exaggerated elegance across the room. "'Tis the way of all French ladies," she intoned, and spun in a circle so fast that her wimple tumbled from her head. Alice laughed so hard that the baby in her arms started to fuss, shaking tiny fists in protest.

Florie put on a tragic face. "Alas. Lufian doesn't appreciate my dancing."

"He will when he grows older." Alice pressed a kiss to the baby's forehead. "Florie, you are such a comfort. Thank you so much for all you've done for us."

Florie dropped into a deep, dramatic curtsy. "You are most welcome."

"Could you..." Alice's voice trailed away, but then she looked at Lufian and managed to continue. "Would you help us once again?"

Florie wrinkled her nose. "To do what?"

Alice slipped one hand under her pillow and withdrew a small twist of paper. "Take this to the copse where you found us," she said. "Hide it in the hollow of a branch."

Florie looked reluctantly at the paper, making no move to take it. "I cannot leave my lady," she said slowly. "But I will ask for permission to send someone."

"I can grant such permission," Catrin said, and both Alice and Florie jumped as if they had been caught stealing. "What is the message?"

Alice glanced from Florie to Catrin, her resolve obviously wavering, but finally held out the paper. Catrin took it, untwisted it, and found herself holding a man's signet ring. It was large, heavy, made of gold and embedded with a single ruby, with Lord Heatherleigh's crest clearly stamped on it. "Where did you find this?"

"I didn't steal it," Alice said quickly. "It was given to me."

"By its owner?"

Alice hesitated. "Yes."

Catrin met the young woman's eyes and held them. "Why?"

Alice stroked her finger over her baby's tiny arm. "I must not say, my lady."

"He asked for her hand in marriage," Florie said. "It was a gift — to prove his sincerity."

Alice lowered her gaze, but not before Catrin caught a glint of satisfaction in her eye. It was understandable, for it was indeed a triumph for a woman of unknown origin to catch the eye of a viscount, but Catrin chose not to comment. She simply lifted the ring and watched the ruby glow in the sun. "So it was a sign of your betrothal, and yet you were going to give it away?"

"I had no choice. I must send a message," Alice said. "Lufian's father is searching for us — I know he is."

"Then tell us who he is, and we can help him find you."

"I cannot. Truly, I dare not," Alice said. "Please understand, my lady — if I tell you, his life will be in danger."

Catrin gazed into her eyes for a long moment, and finally decided that she was being truthful. "Then I will send a messenger to the copse where we found you."

Alice gasped with surprise and joy. "Thank you, my lady!"

"With a *written* message, not this ring. This you should either wear, if you have accepted Lord Heatherleigh's offer, or return."

Alice looked away again, a faint blush on her thin cheeks. "I should return it, then."

Florie's eyes went wide with disbelief. "Why?" she cried. "You would be safe forever with Lord Heatherleigh!"

"He is not Lufian's father." Alice's jaw set tight. "I will not abandon my child's father."

Florie reached out a gentle hand. "What if he abandons you?"

"He will not. I know he will not."

"I hope your faith is well rewarded," Catrin said, over Florie's muttered disbelief. "Now, tell me about the man in the hood."

Alice drew her legs up under her, lips trembling. "Oh, please, my lady, don't ask me that."

Catrin's eyes narrowed. "Alas, I already have."

Alice looked at Florie in hopeless fear, and Florie's sunburned face flushed still deeper red. "He was an old suitor of mine," she said stoutly, and took Alice's hand in hers. "He was trying to force poor Alice to tell him where I was, and she was very brave. She would not tell."

Catrin did not believe a word of it. "He must have been a very determined suitor, to follow you so far."

Florie put on one of her most engaging grins. "Aye, my lady, once a man has met me, he cannot help but love me."

"And yet, you managed to discourage him quite easily, from what I saw."

The grin only slipped for a second. "I — I told him I was married."

Catrin folded her arms. "I see."

"He was devastated, of course, but knew there was nothing he could do, so — so off he scurried." Florie let out an awkward trill of laughter and came forward with her hand stretched out. "Allow me to return that ring to Lord Heatherleigh, my lady. I am sure you have much more pressing matters to attend to."

Catrin surrendered the ring but kept her eye on them both. "Perhaps I do."

CHAPTER FIFTEEN

The heat of the day made the Great Hall close and sticky, even once the evening advanced. It was so warm that Catrin was not inclined to dance, which was rare indeed. Instead, she sat on a bench with a cup of cool wine and tried to stir up a breeze using a goose-feather fan.

She was longing for the childhood joy of swimming in a cool forest pool when Finn appeared at her side, looking flushed and anxious. "My lady, Her Majesty the queen wishes to walk in the garden, and asks that you join her."

"Of course," Catrin said, and followed him out. The gardens at Saintlow Hall were not extensive, and placed rather too close to the scullery, but they were at least cooler than the hall. And, it seemed, quite empty, so Catrin took the opportunity presented. "Before we find Her Majesty," she said, lowering her voice, "prithee tell me if you have discovered anything about Lord Heatherleigh's parentage."

"Aye, I have." Finn paused by a wilting rosebush. "Lord Heatherleigh does not know who his parents are. Some say he does not care, but others claim that he is spending all his time and money trying to find out."

"Is he now?" Catrin murmured, and remembered Lord Heatherleigh's intense questioning of Mistress Blanche at the Charterhouse. She had refused to answer: was it from lack of knowledge, or from determination to keep a secret? "Thank you, Finn."

He bowed low. "My lady," he said, and backed away. Catrin went looking for the queen, and soon found her meandering between the hedges. She was unaccompanied, which was very unusual, and gazing listlessly up at the thin crescent moon.

Catrin curtsied and then fell in next to her, and for several minutes they walked in silence. "The beer is sour," the queen said at last. "And my chamber is half the size it should be."

Catrin nodded. "I fear Saintlow Hall is not truly suited for such a large contingency of guests." She paused. "It makes me wonder why you chose to come, Your Majesty."

The queen turned her head away and increased her pace. "Have you found out anything about Lord Heatherleigh?"

The question brought the diamond ship brooch to glittering life in her mind's eye, but Catrin found herself strangely reluctant to mention it. Torn between her mother's desperate plea for her to keep the secret and her obligation to the queen, she finally chose a different tack. "Did you know he is not the old lord's true son, Your Majesty?"

The queen hesitated. "Aye, I did."

"Is his uncertain parentage why you suspected him?"

The queen toyed with the pearls hanging heavy around her neck. "In part."

"Do you know who his parents are?"

"I have my suspicions, but they have nothing to do with this."

Catrin sighed. "Your Majesty, I will do all I can to help you," she said. "I will search and question and investigate until the end of my days, if you wish. But by hiding the reason for your suspicions, you put blinkers on me and I cannot see my way ahead."

"It is a prince's privilege to keep her thoughts close to the breast," the queen said coolly.

"Aye, it is," Catrin said. "But it may doom my every effort."

The queen chuckled, her displeasure dissipating as quickly as it had formed. "And you do not like to fail in this sort of hunt, do you, my talisman?"

"No, Your Majesty, I confess that I do not. Can you not find it in your heart to tell me who you suspect of being Heatherleigh's parents? Or, at least, tell me what you suspect of Heatherleigh himself?"

The queen hesitated. "The last, I can tell you. I suspect Lord Heatherleigh of … tormenting me, to put it bluntly."

Catrin laced her fingers together and held on tight. "How could he do that, Your Majesty?"

"Before the progress began, I saw a woman … in the distance." The queen's chest heaved in sudden agitation, straining against her tightly-pinned placard. "She wore a black gown and a French hood, and the lace on her wrists was so long as to cover her hands."

Catrin stared at her, confused. "Did she approach you, Your Majesty?"

"No — no, she vanished, when I drew near." A faint sheen of perspiration broke out on the queen's forehead. "But then — I smelled her perfume, in my chamber. And that song we heard in the fog — she used to sing it to me when I was a child. She sang it to me as I fell asleep, and no one knew that, Catrin — no one."

"Your Majesty, please do calm yourself," Catrin said. "I don't understand — do you mean this woman you saw used to sing to you?"

"Yes, she did. You see, that woman —" the queen's voice dropped to an agonised whisper — "was my mother."

Catrin reeled back. It could not be. Hundreds of people had witnessed Anne Boleyn's death; there was no chance that she had survived. "Your Majesty, I fear that cannot be true."

"I know it cannot be true!" the queen shouted, startling a deer in the distance. It bounded away in great leaps over the grass. "My mother is dead!"

"Yes, Your Majesty, she is," Catrin said gently. "But if all these things are truly designed to remind you of her, there is certainly a chance that someone is —"

"Tormenting me!" She clenched her fists tight and pressed them to her mouth. "And I suspect Lord Heatherleigh — partly because of his possible parentage, and partly because of what he said when I told him we would be coming here."

"From what I remember, he simply said that he would be happy for you to visit."

"No, he said 'most happy'. He would be '*most* happy'. That was my mother's motto. For a time, she referred to herself as 'the most happy'. And I have not heard anyone use that phrase since my youth."

"Nor have I," Catrin said absently, her mind already busy trying to fit all the pieces together somehow. This explained why the queen had been so tense of late … and it put their discovery of Queen Anne's diamond ship brooch in a rather harsh new perspective. "Your Majesty, what about the ouche?"

The queen tossed her an impatient glance. "What about it?"

"Did it remind you of your mother when you saw it?"

"No — as far as I know, she did not own such a jewel." The queen passed her long pale fingers over the necklace at her throat. "But the pearls … the 'B' necklace … this is why I was particularly upset when it went missing. It felt like the woman I saw knew I had it, and she has taken it back."

"Someone is trying to unnerve you," Catrin said thoughtfully. "And I wonder if the theft of Lord North's jewels was meant to fulfil the same purpose. Did your mother have any particular affection for diamonds?"

"Not that I have been able to discover, but I dare not ask about my mother too freely."

"Fret no more, Your Majesty, I have no such restriction." Catrin curled her fingers into her palms. "I will find this spectre and end the torment, even if it is the last thing I do."

"Do not make rash promises, my lady," the queen said wryly. "It leads to — what was that?"

Catrin had heard it too. A dull clang as the queen's foot swung forward. Catrin bent down and searched in the dark with her hands, and soon found something smooth and cold lying on the pebbled path. She lifted it up and found herself holding a golden ewer, of the type designed exclusively to pour water for ceremonial handwashing.

The moonlight was just bright enough to show the engraving on the side: the initials 'AR', etched above a falcon in flight and crowned with a royal diadem. "AR, for Anna Regina," Catrin murmured. "The Latin for Queen Anne."

"That is the ewer that was used at my mother's coronation," the queen whispered. "I have heard it described many times."

"A ewer that has long been lost," Catrin said thoughtfully. "So why has it now been returned? To remind you of your heritage, perhaps?"

The queen folded her arms, her shoulders curving inward. "Or to threaten me with it."

When Catrin awoke, Lady Angharad was moving about their room with quiet haste. "I have to return to London, my kitten," she murmured. "Finn has received permission to accompany me."

Catrin rose at once and crossed to the bowl in the corner to splash rosewater on her face. "What is so urgent there that you must go?"

"A child I helped birth has fallen very ill. His parents are frantic."

"Then you truly must leave us." Catrin restrained a sigh. "Does the queen know?"

"Aye, she gave permission through Mistress Blanche." Lady Angharad stopped in the middle of the room, one toe tapping. "I do not wish to leave you in the midst of such difficulty."

"Do not worry, Mother." Catrin slipped out of her linen smock and into a fresh one. "I have grown accustomed to difficulty."

"I know, but it is worse than you think." Her mother folded her fingers into her palms and held on tight. "I spoke to Lord Heatherleigh."

Catrin sat down on the bed so she could pull her silk stockings up and over her knees. "About the diamond brooch we found?"

"Yes. I gave it back to him. It is … dangerous. Too dangerous to be in our possession."

"How so?"

"Lord Heatherleigh told me who gave it to him." Lady Angharad paced back and forth in growing agitation. "'Twas Mary Shelton."

Catrin paused in the middle of tying her garters. "That name is only faintly familiar."

"You may know her best by her first husband's title: she was Lady Heveningham. She is a cousin of Queen Anne, who recently married a man without a title and left court." Lady Angharad brought Catrin her bodice and helped her slide her arms into place, then laced up the back to form the straight, stiff line so favoured by the queen's court. "There are rumours that she became the king's mistress while Queen Anne was still alive."

Catrin smoothed her hand over the satin-covered leather wrapped tightly around her torso. "And you suspect that the rumours are true."

"It would explain why she had a valuable piece of jewellery last seen in King Henry's possession." Lady Angharad held Catrin's farthingale open so she could step into it. "She left court quite abruptly for a time … and some say it was to hide a swelling belly."

"A *what*? Oh, that is dangerous indeed." Catrin held the farthingale in place so her mother could tie the ribbons that secured it around her waist. "If she birthed a child — the king's child — and if it was a boy —"

"He would be our current queen's half-brother on her father's side."

Catrin's spine tingled. "Lord Heatherleigh could be that child. Finn told me that he was left here at Saintlow as an infant, and old Lord Heatherleigh adopted him without knowing who his family was."

"Yes, he certainly could be that child. Mary Shelton would have known old Lord Heatherleigh needed an heir, so she could be fairly sure he would give the baby a home if she left him there. And if she left no information about the origins of the child, her secret would be safe."

Catrin pressed her fingers against her temples. "Until that child grew up, inherited the title and started searching for his true parents."

"How do you know he was searching?"

"Finn found out from the steward, Master Ronald."

Understanding dawned in Lady Angharad's eyes. "When I spoke to Lord Heatherleigh, he confessed that he had talked to Mary Shelton, and she gave him the brooch. But he would not tell me why, and now I understand his reluctance. He might be the king's son."

"And the queen knows that, which explains why she suspects him, and why she is so nervous," Catrin said. "It also explains why she showed him mercy when he lied to her about his political leanings, and why she does not now openly accuse him of stealing the jewels."

Lady Angharad helped Catrin into her kirtle and laced it up with nimble fingers. "Foolish man; he has no idea what a hornets' nest he has stirred up."

Catrin drew in a breath, feeling the familiar restraint on her chest from the weight of her clothing. "He could challenge the queen's position, and cause a civil war."

"I doubt it will come to that. This is all based on rumour and speculation," Lady Angharad said, and brought Catrin her gown. "It could be nothing."

"Possibly," Catrin said. "I wonder what Mary Shelton told Lord Heatherleigh about his parentage."

"He told me that she refused to answer any of his questions."

"That was very wise of her, but makes it strange that she gave him the diamond ship brooch. It is such a distinctive piece."

Lady Angharad helped Catrin into her gown. "It was certainly not from sentiment. He is concerned with its monetary value alone."

"He did mention that he is having financial troubles…"

"Perhaps he mentioned those troubles to Mary Shelton as well, and so she sent him something to help."

"A generous gift, which suggests that she has a reason to be so kind." Catrin drew her fingers over the satin ribbons lacing up her gown, considering. "You said that Mary Shelton was Queen Anne's cousin?"

"Aye, she was."

"I wager Queen Anne hid the child, then. Anne would not have risked her cousin's bastard child taking her own daughter Elizabeth's place, or displacing any son she hoped to have."

"She would have had to hide the child from King Henry, too. He would have proudly acknowledged a son — any son. He made Henry Fitzroy, his illegitimate son by Bessie Blount, the Duke of Richmond."

"So Lord Heatherleigh might be angry that Queen Anne prevented him from taking up his rightful position. And he might feel that Queen Anne's daughter is still holding him back, and might want revenge — the sort of revenge that does not risk his life or position." Catrin rubbed her forehead. "It would explain why he chose to torment the queen with hints and spectres."

Lady Angharad's troubled blue eyes met Catrin's "Will you tell Her Majesty?"

Catrin hesitated. "She must know already. Not about the ship brooch, but certainly of Heatherleigh's connection to Mary Shelton."

"And will you speak to Lord Heatherleigh?"

"Yes, I will. He must stop immediately — the queen could decide to act at any time, and he will be the poorer for it."

Lady Angharad's forehead creased with worry, and then she jumped at a sudden hammering on the door. She went to answer, while Catrin hastily ducked behind a screen to hide her hair beneath her hood. She heard a squeak as the door swung open, and then her mother's voice. "Lord Heatherleigh. Your ears must be burning."

"They're gone!" Lord Heatherleigh's voice sounded thin and shrill. "Mistress Alice and the baby — I went to see the boy this morning and they are gone. There's no trace of them — it is as if they never were."

"Calm yourself, my lord," Lady Angharad said. "Have you asked your servants —"

"Of course! No one knows! They simply vanished!"

"Perhaps they did," Lady Angharad murmured, and her voice took on a dreamlike quality. "Perhaps the forest-folk reclaimed their own."

A pretty thought, but not helpful. Catrin raised her voice so Lord Heatherleigh could hear her. "Or perhaps the baby's father came to claim them. Mistress Alice sent a message to him yesterday."

A loud thump told Catrin that Lord Heatherleigh had dealt a blow to the wall. "No! I will not accept that. No one has a greater claim to them than me, and I cannot lose that child!"

"Calm yourself, my lord," Lady Angharad said sternly. "This is unseemly."

Lord Heatherleigh took a deep gulp of air. "Prithee forgive me, my lady; this shock has unmanned me."

"So I see. You seem very attached to the boy," Lady Angharad said quietly. "May I ask why?"

"You may, but I do not know the answer," Lord Heatherleigh said heavily. "Perhaps he reminds me of my poor babe, dead a full three years now, and his mother with him."

Lady Angharad's voice softened. "I am sorry to hear that, my lord."

"Thank you." Lord Heatherleigh cleared his throat. "I would like Lady Catrin to take up the search. She sees things that others do not."

"She will meet you in the hall as soon as she is ready," Lady Angharad said. "There is much to discuss."

CHAPTER SIXTEEN

The chamber where Alice had slept was pristine. The bedsheets had been removed from the mattress, the blankets folded neatly, the pillow propped up to air. The domed chest in which Alice had stored her meagre possessions was empty but for a single moth, which fluttered up and out the window when Catrin opened the lid.

"One thing is certain," Catrin said. "She does not want to be found."

"But why would she go?" Lord Heatherleigh asked. "She should not travel alone. The poor babe could die from the cold."

Catrin raised one eyebrow. "In July?"

"The nights are chilly," Lord Heatherleigh said defensively. "And he is but a wee thing."

"Have you enquired in the village for anyone who knows Alice?"

"Aye; there is no one," Lord Heatherleigh said, and bent to look under the bed. "She seems utterly alone in the world."

"She does, for I just saw Florie and she told me that the babe's father has not responded." Catrin gazed thoughtfully out the window. "Alice has nowhere to go."

Lord Heatherleigh pulled hard on his beard. "Perhaps someone has taken her — stolen her for his own nefarious purposes!"

"And perhaps she decided to escape the nefarious purposes she discovered here." Catrin folded her arms across her chest. "I hear you offered your hand in marriage, my lord."

"I did, after she refused to let me adopt the babe." Lord Heatherleigh strode across the room to open a cupboard door. He swept a hand over the empty shelves and slammed it shut again. "But once again, I was rejected."

"Aye. I thought at first that it was because she hoped the child's father would come for her." Catrin crossed to the window and settled into the cushioned seat. "But now I wonder if she discovered something about you during her sojourn here."

He opened a chest, glanced in, and let the lid fall. "Such as?"

"Your plans for the queen. Or rather, plans *against* the queen." Catrin folded her hands in her lap. "Have you been plotting, my lord?"

Lord Heatherleigh scowled at her. "You always think the worst of me."

"I have cause to think the worst of you. I know that you have been telling lies about your whereabouts because you were searching for your parents. And I know that you suspect that you are … shall we say, closely related to the queen."

Her knowledge shocked him; he reeled back a full step. "How did you learn of that?"

"The diamonds you are so fond of have betrayed you," Catrin said dryly.

"The brooch? That was a gift, nothing more," Lord Heatherleigh said hoarsely.

"To you, perhaps." Catrin set her hands on her hips. "The queen will think otherwise, and perhaps Mistress Alice thought otherwise as well. Did she hear you talking about your little tricks — the French lullaby, the perfume, the mysterious lady who vanished when the queen drew near, the stolen jewels, the ewer?"

Lord Heatherleigh pulled off his cap and flung it to the floor. "You insult me! I have pulled no tricks!"

"Even though each of them reminded the queen of the family you might share?"

"Even though! I am no jester playing foolish games — nor am I a thief!" He clawed ferociously at his beard. "I acted only so that I might know the truth, not so that I might use it as a weapon."

Catrin was inclined to believe him, but that did not put him in any less danger. "Then give up the search. Let your parentage remain a secret."

"It will be a secret, from everyone but myself," Lord Heatherleigh vowed. "And today, I do not care about who fathered me or why. I care only about Mistress Alice and wee Lufian."

"Very well, my lord," Catrin said, and turned to the door. "I will tell the queen that you will remain here, rather than travelling with us to visit Lord John Grey at Pyrgo. That will allow you to continue to search for them."

"And I will send a letter to Pyrgo by my fastest messenger to apologise for my absence." He bowed briefly and turned on his heel. "Thank you, my lady."

It started to rain as they left Saintlow Hall. The queen immediately called a halt so she could retreat into her litter, while one of the pages took charge of her horse.

Catrin removed her mask so that she could feel the rain on her face, and Florie left her place in the procession to give Lucy her cloak. She put it on with gratitude and drew up the hood with a shiver. "An uncomfortable evening it will be, if we arrive wet and cold," she said. "I doubt Lord John Grey will think to light the fires."

"It is not too cold yet," Catrin said, and cast an eye to the sky above. The clouds were thick and growing darker with each moment, and she knew what that meant. "But we will not be able to avoid a soaking."

"I hope it holds off for at least a little while," Lucy said. "The only path to Pyrgo lies across a river; if it rains too much there could be a flood, and we'll have made this journey for nothing."

As if the clouds themselves had heard her, the heavens immediately opened. Rain came down so heavily that it looked like they were travelling through a waterfall. Even the horses had no hope of seeing the road ahead, and in no time the queen's litter nearly ran into a lone man in black robes, riding a tired grey horse.

"Your Majesty!" the man cried, and the queen rose up on her seat.

"Sir Spirit — Sir William — what are you doing out here?" she cried. "I thought you returned to London!"

"I did, Your Majesty," Sir William said, and drew his horse up next to her. The rising wind flung drops of water from the dripping brim of his hat onto her fur wraps, which she did not appreciate. "I found the coroner, and saw the body Lady Lucy found. It is indeed my clerk."

The queen forgot all about the water drops. "How did he die?"

"A blow to the head," Sir William said. Lucy let out a cry, and immediately Lord Pierrick dropped out of formation ahead of them and circled back to take up a position by her side. Sir William acknowledged him with a nod. "He was found in Fynsburie Field, my lord, was he not?"

Lord Pierrick nodded, and reached out to cover Lucy's hand with his. Catrin shook water out of her eyes. "He was coming from the Strand, was he not, Sir William?"

"He left the Strand for Greenwich Palace. I told him to follow us to the Charterhouse once his business was done."

"It would be faster to go from the Strand to Greenwich by water, and then travel overland to the Charterhouse," Catrin said. "Thus, if he was found in a field outside the city, I would wager that he had completed his business at the palace and was on his way to re-join the court."

"And that suggests that the purpose of the attack was not to steal whatever documents you had sent with him," Lord Pierrick said. "He died for another reason."

"I would agree, my lord," Lord Robert said thoughtfully. "And would I be correct in assuming that he would not have been carrying a lot of money or valuables, Sir William?"

"He would have had a few shillings at most," Sir William said. "However, he was wearing my livery, and it was taken from his body."

"To delay identification, perhaps?" Catrin murmured.

"Or so someone could take his place at court," the queen retorted. "We could have an imposter with us at this very moment."

"I think not, Your Majesty," Sir William said, his grey eyes like flint. "I know my clerks, and I would have noticed that one did not belong."

Catrin replaced her mask, for her cheeks were growing cold. "It is interesting that two bodies have been found in Fynsburie Field recently."

"Two men died there?" Lucy asked, her voice shrill. "*Two?*"

"Yes; when Lady Angharad and I were travelling to the Charterhouse, Lord Robert had just found a vagrant on the path," Catrin said. "What do you remember about him, Lord Robert?"

Lord Robert tugged off his cap and wrung out the rainwater. "Very little," he said, and had to pitch his voice above a fresh onslaught of rain. "I was mostly concerned for the well-being of the queen."

"Perhaps we should investigate him further," Catrin said. "He may have something to do with the clerk's death."

"I want to do it," Lucy said, so suddenly that the queen started.

"Are you sure, little Lucy?" she asked gently. "After so many days … it will not be a pleasant task."

"If it can explain what happened to that poor clerk, I want to do it," Lucy said. "Please, Your Majesty. I see that young man's face in my dreams."

"Then you and Lord Pierrick have my permission to go," the queen said. "And you may take any of my attendants with you, should you need them."

"Thank you, Your Majesty, but I think we should travel with as few people as possible," Lord Pierrick said. "My men Thibaut and Symon will travel with us, and they should be all we need."

"Yes, I agree." Lucy urged her horse out of the procession. "Florie, come back to Saintlow with us to help me prepare. Then you should stay there, where you'll be safe."

Florie turned her horse so she could follow. "Yes, my lady."

Lord Pierrick bowed. "We will return as soon as possible with news, Your Majesty," he said, and left the procession. Their figures disappeared quickly in the downpour, and Catrin silently prayed for their safety.

There were already enough bodies littered about.

The rain grew heavier and the fields turned to mud that splashed the horses' bellies. The procession was further slowed down by swelled streams that would normally be easy enough to ford but had now flooded dangerously. Catrin fully expected the queen to call a halt and return to Saintlow Hall, but she stubbornly pressed on.

It was a bedraggled group that arrived at the intricate iron gates that led to Pyrgo; even Catrin had stopped enjoying the wild ferocity of the storm. The gates themselves hung open, and the low wall on either side was just high enough to prevent anyone from jumping across. The queen's litter could not make it through, forcing her to take to horse.

She kept her chin up as she rode through the gate, but then saw something that made her shoulders drop in abject defeat. Catrin rode up next to her, and knew at once what the problem was. The river on the other side of the gate was a foaming torrent, lapping dangerously at a narrow, rickety bridge. Lucy's prediction had come true: a flood was barring the way to Pyrgo Palace.

Lord Robert rode through the gate behind them. "We must hurry. Within an hour, that bridge will be impassable."

"Is it safe to cross?" the queen asked, her voice pitched so high that it sounded thin and feeble in the roar of the rain. "Should we give up and return to Saintlow?"

"Saintlow is too far away; we need to get into the warm as soon as we can," Lord Robert said grimly. "We will cross one horse at a time. I will cross with you, Your Majesty, and we must go now. Follow us as soon as we are across, Lady Catrin."

"Yes, my lord," Catrin said, and watched with real concern as the queen and her favourite crossed the bridge. Water covered the horses' hooves, but the planks did not break. They arrived safely on the other side and waved her onward, so Catrin urged Ariadne onto the bridge. The mare shied and skipped about in protest, but Catrin soothed her with pets and reassuring murmurs, and she too got across.

As the rest of the procession followed their example, they urged the horses into a trot along the path, which had recently been gravelled so it wasn't as deep in mud as might be expected. Soon an H-shaped manor house, built with grey stone that blended in with the charcoal clouds and washed-out landscape, emerged out of the mist. The queen, Lord Robert, Sir William and several of the ladies went straight through the entrance courtyard, while the harbingers guided the rest of the group toward the stables around the back.

They found a silken pavilion in the courtyard, decorated with fruit and flowers in vivid reds, oranges and yellows. Children in blue silk robes were standing on wooden tiers inside, their faces red with the cold under woven garlands of scarlet and yellow roses. They straightened up at the sight of the queen and broke into song — a beautiful, innocent ballad about the glory of warm summer days amid good company.

A roll of thunder accompanied the first verse, and someone behind Catrin stifled a hysterical giggle.

The queen listened to the ballad with a smile, her dark eyes soft with compassion and pleasure. "Beautiful, beautiful," she said as soon as the song ended — and before another could begin. "What lovely voices you all have."

The children's faces lit up and they bowed almost in unison. Then the tallest one stepped out from the group with his arms full of roses. "We bid you welcome, Your Majesty," he said, and brought the bouquet to the queen. "It is an honour to have you here."

"It is an honour to be here, and what a lovely welcome. My hearty thanks to you all," the queen said. "Now all of you, go inside and get warm."

The children laughed and scattered, and Lord John Grey emerged from the back of the pavilion, his face creased with concern. "Your Majesty, you are very welcome to my humble home. Truly welcome."

"Thank you, Lord John." The queen pushed the dripping feather from her hat out of her eyes. "Will your welcome outlast this storm, or shall you send us on our way after supper?"

Lord John did not answer right away; something at the edge of the courtyard had caught his eye. Catrin glanced over her shoulder and saw a lone figure darting about at the edge of the procession, following each horse until it reached the courtyard, then running back to follow the next one. His features were blurred by the heavy rain, but he was dressed as a man and wore a dark cloak that flicked and waved in the wind. He also seemed unusually agitated, as if he could not believe that so many people were arriving all at once.

Lord Robert frowned. "Is something troubling you, my lord?"

Lord John started, then stroked his hand down his throat as if trying to smooth out his double chin. "No, no. Of course — of course, Your Majesty. We expected — hoped — that you would stay the night," he said hastily. "It would not be wise to travel back in this weather. No, not wise at all."

"We agree," the queen said coolly, "and would welcome a warm fire."

Lord John swept his hand toward the arched door of the manor. "All you need is inside, Your Majesty, and it is an honour — an *honour* — to care for you."

CHAPTER SEVENTEEN

A fire was roaring in the large chamber designated to the queen. Fortunately, Lord Robert and the harbingers had anticipated this eventuality, so they all had fresh clothes and supplies for the night. Catrin, Mistress Ashley and Mistress Blanche helped the queen get changed, while the other ladies helped the servants find places for the chests and boxes. Pallets had been laid out all over the room, in the adjoining chamber, and even in the corridor beyond, so they all had somewhere to sleep.

Once the queen was ready for an audience, she went with Sir William and Lord Robert to the dining chamber and left her ladies to change. Catrin gratefully put on one of her thicker summer gowns, made of a fine dark green wool, and dry stockings and shoes. There was nothing she could do about her dripping hair, though, except replace her hat with a French hood and let it hang down her back to dry.

She and the other ladies left the chamberers to hang the wet clothing by the fire, and went through the library and the great hall to the dining chamber. There, too, a roaring fire held off the damp chill, and better yet there was hot spiced wine and mulled cider. A lady wearing a fixed, unnatural smile was making sure that everyone had something to drink, and she actually brought a silver cup over to Catrin.

"Lady Ashbourne. How lovely to meet you at last," she said. "I am Lord John's wife, Lady Mary."

"It is very good to meet you," Catrin said, and took a grateful sip. The hot spices tickled her tongue and warmed her right down to her toes. "I rather expected you to be travelling with us for this entire progress, as many of the queen's hosts do."

"I had hoped to do so, but —" Lady Mary wrung her hands — "the children — they need so much of my time."

"Oh?" Catrin savoured another sip, wrapping both hands around the warmth of the cup. "How many do you have?"

"Six," she said, and cast a hunted look toward the doorway. "Anthony, my eldest, has been in London, and I am worried about him travelling in such weather."

"It is certainly a bad day to be out," Catrin agreed, and wondered if her son's absence explained the woman's discomfort. For some reason, Catrin suspected that anxiety had long been her close companion … and wondered if there was a reason for it.

"Yes, and now it is growing dark," Lady Mary said fretfully. Then her face froze into a strange expression — half relieved, half apprehensive — as a young man strode in, soaked to the skin. His cloak trailed water over the floor and every bootprint left a mark.

"Father," he said, and it sounded as much like an accusation as a call. "Father, where are you?"

Lord John emerged from the crowd, double chin quivering. "You dare come into this company in such a fashion?" he hissed. "We are hosting the *queen*, Anthony!"

Anthony tossed his head, flinging raindrops in every direction. "I will not dance attendance as you do, Father. Not until I know everything. Not until you explain to me what you did."

Lady Mary abandoned Catrin without a word, skittering over to them on her tiptoes. "Anthony, my sweetheart, prithee do not shame us so," she quavered. "Your father has done nothing wrong."

"Forgive me, Mother, but I fear we differ on what is wrong and what is right," Anthony said. "And I, for one, consider many things more important than our family's *status* in the world."

"It is not *status*, it is *honour* — honour and duty, and our expectations for our son!" Lord John roared. The chatter of a dozen conversations stopped all at once, and many eyes turned in their direction. Including, Catrin saw, the queen's. She did not look pleased, and after such a terrible journey Catrin knew it would take very little to tip her from irritation to rage.

"Your ideals of honour flatter us all," Catrin said hastily, and put on a cheerful smile before she raised her voice. "Good my lord, how delightful that your son wanted so badly to meet the queen, but it looks like he has brought the storm inside! Young Master Grey, we are happy to wait until you have changed."

Anthony sent her an angry look, but his father did not give him another chance to speak. He hustled the boy out of the room, leaving Lady Mary wearing that unnatural smile once again.

"Such an eager boy," she said, to everyone and no one. "He has been looking forward to this so much."

"I'm sure he has," Catrin said, and curtsied before she retreated back through the crowd to the queen's side.

The queen took a sip of her wine, irritation visible in the tense line of her jaw. "Lady Catrin, I suspect that you have poured oil over troubled waters once again. Was the boy planning a rebellion?"

"Aye, but against his parents rather than his sovereign," Catrin said, and refilled her cup from a nearby demijohn.

"Did I see him outside, following the horses?"

Catrin paused, her cup halfway to her lips. "I did not think you saw that."

"*Video et taceo*," the queen said wryly. "I see and keep silent. Was it him?"

"I believe so — at least, he had the same cloak."

"It might be best to ask why he greeted us in such a fashion."

"I will if you wish, Your Majesty, but I think he is merely a hot-headed lad."

The queen chuckled. "They all are, at that age."

Anthony was present at the great feast that night, his bulky frame appropriately dressed in a wine-coloured doublet embroidered with vines and leaves. He escorted Catrin to her seat at the high table, where his parents were sitting on either side of the queen, but he did not speak. Nor did he eat. The hot cockerel broth did not tempt him out of his deep sulk. Nor did the mallard in a mustard and verjuice sauce, the roasted chicken or the pasties of red deer.

Catrin was forced to turn to his mother for conversation. "What delicious food, my lady," she said. "Excellent choices for such a cold and damp day. At last, I feel warm again."

"Many thanks, my lady," Lady Mary said. "But we are not quite finished yet."

"No, not at all. There is more to come, my lady, I assure you," Lord John said, and sent a glare to his scowling son that belied his hearty tone. "Tarts — fritters — gingerbread — and, of course, marchpane. We heard that you are fond of it, Your Majesty."

"I am indeed," the queen said with a twinkle in her eye that told Catrin she was intending some mischief. "But perhaps I should pass it onto your son, as a reward for his fortitude."

Lady Mary made a sound much like a kitten in distress. "His … fortitude, Your Majesty?"

"Yes, I have watched him throughout this meal in great awe." She gave the boy a look that made him sit up straight, as if he had suddenly noticed she was there. "There are not many men in this realm who can so thoroughly resist the charms of Lady Catrin."

Catrin hid a smile. "Indeed, Your Majesty. I was beginning to fear that said charms had been washed away by the rain."

Lady Mary let out a shrill giggle, and the queen chuckled. "Perhaps it is merely that this young man's mind has been captured by something else, Lady Catrin?"

"Yes, surely that is it," Catrin agreed solemnly. "Something very important."

The queen nodded. "Something that makes a young man follow a procession in the rain."

Anthony started. "You saw — you noticed —?"

Catrin leaned close as if to impart a secret. "The queen notices everything."

Anthony drew in a deep breath and bowed his head to the queen. "I apologise if I have seemed rude, Your Majesty, but I do indeed have a great deal on my mind." He glanced out the window at the storm and his brow creased in genuine concern. "Especially today."

"What is causing you such concern?" the queen asked.

"Nothing of any import," Lord John said hastily. "He discovered some truths recently that have disturbed him, that is all."

Anthony's eyes sparked with fresh anger. "Indeed I did," he said. "Did you know, Your Majesty, that my father — for all his talk of proper behaviour and family expectations — is a rebel? It's true! I am the child of a rebel!"

"I did know that," the queen said quietly, and the boy started in surprise. "From what I remember, your father joined Wyatt's rebellion."

Lord John smoothed his hand over his throat, almost shyly. "For love of you, Your Majesty. And for love of your brother's church."

"Yes, we were on the right side that time," Lady Mary said, and let out another piercing giggle. "Unlike my aunt, the Countess of Worcester, who never did learn when to hold her tongue."

Lord John actually buried his face in his hands, and Catrin stared at the woman in astonishment. She could not believe that Lady Mary had pointed out that unfortunate connection. The Countess of Worcester's words had condemned Queen Anne Boleyn to death. Who would try to jest about such a betrayal?

The queen's face hardened into marble, and Catrin hastened to diffuse the situation before she gave voice to her anger. "Ah — it seems we have much in common, Master Anthony. My father was also part of Wyatt's rebellion." She leaned forward to address their host. "Did you know him, Lord John? His name was Dafydd, Baron Aberavon."

Lord John lifted his face, which was now as grey as his name. "I fear not, my lady. I spent most of my time with Wyatt himself."

"That must have been interesting. I hear he was a great poet."

"No, that was his father Sir Thomas Wyatt, who was an important courtier during the time of Henry VIII." Lord John managed a strangled laugh. "The Thomas Wyatt I knew, who led the rebellion, inherited Sir Thomas' passion for justice but not his skill with words. That passion led to his attempt to save us all from Spanish influence in 1554."

Anthony's broad shoulders stiffened. "And what of *his* sons?" he asked quietly. "Are they too men of action, ready to fight for what is right?"

"As far as I know, there is only one still alive," Lord John said shortly. "His name is George, and he lives properly in London with his family. I believe he is in law — at Gray's Inn."

"There are some who would question whether being in the law is at all proper," Catrin said with a smile, trying once again to lighten the mood. The queen acknowledged her efforts with a smile, although she deliberately angled herself away from Lady Mary.

"Let us see this marchpane, then," she said. "It would be pleasant to finish the meal with something sweet."

"Of course, Your Majesty." Lord John waved both hands in the air, and two lines of men in royal livery strode in, carrying platters of fruit, pastries, tarts and gingerbread. Then came a half-dozen men in clothes of wildly contrasting colours, with bells on their shoes and hats. Two of them were juggling, two were playing the drums, and two danced alongside the men who were carefully bearing a plate of marchpane beautifully carved into the shape of Pyrgo's famous iron gates. "Please, enjoy. Please."

Perhaps it was because her pallet was near the door that Catrin heard the voices. It was late; the horizon was grey with false dawn, and all around her the queen and her ladies slept. But the voices grew louder and louder, until she could not help but hear the words.

"Money? Money means nothing to me, Father!"

"It will mean something when you have none, Anthony. Have you forgotten what it was like before the queen restored our name? It was only two years ago! Tell me you have not forgotten the crushing weight of that poverty in two short years!"

"It was the weight of dishonour that crushed me, Father, not the weight of poverty. A fortune means nothing if I am forced to act without honour."

"This is not an act of honour! It is nothing but a hot-headed mistake. A youthful error! That is all! I will not have you throw your life away for something so — so — *foolish*."

"It is not foolish to me! It is the core of my being!"

"Oh, you think that now, but you are thinking with a young man's idealism. Once you grow up, you will realise that I knew what was best for you. I *know* what is best for you."

Anthony snorted. "You think that I will forget, but I will not — be my life long or short. I am leaving now, Father, and I am going to solve this problem before it is too late. It is the right thing to do."

There was a pause, and when Lord John spoke again he sounded old and tired. "Son, I tell you now: rebellion is never the right thing to do."

"If the cause is just, it is the only right thing to do," Anthony replied. "Goodbye, Father."

CHAPTER EIGHTEEN

Lucy and Pierrick found the coroner at his pub, standing behind the trestle table where drinks were prepared, drying tin tankards with a thick cloth. "You're too late," he said. "In summer, we must bury them as soon as the inquest is over. The hairy lad went into the ground yesterday, and the other one two days ago."

"Yes, we understand that. We just need to know more," Lucy said. "What did the jury find in the case of the vagrant?"

The man sent her a kind smile. "You don't need to know about such things, my lady," he said. "It might trouble your sleep and put circles under your eyes."

Pierrick chuckled. "You have it backwards, goodman," he said. "Once a great question has been raised, my lady wife will lose sleep *until* she knows the answer."

The man spread his hands wide. "Then we can all sleep sound, for there is nothing to know, my lord. The jury decided it was death by the hand of person or persons unknown, for both of them."

"What else did you discover?" Lucy asked. "Prithee tell me, how did they die?"

"Very well, then." The coroner set his hands on his lower back, pushing out his stomach. "First, the hairy lad. He died from a blow to the back of the head. The vagrant died from strangulation."

"Could you tell if they knew each other?" Lucy asked.

"There was no obvious connection between the two men, but the soil on them suggests that they were physically in the same area at Fynsburie Field when they died."

"Were there graves for both of them?"

"No, my lady. The jury went out to where the bodies were found — before the storm, thankfully — and found marks showing that the hairy lad was dragged some distance from where he died to where the soil was softer, and then buried in a shallow grave. There were short drag marks around the vagrant; it seems the killer was interrupted before he could move him to the same place and bury him, too."

"We know that the poor clerk was stripped; did the vagrant have anything on or with him?"

The coroner set down the cloth and rummaged in a drawer underneath the trestle, drawing out a roll of thick parchment. He unrolled it and perused what was written with pursed lips. "He had ink on his finger, a few pieces of parchment with words scribbled on them, and a hornbook in his pack."

"A hornbook?" Pierrick asked.

"A teaching tool; you put a piece of paper with sentences on a wooden board, behind a sheet of cow horn which has been shaved thin so you can see through it. Students can then trace the letters without damaging the paper," Lucy said. "It suggests that the man may have been a tutor at some point."

"If he was a tutor, he should have students to care for," Pierrick said. "I wonder why their parents haven't been looking for him."

The coroner shook his head sadly. "I don't think he had a master, or students, my lord," he said. "He was thin, as if he hadn't eaten in days. Tutors usually have at least a few coins to rub together, so if he had a post he surely would have had money for food."

"That's true," Lucy said thoughtfully. "Was there anything unusual on his clothes or his belongings?"

"I'll leave that question to you, my lady," the coroner said, and opened another drawer. He drew out a rough pack with a drawstring top. "That's all he had on him, and his clothes are in there as well."

"Thank you, goodman," Pierrick said, and handed him some coins before he followed Lucy out of the pub. She paused to rummage through the pack, and was immediately saddened by the meagre contents she found.

"Doublet — terribly worn — hosen, stained with dried mud. No shoes, I fear. Here is his shirt…" She pulled it out. "That is odd."

"In what way?"

"It's made of rough lockram." She lifted the sleeve, where white lace on the cuff contrasted strongly with the old, yellowed linen. "And one does not usually add lace to lockram."

"It does seem a waste," Lord Pierrick said. "Is there anything else?"

"Precious little. Here are the papers the coroner mentioned; it will take time to decipher them. A pen and inkpot, which are empty. And that is all." She slid the items back into the pack. "As the sum of a life, it is very sad."

"Despair not, *mon amour*," Pierrick said. "I have been thinking: we might find more if we retrace his steps."

"But we don't know where he has been."

"Not yet, but if the coroner will lend us his apprentice to act as our guide, we can see where he was found." Pierrick shrugged. "It is not much, but it is a start."

Lucy beamed at him. "Agreed."

The rain had long since stopped, but the world was still saturated. Even the sun looked pale as it did its best to shine, and the fields were unpleasant to ride through.

The apprentice led Lucy and her husband to a spot near the path, where the fields were lined by a dark brace of trees. Lucy half-expected there to be signs of a shallow grave, but remembered that the vagrant had been found on the path, not buried as the clerk had been. "'Twas just here," the coroner's apprentice said. "Lord Robert Dudley found 'im, milord. Angry, he was, for the queen were about to pass by."

"So I heard," Pierrick murmured, and glanced up and down the path. "From here, my lady, our vagrant could have been travelling to or from London."

"By foot, since there were no signs he had a horse," Lucy said. "And he was thin, but not starved. He had been eating well, but recently stopped."

"Perhaps he left his money and meals behind in his home village," Pierrick said. "That suggests he was travelling *to* London."

"Yes; a tutor could have earned enough pennies in the city to buy food, so he would not have been so thin had he been leaving the city," Lucy said. "How long can a man travel without eating?"

"A few days at most." Pierrick sucked in his cheeks. "I doubt he could cover more than twenty or thirty miles."

"Perhaps we should travel that far, then, and see if we can find where he came from."

Pierrick shook his head slowly. "There are dozens of villages around London, all within that distance, and we cannot tell from which direction he came. It would take weeks — months even."

Lucy knew he was right. "We must find a way to improve our odds of finding it," she murmured, and the answer came to her in a flash. "The lace!"

"What of it, my dear?"

"We know that the man was not rich, for his shirt was made of lockram," she said. "No one would add lace to such a garment, unless the lace too was not costly."

"Is not lace always costly?"

"It is, unless it has flaws or is a discarded cut from a larger piece," Lucy said. "Such discards can best be found near where the lace is made, for they do not usually distribute them widely."

Pierrick smiled gently. "And I suspect that you know such a place."

"The village of High Wycombe — my mother always orders her lace from the craftsmen there. It is no more than twenty miles away."

He chuckled and cupped her face in his hands. "Then to High Wycombe we shall go."

CHAPTER NINETEEN

Catrin carefully cleaned a fleck of mud from the queen's satin travelling mask while Mistress Ashley arranged the queen's hair in such a way that her hat would sit at a proper angle. Mistress Blanche, meanwhile, finished packing the royal nightclothes in a domed chest and called for servants to come and collect it.

The queen moved restlessly to the window. "At least it is not raining," she said. "But the sky is very grey, and it is not as warm as I had hoped."

Catrin held out the mask to the fire to dry the spot more quickly. "It will be a short ride back to Saintlow Hall, and it should be warmer by the time we arrive. Perfect for a walk in the gardens."

"I am not sure of that; it looks terribly damp," Mistress Blanche said, just as someone knocked on the door. She opened it, and Lord John tumbled in, his eyes wide and wild.

"Your Majesty," he said nervously, and bowed so low he folded himself in half. "You cannot leave my house. No — no — you cannot leave."

The queen turned her coronation ring around on her finger, a nervous gesture at odds with the authority that rang in her voice. "It is our will to depart, Lord John. I suggest you do not attempt to thwart us."

"But — but — the path is more than ankle-deep in mud. Ankle-deep!" Lord John said. "The water is still flowing over the bridge, and has a terribly fierce current."

The queen glanced out the window again. "Is it truly dangerous?"

"Yes, yes." Lord John's gaze slid away from her and alighted for a moment on Catrin before jumping away again. "I sent someone to check and they told me so. It is not wise for you to travel."

"And it is not wise for us to stay." The queen waved a hand to indicate the crowd outside, loading carts and saddling horses. "Surely you are not equipped to provide us with all we need for another day."

"I will manage, Your Majesty. I assure you, you will have all you need."

"Very well," the queen said reluctantly. "Inform the harbingers that we will tarry another day, and send word when a meal has been prepared."

"Yes, yes, Your Majesty," Lord John said, and the relief on his face was enormous. He backed out with another bow, and Mistress Blanche closed the door again.

Catrin smoothed her fingers over the satin mask. "You seem doubtful, Your Majesty."

"I suspect a hidden purpose," the queen said. "Find Lord Robert, my talisman, and ask him to go evaluate the true state of the bridge. That will tell us if Lord John has a darker reason to keep us here."

Catrin thought of Anthony, and his sudden departure for an unknown place. "Or perhaps a darker reason to stop us from going anywhere else."

A generous morning meal was set before them, and came complete with fresh bread, many jugs of ale, salt fish and sweet omelettes, made with eggs, butter, sugar and currants. It was a sign of some impressive husbandry on the part of Lord John and his servants, but the queen did not seem to notice. She ate an omelette and nibbled on some bread, but then moved to the window and stared out at the view to the back of the house, which consisted mostly of fallow fields and tossing trees. Catrin took a cup of ale to her, which she accepted without drinking.

"My brother Edward was held against his will once," she said, and watched a milkmaid pass by, carrying a deep bowl into the kitchens. "And we cannot forget the other Edward, who was taken into the Tower and never seen again."

An overdramatic parallel, but it would do no good to dismiss it. "There is a tale told at Ashbourne, Your Majesty, of someone in much the same circumstance as we find ourselves," Catrin said instead, and lowered her voice into a storyteller's soothing singsong. "It was many, many years ago, when Ashbourne was led by a cruel master, who thought that power was made stronger by fear. Then, one day, a beautiful maiden was caught in a storm and cast up at his front door. The earl took one look at her and fell in love. He ordered his people to give her all the best of what he had, and prayed every minute for her recovery."

The queen gave her an amused glance. "And did God hear his prayers?"

"He did, Your Majesty. The maiden recovered, but once she realised who had saved her she wanted to leave. The earl's reputation for cruelty had spread far beyond his borders, and she wanted nothing to do with him. Her passion humbled him, and he vowed that if she stayed he would become as kind as he had once been cruel."

"Rather a difficult choice for her to make, then."

"Ah, yes. She chose to stay, for she wanted very much to end the suffering of the earl's people. And he was as good as his word; he changed his ways and became in every way worthy of her. And since then, the earls of Ashbourne have been noted for their sense of justice and their concern for their people." Catrin's lip quirked. "Until myself, at least."

The queen chuckled. "I doubt you are at all cruel, my talisman."

"No, I would not be cruel or unjust. However, I sometimes wonder if my lack of experience does as much damage as cruelty would." Catrin sighed. "I have a case before me now where two brothers both insist that their father's will grants them their family cottage."

"Have you seen the will?"

"I have; it is written in a way that makes the father's true intention very difficult to determine. All that is certain is that he left two things of value: a cottage and a rather large farm." Catrin sipped some ale to mask a sigh. "My steward asked me to decide the case on my own authority days ago, but I have not responded. I find it difficult to decide what to do."

The queen started turning her cup between her hands. "Tell the older brother to choose either the cottage, or a piece of land from the farm on which to build a cottage. That will provide both brothers with a home and keep the farm running smoothly."

"Why, that is an excellent solution, Your Majesty. I would never have thought of that."

The queen rested a hand on Catrin's arm. "Yes, you would have," she said gently. "Once you have learned to wield the authority I myself have given you, my talisman, I am sure you will be as fine a lord as any of the ancient earls of Ashbourne."

"Thank you, Your Majesty," Catrin said, and finished her ale. "Now, would you like to play a game of cards to while away the hours?"

"I would, but I must speak with Sir William and my councillors." She gave a great sigh, but her dark eyes sparkled with humour. "Like the business of your manor, the business of the realm is never complete."

Once the queen's chamber was prepared for another night's slumber and the queen's clothing brushed and laundered, there was nothing left for Catrin to do until the evening meal. She could have joined one of a dozen games underway in the Great Hall, or gone to a service in the chapel, but decided instead to brave the elements and explore the garden. It was likely that the queen would feel the need for fresh air once she was finished with Sir William, and it would behove Catrin to know the least muddy paths.

The wind snatched her breath as soon as she stepped outside, but for all its strength and power it was neither harsh nor cold. Catrin wrapped her cloak more tightly around her and stepped out onto the gravel path, which was dry enough that the water didn't squirt between the stones but still wet enough to squeak. Or was that sound coming from the stones? Catrin paused to listen, and heard the sound again. No, it wasn't a squeak under her feet but a cry from afar, drifting in the wind.

Catrin looked around, trying to find the source. The gardens did not stretch far; the ornamental hedges and flowers soon turned into the prosaic rows of a kitchen garden. And then, fallow fields, covered in old golden grass with new green shoots underneath it. A half-dozen outbuildings were scattered about, and there was a ditch to the left, now filled with a rushing stream of water. Could someone be trapped down there?

Catrin hurried through the paths toward the water, and heard another cry. It seemed to be coming from behind her — from the forest beyond the fields. She stopped to listen once again, and jumped when another cry came from much closer to her.

"Lady Catrin!"

Catrin spun toward the house and saw Lady Mary rushing toward her, her nose deeply pink from the wind. "Yes, Lady Mary?"

"I have been looking for you everywhere," she panted. "I did not expect to find you outside on such a day."

"I thought I heard something," Catrin said, and tried again to discern the cry in the midst of the moaning wind. "Are any of your people — or animals — missing?"

"No, we are all safe and sound," Lady Mary said. "Perhaps you heard the villagers talking. His lordship has prevailed upon them to demonstrate their country dances for the queen this afternoon."

"What a lovely idea," Catrin said. "The queen loves learning variations on her favourite dances."

Lady Mary gave a little jump of joy. "Oh, I'm so glad! We were at quite a loss about how to entertain her today, but this should please her greatly."

"Yes, it should." Catrin started to retrace her steps. "So perhaps we should go inside and prepare?"

"Yes, yes, but just a moment. I wanted to show you something first." Lady Mary drew her hand out of the folds of her cloak with a flourish, and suddenly the dull air flashed with cold fire. "Isn't it beautiful?"

It was a golden brooch, with a falcon formed from diamonds at its centre, surrounded by sapphires. Each jewel was exquisitely cut, so it glittered fiercely in Lady Mary's plump white hand. "It certainly is," Catrin said. "But I fear it is not safe to show such a piece; have you not heard of the theft of diamonds from Lord North?"

"I have, but I am not afraid of it being stolen," Lady Mary said. "It's cursed."

Catrin barely resisted rolling her eyes. "I do not believe in curses."

"Nor do I, but my aunt the Countess of Worcester does. She gave it to me because she said that nothing good had come to her since she received it. And, lo and behold — once she gave it away, she managed to find a fine husband."

"Where did she get it from?" Catrin asked.

"It was a gift … after she —" Lady Mary hesitated — "assisted the king in 1536."

So it was her reward for betraying Queen Anne. "I can see why she was not fond of it. But that gives you another reason to keep it hidden; the queen would not be pleased if she saw it."

"Oh, I know. I will put it away again now. I just wanted to show you, for I heard you were fond of sapphires."

Catrin found a smile. "Aren't we all?"

"I prefer rubies," Lady Mary said, and tucked the beautiful, deadly thing away. "Shall we go and see the dancing?"

"Yes, of course," Catrin said, and followed Lady Mary back inside. They found the Great Hall cleared of its tables and benches, and a dozen men and women in simple kirtles and tunics assembled in the centre. The dais at the front of the room had a great oaken chair in place for the queen, and she was perched on the edge of it, with Sir William standing on one side and Mistress Ashley on the other.

"My talisman," she said with a tight smile, when Catrin approached. "Has there been any news of Lord Robert?"

"Not as yet, Your Majesty. But I'm certain he will return ere the dance is over."

"I hope that is true, Lady Catrin," she said, and indicated with a stiff nod that the demonstration could begin.

CHAPTER TWENTY

The dancers were rewarded with cups of ale and wine after their exertions, and some approached the queen to offer their pledges of loyalty. The queen received them graciously, and offered smiles and thanks, but her whole frame was stiff and still. It was like worry had frozen her in place, despite the warmth of music and merriment.

A distant bang made Catrin's fingers fly to the hilt of her *stiletto*. The queen gazed at the doors intensely, and visibly relaxed when they swung open to reveal Lord Robert. His hair was damp, and he wore court slippers instead of boots, telling Catrin that he had taken the time to wash and change before presenting himself to the queen.

He strode in with the sort of confidence that made people step hastily out of his way and bowed before the queen. "Your Majesty."

The queen's cheeks turned pink. "You have long been absent, Lord Robert."

Lord Robert glanced toward Lord John and bowed again. "I apologise, Your Majesty. In my foolishness, I chose to go riding."

"Foolish indeed," the queen said tartly, but her dark eyes showed relief, not rebuke. "Lord John advised us that the way was impassable."

Lord Robert gave a minute shake of his head, suggesting that it was not. But then he sent Lord John a polite smile. "Yes, he was correct to advise that we stay here until the morn."

"And so we shall," said the queen. "Lady Catrin, supply his lordship with a drink. He must be thoroughly parched."

"Yes, Your Majesty," Catrin said, and retrieved a cup that she had already prepared. She took it to Lord Robert, who raised it in a salute to the queen before he drank.

"The roads are passable, but not pleasant," he murmured, over the rim of the cup.

"So why do you think Lord John stopped the queen from leaving?"

"I can think of only one reason, and it is a weak one." He drank again. "I found Lord North and his entourage in some distress in the forest. His horses were trapped in the mud."

That explained the cries she had heard. "Do you think that Lord John was trying to keep the queen here until Lord North could join her?"

"It is my only explanation, but how can it be true? Lord North needed only to follow us back to Saintlow if he wanted to speak to the queen."

"That is true." Catrin accepted the empty cup with a shallow curtsy and returned to the queen. She placed the cup on a tray amongst other empty cups, and passed on what Lord Robert had said in a whisper.

"He is right; there is no reason for such subterfuge simply for Lord North's arrival," the queen murmured. "I do not like this situation, Lady Catrin. Please do ensure that everyone is ready to leave at first light; I do not wish to remain a moment longer than necessary."

"Yes, Your Majesty, but do not fret, I am sure Lord John was simply being cautious," Catrin said. "He is loyal; you have seen proof of that yourself."

"Loyalty is like the weather; one cannot rely on it from one moment to another," the queen said wryly, just as the doors swung open again and revealed Lord North standing there, looking strangely smug.

"Your Majesty," he said in ringing tones that carried throughout the Great Hall. "For the sake of your safety and your kingdom, I must speak to you urgently."

The queen tensed again. "Then speak."

He strode toward her and bowed, and Catrin could tell he was enjoying the attention. All eyes were locked on him, and he liked it. "It is best if we speak privately, Your Majesty."

"If we must," the queen said lightly, and rose from her chair. "We shall retire to our chamber. Lord Robert and Sir William will accompany us."

"Yes, Your Majesty," Lord Robert said, with a bland expression that gave nothing away. But his gaze slid to the back of the hall, where a familiar round-shouldered figure had just slithered in. Catrin recognized him at once.

It was Godfrey Breen.

"Lady Catrin, attend upon us."

The queen's voice carried from her chamber into the Great Hall, despite the noise of dozens of people all waiting for their evening meal. There was a certain scolding note in it, a hint of reprimand, but Catrin refused to blush. She lifted her chin high and swept out of the hall with a flourish.

The buzz of speculation started nearly before she was gone, and Lord North was in the corridor looking similarly gleeful. "Perhaps it is best you have not chosen an emblem," he said with an unpleasant sneer. "It would have been a waste of time."

"We shall see," Catrin said, and entered the queen's chamber. She was standing by the window, watching the clouds break in the sky above them. Catrin sank into a deep curtsy. "Your Majesty."

The queen folded her arms. "Did you know about this Godfrey Breen?"

"I did, Your Majesty."

"Did his claims distress you?"

Catrin smoothed her hands down her skirt and was proud that they did not tremble. "Not particularly, Your Majesty. I intended to look into the matter once we had solved the problem of the stolen jewels."

The queen threw up her hands. "Catrin, I know you to be more intelligent than this. The claim is worthless — any fool would know that."

Catrin hid a smile. "And I did know, Your Majesty. The man Godfrey Breen claims as his father was a traitor to you, so his title is forfeit. Even if he is a legitimate heir — and that has certainly not been established — he holds no claim over the Ashbourne title or the lands."

"Then why didn't you simply tell him that?"

"I wanted to know who had convinced him otherwise." Catrin paused. "And why."

"Ah." The queen paced from one side of the window to the other. "A good question, that. And now we have another question to add to it."

"The question of why Lord North is supporting him?"

"Yes, that is the one. And we must also ask whether Lord John is aligned with them."

"And if there are others." Catrin paused. "Such as Lord Heatherleigh."

The queen fingered the amber beads draped around her throat. "That is an interesting thought. Perhaps it is a two-pronged attack: Lord Heatherleigh works to unnerve me, while Lord John and Lord North work to unnerve you."

"Yes; that may be the truth of it, although I still cannot see why they would take the trouble to work against us in this fashion."

"A house divided against itself cannot stand, as Scripture says," the queen said, and turned her head to look at Catrin directly. "My reign may dissolve if I cannot keep my court intact, and I am at a disadvantage if I cannot rely on my ladies."

The queen's gaze on her was open and steady, but still the words sent a quiver of fear through her chest. "Do you feel you cannot rely on me, Your Majesty?"

The queen chuckled. "Fear not, Lady Catrin, I know I can rely on you. You are still my talisman."

CHAPTER TWENTY-ONE

Catrin ate her evening meal at the queen's table, but she tasted none of it. Her attention was focused on Godfrey Breen, as he moved about the hall with Lord North, speaking to various noblemen. Lord Hunsdon was one of the first; he listened thoughtfully, but not for long. Lord John was next, and he dismissed them both with scorn, which cast doubts on Catrin's suspicion that he was in league with them. Lord Robert glared at them even as they approached, which inspired them to turn aside and speak to Lord Darcy instead, one of the peers Catrin did not know well. She remembered that he would be hosting the queen in August, but that was all.

Catrin lost track of Breen and Lord North then, for she left them behind when the queen's favourites were invited into the smaller dining chamber for the void, a more intimate feast consisting entirely of sweets and fruit. There was no marchpane this night, but a magnificent apple tart had pride of place at the centre of the table.

Lord Hunsdon was one of the first to collect a slice of it, and Catrin watched him bite into the flaky pastry, considering. He had not seemed interested in what Godfrey Breen and Lord North had to say, but he had still heard it. And that offered her an opportunity to find out exactly what their argument was, and whether it was connected to the stolen jewels or the torment that was so unnerving the queen.

She approached him just as he took another generous bite, so he had to chew and swallow rather hastily. "I apologise, my lady. I am over-fond of apples flavoured with cinnamon." A sheepish look crossed his face. "Forsooth, I cannot resist them."

"It looks truly delicious; I will soon follow your example," Catrin said. "I just wanted to ask whether Lord North mentioned anything related to the queen when he spoke to you."

"No, he was too concerned about the redistribution of wealth at court," Lord Hunsdon said wryly. "He seems to think his young squire should be Earl of Ashbourne."

"Did he offer any proof?"

"No, only the suggestion that proof exists." His lips puckered. "I do not think you need fear the boy, my lady. The claim is a weak one."

"Aye, it is, but that does not stop others from believing it." Catrin pushed a lock of hair back into its place under her hood. "Or at least pretending to believe."

"Aye, but just as many will reject his claims outright. I wager you have the support of Huntingdon, Walsall, and at least a dozen others. As well as myself, of course." Lord Hunsdon's gaze sharpened. "And I would appreciate your support in return."

Catrin tilted her head. "For what?"

"I intend to ask the queen to grant me a monopoly on amethysts imported from Germany."

"Oh? I did not realise you were interested in the jewel trade, my lord."

"Amethysts are more deserving of our attention. I believe that it is a neglected market. Can I count on your support?"

She did not see any reason not to agree; no one else was seeking such a monopoly, and it was unlikely to be lucrative. "You can, my lord."

He bowed his head, careful not to tip the tart he still held. "Thank you, my lady."

She curtsied in return, and as she rose she saw a round-shouldered figure sneaking into the room by crouching behind a group of ladies who were too busy chattering to notice him. A mixture of pity and scorn rose up within her, and she crossed over to him as he tried to edge his way toward the tables.

"Such guile and deceit is hardly the act of a nobleman, Master Breen."

He bunched up the muscles of his arms. "As my mother says, deceit is the only option when honesty gets you nowhere."

"You will not get much further with deceit, I assure you." Catrin held his eyes with hers, determined to get answers. "My steward Ned has never heard of you. Nor has anyone asked for the original letters patent for the title."

Breen's dull eyes clouded with confusion, telling her he had no idea what she was talking about. Then he tried to bluster his way out. "I don't concern myself with mere matters of estate business."

"Oh? Then you allow your mother to support you?"

His shoulders sagged, his arms hanging loose in front of him. "Not entirely. I am a baker's apprentice," he said. "But yes … she goes out to work. She cooks in a pub in our home village."

"Does she go by the name of Surovell?"

He seemed completely flummoxed by the question. "Oh … no. She … has a different name."

"Breen, like you?"

He blinked. "No."

"Is Breen her maiden name, then?"

He rubbed the side of his nose. "I think so."

"When did she tell you about the earl?"

"I always knew that she used to be a servant in Ashbourne Manor, before I was born. But I never knew why she left that place until just a few weeks ago. That was when she told me about — about my father."

Catrin linked her fingers together in front of her and kept her eyes on his. "And why then?"

He hunched his shoulders. "I think the apothecary told her to tell me."

"What apothecary?"

"My mother was ill; she had a terrible cough. She stayed home one day, but I went to the baker's, for an apprentice must always go. When I returned, a man was leaving the house. I assumed he was an apothecary, for my mother had a remedy and seemed better. She told me that very night."

"What did he look like?"

"Well dressed; he wore fine leather boots." The young man sighed with envy. "And his cloak was made of satin."

"Have you seen him since? At court, perhaps?"

"No." He tore his gaze from hers to survey the room, and a faint smirk twisted his lips. "But I have seen many others at court, *my lady*. They seem very willing to hear how I have been wronged."

Catrin raised one eyebrow. "Indeed, even grown men occasionally enjoy a fairy tale. But I suggest that you tell your tale no more, and leave this room ere the queen sees you."

"No." He lifted his chin. "I am an earl. I belong here."

He swaggered off, and Catrin let him go. She needed to consider what Breen had said. She doubted that the man who had come to his mother's house was an apothecary; they usually wore robes of such length that no one could see their boots, whether they were fine leather or not. Nor could apothecaries afford satin cloaks; such finery belonged at court, not in remote villages.

Thus, a fellow peer had spun this story for Godfrey Breen. Indeed, it was probably someone she knew at court. It seemed likely that the man had offered Breen's mother money to tell her son that he was special, and she had duly sent him off to claim what was his. It was a hopeless and possibly humiliating errand for the young man, and it would do nothing but cause Catrin some discomfort.

But no, that was not entirely true. It could cast doubt on her status. If enough powerful people demanded that Godfrey Breen receive the title, the queen might be forced into that action. And that suggested that the man in the satin cloak was an enemy.

Who could it be? There were several to choose from. The Duke of Norfolk, still in exile on his home estates after their encounter the previous September. Lord Talbot, who had conspired with him. His status with the queen had not been restored, despite the death of his father making him the new Earl of Shrewsbury. Sir William Petre, one of their future hosts on progress, who may have expected the title of Earl of Ashbourne to come to him.

"What-ho! We have an intruder in our midst!"

The queen's voice cut through the noise of the room, and everyone turned their gaze toward her. Some stood in fear, wondering if they had presumed too much upon their status. Indeed, one or two slipped hastily from the room. But Godfrey Breen stayed where he was at the table, his cheeks bulging with food, and watched the queen approach with round eyes. "No one asked you to come here, sirrah," she said hotly. "How dare you enter this room?"

He swallowed the food with a gulp. "I — I am an earl," he mumbled. "My father was — was — Roger Surovell, Earl of Ashbourne. I belong here."

"You wear a swan's feathers, but I see you for a goose," the queen snapped. "A true earl would not push his way in, but wait to be invited."

Breen's nostrils flared. "I do not wish to be ignored any longer," he said hotly. "I have waited long enough to take my place."

The queen's eyes flashed with fury. "You bold churl! How dare you speak so to the Queen of England?"

The intensity of her anger finally got through to the young man. "I — I am sorry, Your Majesty," he said humbly. "My patron Lord North — I thought he was here —"

"He was not invited, either, as it happens." The queen lifted one slim white hand and pointed to the door. "Now, leave this moment. I do not wish to see your face again."

"But — but —"

Her voice rose to a bellow, and everyone could hear the echo of old King Henry within it. "I tell you now, *leave this house!*"

Godfrey Breen fled. The queen stood there for a moment, chest heaving, and then put on a smile. "Ah, now that has cleared the air. Lord Robert, shall we dance?"

Lord Robert swallowed a grin. "As you wish, Your Majesty."

Hours later, a chorus of voices drew Catrin towards the chapel. She expected such noise from the Great Hall once the wine had been flowing for awhile, but shouts from the chapel were decidedly unusual.

She slipped through one of the half-open entrance doors, and found Lord Robert already there. His eyes were sharp and wary, and he held one finger to his lips to warn her against speaking before he pointed toward a small side-chapel carved into the far wall. Lord North stood there, as rigid and grey as the statue of St Paul that stood behind him. In front of him, with his back to them, Godfrey Breen was pacing like a caged lion at the Tower menagerie, each step a strike against the flagstone floor.

"You made promises to me!"

"And I was absolved of them when you broke your promises to me," Lord North retorted. He seemed remarkably calm, considering that Breen had a sword in his hand. "You pushed yourself in where you did not belong and risked my own status with the queen."

"I do belong!" Breen shouted, and jabbed the air above his head with the sword-point. "I am an earl's son! I am worthy of every benefit!"

"Not until it has been proven," Lord North said. "I told you that. I told you that we would have to take the time to gather support, and you —"

"There is no time! We must act now!"

"Acting now means failure, and that is why I withdraw my aid," Lord North said icily. "Go back to your mother, Breen."

Breen threw back his head and screamed at the ceiling, the echo bouncing around them. "I cannot go back until I have what I am owed. I cannot!"

"You must," Lord North said, and waved a dismissive hand. "And if you behave yourself, another saviour might come to you."

Breen swung the sword, swiping a candle from its holder. It dropped to the ground with a crack and broke into a dozen pieces. "That is not good enough!"

Lord North sent him a cold sidelong glance. "Watch yourself, lad. Lord John Grey will not suffer you to destroy his home. You will find yourself in irons before you can blink."

Breen drew himself up and his body actually quivered with fury. "They would not dare!" he roared, and his voice crept up in pitch with each word until it broke. "They would not dare lay hands on me."

"If you do not calm down, they certainly will lay hands on you — they will throw you into Bedlam," Lord North snapped.

"Bedlam!" The boy started charging mindlessly from one side of the chapel to the other. "No! No! I will not allow it!"

Lord North started to look nervous. Wisely, he backed away before he spoke again. "Stop this, Breen. You show yourself to be a fool, and a dangerous one. Stop it now!"

Breen let out a screech and ran at him with his sword raised to strike, and Lord North darted out of the way just in time. The sword struck the statue with a crunch, and St Paul's hand dropped to the floor. Lord North turned and fled, arriving breathless at Lord Robert's side. "He has gone mad," he gasped. "My lord, do something."

"Not I alone; that would be naught but foolishness," Lord Robert said, and watched in astonishment as Breen started swinging the sword in sweeping arcs and sharp slashes. "By God's wounds, what is he doing now?"

"He is charging at enemies no one else can see," Catrin said, and pressed her forefinger to her lips. "Ferociously."

"Then it is certainly time to send in the guard," Lord Robert said, and raised his hand. Men poured into the chapel, and Breen let out a howl at the sight of them and fled out into the night. The men gave chase, pouring out of the chapel in a single solid stream of grim determination. And then they were gone, and the door swung on its hinges behind them as if waving goodbye. Lord Robert chuckled. "Where can the fool go to escape such men?"

"Far away," Lord North said bitterly. "And that is enough for me."

CHAPTER TWENTY-TWO

Stars were showing shy faces in the sky when Lucy and Pierrick finally arrived in High Wycombe. They rode down the main street with Thibaut riding ahead and Symon behind, and stopped at the first decent inn that they saw. Pierrick helped Lucy down from her horse, and she had to take a moment to get used to standing again.

Oh, how she longed to go back to the palace and simply stay still for awhile.

They walked together into the inn, and found it packed nearly to overflowing. No one came to greet them, so Pierrick went up to the barman. He was standing strangely still, two foaming tankards in each hand and his eyes on the pack that Thibaut carried. "Good e'en, goodman," Pierrick said. "Might we trouble you for a pair of rooms?"

The man swallowed hard and deposited the tankards onto the nearest table. "I fear we are full, my lord. Perhaps they might have room at the Dog and Arrow. It is but a few steps further along the way; you cannot miss it."

Pierrick's eyes narrowed with displeasure, but he turned and left without another word. The Dog and Arrow was, as promised, only a few steps away, but they received the same response there. As they did at the next inn, and the next. They soon found themselves standing bemused on the cobblestones, out of possibilities.

"We must ride on, my lord," Symon said. "'Tis not safe to stay out here alone."

"Aye, I agree, but where can we go?" Pierrick said. "It grows dark, and I do not wish to pitch a tent in the fields."

"I know of an inn on the way to the next town," Thibaut said. "I'm sure we can find a room there."

"Very well." Pierrick let out a long sigh and lifted Lucy back onto her horse. "On we go."

Lucy rose early and called for hot water. She longed for a bath, but doubted that the King's Arms on the outskirts of Downley would have a tub available — or towels, for that matter. She wished she had allowed Florie to travel with them; she was skilled at finding what Lucy needed. The choice to make do with maidservants at inns along the way had seemed wise at the time, but now…

The innkeeper's daughter brought the water so she could wash, and then helped Lucy dress. "Have you travelled far, my lady?" she asked timidly.

"Many miles, and for many days," Lucy said, and could not hide her weariness. "It feels like a journey that will never end."

The maid's hands rested on her shoulders. "And yet, it might end this very day," she whispered. Startled, Lucy stepped smartly away from the girl.

"Why do you say that?"

The maid sent a hunted glance toward the door. "I cannot say."

"Is my husband in danger?"

"I think not, my lady."

"I must see him."

The maid nodded and dropped a hasty curtsy before she led the way out of the room. Pierrick had his own room nearby, and Symon slept outside it. Thibaut had slept outside of Lucy's room — or so she thought. The corridor had been empty when they left her room, she realised. Where had he gone? Oh, if only Florie was there!

Symon jumped up when he saw her. "My lady, are you well?"

"I am not sure," Lucy said. "Has my husband arisen?"

"*Oui*, I am here," came from inside the room. The door opened a moment later, to reveal a Pierrick who was properly dressed but with uncombed hair. Evidently, she had interrupted his morning preparations, but she did not care as long as he was safe. She held out her hands to him and his green-eyed gaze narrowed, flitting from the concern on Symon's face to the timid maiden at Lucy's side to Lucy herself. He knew at once that something was wrong. "Fare you well, my lady?"

Lucy glanced at the innkeeper's daughter. "I fear we have difficulty ahead," she said. The maid's head moved in the faintest of nods, just as a rush of oncoming footsteps confirmed it. Pierrick drew Lucy and the maid into the room and stood protectively in front of them.

"Who is there?" he asked sternly.

"Thibaut, my lord." The footsteps stopped just in front of Pierrick, and Lucy could hear him breathing hard from the exertion. "The horses have been stolen, and with them our supplies. There is nothing left."

Lucy set her hands on her hips and turned to the maid. "And methinks you know why."

"It is that pack you carry," the maid whispered. "The man who owns it is the constant enemy of the men in this village, so they all assume that you, too, are against them."

"We are against no one," Pierrick said. "Indeed, we do not know the man who owns that pack. We have been trying to find out his name."

"Wilkyn Burgh," she whispered. "But please, tell no one I told you. He left High Wycombe days ago, and the men of the villages all around decided as one that they would never allow him to come back."

"Why?" Lucy asked. "What did he do?"

"It is what he did not do," the maid said. "For that, they will never forgive him — nor will they allow him to return."

Lucy met Pierrick's gaze, and understood that he did not want her to tell the maid about Burgh's death. "We don't want to bring him back here," Lucy said. "We just want to talk to the people who knew him."

"Then you will have to go to High Wycombe," the girl said. "He had a post there ... with a woman named Joan."

"And how can we get there?" Pierrick asked, irritation sharpening his voice. "We no longer have horses."

The maid spread her work-roughened hands. "I cannot help you," she said, and glanced down the hall. "But ... perhaps it would be wise to visit the forest this afternoon. There is a lovely brook just past the stables; many people follow it and take pleasure in the trees and flowers they see."

"Perhaps we will," Lucy said, and sent her a silent thank you with a smile. "Once we have eaten, of course."

The maid bobbed a curtsy. "I will inform the cook," she said, and scurried away.

Queen Elizabeth was as good as her word; they left Pyrgo at first light. By then Catrin had been up for hours, ensuring that all the ladies' personal items were collected and properly packed, and all the chests and coffers safely loaded onto the carts.

Only once she had the assurance of the ushers that all was secure did she don her travelling cloak and hat (now dry, fortunately) and go in search of her beautiful bay mare Ariadne. The stableboys had taken good care of her, so Catrin rewarded them with coins before she rewarded Ariadne herself with a fresh crunchy carrot. Then she took her seat and urged the mare into the procession.

They were all in place when Lord John, proudly attired in a grey silk doublet, escorted the queen into the courtyard. He helped the queen mount her horse and steered it into place, and then moved forward to a spot in the procession where a boy in his livery was holding his horse.

Then they waited, while the harbingers galloped around them and the yeomen made sure the queen was safely surrounded. The sun climbed higher in the clear blue sky, warming the stone all around them, and Catrin donned her mask before her skin began to burn. And then, finally, the call of trumpets told them all it was time to go and they rode out of the courtyard together.

Immediately the queen gave a great gasp of astonishment. The road was lined with people, rows of them, stretching far into the distance. The Grey family was first: Lady Mary sat side-saddle on a glossy brown mare with her children on either side. The two eldest held a large banner with the Grey family crest on it, while the little ones on their ponies waved colourful flags in the Tudor green and white.

Anthony, Catrin noted, was not there.

Beyond the family stood the servants, wearing their lord's badge and armbands, waving flags and handkerchiefs so that the road was a whirl of colour. Beyond that were Lord John's men, resplendent in their lord's grey and blue livery. And beyond that, the villagers. Dozens of them, cheering for the queen, with children all around them dancing with excitement.

Lady Mary joined the procession, taking a place by Catrin's side. "A fine surprise, is it not?" she laughed. "Lord John was up all night putting everything in place."

"It is a spectacle indeed, and I know it has pleased the queen," Catrin said. "Will you travel with us all the way to Saintlow?"

"Nay, indeed, I will return once you have crossed the boundary lines at the edge of our estate," Lady Mary said. "My children will need me."

"I'm sure they will." Catrin hesitated, but had to ask. "Have you had any … unpleasantness this morning?"

Lady Mary's smile stiffened into that unnatural grimace. "What do you mean?"

"Thefts." Catrin lowered her voice. "Have you checked that your brooch is still in place?"

"Oh! Yes, of course. There was no difficulty there," Lady Mary said, with evident relief. "I thought you meant … but never mind that. Isn't it a lovely morning?"

"Yes, it is." Catrin sent her a sideways glance. "Thus far."

As if the words had drawn out trouble, the queen let out a cry of outrage. Catrin rode forward at once, guiding Ariadne to a place beside her. "What is it, Your Majesty?"

The queen pointed. "He defies me again!"

It was Breen, standing stock-still amongst the dancing, laughing crowd. He was glaring at Catrin, a flat stare full of hate but empty of understanding. "Catrin Surovell — you are a thief!" he cried. "You are a false councillor! You pour foul poison from a fair ewer!"

"Enough," the queen hissed, and waved two yeomen forward. "Ensure he does not come near us again."

They nodded curtly and plunged into the crowd, which was forced to scatter before their giant warhorses. Several children screamed in fright, and the queen immediately reined in her horse. "Good people, be not afraid," she said, in those ringing tones that could carry far over open ground. "I seek only your safety and succour, for you are my beloved servants."

"Bless you, Your Majesty! God save you!"

The shout came from many throats, and the queen removed her mask so they could see her smile upon them. "God save you, my good people."

Cheers arose again, and several women and children came forward with bouquets of flowers in their hands. Meadow flowers, Catrin noticed. Red poppies, white and yellow daisies, delicate pink vervain, bluebells cheerfully bobbing their heads on their long stems. The queen took them all, enfolding each bundle in her arms until she was nearly buried in blossoms. "Thank you, thank you all," she said, and urged her horse onward as she nodded and waved and smiled until they had left the crowds behind.

Only then did she hand the flowers to Mistress Ashley. "Put them by my bed at Saintlow," she said. "They are too beautiful to be discarded."

"Yes, Your Majesty."

"I wonder what we will find there," the queen said, and watched a rabbit race across the fields. "Hopefully there will be a new supply of beer, at the very least."

"I hope Lord Heatherleigh managed to find Mistress Alice and Lufian," Catrin said. "He seemed enormously worried about them."

"Yes; it is a strange attachment, that," the queen said. "I do not know what to make of it."

"Nor do I," Catrin said. "But I know he wants to adopt the child."

The queen sent her a sharp glance. "Do you think he will?"

"I am not sure, but I wondered if you would approve of such a decision."

The queen considered it for a long time. "I would, but only if the child's father rejected him outright."

"That seems a fair restriction. Lord Heatherleigh was going to look for the father; I wonder if he has had any success."

"I doubt he wants to succeed," the queen said dryly. "Perhaps you should add that to your ever-growing list of questions for him to answer."

Catrin smiled at her. "I would rather gallop headlong over this great green vale, Your Majesty. It seems the sort of day for such abandon."

The queen laughed and urged her horse to a trot. "It does indeed."

CHAPTER TWENTY-THREE

They approached Saintlow Hall at a gallop, forming a wide oval with the queen in her emerald travelling costume at the centre. All around her, the satin cloaks and gowns of her courtiers and ladies flashed in the sun, and the yeomen of the guard circled them all, swooping in and out in wide curves. They thundered triumphantly into the courtyard — and immediately their triumph collapsed. There were no stableboys to take the horses, no courtiers or guests to welcome them, and no Lord Heatherleigh. The entrance courtyard was awash with foetid manure that had been pounded into the stone by the rain, and debris of every sort had piled up in the gardens.

The queen reined in and stared in astonishment as a piece of torn ribbon drifted lazily past her, fluttering in the breeze. "What sort of a welcome is this?"

"'Tis no welcome at all," Sir William Cecil scowled. "Lord Heatherleigh knew we were returning today, did he not?"

"I sent a messenger to inform him," Catrin said. "Also, I believe some of the harbingers returned ahead of us — look; is that not one of them?"

"It is Master Blacquier." Lord Robert narrowed his eyes at the man riding slowly toward them through the gate that led to the stables. "What-ho, sirrah! Explain yourself!"

Master Blacquier rode over to them, or rather, the horse decided to come in their direction. The man himself seemed too shocked to direct it. "Good my lord," he said, and wiped a hand over his mouth. "Good my lady."

Lord Robert flushed with instant fury. "What? Do you not see that the queen is among us?"

"Hold," the queen said quietly. "He seems … disturbed. I think there is something deeply wrong."

Master Blacquier nodded, his eyes fixed and staring. "They're gone — they're all gone. I don't know why … or where … they're just … gone."

"Who is gone?" Lord Robert asked.

"Everyone." The man gulped. "It is as if they all disappeared. All at once."

"That cannot be," the queen said. "There were hundreds of people here when we left. Mostly Heatherleigh's dependents, but many of my people as well."

"Gone, all of them. And the tents are gone, too," he said. "It's like the court was never here."

"If there is no sign of them at all, I wager they left before the rain stopped," Catrin said. "Such a storm would easily wipe out all footprints and stake-marks."

"But why would they leave?" the queen asked. "Where would they go?"

"There must be an explanation," Lord Robert said grimly. "I will look inside; perhaps they left word."

"I will come with you," Catrin said, and jumped down from her horse before he could protest. He paused for long enough to ensure that Sir William would look to the queen's safety, and then he and Catrin walked up to the front door.

The door handle turned, but it would not open. Lord Robert put his shoulder to it, and finally forced it open just enough for the two of them to squeeze in. And then it shut again, as quickly as if a hand had forced it.

And indeed, one had. The dead white hand of a man in guard's livery was still pressed against the wood, as if even in death he had tried to fulfil his duties. The rest of him was slumped in a heap on the floor, and flies were buzzing around the dried blood on his chest.

Lord Robert drew his sword and Catrin her *stiletto*, and they advanced at a cautious pace into the Great Hall. They found the bowls and plates from a meal scattered around the tables, and the benches around them at awkward angles, as if they had been hastily shoved aside. Several cups had been knocked over, and the contents had formed pools on the table before they dripped down onto the floor.

Catrin rested her fingertip on one such pool. "Still slightly sticky," she murmured, and wiped her finger on the wood. "Methinks this happened yesterday."

"It could have been the day before, right after we left," Lord Robert said. "It looks like a morning meal, rather than a supper."

"Aye, but we did not have boiled beef," Catrin said, and pointed at a platter at the centre of the table. The fat had congealed on it, forming white greasy blobs. "It must have been yesterday."

Lord Robert nodded reluctant agreement and pointed toward the fire. "What is that?"

A figure was slumped against the brick surround. Immediately Catrin felt a cold, brittle reluctance to go any further, but she forced herself to follow Lord Robert over to the hearth. She soon saw that the figure had a pair of torn stockings on her lap and a needle in her hand, but it was her wild red hair that told Catrin who she was.

A rush of tears nearly made her choke. "It's Florie. She's been stabbed in the back."

"This must have been an attack of great speed and fury, for the poor girl not to have had time to hide," Lord Robert said soberly. "I am sorry, Lady Catrin."

Catrin forced her throat to clear. "It is Lady Lucy who will be most grieved."

"I suspect that grief will find us all," Lord Robert said heavily, and led the way out of the Great Hall and into the next room. It too was empty, as was Lord Heatherleigh's privy chamber and several other smaller chambers. The small dining chamber at the end looked much the same as the Great Hall, except that there were two or three kinds of meat sitting neglected on the tables instead of one, with serving-forks still stuck in them. And a man lay near the fire, unmoving, his sword still in his hand and his throat a mess of blood. Catrin recognized him: it was the good Viscount Walsall, who had been so kind to her. She covered him with a cloth and pressed onward.

They retraced their steps through the Great Hall and into the other wing, which led toward the queen's chambers and the chapel. A maiden's crumpled figure lay unmoving outside Heatherleigh's chamber, blood on her back telling a terrible tale. She was the only one left: the ladies' chamber was empty, as was Heatherleigh's own chamber and Lord Robert's. The beds looked like they had been slept in, and there were fresh linens lying on the floor, as if the maids had been interrupted in the middle of preparing the rooms for the day.

The queen's chamber was similarly disturbed. The fire in the privy chamber was out and the ashes scattered. An old and filthy towel was lying in the corner, next to a stinking chamber pot. In the bedchamber, the bedding had been flung in every direction and there were leaves and mud all over.

Lord Robert retrieved a broken lute string from the glossy plank floor. "Someone has certainly been here."

Catrin drew closer to the bed and bent over the pillows quite reluctantly. The sour smell that arose from the linens made her nostrils burn. "Someone *slept* here," she said, and noticed an odd unevenness to the mattress. She had helped the chamberer prepare the queen's bed three nights before; she had noted then its smooth quality. "And they may have left a trap."

Lord Robert took her hand even as she reached out. "Let us not risk the maidenly hand," he said dryly, and used his sword to slice the sheet in twain.

Beneath the shredded linen, the mattress began to sparkle. Catrin gasped. "Diamonds!"

"A dozen of them at least," Lord Robert said grimly. "By Christ's own wounds, this grows more grim by the moment."

Catrin collected the diamonds, finding a total of fifteen — including five that were still embedded in a silver chain. "They must be the diamonds stolen from Lord North. Not all of them are here, but…"

"But there are enough of them to suspect that the man who slept here is our thief." Lord Robert shook his head. "They must be worth a fortune — why would he leave them here?"

"I cannot imagine." Catrin searched about for something to hold them in, and finally folded them into a scrap of parchment for want of anything better. "Should we send a messenger to Lord North?"

"We can do so if you wish," Lord Robert said, and then his dark eyes narrowed and he pointed at some smudges on the floor. "Are those footprints?"

"Yes, they are." Catrin stored the parchment in her purse and tightened the drawstring. "They lead out of the room — toward the great hall."

Once again Lord Robert led the way, and it was not an easy path to follow, twisting and turning all through the house. They soon realised that there were two sets of footprints, one set left by rough boots and the other a softer shoe. The shoes were nowhere near as muddy, and thus harder to track. But once they were outside, and the path led through the gardens, the wrecked plants and churned mud made it easy to follow the trail to the unfinished building near the west wing of the house. Bricks and tools were scattered about outside, and as they cautiously approached they heard something that sounded remarkably like … singing. The mournful, drawn-out notes of a minstrel song, sung sloppily so that the words were all but indistinguishable.

Lord Robert kicked a trowel out of the way and pushed into the unfinished building through a space between the scaffolds. A man in a rough tunic and filthy breeches leapt to his feet, swearing with the full-throated relish of a man who was very, very drunk. "How dare ye disturb me! What the hell —"

"Yellow-bellied churl, sit yourself down," Lord Robert snarled. "Who are you?"

The man bowed so low his hat fell off, then slumped back down in the dirt. Catrin answered for him. "I believe he is Lord Heatherleigh's steward, Master Ronald."

"What is he doing here?"

Master Ronald's eyes filled with tears and he reached blindly for a demijohn sitting crooked in the dirt by his right hand. "Guarding my lord, I am, and I will do so until my last breath."

"Codswallop," Lord Robert said, and swept an arm to indicate the dirt floor and half-built walls inside their skeleton of scaffolds. "There is no one here."

"Lord Robert." Catrin rested a hand on his arm and pointed to the far corner, where a rectangle of dirt was freshly disturbed. "I fear there is."

CHAPTER TWENTY-FOUR

Catrin waited outside the unfinished building while three of Lord Robert's men dug into the dirt inside. The steward was with her; he had hidden himself in the lee between the scaffolding and the wall, but at least he was sobering up.

"It was like a demon had descended upon us all," he said fitfully. "We heard the most terrible screaming and howling, and then we saw a man with pearls and gold at his throat, dressed all in red —"

Catrin had long run out of patience with such fairy stories. "With horns and a tail, I wager."

"I did not see a tail," he said, in a tone that suggested there may well have been one. "But he was wild, my lady — wild and evil. One of the chambermaids went into the queen's chamber to air it and ran out screaming, with the demon at her heels. He cut her down with a knife to the back and then started chasing people all over the house — snarling — screaming — hewing down any who tried to resist him. Lord Heatherleigh chased him while most people fled."

"When did Lord Heatherleigh start to chase him?" Catrin asked.

"My lord came flying out of his chamber once he heard the noise, my lady."

"His own chamber? Not the queen's?"

"No, he came from his own chamber, I am sure. Then he chased the demon all over the house, fighting to save his people." The steward let out a sob. "My good lord … may God take him into his kingdom."

"Amen," Catrin said. "Then what happened? Did the demon vanish in a puff of smoke?"

"Once it was quiet … I came out here and found my lord Heatherleigh … dead. Run through with a sword — or maybe a dagger — and half-buried, as if the demon had dropped him in the hole and then run away. I … I finished the job. It seemed the decent thing to do."

Catrin's attention was caught by movement at the edge of the forest. She was too far away to see what it was, but she kept a wary eye on it, and her ear on Master Ronald. "Why didn't you run for help?"

"When I found myself alone, I assumed that's what everyone else had done," he said, and let out another sob. "Where is my jug?"

"You have had enough," Catrin said, just as the movement at the edge of the forest grew clearer and she could tell that it was people. Men, women and children, all moving cautiously in small groups, ready at any minute to turn and run. It was both a relief and a sorrow, for Catrin knew what they were returning to. "Ah, the frightened folks return."

She heard a faint scrabbling behind her, and Master Ronald emerged from his hiding-place with hope drying the tears in his eyes. "There is the head laundress, with her girls — the stableboys — and — there! I see all but one of the scullery maids."

"Perhaps the other is too afraid to return."

"No, she is dead." Ronald scrubbed both hands over his face. "I saw her fall before the demon; he stabbed her through the belly."

Catrin felt sick, but she made herself focus on the people that crept toward them. None of them, she noticed, looked like members of the queen's court. "Do you recognize any of the others?"

"All of them," Master Ronald said happily, and then clapped his hands with joy. "And there is my wife Helen — my heart's root!" He ran out into the field and threw his arms around a woman with iron-grey hair that reminded Catrin of her mother.

She took a moment to be grateful that Lady Angharad and young Finn were safely back in London … and then she wondered. Was this strange and violent attack the reason Lord John had kept the queen in Pyrgo? Had he known of it, and tried to keep her safe?

Catrin went back into the unfinished building, and found Lord Robert's men lifting the limp form of Lord Heatherleigh out of a shallow grave. His eyes were closed, and she was grateful for that. It was difficult enough to see his jaw so slack, his thin form so lax. Indeed, she had to look away for a moment to keep her composure, and that was when she saw something in the dirt where he had lain. "Behold," she said, and approached the makeshift grave from an angle that did not block the light on the small object she saw. From its gleam, she suspected she knew what it was.

"My lady, the ground there is rather unpleasant," Lord Robert said. "Are you sure —?"

"There is something there, my lord," she said, and bent over the churned-up earth. In the midst of it all something gleamed, white and pure. She plucked it out carefully, and found herself holding a perfect teardrop pearl.

"God almighty," Lord Robert said, in a hushed voice. "I don't believe it."

Catrin picked up a stick and pushed around more of the dirt, and soon found two more identical pearls, with gold clasps and hoops where they had once attached to a larger piece. Once they lay together on her palm, there was no mistaking them. "Lord Robert, I think we may have found the queen's necklace," she said quietly. "Or what is left of it."

"So Lord Heatherleigh was the thief," he said flatly. "He was the one who left the diamonds in the queen's chamber."

"No, I think the man who killed him stole both the diamonds and the necklace. He left the diamonds behind, but I think he kept the necklace. Master Ronald just said that the 'demon' who attacked them all wore gold and pearls at his throat."

"Then why are the pearls here?" Lord Robert shook his head and answered his own question. "The necklace was damaged in the struggle, and the pearls fell into the makeshift grave."

"I think that is what happened, yes."

Lord Robert swiped at the sweat on his forehead with the back of his hand. "I am glad of it, it must be said. I did not want to think that Heatherleigh had fallen so low."

Catrin folded her fingers over the pearls, hiding their serene gleam. "Nor did I."

"How many dead?"

Catrin adjusted the poultice on the queen's forehead. "Six, including Lord Heatherleigh himself."

The queen let out a tiny, mournful sound. "How many were my people?"

"Two." Catrin crossed to the window and tucked the blanket more firmly against the glass, to keep out all the light. When the queen had a headache, light was the greatest enemy. "Viscount Walsall, and Florie … Lady Lucy's maid."

"Have we found the rest of my people?"

"Not yet," Catrin said. "Lord Robert sent two yeomen to Pyrgo, and two to the next planned stop in your progress, to see if they fled to either place. He fully expects to find them in one or the other, for their journey seems planned and orderly. They took the time to gather all their belongings and take the horses and carts with them."

"While Heatherleigh's people simply fled to the woods." The queen pressed a trembling hand against the poultice, and the fresh lemony scent of vervain and wormwood rose around them. "Has Alice returned with them?"

Catrin poured some small ale into a silver cup and carried it to the queen. "I'm afraid there is no sign of Alice, or her son."

"I wonder if the attacker was the child's father, and he thought Heatherleigh was trying to keep Alice and the child away from him."

"I couldn't find any sign that Lord Heatherleigh found Alice or the child, but I have not yet finished searching the grounds."

"Poor Heatherleigh," the queen murmured. "And those poor people … ambushed and murdered in their home. Who could possibly have done this — and why?"

"We still have no idea, I'm afraid."

"Go and finish your search outside, then," the queen murmured, and rested her cheek on her pillow. "And send Mistress Ashley to wait upon me."

"Yes, Your Majesty," Catrin said, and slipped out of the room at once. They had put the queen in Catrin's chamber, as it had been the least disturbed, while Mistress Ashley and Mistress Blanche supervised the thorough scrubbing of the queen's chamber. Mistress Ashley was happy to take Catrin's place with the queen, and Catrin was happy to return to the search.

Lord Robert had pressed some men into service to take care of the bodies, planning to store them in cellars until a coroner could come. Others were given the task of cleaning the manor and restoring it to order. Still more were searching the gardens and buildings, looking for anything that might help explain what had happened.

Catrin returned to the unfinished kitchen, and bent to examine every inch of the dirt floor. The grave had been filled in again, so she could get close to the far side, and the shallow U-shape that would have become a window had the walls continued to rise. Was that dried blood, soaked into the brick? It was. Just a small dot, but when she looked out over the wall she saw a splash of it on the ground. That suggested that it belonged to someone who had left the building that way — possibly the attacker, if Lord Heatherleigh had managed to injure him.

He may have left a trail that would lead them straight to him.

She stepped over the unfinished wall, a feat she could not have managed had she not still been wearing her split riding skirt, and examined the blood on the ground. The splash pointed west, toward the forest, so Catrin moved away from the building, scanning the ground until she found another splash. And another, still further away from the half-finished window.

She soon found herself amongst the trees, and paused for a moment to listen. Her father had taught her the language of the forest, and how to move in such a way that she disturbed as little as possible. It served her well as she followed the drops of blood, for they grew fainter and less frequent the farther she went, but eventually they led her to the lee side of a small hill. A rough lean-to had been erected from some gnarled sticks and a beautiful green cloak that Catrin recognized as belonging to Lord Heatherleigh. Inside were the ashes of a fire and a jumble of items: a single boot, a ragged cloak stained with blood, and a knife. It was clean but for some smears near the hilt, but there was no way to know if the smears were from a human, an animal, or possibly even a plant. Forsooth, they could have been left when the knife's owner had crushed some berries.

One thing she knew for sure was that the attacker was not there. Annoyed, Catrin rolled up the knife and the boot in the blood-stained cloak, and started to walk away. Something made her stop, though, and go back to retrieve Lord Heatherleigh's cloak. She remembered how proud he had been of its gleaming green satin, and could not imagine that he would have wanted to see it used in such a manner. Perhaps it was foolish sentiment to retrieve it for such a reason, but she did so nonetheless.

She retraced her steps back to Saintlow, trying her best to prevent or erase any signs of her passage on the lichen-covered rocks and springy moss. It was perhaps her determination to move silently that alerted her to another sound: stones crunching under a heavy foot. Someone was coming, and he did not seem too concerned with keeping his presence a secret.

She slid silently into the small space between two young beech trees and bent low, below eye level. Crunch, crunch … crunch. The footsteps were louder, but slower. Something may have alerted him to her presence, although she wasn't sure what. She wore a dark blue riding costume that blended quite well into the shadows of the trees, and she was downwind of him so her scent should not have alerted him.

A stray ray of sun drifted through the trees and lit up the length of her arm, making the gold embroidery at the cap of her sleeve glitter. Hastily she pressed her hand against the spot, but knew it might be too late. The footsteps stopped entirely, and the forest was silent once more.

Catrin breathed lightly through her mouth to keep him from hearing her and turned her head slowly from side to side. There — to her left — she saw him. From this distance he was but a shadow in the trees — a massive shadow, which held itself stiffly as if it hurt to move. Was there something familiar in that bulky frame? Could she be looking at the rounded shoulders of Godfrey Breen — or even the thick proportions of Anthony Grey?

She watched and waited, while the shadow did the same thing. She could see his head swinging from side to side, trying to see through the trees despite the thick foliage. And then, abruptly, he gave up and moved onward, away from Catrin and toward the lair she had found.

She waited until his footsteps had begun to fade before she left her hiding place, and then she moved quickly in the opposite direction. It felt like hours before she emerged next to the unfinished kitchen, but it could not have been more than a few minutes. Just as she started for the house, a sudden howl in the forest silenced the birds and made her spine tingle.

Someone had noticed that his belongings had vanished.

CHAPTER TWENTY-FIVE

Lucy and Pierrick broke their fast at a leisurely pace, while Symon lurked by their side and Thibaut made a show of searching for the horses and interrogating the innkeeper. The innkeeper was not helpful; he seemed to find their predicament remarkably amusing, as did several of the other men who gathered in the pub for some bread and cheese once the morning had worn away.

Lucy knew that she and Pierrick had to act worried and upset, to save the innkeeper's daughter from suspicion, and in truth she was growing anxious. The men grew more bold with every tankard, and she did not like it. "They are rude," she murmured to Pierrick, under cover of retrieving another piece of bread.

He sipped from his own tankard, his gaze fixed on the loudest of the men with no sign of anger or frustration. Just cool, implacable focus. "They are indeed."

The innkeeper went over to one of the tables of men with a jug in hand, and the loudest man grinned at him. "Good morrow, John-a-bounty," he said cheerfully. "What say you?"

The innkeeper considered the question gravely, but with a twinkle in his eye. "What say I? Why, I say what I have always said: no good comes of associating with a cursed queen."

"Or Frenchmen," another man muttered into his cup, and set off a roar of laughter.

A spark of anger lit in Pierrick's eye, and Lucy set a pleading hand on his arm. "Prithee, let us go. We need not endure this any longer; it is afternoon."

"As you wish, my lady," Pierrick said grimly, and led her out of the room. More laughter followed them, and Lucy kept tight hold of her husband's arm to stop him from returning to answer the insult. They followed the instructions they had been given, circling the stables until they found the brook and then following it upstream.

As promised, it was a lovely place. Clear water flowed over white round stones, while young trees danced in the breeze all about them. Lucy would have quite enjoyed it, had they not been anxiously searching in every direction while they walked.

"Someone is following us," Pierrick murmured. "I can see a figure through the trees."

Lucy tried to follow his gaze without being too obvious. "I see it. Whoever it is, they are quite small," she murmured. "Perhaps it is a child — or a maiden."

"Could it be the same *petite femme* we spoke to this morning?"

"She would not need to follow us; she knows where we are going."

"So she does," Pierrick murmured, and abruptly lifted his head and sniffed the air. "I smell horses."

So did she. It was not a pleasant smell, but it was very welcome at that moment. "I think I see them — there, in that clearing."

Pierrick pushed through a brace of holly bushes, and was greeted with a welcoming whinny. His horse, Swiftsure, bobbed his head with pleasure to see him, and Pierrick stroked his nose with delight. Lucy's horse, a white mare named Lily, was more aloof, but she too seemed pleased that she was no longer alone. The other two snorted in protest, but were soon soothed by Pierrick's gentle touch.

Lucy took apples from her purse and fed them all, and they gobbled them up with pleasure but not desperation. "I think they have been well fed," she said. "And it seems that no one hurt them."

"No one here would hurt a horse."

The voice was light and gentle, but still Pierrick jumped back and drew his dagger. A young woman stepped out of the trees with her hands raised, and dropped an awkward curtsy. "My lord. My lady. I'm sorry; I did not mean to startle you. I just wanted to assure you that your horses were well cared for."

"If they had been hurt, I would have visited the same injuries on every blackguard in that inn," Pierrick said grimly. "Now explain yourself; why have you been following us?"

"I need to speak to you," the young woman said, and lowered her hands so she could take tight hold of her skirt. There was something in her eyes that told Lucy what she was about to say, and she reached out to take the woman's trembling hand in hers.

"You know Wilkyn Burgh," she said. "And you love him."

"I do … I do. I know he is not what they say he is." Tears started trickling down the young woman's rosy cheeks. "He is clever, and kind, and very sweet."

Pierrick sheathed his dagger. "So why do people think him an enemy?"

She ducked her head and her chin trembled. "I cannot say."

"I wish you would," Lucy said gently. "For we have sad news, I fear. Master Wilkyn was found murdered outside London. That is why we have been trying to find out who he is; we want to find the person who killed him."

The young woman reeled backward and landed against an oak tree with a dull thump. "D-dead? He is dead? Oh, I knew it! I knew it! My poor love!"

"You knew it?" Lucy asked. "What made you suspicious?"

"Wilkyn took a post caring for a madman, and people hated him because he could not control the man. The man stole from people in the villages around his home and attacked them when they tried to stop him, or when they tried to force him back into his home. Some people even thought that Wilkyn encouraged the man to steal, to gain money for himself." She wrapped her arms around herself and rocked back and forth in abject misery. "I was sure they would hurt my Wilkyn, for they dared not attack the madman."

"Who is this madman?" Pierrick asked intently. "Perhaps it is he who attacked Wilkyn."

"I do not know his name; Wilkyn did not want any connection to form between us. He thought it would be dangerous for me if the madman knew I existed. But I know that he lived in High Wycombe, and I know he stole these." She drew a wooden box from the satchel that hung at her side and handed it to Lucy. Lucy opened it, and found inside a stack of folded paper, old and turning brown at the edges, bound in two bundles with frayed twine.

She lifted out one bundle, and saw faded ink and crumbling wax seals. "Are they letters?"

"Aye, they are, and when Wilkyn found them in the madman's possession he took them at once and asked me to keep them safe." She hesitated, and for a moment it looked like she was about to take them back. "He said they were more dangerous than fire and gunpowder."

Pierrick sucked in his cheeks. "We must take them to the queen."

The young woman gazed at the box longingly, fear and sorrow mingling in her eyes. "If you must, my lord."

Lucy rested a soothing hand on her wrist. "If she allows it, I will bring them back to you."

"No need," the woman said, and a single tear slipped down her cheek. "Without Wilkyn to protect me, I do not want the madman to think I have them."

"That is very wise," Pierrick said. "Would you like us to escort you back to the village?"

"No, thank you; I must go a different way, or they will know I came," the young woman said. "And I don't think it is wise for you to return, either."

"No, we shall not return if you do not need us," Pierrick said. "We will meet my men and go at once to High Wycombe."

"May God go with you," the woman said, and faded back into the forest.

Thibaut kept Wilkyn Burgh's pack out of sight when they arrived back in High Wycombe, and perhaps that was why they found someone willing to talk to them. The golden coin in Pierrick's hand might have helped, too, for the young man who stopped did seem very focused on how it gleamed in the late-afternoon sun.

Pierrick casually flicked the coin between his fingers. "I hear you have a madman among you."

The young man let the basket of kindling on his shoulder fall to the cobblestone street. "We had one, m'lord, but haven't seen him in more'n a fortnight."

"Did he have a keeper?"

"Aye, Wilkyn Burgh is his name." The young man scowled. "He's no 'keeper', though. Couldn't 'keep' any sort of control. And he went missing soon after Alban did."

"Alban. Is that the madman's name?"

"Yes, my lord."

"Where did he live?"

The young man jerked his chin in the direction of the Dog and Arrow. "Behind the pub, there. With Joan." He grinned a lopsided grin and picked up the basket, centring it on his shoulder. "Beware of her, m'lord. She's no less mad than Alban, and she's been worse since he left."

"Thank you," Pierrick said, and handed him the coin. The young man bowed his thanks and strode on, and Pierrick jumped down from his horse. "Perhaps you should stay here, *mon amour.*"

Lucy held out her hands so he could help her down. "And perhaps not."

He gave a wry chuckle and helped her reach the ground, and they walked together up the lane toward the Dog and Arrow. Thibaut followed them; Symon stayed with the horses, quietly loading a crossbow bolt.

They turned onto a space so narrow it could not truly be called a lane, where the cobblestones were uneven and coated in all kinds of muck. Lucy lifted her skirt to keep away from the worst of it, and did her best to tiptoe between the muddy patches.

Then she forgot all about her skirt when a woman's screech rose from a small wattle and daub house behind the back wall of the pub. "I'll kill him! Damn him to hell, I'll kill him!"

Thibaut tried to hold Pierrick back, but he drew his dagger and pounded on the door. The screeching abruptly stopped, and a woman in a ragged brown kirtle pulled it open with a curse Lucy had never heard before. "Keep a civil tongue in your head," Pierrick snapped. "There will be no killing today."

The woman thrust her sizeable jaw forward. "Not even a *lord* can stop *me*," she declared, and her black eyes glittered with malice. "And what the hell do you care if I kill the entire cursed village?"

That was a reasonable question, really. "We are looking for Alban," Lucy said. "Does he live here?"

"He's not here, and if he ever shows his face again it will be the last thing he does," the woman said. "I'll kill him, I tell you. Kill him dead."

It was obvious that no one could persuade her otherwise, so Lucy did not try. "Are you Joan?"

The black eyes swept over Lucy's pale blue travelling-costume and her lip curled. "Yes, I am, my lady," she said with exaggerated courtesy. "Welcome. Welcome to my humble home."

Lucy decided to pretend the sentiment was sincere. "Thank you, goodwife. Tell me, are you married to Alban?"

"Married to him? God forbid!" The shrill screech sent several mice scurrying from their nests in the thatch above their heads. "He could never get himself a wife! No one would have that staring, bug-eyed knave —"

"His mother, then?" Lucy asked, and could barely hear her own voice over the ringing in her ears.

"The only one he knows," Joan said, and let out a cough so violent her chest heaved. "And after I have cared for the bastard for his entire damned life, he had the audacity to steal from me!"

"What did he steal?" Pierrick asked.

"My retirement! The comfort of my old age!" Her voice cracked and tears welled in her eyes. "I'll have nothing now — nothing!"

"But *what* did he steal?" Pierrick asked again.

"What does it matter? It's gone — all gone." She swiped the tears from her cheeks, her dirty fingers leaving dark smudges. "I had it all hidden so carefully, but that thrice-damned man found it and took it all. Then he ran, like the coward he is. I swear, I will slice off his beard with a dull blade and —"

"Do you know where he went?" Lucy asked.

"If I knew, I would have dragged him back here behind a horse cart, and whipped him all the way." She coughed again and it made her breathless, but her fury kept her talking. "And Wilkyn with him — damn them both."

Lucy and Pierrick shared a glance. "I'm sorry to tell you that Wilkyn is dead," Lucy said gently. "That's why we're here — we're trying to find out who killed him."

"Find Alban, then," Joan said grimly. "There's nothing that bastard wouldn't do."

"We will," Pierrick said. "And it would help if you told us your surname."

An unpleasant smirk thinned her dry lips. "Sandys. Now leave me alone," she said, and slammed the door hard enough to make the greased paper in the windows crackle like the cry of distant crows. Pierrick stared at the wooden door in astonishment. "The impudence! How dare she speak to us in such a manner?"

"She's frightened," Lucy said. "There is a reason she does not want us to find out any more about Alban … a secret she feels she has to keep."

"How do you know?"

"By how carefully she ensured that we know little more now than we did before."

"Should we insist that she explain herself?" Pierrick looked at the door consideringly. "It would not take much to get inside."

Lucy bit her lip. "I do not think we could make her tell, unless we caused her harm, and I don't want to do that."

"Nor do I."

"Let us return to the queen with what we know, then," Lucy said. "She can then decide whether we need to find out more."

"With a will." Pierrick plucked a purse from his belt and handed it to Thibaut. "Purchase supplies enough for a day; we will leave at dawn."

"Yes, my lord."

CHAPTER TWENTY-SIX

The afternoon was waning when Lord Robert decided it was safe for the queen to venture out into the gardens. A thorough search had yielded no one in the forest, injured or otherwise, and the searchers had more pressing matters to deal with at the manor. Everyone there was settling slowly back into their familiar routines; women were tidying the rows of vegetables in the kitchen garden while men repaired trellises and turned over the soil. Boys were vigorously sweeping the worn paths between the outbuildings, and the clang of bells indicated that someone was leading the cows home for milking. Best yet, for Catrin's insides were cramped with hunger, the scents of roasting meat and baking bread were drifting over the gardens from the kitchens, where Catrin and the queen could hear the rattling of dishes, the thump of knives, and even some chatter and chuckles.

"I confess," the queen murmured, "although I mourn him as I should, a part of me is relieved that I no longer have to be afraid of all the possibilities surrounding the fathering of Lord Heatherleigh."

"That is understandable," Catrin said. "They were very frightening possibilities."

The queen cast her a sidelong glance. "And you are one of very few who know about them, my talisman."

"Yes, I thank you for the privilege, Your Majesty," Catrin said. "Fret not; I will prove worthy of your trust in me."

"You have thus far," the queen said wryly. "In this past year, you have become a great keeper of secrets."

"Aye — but *for* you, not *from* you."

"As it should be." The queen plucked a daisy from its stem and twirled it between her fingers. "Did the items you found in the forest tell you who the stranger was?"

"Only that he was certainly the attacker; it was Lord Heatherleigh's cloak that he was using as a tent, as I suspected. The other cloak was liberally stained with blood, and some had long since dried, so it seems that these victims were not his first."

"How —" Suddenly the queen froze. "Who is that?"

Catrin peered down the path, where a portly man was ambling toward them carrying a shield. He wore a helmet with an overlarge plume of feathers down the centre, and a breastplate over a woollen tunic that reached his chubby knees. Below that, sandals were elaborately tied with leather ties over his calves.

In light of all that had happened, he looked nothing short of ridiculous, as if the jolly village baker with a square beard had joined a masque as a warrior only to wander into a real war. "It is an ancient Greek, it seems, visiting us from the distant past," Catrin said solemnly, and held back a smile with an effort. "Perhaps he thinks we are in need of his services."

The queen flung the daisy away. "How dare he make light of the circumstances we are in?"

"I wager he was part of an entertainment planned for your return by Lord Heatherleigh, and has not heard about what happened," Catrin murmured. "Stay here, Your Majesty; I will explain."

The queen folded her arms. "Prithee, do so quickly."

Catrin advanced down the path, and the 'warrior' drew a sword that shone like steel but made a flattened clang like tin. "I am Ares, the god of war!" he cried. "I have come to join the hunt."

"I fear the hunt has ended, in the sense that it never began," Catrin said. "We have had a tragedy here — perhaps you have not heard?"

The warrior ignored her entirely; his eyes were all for the queen. He went down on one knee in a show of devotion and pressed his fist against his heart. "Whoso list to hunt, I know where is an hind, whom I will capture and love forevermore. Great travail hath wearied me so sore, and I have sacrificed, denied myself, accepted small defeat for a later victory. Victory! Now I am blessed my love, my bride to bind. Yet may I —"

"I fear you may not," Catrin said firmly, for she could feel the heat of the queen's displeasure on her back and knew the whole performance needed to end. "You speak well, goodman, and the queen is grateful for your efforts, but this is not an appropriate time."

The man flushed red and jumped to his feet. "I have waited long for this day, my lady, and must have my prize."

Ah, of course. He wanted his payment. Catrin retrieved some pennies from her purse and held them out. "That is all the prize we can offer today, goodman."

The man took the coins, staring at them bemused. "This is not the hunt I planned."

"I am sorry your plans are thwarted; perhaps we can hear the whole speech another day," Catrin said. The queen huffed out an impatient breath and Catrin caught her striding back to the manor out of the corner of her eye. Two of her guards stayed behind, staring with displeasure at the man and his imitation sword. "For now, it is time for you to go."

He turned away slowly, his gaze still fixed on his plump palm. "I will heed your words, my lady."

Catrin turned away, before the absurdity of the situation made her laugh. "Thank you, goodman."

"A diamond noose…?"

The words, though whispered, carried down the corridor and made a nearby page start with fright. Catrin sent him a reassuring smile and edged closer to the queen. "What did you say, Your Majesty?"

"I was just thinking about the woman I saw, who wore the French hood… She had a necklace wrapped so tightly around her neck it looked like a diamond noose." The queen pressed a hand to her own throat. "Perhaps her appearance was not a threat but a warning — a premonition of my own fate."

"'Tis more likely that it explains why the thief only stole diamonds, Your Majesty," Catrin said gently. "To remind you of that figure."

"I did not need reminding; she is someone I shall never forget," the queen said. Lord Robert appeared at the door to the library, and she raised her head and visibly shook off her melancholy. "Has everyone assembled, my lord?"

Lord Robert bowed low. "Yes, Your Majesty, and we await your presence with great eagerness."

"Very well," the queen said, and swept through the door with all the elegance and confidence that was needed on that particular evening. The room was sparsely populated; only those who had travelled with her to Pyrgo were there to honour her. She had also invited the highest-ranking of Lord Heatherleigh's people, but both they and Sir William Cecil had thought it best for them to eat with everyone else in the dining chamber, and mourn their losses in their own way.

Catrin took her place at the queen's table and greeted the others without really thinking about what she was saying. The queen's words had brought a vague, half-forgotten memory to mind, and she wanted to capture it before it drifted away again. A diamond noose … a woman dressed as the queen's long-lost mother ... a French song floating through the mist ... the tangy, musky scent of perfume.

The food came, served in beautiful silver bowls and on platters but lacking any sense of show. It was a clear sign that ceremony and celebration had been abandoned, but Catrin did not care. Her mind was busy with the problem as she sated her hunger with stewed beef and onions and soft white bread. Poetry ... love ... the pursuit of passion ... two poets talking of hunting and hinds. First, the poet outside the queen's window, and now 'Ares', who had been so determined to complete his hunt.

Suddenly Catrin lost her breath. That was it! Like Ares, the musician who had recited poetry outside the queen's window had mentioned a hind. Not in the literal sense, where the hind meant a female red deer, but as a symbol of an elusive and desirable human woman.

She tried hard to remember more of the poem, but only random words came to mind. *A hind ... graven with diamonds ... written her fair neck round about... Wild, wild ... though I seem tame ... noli me tangere.* That last was a Latin phrase; she had heard it before but didn't know what it meant. She would have to ask Lucy.

A page came in and whispered to Lord Robert, whose eyes started to twinkle. He dismissed the page and turned to the queen. "I have good tidings, Your Majesty."

"And welcome they would be," the queen said.

"The yeomen I sent to Ingatestone Hall have returned, and they report that your people are there, safe and secure. Would you like me to order them to return?"

The queen let out a long breath of relief. "My first thought is that I would like to join them rather than have them join me, and as quickly as possible. However, we cannot leave yet. We should wait for the coroner to arrive, and ensure that all is safe here before we leave." The queen hesitated. "Should we not?"

"That would be wise," Lord Robert agreed. "But if you would like to leave tomorrow, waiting for the coroner will delay us by a mere hour or two, Your Majesty. We could be in Ingatestone by early afternoon."

"Truly?" the queen asked. "The lanes have recovered quickly from the storm, then."

"Yes, they were most difficult to traverse before the rain had fully stopped." He chuckled. "That is why Lord North and his entourage got into such difficulty on their way. I found them attempting a shortcut off the road to London that revealed itself to be a pond, not a path."

Several men chuckled, but Catrin was immediately arrested by an unpleasant thought. "I thought they were close behind Pyrgo when you found them struggling."

"No, they had not made it that far." Lord Robert raised his cup so a page would come and refill it. "Indeed, they were so far away we nearly didn't see them at all."

"I see," Catrin murmured. That meant that they couldn't have been the source of the cries she had heard. But who else could have made such a sound? Even considering the possibilities made her uneasy, leading her to wonder once again if Lord John Grey was behind it all. He could not have attacked Lord Heatherleigh, for he'd been with them in Pyrgo when the attacker had been rampaging through Saintlow Hall. However, he could have sent someone.

Whom would he have sent? Would Anthony have taken on such a task? He did not seem open to such dishonourable acts as theft and murder, but he could have been tricked into believing that Lord Heatherleigh had caused an injustice. And then, with his youthful idealism and passion, he would have moved swiftly to avenge it.

Sir William leaned closer to her, his brow furrowed over clear grey eyes. "You seem distracted, my lady. Is all well?"

"Perhaps," Catrin said slowly. "But I find myself wondering if Lord John Grey has had something to do with all of this, my lord. Do you know any reason why he would arrange an attack on Lord Heatherleigh?"

"As it happens, I do." Sir William sat back in his chair with a long sigh. "You know of Ethel, Lord Heatherleigh's wife?"

"Aye; I hear she died in childbed, and the babe with her."

"Yes, and some think she should never have been with child, for she was weak and sickly from childhood." He paused. "Including Lord John Grey, whose sister she was."

It was astonishing, how a single fact could answer so many questions in one fell swoop. "So he would have reason not only to kill Heatherleigh, but to make him look guilty of something he had not done. It would be a fine revenge, to not only end his life but also ruin his reputation."

"I suppose so, yes." Sir William frowned. "You are thinking of the constant reminders of the queen's mother. The queen has confided in me about her fears of the spectre that she saw."

"Yes, and the theft of the necklace that she held so dear." Catrin fingered the pendant she wore, feeling its weight and the flat, round loops of the chain. "It seems unnecessarily cruel, to take that from her."

"It was unnecessarily cruel." Sir William's gaze drifted upward, as if he was remembering. "As was this attack on Saintlow, and the murder of Lord Heatherleigh."

Suddenly Catrin found her throat thickening with tears. "This attacker has much to answer for, my lord."

"And answer for it he will, my lady." Sir William's grey eyes hardened to flint. "In the dungeons of the Tower, if I have my way."

CHAPTER TWENTY-SEVEN

The following morning saw the harbingers counting the carts and checking their contents while servants darted about in all directions, carrying goods and chests and coffers. Stableboys lined up in the courtyard, each one struggling to control several saddled horses who moved restlessly about, stamping their feet with impatience.

The queen, however, was not yet ready. She had sent a half-dozen ladies scurrying around in search of her silk travelling mask, for the satin one would not do.

Catrin suspected the silk mask was already packed on a cart, but pretending to search gave her the opportunity to walk through the house one more time. It had been cleaned since that terrible day, so the mud on the floors was long gone and the rooms were all being put to rights. Even as she wandered away from the queen's chamber, she could see maids going into the rooms, stripping the linen from the beds and shaking the pillows free of dust.

Only Lord Heatherleigh's own chamber sat still and undisturbed. Catrin slipped inside and idly drew her finger over the door of the cupboard by the window, leaving a clear trail in the gathering dust. The giant Bible still sat on the shelf, almost too big for the space, its ancient leather worn and cracking. A piece of paper had nearly slipped free of it, and Catrin went over to tuck it back into place, uninterested in its contents until she saw the first lines:

In the name of God, amen. 15 July, the year of our lord 1561. I, Griffin Petre, Lord Heatherleigh, of Ilford parish and the manor of Saintlow, whole of body and constant of reason and remembrance, doth make and ordain my last will and testament as shall follow. First, I bequeath my soul to almighty God, my maker and redeemer.

A long list of small bequests followed, which was unusual. One usually began a will with the greatest bequests, such as an estate, property, valuable pieces of furniture or even livestock. Lord Heatherleigh had started with the list of bequests for his servants, outlining their pensions in great detail. And then came the great bequest, one Catrin could not believe was truly written there:

According to the rights and privileges outlined in my letters patent, it is within my gift to choose the heir to my lands and titles. And thus I choose to leave Saintlow Hall, with all the rents, goods and chattels not heretofore distributed, to the child Lufian under the guardianship of his mother Alice. I also choose to grant the said Lufian the title of Viscount Heatherleigh, with all the rights, privileges and responsibilities of that rank.

Heatherleigh had given a poor and homeless child all he had, and by doing so he had burdened the babe with the financial troubles Heatherleigh himself had struggled with. Undoubtedly this was not his intention, for he had not intended to die so soon after making this will. He had intended to sell the diamonds from the ship brooch and restore his —

The ship brooch. Catrin had not seen it since her mother had first found it. She had said that she had returned it to Heatherleigh due to the danger of being found with it, but since then there had been no sign of it. Surely it was carefully hidden… Heatherleigh was no fool. But was it hidden well enough to keep it safe until Lufian was found and united with his inheritance?

It was best to check, so Catrin moved swiftly through the room, searching every corner that could possibly hold a palm-sized brooch embedded with diamonds. It was only when she slid under the bed that she found it — a clever hiding space built into the wall. Inside lay the ship brooch, nestled in a velvet-lined wooden box.

Catrin slid out and moved the bed so that its leg blocked the hiding place all the more. The brooch was safe enough there, she decided as she brushed her skirt clear of dust. Lord Heatherleigh had hidden it well.

Unless … the Bible caught her gaze again. It had several pieces of paper tucked among the pages — indeed, it was bristling with them. Could Lord Heatherleigh have left some clue to the brooch's location, some way to remind himself where it was? If so, there was danger there.

She went over to the Bible again, pinched another piece of paper between her thumb and forefinger and pulled it from between the pages. Once again, she was astonished. It was a letter from Mary Shelton, refusing to answer Heatherleigh's questions but offering aid if he needed it, 'due to their close kinship'. A dangerous letter indeed, especially if the queen's enemies were to find it. And it made her wonder what other dangers lay between those ancient pages.

"Lady Catrin?"

Catrin jumped and her fingers clenched, wrinkling the paper. There was a servant in the doorway, looking curious. "Yes?"

"The queen is ready to depart."

"Very well." Catrin eased the paper back into its place and gathered the Bible up in her arms. "So am I."

Thibaut and Symon seemed pleased to leave High Wycombe; they set a strong and steady pace that soon took the four of them into the countryside. Many miles passed without incident, while Pierrick sang French ballads and Symon told minstrel tales.

Lucy took the opportunity to look carefully at the papers that they had found in Wilkyn Burgh's pack. They seemed like random notes, scribbled hastily. Each block of lettering was coloured slightly differently, suggesting that they had been written at different times using different batches of ink.

1527? 1530?
1525 — King of France captured
Easter 1526
December practicality defeats passion…

She could make no sense of that. It seemed a strange list of dates that did not connect. However, there was a passage below them that tugged at her heartstrings.

Poverty is the foul hag that keeps me from my fair lady; my hands are desolate but my heart o'erflows
This is what started it.

Had Wilkyn written that? There were no crossings-out or re-writings as there were in the first list of dates, which made Lucy think that he had copied it from somewhere else. One of the letters, perhaps? And she could assume that he had added the second line himself, based on its similar tone to other such notes. One was scribbled in the very corner of the page: *10 from the man, 12 from the woman — surely she is not the one.* Another said: *It can't be her!* And finally, the last note: *Alas, the poem is true. A poacher, not a hunter.*

Lucy shifted the papers around, suddenly aware that the sun was glaring off the sheets, and flies had started buzzing around the sweat on the horses' flanks. Her side saddle was growing distinctly uncomfortable, and her clothes were too warm for the day.

She lifted her mask so she could wipe moisture from her brow. "How much longer, do you think?"

"Ten or fifteen miles at least," Pierrick said absently, and squinted at something on the horizon. "What is that?"

"A man, I wager, my lord," Symon said tensely. "Shall we chase him off?"

"Hold, for now," Pierrick said. "He is not coming any closer."

Symon loosened his sword in the scabbard. "Nor is he going away, my lord."

Pierrick acknowledged that with a nod, and put one hand on his hilt. They drew close to the figure, and Lucy felt her heart flutter. He was very large and bulky, and his gaze was disconcertingly steady. He also had blood on his doublet, and held his left arm stiffly as if he was injured. But he did not threaten them, so she decided to err on the side of courtesy. "Greetings, goodman."

"Good morrow, my lady," the man said, in a surprisingly rich and beautiful voice. His gaze drifted southward, and fixed on the notes Lucy carried in her lap. "Are you travelling to join the court?"

"Yes, we are," Lucy said, too soon to see Pierrick's warning glance. "I — I mean … perhaps we are. We have not yet decided."

"If you decide to join the queen, be aware that they have progressed to Ingatestone," the man said, and stepped closer. "That will add to your journey, I fear, but give it a happier conclusion."

"Thank you, goodman," Pierrick said coolly, and tossed some coins into the air for him. "We are grateful for your help."

The man caught the coins deftly with his right hand, while the left darted out as quick as a snake and grasped the papers on Lucy's lap. He would have been able to take them, too, if he had not been injured. He cried out in pain as she pulled them out of his grasp, then immediately turned and fled. He was gone so quickly that none of her companions had a chance to draw their swords.

Lucy gathered up the notes at once and slid them into Master Burgh's pack, her fingers shaking. "Why would he try to take these?"

"He must have thought them valuable," Thibaut said.

"But he doesn't know what's in them." Lucy tucked the pack safely away in her saddlebag, just in case. "And nor do I, if the truth be told. All I have learned is that they seem to refer to the letters."

"Yes, the letters Wilkyn thought were so dangerous." Pierrick gave her a long, steady look. "And I suspect he was right."

As the queen's procession drew close to Ingatestone Hall, the trees along the road thinned and they could see fields of wheat beyond, slowly turning from green to gold. The warm summer breeze made ripples in the tall waving stalks, and captured Catrin's attention so thoroughly that she did not notice when gravel suddenly took the place of the soft earth beneath them.

The horses perked up their ears at the crunch, and seemed pleased that they had an easier surface to walk on.

Lord Robert glanced at Catrin. "This must have cost our host a great deal of money."

"It's Sir William Petre, is it not?" Catrin asked, and Lord Robert nodded. "I hear he is very wealthy."

"Or rather, his wife is — as was the wife before her," Lord Robert said. "I wager he will welcome us with enthusiasm, for he is more openly against the queen's religious settlement than most."

"Ah, yes. So he will provide a display of loyalty — with emphasis on the display," Catrin murmured. "Petre — like Griffin Petre, Lord Heatherleigh. Are they related?"

"Very distantly," Lord Robert said. "So distantly no one quite remembers how the connection was forged."

"I imagine there was a marriage involved," Catrin said dryly, and drew in a breath when they came around a bend and got a clear view of the path ahead. It was lined with banners in the Tudor colours of green and white, interspersed with cinquefoils of azure blue and white scallops from the Petre coat-of-arms. The choughs from the coat-of-arms were present as well, but they were live rather than painted: black birds like small crows, with red feet and beaks. They flew around and between the entire procession, letting out strange hoarse sounds that hovered between a squawk, a squeak and a croak. Some of the ladies hid their heads in fright when they flew close, but Catrin watched them swoop about with a vague sense of envy for their freedom.

The house came into view — a massive square structure made of smooth grey stone. There was no gatehouse; the edifice itself was enough to protect its inhabitants. It was two storeys tall, plus a parapet on top that was patrolled by armed men in Sir William Petre's livery. It would have been intimidating, but every available surface was draped with bright, cheerful flags, and banners placed around the edge of the courtyard snapped and whipped about in the breeze. Better still, dozens of people were spilling out around the two sides of the building from the grounds behind the house. Familiar people, dressed in the silks and fine linen of a royal summer court, with gold and silver embroidery making patterns of light in the sun. The sparkle dazzled the queen's procession as they galloped into the courtyard.

The queen let out a cry of joy and pressed one hand to her lips. "They are my court — my people!" she cried. "I know them all. Thank God they are safe."

Lord Robert glanced uneasily around at the deep forest surrounding the house. "Your Majesty —"

"Tush, Robin. Listen," the queen said, as a round of applause filled the air and songbirds joined in with joyful trills and cries. The queen reined in and dropped to the ground without waiting for assistance, spreading her hands wide. "My people — glad I am to see you safe from harm. I thank God for your preservation, and pray He will always protect you from all danger."

The applause swelled again, and a man approached the queen using a cane to propel his hunched figure forward.

"Your Majesty!" he cried, his face beaming lantern-bright. "What a great privilege and delight to see you!"

"Sir William Petre," the queen said, with genuine affection. "It is good to see you as well."

"Great and glorious Majesty, honoured and noble queen, beloved and beautiful lady. I offer my humble home to you, to treat as yours, for all I have is by your gift," Sir William Petre said. He attempted to speak with the expected volume and grandeur, but his aged voice cracked and fell to nothing within ten feet. Behind Catrin, the great company who could not hear him shifted restlessly. A page took up the call, as per usual, repeating his words. Faintly, many feet further back, Catrin heard another page repeat the words of the first, and wondered at their accuracy.

"We accept your gift, as we accepted your great service as Secretary of State in years past," the queen said. "And we return your home to you, in a heartfelt thank-you for your hospitality."

"You are most welcome, Your Majesty," Sir William Petre said, and his watery eyes took on a cast much like a mournful puppy. "I am truly sorry for the difficulty of the past few days, and I hope that you can look on this time in my home as a respite and a delight."

The queen threw back her head and regarded the mass of solid stone before her, with its decoration of dancing cloth and double set of wine-red doors. "I believe I will, my lord. I have not felt so safe as this in many days."

Lord Robert sent Catrin an uneasy glance, and she inclined her head in silent acknowledgement. Surely the queen was safer surrounded by her court, but that did not mean she was safe. "Your Majesty," Catrin said, and her voice carried easily throughout the courtyard. "Would you like to go inside and take your ease?"

"I would," the queen said, with a single hot glance that told Catrin that the queen knew what she was thinking. "It has been a long journey, though a pleasant one."

"One moment, Your Majesty. I have a gift for you," Sir William Petre said, and took one hand from the handle of his cane. A young man responded to the wave of his hand, bearing a small coffer with brass fittings on a red velvet cushion. He held it up and sunk low in a bow, and the queen lifted the lid carefully before peeking inside.

"Why — how beautiful!" she cried, and lifted out a necklace of gold filigree. The delicate tracery formed a series of roses, and at the centre of each one was a blood-red ruby. "I thank you sincerely, my good lord," she said. "And I intend to wear this lovely thing at supper tonight."

"I look forward to that, Your Majesty," Sir William Petre said with another bow. "And now, please follow me. I will show you to your chamber personally."

The queen sent another glance in Catrin's direction, and this one told her clearly that she was to follow. "Thank you, my lord."

CHAPTER TWENTY-EIGHT

The queen was pleased with her rooms, even though a door connected her bedchamber to Sir William Petre's. He made a game of locking it and giving her the key, which amused her so much that it delayed her preparations for the evening. It was a long time before Catrin could extract herself from her duties with the queen and go to her own chamber to find fresh clothes for the evening meal. She was sharing with several ladies for this leg of the journey; the luxury of having her own chamber was no more. But she had a high bed with a thick pallet, and her chest had arrived safely, so all was well.

Catrin drew a key from its chain around her neck and unlocked the padlock, setting it aside with a rattle. The lid lifted easily, as always, revealing the red silk gown she usually wore in the evening, the linens that she changed regularly, the combs and toothcloths, the books and quills and inkpots, the —

They were gone. Catrin stared at the empty space in her chest where a canvas bag containing two cloaks, a boot, and a knife had once lain. She leapt to her feet and strode out to the hall. "Page! Page!"

A tall youth ran toward her from the end of the corridor, his oversized tunic flapping against his knees. "Yes, my lady? May I help you?"

"There are items missing from my chest." Catrin strode back into the room and snatched up the padlock. God's heart! There were scratches around the lock she had not noticed. "Who brought the chests into the chamber?"

The page's gaze darted from side to side. "I — I, um, do not know, my lady. Would you like me to make enquiries?"

Catrin seriously considered it. The missing items were important, after all — they were proof of what she had found in the forest. "Can you or anyone tell me who would have had access to the cart on which this chest travelled?"

The page hastily swallowed a chuckle. "On a day like today, my lady, methinks only God himself could tell you that."

"I suspected as much," Catrin said, and flicked the chest shut with a bang that echoed through the chamber. "Tell the usher to send a messenger to Saintlow Hall. Ask if I left a canvas bag there."

"Yes, my lady," the page said, and darted away with all haste. Catrin sat down on the bed and smoothed one hand over her travelling-skirt, allowing the softness of the fine wool to calm her mind. There was no purpose in searching further for the contents of that bag; it could have vanished at any point during the eleven-mile journey between Saintlow and Ingatestone. Nor did she have any particular need to keep hold of those items; she had already gleaned all she could from them.

But the theft itself was significant. It meant that Heatherleigh's attacker had not fled as they had hoped. He was still hidden amongst them.

Safety at Ingatestone, it seemed, was an illusion.

The dining chamber was decorated with new painted cloths that were so intricately designed that they looked like hand-stitched tapestries. They boasted colours that Catrin had never seen before and were tipped with gold, so that they glittered in the lantern light. It was difficult to draw the ladies away from them; even the queen was intrigued by their artistry.

The marshal of the hall, who was much more cheerful than the sour-faced man in Lord North's household, managed to get them all seated in the proper order of precedence, and then the almoner came in, followed by his servants. Each carried a large shallow silver bowl, and looked properly solemn as they held it out to the guests. "Remember the poor," they intoned. "Remember the poor."

Catrin retrieved some coins from her purse and let them fall into one of the bowls with a clatter. As always, she wondered how many of those coins actually made it to the poor, a question that was all the more difficult to answer at Ingatestone. Usually one could see the poor gathering at the gatehouse of a manor house once the feast began and watch the almoner distribute coins and food, but Ingatestone was a massive hollow square and served as its own gatehouse. The poor were most likely sent around to the back, near the chapel, and not allowed to linger in the tidy courtyard with its fluttering flags.

Even as the thought came to her mind, Catrin saw four people emerge from the dusky half-dark and enter the courtyard as if they belonged there. No one sent them around to the back, for they were certainly not poor. They looked worn out, but they were dressed for court, and one was a woman.

Catrin rose to her feet with such haste that the queen looked up in surprise. "What troubles you, my talisman?"

"I must ask to be excused, Your Majesty. I believe I see Lord Pierrick and Lady Lucy returning."

"Go, then, and greet them heartily on my behalf," the queen said. Catrin curtsied with a word of thanks and hurried out of the chamber and into the Great Hall. The noise of hundreds of voices immediately assaulted her ears, and she had to weave around dozens of people who were busy drinking ale and tearing into loaves of bread. Dogs darted merrily around her feet, begging for scraps. They made her stumble more than once, but still she reached the door just as the steward did. He looked somewhat confused to see her, but bowed low nonetheless. "Do you need something, my lady?"

"I too wish to greet these arrivals."

"Very well, my lady."

"I suspect that they are very weary, and will need to retire at once."

He waved a hand at a nearby page, who immediately rushed away. "We will ensure their chambers are well prepared, my lady."

"Thank you," Catrin said, and waited impatiently through the ceremony of greeting the new arrivals. The steward welcomed them on behalf of Sir William Petre, servants took away their packs, stableboys arrived to help with the horses — it seemed an age before Catrin could push through all the people and find her friend. "Dearest Lucy, I am so glad to see you."

"Catrin." Lucy clung to her for a moment, and Catrin could feel her trembling. "It seems so long since we have seen you."

"You have travelled far, I suspect."

"And learned much. The vagrant's name was Wilkyn Burgh."

Catrin took both of Lucy's hands in hers. "That is very good, but I must tell you —"

"He was the keeper of a madman named Alban, and we think Alban killed both him and the clerk."

"I understand, but —"

"Alban was in London when the progress started, but we have not yet learned where he went after that."

"Lucy —"

"There is more, but first I must wash away the dust of travel." Lucy straightened, glancing around the empty courtyard. "Where is Florie? I would like her to fill a bath."

Catrin could not hold in a wince, and Lord Pierrick noticed. "What is it?" he asked, drawing near with a frown. "Is Florie ill?"

Catrin took a deep breath. "I have some sad news. Saintlow Hall was attacked by a man we have not yet found. He killed several people there. Including, I'm afraid … Florie."

Lucy let out a cry, and Lord Pierrick's jaw tightened. "Where is her body?"

"At Saintlow."

"I must arrange for burial." Lord Pierrick rested a hand on Lucy's back. "Are you content to stay with Lady Catrin, my love?"

"Of course," Lucy said quietly, and fainted.

"Catrin?"

The tiny voice came out of the darkness. Catrin rose from her seat near the dying fire and went over to the bed where her friend lay propped up with pillows. "What is it, dearest?"

"Where is my lord Pierrick?"

"He is still making arrangements."

"Oh." Tears filled Lucy's eyes, and she wiped them away half-heartedly. "Have our things been brought in? I need something from the saddlebags."

"Yes; your packs are right here by the door. What do you need?"

"The wooden box. Please get it out and open it."

Catrin did so, and found two parcels of parchment, hastily bundled together. "What is this, dearling? Some correspondence you need taken care of?"

"No, it is something Wilkyn Burgh took from Alban. It may be why Alban killed him."

Catrin rifled through the pile. "They seem to be nothing but letters."

"And yet Master Burgh thought them dangerous." Lucy rested her head on the pillows. "There are notes as well, but I could make nothing of them. I hope you will have better fortune."

"I will try, dearest," Catrin said. "But first, I think I must find you some food."

Lucy pressed both hands to her stomach. "I am not very hungry, but perhaps … some bread and wine?"

"Yes, that sounds just right." Catrin set the box on a nearby stool. "I will find the usher assigned to your rooms and request it, and then I will be back."

Lucy nodded wearily, and closed her eyes again. Catrin slipped out of the room and went in search of the usher, but before she had walked even half the length of the corridor, she found someone whose presence was entirely more surprising. "*Finn*? What are you doing here?"

Finn bowed. "Lady Angharad sent me with a letter for ye. She has been very worried."

Catrin shook her head in wry amusement. "She needn't be; I sent her a messenger to tell her that I was safe."

Finn's bright eyes took on a sceptical glint. "Safe, my lady? Truly?"

Catrin's lip quirked. "Perhaps I should phrase that differently. I am as safe as possible."

"I fear that will not make her feel better." Finn held out a folded parchment stamped with the Aberavon seal. "Maybe I should stay with ye and guard your back against … against whoever attacked Saintlow."

The earnestness on his youthful face made her heart ache. "I would prefer it if you returned to London and protected my mother."

"I can do that, my lady," he said. "If ye be sure the greater need is there, not here."

"I am sure. I need to know you're both safe; that is what I need most," Catrin said, and opened the letter. It was certainly her mother's handwriting, but the words did not form straight lines on the page, suggesting she had written it hastily.

Dearest Catrin,

I must tell you a very great secret. Alice and the babe are with me, in London. Alice asked me to help her disappear from Saintlow, because a man found her there — a man she had met in London before her child was born. He was bearded and had bulging, staring eyes. He paid her to dress as Anne Boleyn and allow the queen to see her, and she agreed only because she was so desperate for money.

Do you remember when I told you that I made the bedsheets she lay on? It was he who gave them to her, back in London when they first met. She said they were strangely creased, as if they had long been used to wrap objects. One such crease was a circle with a lip, and that reminded me of the ewer you found. Could it have been wrapped in them?

Alice does not want me to tell you this next part, for she is still very afraid of this man, but the fairies have told me that you need to know. The man said that the sheets had originally been intended for a woman with child, so he would give them to her and find another tie to bind. Neither of us know what that means, and it was not unusual for this man to say such unfathomable things. He used to sing French ballads she couldn't understand, and recited disjointed bits of poetry. Once she overheard him muttering, 'Wilkyn had to die; I could not spare him. Wilkyn and the bear; they both had to die.'

I do not know if any of this makes any sense to you, my kitten, but I know I had no choice but to tell you. Please, please be safe.

Your loving mother,

Angharad

Catrin shook her head, bemused. "Mistress Alice and Lufian were gone before my mother left. How did they manage to travel so far on their own?"

"They were not on their own," Finn said, and grinned his sideways grin. "Lady Angharad has friends everywhere. Did ye not know that?"

"Friends, or fairies?" Catrin asked wryly. "But no matter. I am glad Mistress Alice is safe, and all the more glad that she was not at Saintlow when it was attacked." She read the letter again, considering each fresh bit of information. "I must speak to Lady Lucy. You go and find some food and get some rest, and in the morning return to London."

"Yes, my lady. If you're sure —?"

She didn't wait to hear the rest of it; there were too many questions she needed to ask. Instead, she returned to Lucy's chamber and handed her the letter from Lady Angharad. "This gives us some insight, does it not?"

Lucy's clear blue eyes flicked over the words, and slowly colour returned to her face. "The man who frightens Alice must be Alban. Joan said that he had staring eyes and a beard, and she suspected that he was the one who killed Wilkyn Burgh."

"It is more than a suspicion now; this confirms it." Catrin pressed her fingers to her temples. "If I remember aright, you told me that the coroner believed Wilkyn Burgh and the clerk were killed at the same time."

"Yes, that's true," Lucy said. "And in the same place, because the same soil was found on both their bodies."

"So it is fair to assume that 'the bear' Alice overheard him muttering about was the clerk," Catrin said. "We suspected he was killed for his livery or his money, but now I think it was simply because he witnessed Master Burgh's murder."

"I would agree with that, yes."

Catrin read her mother's letter again. "This also suggests that Alban has been the one tormenting the queen with reminders of her mother."

Lucy pushed herself upright. "Yes, the songs from France and using Alice to pose as Queen Anne makes that very likely. But what did the man mean by the 'tie to bind'?"

"I do not know."

"It sounds somewhat menacing."

"Yes." Catrin folded the parchment and tucked it away in her purse. "I noticed that."

CHAPTER TWENTY-NINE

When the morning meal was nearly over, Sir William Petre arrived at the queen's table so suddenly it was like he had appeared from nowhere. Catrin was still trying to discern how he had done that, considering his age and reliance on his cane, when he bowed low before the queen. "Your Majesty, there is a battle about to begin."

The queen raised one eyebrow. "Are we in danger?"

"I hope not." A look of great mischief crossed the old man's face. "But there is a possibility that we shall be overwhelmed by the number of ships approaching."

"Ships?" The queen glanced out the diamond-pane windows at the gravel and the trees and the green rippling fields. "Here?"

"Aye, Your Majesty. Do please come."

"Of course." The queen set aside her cup and rose. "One should never refuse to watch a naval battle on dry land."

Several people chuckled at that, and most of the court followed them out of the manor. Lucy slipped in next to Catrin, and sent her a small smile as they walked down over a sloping expanse of grass and into a thick growth of trees. There they found a royal pavilion which was draped with warm orange and yellow silks, beside a large oval pond, with waters that glittered and rippled in the sunshine.

On the pond was the invading fleet — two dozen wooden sailing ships that bobbed about in the breeze, straining their anchors. Each one was no more than a handspan high, and painted like the great fighting ships of the Royal Navy, both past and present. Catrin could only recognize two — the *Henri Grâce à Dieu* and the tragic *Mary Rose.*

Sir William Petre raised his voice so it carried through the crowd. "We are about to have a mighty battle. These ships will race to the end of the pond, enduring many attacks from the shores. The first to arrive safely in port will be declared the victor, and its owner will earn a great prize."

There were squeals of delight from the ladies, and one young girl actually began to jump up and down. "May I own a ship? Oh, please, may I?"

"Of course," Sir William Petre said. "But first, the queen shall choose."

"I wish to sail my great ship the *Elizabeth Jonas,*" the queen said at once. This roused a cheer from the men, for the new galleon was the pride of the navy. Lucy, however, was less impressed.

"I do not wish to play this game, Catrin," she whispered. "I would rather find a shady spot and rest."

"Let us wander back toward the house, then," Catrin returned. "I have a question for you anyway, and this is not the place to ask it."

"Very well," Lucy said, and they slipped out from the crowd. No one noticed them go; competition was fierce to be one of those who 'owned' a ship.

The air smelled faintly of roses as they climbed the slope, and that inspired them to follow the scent, wending toward the south and the chapel that was attached to the long gallery. It was surrounded by roses, and the morning sun had not quite reached the far side of it. Lucy and Catrin found a bench on which to settle, and Lucy relaxed against the cool stone with a contented sigh.

"Much better," she murmured. "Now you may ask your question."

"It is quite simple: what does *noli me tangere* mean? It sounds vaguely familiar … perhaps from my childhood … but I cannot remember."

"It means 'touch me not'," Lucy said promptly. "You may remember it from the days when the Bible was read in Latin. Christ said 'touch me not' when he first appeared to his disciples, after the resurrection. Where did you hear it?"

"A poet shouted it below the queen's window. I also heard the words: 'And wild, wild though I seem tame.'"

"I believe I have heard that before," Lucy said thoughtfully, and murmured the words again. "Yes, I'm sure it comes from a poem I have read… I will try to find it."

Catrin broke off a rose and handed it to her friend. "Thank you, dearling."

Lucy buried her face in the petals and drew in a deep breath. "Florie loved roses," she murmured, and tears welled in her eyes. "Poor Florie. She did not deserve to die that way."

"None of them did," Catrin murmured. "That is why I am doing all I can to find their killer."

Lucy gazed at her for a long moment. "Alban. It must be Alban."

"Yes, it must be." Catrin pressed a fingertip against the stem of a rose until the thorn pricked her skin. "I do not know where he is, or why he has done all this, but I will find out."

Lucy thought about it for a moment, then let out a sigh. "I confess, Catrin, that none of his actions make sense to me. Why remind the queen of her mother? Why attack people in their home?"

"Those are not the only questions. Why leave the queen an ouche that means nothing to her, and steal diamonds that matter even less, only to leave them behind?" Catrin rose from the bench and paced in circles on the path. "It is like he is leaving the queen a message that none of us can read."

"Literally," Lucy said.

Catrin came to an abrupt stop. "What do you mean?"

"The letters I gave you yesterday. Alban had them, right before all this began. And Master Burgh tried to decipher them, before he left High Wycombe to search for Alban."

It was so obvious. Catrin could have kicked herself. "They might be the key to all of this. Pray excuse me, dearling — I must go and read those letters."

"Not yet … please, not yet." Lucy rested her cheek on the bench. "I beg you for a few more moments of peace first."

"Of course. I understand." Catrin took firm hold of the back of the bench to stop herself from departing at once. "Rest now. You're safe, and we — what is that?"

Lucy buried her face in rose petals. "I don't see anything."

"That is because you are not looking, dearling." Catrin circled the bench so that she stood on the far side of the rosebush. Taking the blossom for Lucy had revealed a strange dark patch on the ground behind it, one which stretched to the chapel wall. "It looks as if something has worn the earth smooth."

Lucy glanced at the patch dubiously. "It's a garden. Perhaps the workers smoothed it themselves."

"It's a triangle, but with one curved edge," Catrin murmured. "I'm sure I've seen such a shape before, but I can't —"

"What-ho! What are you doing there?"

Sir William Petre had circled the chapel wall and was limping toward them, annoyance showing in a red flush across his cheeks. Lucy immediately rose to her feet. "Oh, sir — we're sorry —"

"We're just admiring the garden," Catrin interrupted smoothly, and bent to press her face against a rosebud. "It is truly delightful, my lord."

Sir William Petre waved his cane at her. "Come out from there at once. You might damage something."

"Of course," Catrin said demurely. "I would not want to cause any upset."

He snorted. "That is not what I hear, Lady Catrin. Now — both of you — remove yourselves. Go and watch the rest of the race."

Catrin joined Lucy, keeping her gaze on the path for fear her eyes would reveal her vexation. "As you wish, my lord."

CHAPTER THIRTY

There was to be a grand feast that evening, with noble guests arriving from miles around, spectacular food, and sweets of unprecedented delicacy. Indeed, there were rumours that Sir William Petre's confectioners had constructed an entire castle of sugar as a centrepiece, so everyone was expected to measure up to all this extravagance. And that meant that the queen had to be more splendid still.

In mind of this, Catrin and Lucy decided to change into their own finery early, so they would be free to help the queen prepare. They went first to Lucy's chamber, so that Catrin could help her dress in her favourite pale green silken gown.

"We must ensure that my hair is firmly pinned up underneath my hood, too," Lucy said as they walked along the corridor. "As a married lady, I can no longer let it lie loose on my shoulders, as you do."

Catrin gave a great dramatic sigh. "How sad, that we must hide the golden curls that have inspired the lovesick poetry of so many courtiers."

"Not as many as those who write to praise your eyes of forget-me-not blue," Lucy teased. "But it is no loss. None of those poems had any literary merit."

"I don't know — remember the one that compared your skin to freshly made cheese?" Catrin asked. "That was, at the very least, creative."

Lucy laughed as she pushed open the door to her chamber, but the sound ended in a choked gasp. The blankets had been pulled from her bed, the sheets ripped. Her chest was open, linen and gowns spilling out. Her books were lying about in heaps, some of the pages ripped out and scattered across the floor.

"Oh, woe," Lucy whispered. "Alban. It must be Alban. He's looking for the notes."

Catrin stared at her, dumbstruck. "How do you know?"

Lucy sniffed back tears. "We saw him on the road on the way here. We thought he was just one of those men who follow the court on progress, and direct others for a few coins. But then he tried to steal Master Burgh's notes."

"Tried to *steal* —" Catrin flung her hands up in the air. "Why did you not tell me this yesterday?"

"At the time, we did not realise who he was. And then … I could think only of Florie." She picked up a torn book of poetry and cradled it in her arms as she started to weep. "So much … so much has been destroyed."

Catrin knelt and drew Lucy into her arms, soothing her with murmured assurances she did not herself believe. It was true; so much had been destroyed. And still the destroyer remained just out of her reach.

Lucy was still feeling rather shaky when she left her chamber to go and help the queen. She passed the ladies' chamber, where Catrin was preparing for the evening, and took the stairs from the upper gallery down to the main floor. The queen's rooms were off the gallery, with a privy chamber first and a bedchamber within. It was rare for the queen and her ladies to be so separated, but the square stacked design of Ingatestone Hall made it necessary.

The yeomen of the guard let Lucy pass into the privy chamber without challenge, and she approached the open bedchamber door with an absent smile for the lords and ladies scattered about. Most were strangers, attending only for the evening; Lord Robert was the only one she recognized. He was sitting on a cushion in the corner, reading a sheaf of parchment pages with great intensity.

Faint voices floated out from the bedchamber, and Lucy paused, wondering if she should interrupt. The queen was speaking, telling someone all about the horror they had found when they had returned to Saintlow Hall. She also mentioned the strange determination of Lord John Grey to keep the court at Pyrgo, and the constant reminders of her mother that had tormented her for days: a lady in a diamond noose ... Queen Anne's perfume ... a golden ewer with the former queen's symbol ... a song sung in French with lyrics that made Lucy's heart ache. "I know that there is danger in going on progress," the queen said, and let out a long sigh. "But this is not the sort of danger I expected. It seems that someone wants me to feel afraid."

"Someone wants you to wallow in the sorrow of your youth," a man said. Lucy recognized his voice immediately; it was Sir William Petre. "And I think that same someone is obsessed with your mother."

"Yes, that seems the central theme of all this difficulty."

"Perhaps it is someone who was once obsessed with finding her own mother." Lucy's heart skipped a beat. Surely he didn't mean Catrin? The queen said nothing, and that seemed to encourage Sir William Petre to continue. "Lady Catrin defied you to find Baroness Aberavon, did she not?"

"'Defied' does not quite describe it, my lord, and I am sure of Lady Catrin's loyalty."

"I know you are, Your Majesty, and it is not her loyalty I question. It is your trust in her wisdom. After all, Lady Catrin would not be the first to find a creative way to convince you to follow the path she has chosen for you." The queen was quiet again, and Sir William Petre took advantage. "There may be many explanations for these events, but she has pushed you to believe in only one. She has chased an attacker no one else has seen; she has found objects where other eyes found nothing. Does that not seem suspicious to you?"

A long pause. "I suppose it does."

"I wonder, Your Majesty, if you should not step back from Lady Catrin, and consider whether her counsel has been as good as it has seemed."

"Perhaps you are right, my lord," the queen said quietly. "I have often found treason in trust."

"So you have, Your Majesty, but many others are here to help you," Sir William Petre said soothingly. "Allow me to confer with your councillors, and then we will speak again on these matters."

"Very well, my lord. Until then."

"Until then, Your Majesty."

Lucy hastily retreated from the doorway just as Sir William Petre appeared. He limped his way past her but had not gone far when an elderly woman approached him with hopeful eyes. Clearly thinking he was out of earshot, he said, "Good evening, my sweet heart." He rested his free hand on the woman's shoulder and leaned close to her ear. "We shall end this tyranny once and for all."

The woman smiled. "So the plan is in motion?"

Sir William Petre didn't respond, but his smile said it all. "I will see you anon, my dear."

Catrin noticed Lucy's agitation while they were all waiting to be called into the dining chamber for the feast, but the crush of people was too great to allow them to talk. Nor was there a chance while the food was arriving, for there were dozens of dishes being carried all about the room with great ceremony. Including, to Catrin's astonishment, a roast peacock served with its feathers re-inserted, so it had a halo of green and blue all around it.

It was only when a select group was moving to a smaller chamber for the void that Lucy managed to dart through the crowd and catch Catrin's arm. "Catrin, I think you're in danger," she whispered. "Sir William Petre is conspiring against you."

Immediately Catrin led them to a panelled niche set into the wall so no one could overhear. "How?"

"He has eroded the queen's trust in you, and I overheard him talking about a plan to 'end this tyranny'. Very dramatic and overstated, of course, but still —"

"I wonder if Lord North or Godfrey Breen poisoned him against me," Catrin said, and weariness suddenly washed over her. "Oh, what I wouldn't do to be safe from such intrigue. Perhaps I should return to Ashbourne and let the villains of the court do what they wish."

Lucy's blue eyes widened. "Would you do that, truly?"

Catrin actually considered it for a moment. Only a moment, but that was certainly more than she had ever considered it before. "I could not desert the queen ... but then, if she starts to think ill of me, it would not be desertion but self-preservation."

Lucy bit her lip. "So is that what you are going to do?"

"I don't know." Catrin's mind was full of possibilities, but no solution emerged from the tangle. "I need a quiet place to think. Prithee give my excuses at the void; tell them I have a toothache."

"I will, if that will help."

"I hope it will," Catrin said, and squeezed Lucy's hand in thanks before she walked away, leaving the noise and chaos behind.

The ladies' chamber, in contrast, was quiet and empty, allowing her to consider the problem at hand. Sir William Petre was conspiring against her, which meant he had joined the ranks of men such as Lord North and Godfrey Breen. But why? What did they hope to accomplish?

It was an impossible question, and only one of many that buzzed like angry wasps in her mind. Indeed, it was not even the question that most concerned her. What she wanted most was to find the man who was tormenting the queen and killing innocent people. If only the answers would come to her as the diamonds had.

A sudden thought gave her pause. What if they had — through the letters Lucy had found? She had been right that afternoon when she pointed out the importance of the letters; they were the catalyst for all that had happened since. Through them, she might be able to determine why this Alban had started his evil journey, and that might tell her where he intended to go next.

Hastily she lit a candle to give her enough light to read by, and pulled out the bundle of letters she had hidden under her mattress. It was easy to see that they were love letters: one bundle was written from a woman to a man she called 'my champion'. The other was the man's replies, which referred to the woman as 'my untamed heart'. No names were used, although they occasionally referred to someone as 'the challenger'.

She started by looking through them quickly, flipping through several pages in rapid succession.

Ours is a love so pure I fear it does not belong on this earth. Are we doomed to failure, my own heart's root? Tell me we shall live our lives together.

…for you are precious. Too precious to throw your life away on someone unworthy of you.

I think often of our moments in hidden corners. Your lips are a delight sweeter than honey.

I know you will soar like a great hawk someday, my love … the world will know your name.

Catrin sighed. If there was any significance to these letters, it was certainly buried deep in sentiment. And there seemed to be no obvious chain between them, nor any obvious signs of a cipher or any hidden meaning. If only her mother was there: with her skills at deciphering secret messages, she might have found something. To Catrin they were just … love letters. Nothing more, nothing less.

She sighed and hid the bundle away again, then blew out her candle and lay down. Her bed faced the windows, which showed the sky coloured in intense pinks and blues as the sun finally slipped below the horizon. Her mind drifted to Ashbourne … its tall red brick walls and octagonal chimneys … the nearby river, rushing constantly under the ancient yellow-stone bridge … the rolling fields and thick forests. It would be warm there too, but under the trees the air would still be fresh and cool. And she could wade in the streams barefoot, because no one would be there to be shocked by it.

"Ashbourne…" she murmured, and fell asleep.

CHAPTER THIRTY-ONE

Catrin's dream drew her along a mossy path beside a wide shallow river. It felt so real; she could smell the fresh pine, hear the water bubbling over rounded golden stones. But she knew she was dreaming, because the man who walked by her side would never walk with her again. "Father."

He turned his head and his lip quirked in that sideways smile she knew so well. "Speak softly, kitten, and you will see something remarkable."

She slid her hand into his. "I see something remarkable now."

He squeezed her hand, then drew her off the path, toward the water. They came to rest behind a weeping willow, and he set both hands on her shoulders to turn her slightly outward so she faced a crane on the far bank. It stood motionless in the water on one leg, its other leg drawn up underneath it and its head up, beak pointed toward the moon. "He is on guard," her father whispered. "See — he holds a rock in the crook of the leg drawn up under him. If he starts to fall asleep, it will fall and rouse him again."

"How clever." The crane turned its head toward her and she pressed her fingers to her lips, afraid she had disturbed him. "He is very brave."

"And he never gives up." Her father kissed the top of her head. "Remember that."

The crane stared at something over her shoulder, his black-eyed gaze so intense it made her shiver. She turned to see what he had seen, just as a door appeared at the side of the path — a door that was not attached to any wall or archway.

There was a whoosh and a flurry and a great splash of water, and then the crane flew over her head in a straight path right toward the door. She cried out in concern, sure it would break its neck on the unyielding wood, but the door swung open just in time and the crane flew through and disappeared.

Catrin found herself staring at the scratches in the earth the door had made as it opened. It had marked out a triangle — a triangle with one rounded side.

And suddenly she knew exactly what to do.

She woke with a gasp, and found the room fully dark. It was late, but most of the beds were still empty. One person slumbered on a pallet near the door, but fortunately she did not so much as stir when Catrin rose and lit a candle. Indeed, she began to snore as Catrin wrapped up in a dressing gown and put on her softest slippers, and did not notice when Catrin slipped from the room.

Catrin tiptoed down the stairs and along the gallery, leaving the manor through the door at the far end. It brought her to the garden, where the air was tingling with the sweetness of jasmine as the white star-shaped flowers opened to the night. So strong were they that Catrin could not discern any other flower, until she brushed against the damask roses by the lee side of the chapel and was suddenly drowned in their deeper, richer scent.

She found the rounded triangle on the ground almost immediately, just behind the bench where she and Lucy had sat to rest. It was the mark a door made when it scraped along the ground; she was sure of that now, even though she couldn't see a door. And she was equally sure that Sir William Petre had been very anxious to keep her away from that spot.

She slid her fingertips along the stone wall, alert to any change in texture or shape, but there was nothing at eye level.

It wasn't until she bent low that she noticed a hollow shaped exactly like Sir William Petre's cane. She slid her fingers inside and felt something smooth; when she pressed it, there was a rumble below her feet that made her jump back. A large stone in the wall swung outward and a rounded arch appeared, with uneven stone steps leading downward.

Catrin took a breath to steady her nerves and placed one slippered foot on the top step. There were no further creaks or rumbles, so she dared to descend further, counting the steps as she went. *Two, three, four … ten, eleven … twenty, twenty-one, twenty-two.*

When she reached the bottom, the air was distinctly cold and damp, and the earth felt soft beneath her feet. There was a torch in a sconce to her left, its embers glowing faintly. She pulled it from its place and used her candle to encourage the flame, which flared up enough to reveal bundles of twigs, each one wrapped in a waxy cloth, sitting ready on the floor.

She added one bundle to the embers and the torch flared up with a hiss, showing her three rounded doorways filled with shadows that wavered and shifted in the flickering light. She blew out her candle to save it and moved first toward the left, holding up the torch so she could see the tunnel twisting and curving before her. It seemed to have no end, but she followed it for as long as she dared before she retraced her steps. There was nothing there; just earthen walls and a damp floor.

Back at the staircase, Catrin peered down the centre tunnel before advancing several paces. She found rough doors held fast by rusting locks, and like the first tunnel it seemed to stretch on endlessly, sinking deeper and deeper. She turned back when the chill started to remind her of the grave.

The right-hand tunnel looked like it was the one used most. The doors that stretched along it were whitewashed and the locks free of rust. One of the doors hung open, and she was relieved to see the familiar outline of wine barrels and casks of ale.

Unlike the others, the right-hand tunnel didn't have any turns, and it didn't seem to sink as quickly. Also, to her surprise, it did not take long before she found herself at the end of it, facing a large arched door with a heavy iron bar holding it shut. Part of her did not want to know what was behind that door, but still Catrin fit her fingers into the ring on the bar and slid it free from the pocket that held it. The rattle of iron against iron in that silent space made her jump, and her fingers were shaking when she pushed the door open.

It swung open slowly, revealing a scene Catrin only vaguely remembered from her childhood — a scene of images and colour and rich hangings. It was a chapel, decorated as all chapels had been decorated during the time of Queen Mary. There were elaborate paintings on every wall depicting heaven and hell, all designed to draw the eye to the altar at the east end. It was covered in cloth of gold, and a silver crucifix sat on top, with a gold base and rubies embedded in each of Christ's wounds. On one side of it a golden chalice sat ready to hold the blood of Christ, and on the other a ciborium to hold the body. A rosary formed from ebony and diamonds wove like a serpent around them.

Sir William Petre, it seemed, held firmly to the old religion — something long suspected by the queen and her court, but never proved. Catrin now had the proof — and if she used it, Sir William Petre would lose his status, his home and his wealth. She could destroy him with a word.

She had no desire to destroy him or any man, but nor was she willing to be destroyed. So this was a secret she would keep.

Until the right moment.

Catrin, Lucy and Lord Pierrick were summoned to attend the queen early the next morning, but when they arrived at her chamber she was not yet ready to receive visitors. So they waited in the gallery, looking out through diamond-paned windows at the flowers tossing in the fresh breeze and the clouds sliding rapidly over the sun.

Catrin slid her foot over the flagstones, thinking of what lay beneath. "Lucy, are cranes used in heraldry?"

"Yes," Lucy said, and rose from the bench on which she was perched. "They represent vigilance, justice and longevity. Why?"

"Mere curiosity." Catrin started to wander along the length of the gallery. "Does Sir William Petre have any connection to Godfrey Breen?"

"None that Sir William Cecil or his clerks could find," Lord Pierrick said. "Whatever Sir William Petre's reasons for plotting against you, they are not related to Breen's claim to be Earl of Ashbourne."

"I suspected as much," Catrin murmured, and lifted her head when Mistress Ashley arrived. She ushered them into the queen's privy chamber without a word, and left again just as silently. Meanwhile, the queen herself sat stiffly in a cushioned chair near the window, with Lord Robert on her right and Sir William Petre on her left.

Lord Robert, Catrin noticed, looked worried.

"Your Majesty," Catrin said, and sunk into a deep curtsy.

The queen ignored her. "Lord Pierrick — Lady Lucy. How deeply I regret the loss of your servant in the attack on Saintlow."

Lord Pierrick bowed low. "Thank you, Your Majesty."

"We have learned much since we last saw you, Your Majesty," Lucy said, and gave a somewhat unsteady curtsy that showed her nerves. "The man we thought was a vagrant was a tutor by the name of Wilkyn Burgh. He was killed by the man in his charge, who was called Alban."

"How do you know?" Sir William Petre asked sceptically.

"We met his mother in High Wycombe," Lord Pierrick said. "She was quite certain that Alban would have killed Wilkyn Burgh if Burgh had tried to thwart him in any way."

Sir William Petre shivered. "High Wycombe, you say?" he asked, and drew his cloak more tightly around his neck. "What was the mother's name?"

"Joan Sandys," Lord Pierrick said. "I believe she knows more about Alban's schemes than she said, but did not want to share them. We could have applied further persuasion, but did not want to do so without the queen's permission."

"And I do not give it," the queen said. "I see no connection between the court and this man Alban, and thus there is no reason to disturb his mother."

"But Alban also killed Sir William Cecil's clerk, John — known as Ursus," Lucy said. "Isn't that a connection?"

The queen's fingers curled around the arms of her chair. "Not unless it tells me who attacked Saintlow, killed Heatherleigh and stole jewels from my host."

"But it does," Lucy cried. "Alban is mad. Mad enough to kill, steal the diamonds, *and* attack Saintlow."

Lord Pierrick rested a warning hand on Lucy's shoulder, and Catrin stepped in. "If I may, Your Majesty," she said. "I received a letter from my mother, who is now protecting a woman who knows Alban, and is frightened of him because she heard him talking about killing Wilkyn Burgh and the clerk."

"I remain unmoved. That has nothing to do with my court or my people," said the queen.

"But the woman is Alice, Your Majesty," Lucy said. "She fled your court because Alban found her, and wanted her to play the same role at Saintlow that she played in London."

"A role? What do you mean?" Lord Robert asked.

Catrin kept her eyes on the queen. "It was she who pretended to be your mother, Your Majesty. After that, Alban provided the rest of the reminders himself."

Sir William Petre threw up his hands. "Do you see, Your Majesty? At every opportunity, Lady Catrin refers to your mother! It is *she* who wants you to dwell on this painful past, not some unknown madman!"

"No!" Lucy cried. "It is not Catrin — it is Alban! He is the one who stole the diamonds, and sang the French ballad, and used the perfume —"

"Enough! I will hear no more of this," the queen said, and swept out of the room without further ceremony. Catrin dropped into a curtsy just in time, and a fold of the queen's skirt slapped against her elbow. For some reason, that carelessness was almost as hurtful as the queen's rejection.

Lord Robert and Sir William Petre followed her out, and the door shut behind them with a terrible finality. Lucy burst into tears. "Oh, woe — is she terribly angry? Will she send us away?"

Lord Pierrick pulled her into his arms, his brow deeply creased. "Fear not, *mon amour*, I am sure it will not come to that."

"But Sir William Petre has convinced the queen that Catrin is deliberately misleading her!"

"Then we must prove otherwise," Catrin said bleakly. "Lord Pierrick, I beg you to go out with the court in whatever they do today. Find out who is saying what, and what people believe."

"With a will, my lady."

"Lucy, I'm going to return the notes and letters to you and ask you to look at them again," Catrin said. "I could find no meaning, but if you look at them both together, you may have better fortune."

"I'll do my best." Lucy wiped her eyes dry with a sniff. "What are you going to do?"

Catrin smoothed her hair under her hood. "Convince Joan Sandys to come to Ingatestone."

After the morning meal, the entire court — Pierrick included — went out on the hunt. Ingatestone Hall was left almost empty, but humming with a sense of quiet purpose. Servants bustled about changing linens on the beds and carting laundry back and forth. Sir William Cecil's clerks busied themselves with the business of the realm. Sir William Petre limped through the chambers with his steward and the marshal of the chamber, planning the afternoon's entertainment.

Lucy took the wooden box of letters to the gallery, where there was enough light to read and she could examine the letters on the windowsill without disturbing them too much. They seemed all the more fragile now that she had a chance to really look at them; the edges crumbled as she untied the twine that bound them.

"What are you looking at, Lady Lucy?"

Lucy jumped, and her first instinct was to sweep the letters into a bundle and hide them. But then she saw familiar warm grey eyes and a long-held trust took sway. It was Sir William

Cecil, and she knew he would not betray her. "Letters which have been called more dangerous than fire and gunpowder."

Sir William sat down on a clear space at the edge of the windowsill, careful not to disturb the crumbling paper. "I suspect, then, that you are on a different kind of hunt than the rest of the court."

Lucy nodded. "My husband told you what we discovered about Ursus, did he not?"

"Yes." The grey eyes dimmed with sorrow. "The poor lad lost his life because he witnessed a murder."

"Yes, and the murder he witnessed was committed by the man who stole these letters — a man called Alban. He killed his tutor, Wilkyn Burgh."

Sir William frowned. "Did Master Burgh try to take them from Alban, and that's why Alban killed him?"

"No; we think Alban killed Master Burgh simply because Burgh tried to force him to return to his home. By that time, Burgh had already taken these letters from Alban; he knew they were dangerous."

"Dangerous enough to kill for?" Sir William rested a finger on one brittle piece of twine. "They do not look as valuable as that."

"I think they are. I think that Alban found something in them: something that prompted him to steal from his mother, run away from his home, kill Burgh for trying to stop him, and possibly stage the attack at Saintlow." Lucy took a deep breath. "Lady Catrin thinks he is also the one who has been reminding the queen of her mother, although she does not yet know why he would do so."

"And you are searching for evidence to support this idea?"

"Yes, and for any reference to diamonds or the queen's 'B' necklace, because they were both stolen." Lucy bent over the letters again. "Oh, and for anything relating to an alabaster cup or a jewelled ouche, because they too have been part of this strange tale even though the queen does not remember either one in connection to her mother."

"I see," Sir William said. "It is a weighty task indeed. May I be of assistance?"

"I would be most grateful."

Sir William smiled. "And I would be honoured."

CHAPTER THIRTY-TWO

Lucy cast a letter down on the pile, and a large flake broke off and drifted sadly down to the floor. "These letters are all just love-talk."

"Most of them, yes," Sir William said. "But even love-talk could be useful if we understood who was speaking."

"It is impossible to know that. They never use names."

"I found one where the woman calls the man her Abelard, but I doubt that was literally his name," Sir William said. "I suspect she refers to the philosopher-priest Abelard, who loved a woman named Heloise and suffered for it."

"Yes, theirs was a forbidden love, which would be a helpful hint if forbidden love was not so common," Lucy said. "These letters could have been written by any of a hundred couples, from a milkmaid in love with an usher to an innkeeper's son who was rejected by the butcher's daughter."

"I do not think so — the language shows that these people were well educated, and they seem very aware of all the great events of the day." Sir William pointed at one letter, written by the man. "In that one, the man claims that he has been captured by the woman as thoroughly as the King of France was captured."

That gave Lucy pause. "That happened in 1525, did it not?"

"Yes, it did. How did you know?"

"It is mentioned in Master Burgh's notes." Lucy cupped her elbows with her hands and wandered around the gallery, thinking hard. "If we say that these letters date from that time, and that the writers' style and knowledge makes them part of the nobility, we can argue that they must have been members of King Henry's court."

"Or one of them was, at least. Not, I would guess, the man," Sir William said. "I read a line about poverty being a foul hag in one of his letters. He says that he would declare his love to the world if it were not for his poverty."

"According to his notes, Master Burgh thought that was the first letter — and that makes sense, for it is the least specific." Lucy shifted around the letters and soon found the one she sought. "I think this is the response to it. She says that poverty is only one of the reasons not to declare their love."

Sir William frowned. "Status, perhaps?"

"Or maybe she was betrothed."

Sir William shook his head. "I read one letter where she says she is free of any entanglements of marriage, but not of love." He found it quickly, and read the passage aloud, finishing with: *"It is like the song I sang to you — 'it is right that I love you, without blame.'"*

The words were familiar, but Lucy knew she had heard them a different way. Or rather ... in a different language. "In French, that would be *'c'est drois que je l'aime, sans blame.'"* She bit her lip. "Isn't that the song that the queen heard someone singing in the fog? The song that her mother used to sing to her?"

"It is." Sir William turned pale. "But ... but surely, the woman who wrote these letters can't be Anne Boleyn."

"I think Master Burgh had the same thought, my lord. He wrote 'it can't be her!' in his notes — but I can't agree." Lucy hastily sifted through the letters in search of another passage she had read. "Here the man refers to the scent the lady wears — mint, lavender and musk. The same scent Anne Boleyn wore, which someone left in the queen's chamber."

Sir William gazed at the letters for a long time, a faint crease between his eyebrows. "If this is true, then these letters could prove Anne Boleyn had a lover while King Henry was courting her." He flicked through the pages, his grey eyes sharp with suspicion. "That could make the royal marriage void and our queen a bastard."

"I don't think it is as bad as that," Lucy said. "The king declared himself in Shrovetide, 1526, did he not?"

"Yes, but Lady Anne herself certainly knew of the king's interest long before then."

"Then that explains *these* letters — and I suspect that they were the last ones." Lucy held up two of them, first the man's, then the woman's. "They say that they are not going to see each other anymore, or write, or even acknowledge each other in public. The man promises to set the hind he has captured free from his love, because the 'challenger' has defeated him, her 'champion'."

"I read her response to that," Sir William said. "She thanks him, and says the jewels they exchanged will always remind them both that their love was real and pure."

"So he gave her up despite his love for her, because the king was interested in her as well." Lucy let the letters fall from her hand. "That's really rather sad."

"And, as you suspected, very dangerous." Sir William sighed. "Even if we can prove that these were written before Shrovetide 1526, and thus the relationship was over before Anne Boleyn became the king's mistress, it still calls her chastity into question. And that weakens our queen's position on the throne."

"Perhaps that is why Alban has been sending the queen all these reminders of her mother. He read the letters, and decided to damage her by bringing them to life."

"If that is so, he may well succeed." Sir William stood up. "Perhaps it would be best if I took charge of these letters, my lady."

Lucy hesitated. "You won't destroy them?"

"No, but I may study them further."

"Catrin might need to see them."

"I promise to make them available to her." He smiled. "You can trust me, Lady Lucy. Like you, I am loyal."

"Yes, I know," Lucy said, and returned the letters to their box before she handed them over. "Thank you, my lord."

He bowed, his grey eyes sparkling silver. "You are most welcome, my lady."

Wherever she went, the skin on the back of Catrin's neck prickled. It felt like everyone was watching her — whispering behind her back — planning to move against her. It made her fingers itch to draw her *stiletto*, but she refused to give in to the urge. Instead, she swept past gossiping ladies with her head held high on her way out to the gardens, and greeted passing courtiers with light-hearted charm.

Her pace was quick, so she soon found herself far from the house, wandering the paths of a young knot garden, where a lad was out walking with his sweetheart. The woman kept trying to talk to him, but he seemed determined to show off his poetic skills, and often interrupted her with theatrical quotations. He reminded Catrin of the poet-musician outside the queen's window, and the man dressed as Ares. They had been equally as determined to impress a lady, and they had chosen the queen as the elusive hind to hunt. A hind who could not be captured, for she was wild and free and —

A shiver ran down Catrin's spine. Was it suspicious that both men had used the same metaphor for the queen? Indeed, their poetry had had similar themes. A captured love, set free and lost for the sake of a later, greater victory.

She turned on her heel to retrace her steps, and caught sight of someone rushing toward her out of the corner of her eye. Immediately she spun on her heel, braced and ready to meet their attack.

Lucy skidded to a stop at the flash of a blade in the sun. "Catrin — it is just me."

Catrin immediately sheathed her *stiletto*. "I do apologise, dearest. I am just feeling … overly cautious, shall we say."

Lucy blinked wide, innocent eyes. "I understand. A hostile madman would have that effect on most people, I wager."

Catrin's lip quirked. "Thank you for understanding."

"And you do look worried." Lucy tilted her head. "Have you found any answers?"

"I have found only questions." Catrin pressed her fingers to her temples. "And right now I am thinking of poets and their poetry, and that seems simply foolish, in the light of all that has happened."

"Maybe not, dearling. I went looking for the words you mentioned to me, about the hind and the diamond necklace. I also looked for the words that Ares said: 'whoso list to hunt, I know where is an hind, whom I will capture and love forevermore.'"

"Did you make any sense of it?"

"All those phrases came from a poem by Sir Thomas Wyatt. They were changed a bit, but —"

"Thomas Wyatt of Wyatt's rebellion?"

"No, his father. The statesman."

"So both Ares and the musician who followed us stole their poetry from the same source," Catrin said slowly. "And they were both large men, with square beards and a certain skill for recitation."

"Ooh — could they be the same person?"

"It is possible," Catrin said slowly, but then shook her head. "But even if they are, it might mean nothing. Both Lord North and Lord Heatherleigh could easily have hired the same poet to perform for the queen."

"That is true." Lucy sighed. "There are not a lot of players in the realm, and many of them travel to different great houses to offer their services."

"Yes, that is true. So it leads us nowhere. We must take another tack." Catrin circled the knot garden, her feet crunching on the gravel. "Did you find out anything from those letters?"

"Yes, with Sir William Cecil's help. We think the letters were between Anne Boleyn and a lover. They exchanged jewels and other gifts, and when they chose to end their liaison, he gave her a necklace to remind her that he would always love her." Lucy huffed out a frustrated breath. "Unfortunately, we could not determine what the necklace looked like, or what happened to it."

Ours is a love so pure I fear it does not belong on this earth. The words from one of the letters rose in Catrin's mind, and suddenly everything became clear. "I would wager it was made of gold and pearls, some of which were recently found in the grave of a man who tried to stop the thief."

Lucy pressed her fingers to her lips. "Do you mean … Queen Anne's 'B' necklace?"

"I do. Pearls represent purity, and I remember from reading the letters that the two writers claimed several times that their love was pure."

"A 'P' may have been a better choice than a 'B', then. After all, what did the Boleyn name have to do with it?"

"Nothing at all, I wager." Catrin let her gaze rise thoughtfully to the sky. "Everyone assumes that the 'B' in Queen Anne's necklace stands for 'Boleyn', but it could easily stand for 'Beloved'."

Lucy flung her hands into the air in frustration. "I should have thought of that."

"And that is why the necklace was so important to Queen Anne that she would not let her child play with it, and why wearing it made her sad."

"It reminded her of the man she loved and lost." Lucy's lip trembled. "How tragic."

"Yes, and very strange. Why would Alban take the 'B' necklace from the queen if his goal was to remind the queen of her mother?"

"That is true — it would make more sense if he put it on display," Lucy said. "And how did he even know that the queen had that necklace?"

"A fine question indeed. We should look into that right away."

Lucy glanced uneasily over her shoulder. "But it is time for the afternoon's entertainment. I hear there is to be a play … and the queen will be suspicious if we are not there."

"Then we must attend. But first, I must speak to Lord Hunsdon." Catrin turned back to the manor. "There is much still to be told in this tale."

Lord Hunsdon was in the gallery as she passed through, his long lean figure in its black doublet and hose taking up the entirety of one window-seat. He was speaking with Sir William Petre, who looked less than pleased to see Catrin pass through the doors. "Do you need something, Lady Catrin?"

"I wish only to speak to Lord Hunsdon, and I am content to wait," Catrin said, and could not resist a brittle smile. "As before, I do not wish to cause upset."

Sir William Petre snorted at that, and resumed his conversation. Obviously, he still considered Catrin's loyalty to be nothing but disguised ambition, and that made Catrin wonder who could have given him that idea. Lord Heatherleigh was unlikely to have spoken against her in such a way, and Lord North's dislike of her was focused entirely on her status as countess; her personal actions did not matter to him.

It was possible that he had heard Godfrey Breen's assessment of her character, but less likely that he would give the opinions of a baker's apprentice any weight. So, perhaps he had come up with these accusations all by himself. Perhaps he was afraid of her, or what she might discover. Perhaps his threat to end her 'tyranny', as he called it, was a plan to destroy her for no other reason than to save himself, and keep his secrets safe. Both the secrets she knew … and those she hadn't yet uncovered.

She watched him as he moved off, leaning heavily on his cane, and decided the time had come to defend herself in any way she could. Which brought her back to Lord Hunsdon, who rose to his feet and bowed as she drew near. "My lady Ashbourne."

She curtsied with a smile. "My lord."

He took hold of the black satin ties at his collar, playing absently with the golden aglets at their tips. "The queen granted my monopoly, and I suspect I have you to thank."

"Oh, yes — I spoke to her about the amethysts several days ago." It seemed an age ago and in truth, she had forgotten about it.

"I thought as much. I am in your debt, my lady."

Catrin smiled at him. "Are you, my lord? Mayhap I can ask you a question then."

"Of course, my lady."

Catrin moved a little closer and gazed up at him through her lashes. "It is a question that might seem perilous, so if you are concerned for your reputation, you need not answer."

Lord Hunsdon chuckled. "I will take the risk, my lady."

"Our host Sir William Petre ... do you know when he first rose at court?"

"Ah, not by memory, my lady, for I am not old enough. But I was told that he started in the early 1520s and became Secretary of State for King Henry in 1544."

"Was he an enemy of the queen's mother?"

He seemed surprised by the question. "No, indeed. He rose in royal service due to the patronage of the Boleyn family."

"And yet ... he did not fall when Queen Anne did."

"No," Lord Hunsdon said slowly. "No, he did not."

"That is very interesting."

"Perhaps." Lord Hunsdon raised one eyebrow. "Is that all you wanted, my lady?"

"I fear not, my lord. I also need to borrow two of your fastest horses." Catrin sent him a demure look from under her lashes. "And two men to ride them."

Catrin and Lucy walked into the Great Hall, where the benches in the hall had been rearranged in rows, all facing a large platform at the front. The queen's chair was on the right of the platform, to give her the best view of the upcoming revels and some fresh air from the doors leading to the inner courtyard. It had grown very warm, and any breeze was welcome.

Catrin was shown to a place on a cushion next to Lucy, which was further from the queen than she was usually placed. Sir William Petre was already there, in a chair on the left of that reserved for the queen, and that offered Catrin an ideal opportunity. She gave a shallow curtsy, and then lifted her gaze to meet his. "Good afternoon, my lord."

He inclined his chin in an imitation of deference. "My lady."

"I did not see you at the chapel yesterday."

"I had to attend to business. You may not realise, being a lady and a courtier, but there is much to consider when hosting the queen."

"And much to hide." Sir William Petre stiffened as Catrin tapped her foot to indicate the space beneath. "Or so I am told."

Colour infused his grey face. "Vile asp," he hissed. "First you pour poison in the queen's ear, and then you threaten me?"

"I do not threaten; I merely defend myself," Catrin said. "You need not worry, my lord. I will speak only if it will save my life or my position."

His fingers clenched on the head of his cane. "You are an evil temptress, and if you speak against me, I will declare it to the world."

"That creates a delicate balance between us, then." Catrin rested a single fingertip on the papery skin on the back of his hand. "You are safe from me as long as I am safe from you."

"You are not safe," Sir William Petre said, but his voice cracked with fear and told her that she need no longer needed to be afraid. "I will end your influence over the queen if it is the last thing I do."

Catrin did not answer; there was no purpose in antagonising him further. She simply crossed in front of him and took her seat, aware of Lucy's wide eyes. "Dearest, do you remember what I said about rumours?"

"Yes," Lucy said slowly. "You said they were a useful weapon."

Catrin leaned back into the thick cushion and allowed herself a smile. "So is knowledge."

CHAPTER THIRTY-THREE

The actor, resplendent in a crimson velvet doublet and emerald hose, paced the length of the platform while his voice thundered all the way to the back of the room. "Under fear's dark weight do I wander this night, for once burned a man holdeth not his hand to the flame ... unless a greater fire burns within."

Lucy leaned forward, so absorbed in the actor's torment that she placed her head in his path and he had to leap out of the way. Catrin found that rather more amusing than the play itself, which was about a man who discovered that his lover had been unfaithful with his dearest friend. Then the friend died, and the cuckolded man agonised over whether or not it would be safe to take the lover back again.

The answer seemed obvious to Catrin, so she was not particularly interested.

"It comes to this: I love Isabelle," the actor declared, and swung his arm out to indicate the actor on the far side of the stage, a boy dressed in a silken gown with glass for jewels to show he was playing a female. Thus indicated, 'Isabelle' clasped her hands in desperate hope, and he strode across to her, pulling a wooden box from the overlarge purse swinging at his belt. "Thus I give this gift, my heart, yours once and now again."

Lucy gave a little sentimental sigh, but the queen did not respond. Sir William Petre did not notice either reaction, nor did he seem concerned that the queen was not engaged. He had abandoned his duties as host, sinking deeply into himself after speaking with Catrin, his gaze fixed on the reed mats at his feet ... and perhaps the tunnels that curved and twisted below them.

Isabelle reached out her hands, but did not take the box. "Mine ears drink thy words eagerly, dearest Antonio, and yet I burn with such guilt. I am not worthy of your love, though I love thee completely, deeply ... hopelessly." She gave a great sigh. "Give this gift instead to a lady wise and true, brave and noble —"

The actor seemed to become suddenly aware of the queen's presence, and moved toward her as if compelled by Isabelle's words. Isabelle raised a hand toward the queen, as if sending him toward her: "— and deserving of all love and devotion," she finished, and buried her face in her hands to hide her tears.

The actor knelt at the queen's feet and held up the box, and a spark of interest lit in the queen's eye. "For me?"

The actor bowed his head. "With my whole heart, noble queen."

"The gift I accept, but I return your heart to Isabelle, for I know she will now ring true," said the queen, and a smattering of appreciative applause flowed throughout the watching court. Catrin herself was quite impressed; not everyone could fall into the style of dramatic blank verse with no warning, and include a play on words besides.

The queen removed the lid of the tiny box, and Sir William Petre came back to the present as if the motion had called him, straightening in his chair with a satisfied smile.

It vanished when the queen let out a strangled sound partway between a scream and a wail. "How — where — has it been you all along? How dare you?" she cried, and thrust the box at Catrin before she fled through the door. The hall dissolved into chaos; the actors retreated, their faces frozen in horror; Lord Robert ran after the queen; Sir William Cecil called in the guards to stop people from following him. Only Lucy and Mistress Ashley were allowed through; even Mistress Blanche stayed, guarding the door to the courtyard and snapping at all comers like an angry spaniel.

Sir William Petre turned on Catrin, tearing the box from her hands. "What have you done?"

"What have *you* done?" Catrin demanded, and snatched it back. Something rattled against the sides of the box, and when she glanced down she lost her breath.

It was the diamond ship brooch, lying crooked on a bed of velvet.

"That — that —" Catrin made herself pause, taking several deep, steadying breaths. "This item was last seen at Saintlow, Sir William Petre. It belonged to Lord Heatherleigh, and he held it very dear."

The name caught the attention of Lord Pierrick, Lord Hunsdon and several of the queen's guards, and Sir William Petre turned pale as they advanced toward him. "I barely knew Heatherleigh. I have never even been to Saintlow," he said. "And I had nothing to do with what happened there."

"Then explain how this came to be here, my lord," Lord Pierrick demanded flatly. "Now."

"My goldsmith sold it to me," Sir William Petre said nervously. "He brought my new gold chain from London just yesterday, and told me a man had offered it to him at an inn along the way."

"Did he describe the man?" Catrin asked quietly.

"He said he was ordinary, but did not blink. My goldsmith thought him simple. He assumed the brooch was stolen from the man's master and felt no guilt at giving the man a tenth of its value."

"I suggest you find an honest goldsmith," Catrin advised, and turned her back on him so she could face Lord Pierrick. "This means that Alban must have returned to Saintlow recently, for that brooch was still there when we left. I thought it safer to leave it there."

Lord Pierrick's lips firmed. "I will send a messenger to see if the residents are safe."

"That would be wise, but I would guess that they are all quite well." A chill ran down Catrin's back. "Alban is here."

The queen charged up and down the length of her bedchamber, shouting to the skies that the people who owed her the most did nothing but betray her. She flung herself onto her bed and mourned that she was slain by grief, and then she rose up and paced, sliding her rope of pearls through her fingers so they clicked-clicked-clicked one against the other.

This went on for hours. Catrin waited in the privy chamber, the ill-fated diamond ship brooch in its box in her hand. She listened while Mistress Ashley tried a hot posset, Mistress Blanche offered perfumed cloths for the royal head, and Lucy tried to cajole the stricken queen with riddles and wordplay. Nothing worked, but she did eventually grow weary of her own anger.

"Lady Catrin, attend upon me."

Catrin slipped into the room and kept her eyes carefully cast down. "Yes, Your Majesty?"

The queen lay back amongst her pillows and gave her a long, steady look that was neither friendly nor hostile. "I wish to hear a Welsh lullaby."

"Of course, Your Majesty," Catrin said, and sang the one the queen requested most often. Lucy smiled as the queen rested her head on the pillow with a small sigh, and both Mistress Ashley and Mistress Blanche sank into chairs with great relief.

When the lullaby finished, the queen waved her hand to request another. This time, however, it did not seem to relax her. She sat up halfway through. "Heatherleigh had that brooch, didn't he?"

Catrin broke off mid-lyric. "Yes, Your Majesty."

"And I suppose it was given to him by Mary Shelton."

"Yes, to help him restore his fortunes."

"So he did guess who his parents were." The queen slid her pearls through her fingers again — click-click-click — and then pulled the necklace over her head and tossed it aside. "I would accuse him openly of tormenting me, were he not in his grave."

Catrin retrieved the pearls and handed them to Mistress Blanche for storage. "I do not think he was your tormenter, Your Majesty."

The queen rose, pacing restlessly back and forth. "You think that the true culprit is this man Alban."

"Yes, I do, Your Majesty."

"But you don't know why."

"I still intend to find out why."

She frowned. "I must accept that you were right, my talisman. The connection between it all is my mother."

A knot of tension at the base of Catrin's skull dissolved at this use of her nickname. It seemed that she was restored to favour. "Yes, although the connection itself is not yet clear."

"Nor is the identity of this Alban."

"No, it is not. We know that he is large, bearded and has a habit of staring without blinking. His left shoulder was also injured recently; I assume it was during the skirmish with Lord Heatherleigh."

"That could describe nearly anyone." She froze suddenly, and then turned slowly on her heel to face Catrin. "That could describe Godfrey Breen."

Catrin linked her fingers together. "Could it, Your Majesty?"

"Of course! Think of it! Godfrey Breen could have been the one who fought with Lord Heatherleigh; I had banned him from court the day before the attack happened, so he could have gone to Saintlow, and he would have been angry. He was also large and bearded, and he first arrived at court just before Lord North's diamonds were stolen."

"Yes, that is true," Catrin said slowly, deciding it was best not to openly disagree. "But do you truly think that Breen had the wit to put together such a plan?"

"Of course not. But his friends — people like Sir William Petre and Lord North — could have done it easily, knowing that to weaken and unnerve me would increase their own strength." Her face darkened. "I wish to see Sir William Petre right away. Send also for Lord Pierrick."

"I will fetch them, Your Majesty," Lucy said.

"No, Blanche will go." Mistress Blanche curtsied and left the room. The queen crossed the room to Lucy. "You said that Alban met you as you were returning to court."

"We believe it was he, Your Majesty," Lucy said anxiously. "Because he tried to steal some papers that only Alban would consider valuable."

"Have you ever seen Godfrey Breen?"

"I fear not, Your Majesty."

The queen huffed out a breath of frustration. "Has *anyone* seen both men?"

"That rather depends on Sir William Petre's role in all this," Catrin murmured.

"You suspect him?" The queen let out a harsh laugh. "That is fair enough, I suppose; he suspects you."

Catrin spread her hands wide. "I suspect only that he knows more about Alban than he has told us, Your Majesty."

"Or at the very least, more about these constant reminders of my mother." She hesitated, then held out an imperious hand. "Let me see that cursed brooch."

Catrin fetched it from the privy chamber, and the queen took a deep breath before she opened the box. She stared down at the glitter within, pain and sorrow drawing lines on her face, and then Sir William Petre and Lord Pierrick arrived and she shoved the lid back into place.

Both men gave proper courtly bows as they entered, bending low over an extended foot and sweeping gracefully out and downward with their right hands. The queen dropped the box onto a nearby table. "Lord Pierrick, I wish for you to fetch Joan Sandys and bring her into my presence as soon as possible."

"Ah —" Lord Pierrick bowed low once again. "I believe Lady Catrin has already sent men to fetch her."

"Very well; you shall take charge of her once she arrives. Sir William Petre."

Sir William Petre used his cane to push himself back upright. "Yes, Your Majesty?"

"Do you know Alban Sandys, or Godfrey Breen?"

Sir William Petre blinked in what looked like honest confusion. "No, Your Majesty."

Her sharp black gaze bored into him for an endless moment, and then she waved her hand. "Then you may leave us, and I shall not see you until the morrow. I shall be dining in my rooms tonight."

He winced, but bowed in acknowledgement. "As you wish, Your Majesty. Is there anything else I can do for you?"

The queen seized the tiny box and threw it at him. It came dangerously close to the old man's face; only Lord Pierrick's quick reflexes saved him from injury. He snatched the box from the air and handed it to Sir William Petre without even a change of expression.

The queen chose not to notice this last-minute rescue. "Take that away," she said coldly. "I never wish to see it again."

CHAPTER THIRTY-FOUR

Catrin and Lucy were amongst those chosen to join the queen for supper, and it was not a merry meal. The queen ate silently and retired early, and her ladies felt it prudent to follow her example rather than join the revels.

Catrin, however, could not sleep. She watched a line of moonlight crawl slowly across the plaster wall for a long time before she gave up and went to her chest in search of something to distract her. Her eyes fell on Lord Heatherleigh's Bible, and she lifted it out with an effort. It was huge, definitely designed for a parish church rather than personal use. She had to set it down on the bed to open it, and at once she found proof that it was indeed a parish Bible. The first few pages listed the births, marriages and deaths for somewhere called Witherington, stretching back to 1500.

Catrin turned the page, and caught a folded piece of parchment as it slid out. She was about to open it when a particular entry in the Bible caught her eye:

5 April 1542 — son Godfrey Breen born to Titha Jones

So Godfrey Breen's mother was named Titha. Lady Angharad had said that Roger Surovell's mistress had a name that started with 'J', not 'T', making it less likely that Godfrey was Roger's son. But it was still not impossible; Lady Angharad could have misremembered the mistress' name, and it was significant that a father was not listed in the birth record. To truly prove that Roger had not fathered Godfrey, Catrin needed proof that Titha Jones had been in Witherington, not Ashbourne, in the months before Godfrey's birth.

Catrin returned to the front of the Bible and searched line by line, tracing her finger over the thick parchment until she found what she needed.

18 August 1541 — married, one John Nathan Jones to maiden Titha Breen

People usually married in their own parish, so even if Titha Breen had once worked in Ashbourne she had certainly left it before she was married, and before she quickened with child. That was proof enough for the queen, Catrin was quite sure. Her position was safe.

The relief that washed over her was quickly swallowed by fresh concern. Lord Heatherleigh had had this Bible. He had held the proof that Godfrey Breen was not the son of Roger Surovell, and never had any claim to Catrin's title. Why had he not shared it with her? Had he known of Breen's attempt?

Could he have *caused* Breen's attempt? Breen had said that the man who came to his mother's cottage wore a satin cloak, and Heatherleigh had always been very proud of his green satin cloak. He had been wearing it the very first time she saw him, in fact, when he was riding in the opening procession for the queen's tournament.

But why would he tell Godfrey Breen to make this claim, and yet keep hold of the proof that it was false? Did he hate her that much? Was it revenge because she refused his suit? He had not seemed angry, and he had not yet fully accepted her refusal. Indeed, he had seemed determined to change her mind — giving her gifts such as a chamber of her own, and paying close attention to her needs. Had it all been play-acting? Had he hated her, down at his core?

She had no feelings for him, but still the thought disturbed her. Had she agreed to marry him, she could have found herself at the mercy of a man who could present two different faces to the world... It was terrifying to think what could have happened: how her life could have changed so quickly for the worst, once she was bound to such a husband.

Catrin forced the thought from her head, but still her fingers were shaking as she kept searching through the Bible. Then she opened up the parchment she still held, and everything changed once again. It was a letter from the priest in Witherington, and seemed to be a pointed reminder that Heatherleigh had promised to return the parish Bible.

...for, my good lord, there have been several births that have not yet been recorded, and I am sure that the summer weddings will soon begin. But do not fear; I understand that you need to prove your sincerity and good faith to your lady, and save her from this great difficulty.

I regret only that I did not have the opportunity to explain to young Godfrey that this tale of his noble birth is false before he left. I could have prevented this entire difficulty, for I remember his birth. It took place not more than a fortnight after his father went missing. He drank too much at the pub, left to walk home, and was never seen again.

Some think that he fell in the river and drowned. Godfrey's mother Titha was so angered by his death that she gave her son her maiden name and refused to tell the boy anything about his father.

So Heatherleigh had hoped to cast Catrin in the role of damsel in distress. He had planned to call her status into question, and then triumphantly appear with the proof that would save her. He had not been driven by hate or revenge, but love. No, such manipulation could not be love. Desperation, perhaps. Even a strange sort of devotion, but not love.

A chill ran through her. Had Breen found out that Heatherleigh had played him false? She knew him to be violent and dangerous; it was not difficult to imagine that he had been the one to wreak such destruction at Saintlow, and then flee from the consequences of his actions.

But the attacker of Saintlow had also stolen diamonds from Lord North. Their hiding-place in the queen's bed suggested that he had stayed there for the night and been discovered in the morning, a discovery that led to the attacker's fit of rage and the murder of so many. Could Breen have stolen the diamonds?

She didn't know.

It was unsettling, how confused she was. She had been so sure that all the events of the past week had been the work of one man — one madman. But what if she was wrong? What if Alban Sandys, though guilty of the death of Ursus the clerk and Wilkyn Burgh, had had nothing to do with the attacks on the queen? Had she, Catrin, told the queen a falsehood? Would Alban suffer for crimes he had not committed, while a murderer roamed free? She put the Bible and its papers back in her chest and went to bed, determined to forget the entire idea.

But it was many hours before she managed to sleep.

Catrin rose and dressed with the help of a chamberer, and went out into a perfect summer morning. The birds were singing, the sun was just warm enough, and the grass released a soft, fresh scent with every step. Perfect, Catrin decided, to bring the queen back to good humour.

"My lady Catrin."

It was Lord Pierrick. He was crossing the garden toward her, and with him was a woman in a muddy brown kirtle, with tangled tendrils of hair escaping from her wimple and her dark eyes blazing with anger. Catrin paused and folded her hands before her. "Joan Sandys, I presume."

"Yes." Lord Pierrick scowled at the woman. "And she is not being very helpful."

Catrin tilted her head. "Not a particularly wise decision, when one is about to meet the queen."

The woman coughed into her hand. "I don't got nothing to say."

"Perhaps we should speak to your husband, then."

"He's dead."

"Would another of your children be willing to speak for you?"

Joan jolted as if the question had hurt her, and some of the anger faded away. "My only child died at birth."

Interesting. "So Alban is not your son, as you told Lord Pierrick."

Joan scowled. "No … the blackguard is my brother."

"Meaning that his surname is not Sandys."

"No, it's Wyatt."

"And is your brother mad?"

She let out a snort of laughter. "Of course! Each day he believes something different. He is a warrior — a poet — an alchemist — a man of God — an ancient hero — a courtier. All with one common trait: each one makes him out to be far greater than he could ever be."

"Is he young?"

She seemed to think that was an odd question. "No."

Then he was not Godfrey Breen. "That means that he has long been living like this. Why would he suddenly leave his home and kill his keeper?"

Joan shrugged. "Master Burgh must have tried to stop him from doing something he wanted to do, or told him his beliefs were false. Either one would send him into a great fury."

Catrin tilted her head and regarded her for a long moment. "Are you afraid of Alban?"

All of the woman's defiance disappeared at once. "Yes," she said, and her lower lip trembled. "I have lived in fear of my brother my whole life, and now he has stolen all I have and left me penniless, without even his poor protection."

"What was stolen?"

"A very valuable ouche, a long diamond necklace, a golden ewer —" She paused, wheezing. "A — a rose made of rubies, and a silver locket."

"What about letters?" Lord Pierrick asked quietly.

"Oh — yes, some letters bound with twine. I never read them." She scowled. "Master Burgh got hold of them, though. He kept asking questions about them."

"And did you answer?"

Joan stiffened with sudden wariness, and glanced sideways at Catrin. "No, I didn't. I promised I wouldn't when I was just a girl, and I never have."

Catrin's spine tingled. "Someone asked you to promise not to tell anyone about those letters?"

"I was told not to talk about any of it — the letters, the ewer wrapped in the bedsheets, the jewels. They were mine only as long as no one knew I had them." A tear trickled down her cheek. "And now they're lost forever."

"Who told you not to talk about them?"

"A man who served Queen Mary. I do not know his name; no one ever told me."

"Does your brother know his name?"

"He might." The implications of that made her shiver. "He might."

"Joan, we must stop him. Where has he gone?"

"I don't know." Joan coughed again and slumped against Lord Pierrick, forcing him to hold her up. "By God's wounds, I swear it — I don't know."

Catrin settled her hood more firmly behind her ears, her mind racing. "You will have to tell all this to the queen, Joan."

Joan shrugged listlessly, and Lord Pierrick put a firm arm around her shoulders, forcing her upright. "Has the queen arisen?" he asked.

"I doubt it, but I will go to her nonetheless," Catrin said. "Can you find a secure place for Joan until she is ready?"

"Oh, I'm sure Sir William Petre has a cell she can borrow," Lord Pierrick said grimly, and forced Joan toward the side of the manor house. Catrin left him to it and went inside through the gallery, as it was the shortest path.

The esquires of the body who took charge at night were standing firm at the door to the royal bedchamber, looking somewhat bored but reasonably alert. The younger of the two opened the door for her, and she thanked him with a smile as she passed into the bedchamber.

All at once, her every sense was alert. The fireplace was dead and cold, the air close and still. Worse, the bed was empty. The coverlets were peeled back, revealing rumpled white sheets but no sign of the queen — or her bedfellows.

Catrin swallowed the cry that rose to her lips, forcing herself to think calmly. Could the queen have risen early as well, and gone for a walk as Catrin herself had done? Not without Catrin seeing her — unless she went to walk at the front of the house. It did not seem likely that she would choose a gravel courtyard over the gardens, but surely it was still more likely than the horrible possibility that had been Catrin's first thought.

She was ready to run out to the front of the house when a faint moan stopped her short. She hurried toward the sound, circling the bed to find a figure lying with limbs akimbo on the floor, in the midst of a mess of blankets.

Catrin dropped to her knees in front of the figure and took hold of her shoulder, praying desperately that it was the queen. But no — the bruised and battered face that turned up to her was unmistakably Mistress Ashley. "By God's wounds, mistress," Catrin gasped. "What happened?"

Tears leaked from the swollen eyes. "It was so fast — so fast—"

"Where is the queen?"

Mistress Ashley shot upright, immediately rigid with panic. "Is she not here?"

"No — neither she nor Mistress Blanche."

Mistress Ashley let out a scream that nearly deafened Catrin for life. Catrin clapped her hand over the woman's mouth and hissed out a warning. "Tush! Tush, you silly woman! If the whole palace learns of this, there will be panic and riots like we have never seen. We must keep it quiet."

A hard hand pounded at the door. "What's happening? What's wrong?"

Catrin hurried across and opened the door with her most charming smile in place, making sure to block the sight of the empty bed from the esquire who stood there. "I saw a mouse," she said limpidly, and fluttered her lashes. "The queen is already up and dressed, and wishes to see Lord Robert, Lord

Pierrick, Lady Lucy and Sir William Petre. Could you send a page for them, please?"

He nodded reluctantly and slouched off, and Catrin crossed the room to the ewer that stood under the window. She filled a bowl with water and carefully washed Mistress Ashley's wounds, then helped her to a seat in a cushioned chair. Mistress Ashley muttered protests all the while, insisting they needed first to find the queen, but she was clearly too weak to put up much resistance.

A gentler knock heralded the arrival of the others, and Catrin opened the door just wide enough to let them in. "This is highly unusual, my lady," Sir William Petre huffed. "I cannot imagine that the queen truly wishes to see me so —"

"God's wounds," Lord Robert interrupted, and pointed a shaking finger at the bed. "She is not here."

"Someone attacked us," Mistress Ashley wailed. "It was so fast — I was asleep, and then I felt a blow that made me dizzy."

"Oh, woe," Lucy murmured, and ran over to enfold her in her arms. "You poor dear lady!"

"I — I — I tried to rise, but another blow rendered me helpless. I heard the queen cry out — oh, God protect her! — and I heard a flurry of movement, but I could not move. Blanche, too, cried out, and I called her name, but she didn't answer."

Lord Robert's face turned red with a fury so great that it frightened even Catrin. "Someone has taken our queen. Damn the bastard! I will tear him limb from limb."

"It cannot be," Lord Pierrick said. "No one would dare touch a sovereign queen. To do so would make any man a fool."

"As my mother says, desperation makes fools of us all," Catrin remembered, and felt her heart flutter in her chest. "We must find the queen immediately."

"Yes — yes. We must raise the hue and cry," Sir William Petre said shakily. "Question the guards — bring more men from London —"

"If we do, the world will know it and the queen will never be safe," Catrin said sharply. "She will live her life under a shadow, and there will always be people who will say that the queen who came back was not the same as the queen who went away."

Lord Robert went rigid, and looked angrily at Catrin. "Lady Catrin, it sounds very much as if you wish to keep this vile act a *secret*."

Catrin faced him squarely. "And so I do."

He glared at her, but the anger leaked slowly away, replaced by resignation. "You are right. From what I know of Elizabeth, she would prefer to die than suffer the damage to her image and reputation that you describe."

"So — no matter what happens — no one can ever know what happened last night." Catrin looked from Lord Pierrick, to Lord Robert, to Lucy, to the quivering face of Sir William Petre. "Are we agreed?"

They nodded mutely, each horrified eye still fixed on that empty bed. "Very good, then," Lord Robert said grimly. "Let us find our queen."

"How?" Sir William Petre asked blankly. "I — I cannot think where to begin."

"Let us start with the most obvious problem: how did the blackguard — or blackguards — get her out of the room?" Lord Pierrick asked. "Through a window?"

"All locked from the inside," Catrin said.

Lord Robert drew his fingers down his beard. "Could they have got Her Majesty past the esquires?"

"Not without a fight," Lord Pierrick said. "And there are no signs of that."

Perhaps they did not get the queen past them at all. Catrin looked at Sir William Petre, who glanced once at a panel near the fireplace and then hastily away. Catrin considered, but did not mention it. "Distraction, perhaps?" she suggested instead, and Sir William Petre sent her a surprised glance. "After all, our blackguard would first have to get Mistress Blanche away before they could come near the queen."

Fresh tears fell down Mistress Ashley's cheeks. "Perhaps they killed her," she sobbed. "Perhaps her body lies somewhere in this manor, even now."

That was a possibility that put fresh determination into the faces around her. "Sir William Petre and I will question the guards — subtly, of course," Lord Robert said. "Lord Pierrick, Lady Lucy, if you would be so kind as to start searching for Mistress Blanche. Lady Catrin —"

"I have a possibility I must explore," Catrin interjected smoothly. "Then I will return here and help Mistress Ashley keep all enquiring souls away."

"Very good," Lord Robert said. "Let us all return within the hour to share what we have found."

CHAPTER THIRTY-FIVE

Lucy left the chamber with her husband, determined to do all she could to help find the queen. But when she saw the vast empty space of the gallery, her legs went weak with a sudden flood of horror and despair. There were so many rooms and corners and corridors to search ... and so little chance of success. "Oh, what a terrible task! Whatever shall we do?"

"Start in the gardens," Pierrick said grimly.

"Why?"

Pierrick pushed the toe of his shoe into the flagstones beneath them and deliberately did not meet her eyes. "Freshly turned earth is less likely to be noticed there."

Lucy stared at him, freshly horrified. "You assume that Mistress Blanche is dead."

"It is the more likely scenario."

"Even though Mistress Ashley was not killed?"

That gave him pause. "It's true — he did not kill her. Why would he spare one and not the other? It would have been faster and more efficient to kill them both."

"But he didn't. He incapacitated Mistress Ashley, and then left her. And maybe that means he spared Mistress Blanche too." Lucy spun on her heel, gazing in every direction for cupboards, chests, wardrobes — anywhere large enough to fit a full-sized woman. "We should look for places he could have hidden her inside the house."

"Yes." Pierrick squared his shoulders. "He would not want to take time to hide her far away. His goal, after all, was the queen, and she could have woken at any time and called for her guards."

Lucy opened a large wooden chest, and then let the lid fall with a bang when it showed her nothing but folded blankets. "The chamber next to the queen's is Sir William Petre's, and beyond that is Lord Robert's."

Pierrick started down the corridor, and in his distracted state barely avoided a collision with a maid carrying a bowl of washing-water. "Is there not a room between Sir William and Lord Robert?"

Lucy scurried after him. "Oh — yes — a closet of some kind. I think Sir William Petre uses it for storing clothing. It's here — see? Right here."

"And there are connecting doors from the queen's room through Sir William Petre's room to this one."

"But they were locked," Lucy said. "That is why the esquires were satisfied to stay in the outer chamber."

"Locks can be broken, *mon amour*. This is the perfect place," Pierrick said, and tried the door handle. It opened easily, revealing a plain room with wide, worn wooden planks for a floor and rough brick walls. There were four large wardrobes towering over them, two on either side, and one door wasn't quite shut.

Lucy pulled it wide, and gasped at the sight of Mistress Blanche, her wrists and ankles bound with strips of linen, and more strips tied around her mouth and over her eyes. She reached out to help her, and the poor woman let out a shriek as soon as she felt Lucy's touch. "All is well, mistress, all is well, it's just Lady Lucy. I'm here to help you."

Mistress Blanche just moaned, and Lucy couldn't tell if she understood or not. Pierrick drew his dagger and cut her bonds, while Lucy unwound the strips over her mouth and eyes. Mistress Blanche was not bruised and battered as Mistress Ashley was, but her face was rough and pink, and her lips swollen. "The queen — the queen —" she mumbled, and pressed shaking fingers to her cheeks. "Is she well? Has anyone hurt her?"

"She is missing, mistress," Pierrick said.

Mistress Blanche let out a cry, and Lucy hastily shushed her. "Prithee tush; we are trying to keep it a secret. What happened — do you remember?"

"I was sleeping — all was quiet." She took a deep breath, coughed and tried again. "Then I thought I could smell the forest. I opened my eyes, and a man without a face was leaning over me. He had his hands around my neck, so I could not speak, and he squeezed until I lost my senses."

"A man without a face," Pierrick said. "Undoubtedly he wore a mask of some kind."

"Yes, but I could tell he had a beard," Mistress Blanche said, and her famous fierceness suddenly asserted itself. "If he hurts my queen, I will tear out every hair!"

"You will not be alone in meting out slow torture," Pierrick said grimly. "But first, we must ensure that no one discovers that the queen is missing. You must go back to the queen's chamber and pretend all is well."

"Yes … I can see why that would be best." Mistress Blanche passed her hand gingerly over her throat. "I will go at once."

The tunnels held no terror for Catrin anymore. She walked through them quickly, trying every door, taking a new torch from the sconces on the wall whenever hers burned low. Some tunnels twisted away from the queen's chamber, leading toward the Great Hall and the front courtyard. Others ended abruptly in a wall of dirt, as if the tunnellers had lost interest. Only one followed a path parallel to the gallery and then turned abruptly right, as if to follow the corridor above. It was lined with doors, and when she tried the first one, Catrin found a set of stairs, thick with dust in the corners but swept clean at the centre. Her heart thudded once, and then she climbed the stairs at a slow, steady pace, looking in all directions for a threat of any kind.

Nothing. It was all dust and worn-out wood — until a flash of light caught the torch flame. Catrin turned toward it and the flash became a steady twinkling light that formed the shape of a falcon. It was Lady Mary's brooch, lying on the step as if it had always been there.

Catrin's jaw firmed. She picked up the brooch and continued up the stairs, and was unsurprised when the air grew warmer and the musty smell faded in favour of the scent of old lavender and smoke from a long-dead fire. A small door appeared in the torchlight, quite narrow and short, and Catrin spied a piece of white linen caught in the latch. She plucked it out and speared it on the pin of the brooch, then pushed the door open.

She was in the queen's bedchamber. As expected. The bed had been made, the floor tidied, the windows opened to freshen the room. Just as always.

Catrin crossed to the fireplace and put out her torch in the ash bucket, then she opened the door that led out to the privy chamber. Lucy was sitting next to Lord Pierrick across the room, pretending to embroider a cushion. Lord Robert and Sir William Petre were standing in the corner, talking in low voices, and Mistress Ashley and Mistress Blanche were hovering just in front of the door. They stumbled back in shock when Catrin opened it, and Lucy dropped her embroidery. "Oh — Catrin! We didn't see you go in there!" She scrambled to retrieve her cushion and glanced around at the ladies sitting idly on stools and cushions all around them. "Is the queen still … resting?"

"Yes, she is," Catrin said easily. "She thinks she may be developing a toothache."

Mistress Ashley nodded vigorously. "Yes, yes — she said as much to me last night."

"I'll find some cloves for her to chew; that always cures a toothache," Mistress Blanche said, but without her usual vigour. She looked, indeed, quite weak. Catrin noticed the bruises on her neck, guessed what had happened, and though she was pleased Mistress Blanche had been found, she had to tamp down a cold wave of anger.

"Lord Pierrick," she said, and forced her tone to remain mild and even. "The queen said she would enjoy hearing you play the lute, and would appreciate a visit from Lord Robert and Sir William Petre."

Pierrick rolled up the scroll he had been studying with a single quick turn of his wrists. "I will fetch my lute at once, then, and return anon," he said, and strode out of the room. The rest of them retreated to the queen's bedchamber, and gathered in a tight knot in the centre of the room.

"How did you get into this room? I know full well you did not pass me; I was standing in front of the door to the gallery." Lord Robert went over to try the door that led to Sir William's Petre's chamber. Lucy looked surprised when it opened. "Through here?"

"No." Catrin pointed to the panelling by the fireplace. "I found a tunnel, leading from this room to the entrance to the cellars at the far side of the courtyard," she said. "Our villain could have easily spirited the queen not only out of her chambers, but out of the manor itself."

Lord Robert turned to Sir William Petre. "Did you know of this tunnel?" he asked tightly. "If so, we could have prevented this."

"No," Sir William Petre said, and glanced at Catrin. She held his eyes with hers and watched a range of emotions flutter across his face. Relief, fear, guilt. None of them nearly as intense as what he should have been feeling.

She looked away from him, disgusted. Lord Robert took several thoughtful steps around the room. "I would wager," he said slowly, "that the attacker rendered Mistress Blanche unconscious first. It would be a silent crime, and he could lift her out of the bed and remove her to that wardrobe room without rousing the other two, alerting the esquires or disturbing Sir William in his chamber. Then he returned and struck Mistress Ashley, stunning her so that she could not raise the hue and cry. And then he took the queen."

"But how?" asked Sir William Petre. "How did he get her into the tunnel? Would she have obeyed him, if he threatened her with a weapon of some kind?"

Lucy's lip trembled. "Perhaps he did the same to her as he did to Mistress Blanche."

With that thought, Lord Robert's face turned a sickly grey. "Let us speculate no longer. We must go and look for her."

"Wait," Catrin said. "First, we must think. I think we should return to the letters, and find in them all references to —"

"That is naught but a waste of time," Lord Robert said. "We must focus on the facts at hand, not the misty possibilities of the past."

"The facts support me, I assure you," Catrin said coolly, and held out her hand to show the diamond and sapphire brooch cupped in her palm. "I found this in the tunnel. It belongs to Lady Mary Grey, Lord John's wife."

Lord Pierrick joined them just as she said it, and a faint smile crossed his features. "Surely you do not suspect Lady Mary as the villain of this piece."

"Not at all. I still believe the villain to be our madman — Alban Wyatt — and I think that this brooch proves only that he has recently been to Pyrgo." Catrin spread her hands wide. "He may be doing the same as he did at Saintlow. There, he made Lord Heatherleigh seem the guilty party, which led the queen to ask me to investigate him. Now, he is making the Greys seem guilty."

Lord Pierrick strummed a few absent chords on the lute. "But perhaps the Greys *are* guilty. You mentioned earlier that the son, Anthony, seemed dissatisfied with his lot, and the father was acting strangely when you were there."

"I thought the Greys had cause to try to hurt Lord Heatherleigh, yes. However, I do not think that they have any reason to steal our queen," Catrin said. "Especially since they could have taken her captive far more easily while she was in their own home."

"I suspect Lord North," Lord Robert said. "He is hostile to the queen, and actively tried to weaken her position by questioning her decision to ennoble you, Lady Catrin. Also, his support of Godfrey Breen led to much trouble, and it may be only the beginning."

"But neither Lord North nor the Greys were involved in all the references to the queen's mother," Catrin said. "That brings us back to Alban Wyatt. His possession of those letters show that he was —"

"I doubt one has anything to do with the other," Sir William Petre said. "I have always said that these references to the queen's mother mean nothing."

Lucy bit her lip. "I think you're wrong, my lord. There have been too many to dismiss them like that, and they closely follow the letters that Sir William Cecil and I deciphered, which simply must be significant."

"And, it must be said — Alban Wyatt is mad," Lord Pierrick added. "And that is the sort of person who would think it a good idea to capture a queen."

"Such speculation is getting us nowhere, and I can no longer sit and do nothing," Lord Robert snapped. "Lord Pierrick, go to the Charterhouse and see if Lord North knows aught of this matter."

"Yes, my lord," Lord Pierrick said. Lucy crossed to him and took his arm, and he nodded once with a smile. "We shall be on our way within the hour."

"I am going to Pyrgo to speak to Lord John Grey," Lord Robert said. "If you wish, Lady Catrin, you may accompany me."

Catrin pressed her fingers against the hilt of her *stiletto*. "I do so wish."

"Very well. Let us all meet again as soon as possible — at Saintlow Hall, I think. It lies between the two houses."

Lord Pierrick agreed and escorted Lucy out. Lord Robert strode out with them. Catrin started to follow, then turned to look at Sir William Petre. He was looking at the hidden door with something very like regret on his face, and it felt significant, at that moment. "Do you feel the need for confession, my lord?"

Sir William Petre stared at her for a long moment, but he did not answer directly. "You did not tell them about the chapel."

"I did not need to tell them; the queen is not there."

"No, she is not," he murmured, and leaned heavily on his cane. "I do not work against her, Lady Catrin. I accept her as sovereign. I am loyal."

"You have allowed her to be taken from your home." Catrin shook her head. "That is not loyal."

"I had nothing to do with that!"

"Oh, yes you did." Catrin pointed at the hidden door. "It was your secrets that made this vile deed possible."

He clenched his teeth, his breath whistling out between them. "Do not question me, stripling. You are too young to know that some secrets must be kept."

"Yet I am old enough to know my sacred duty. And that is to aid and protect my sovereign queen, even if it costs my own life."

"And well it might."

Catrin turned away from him. "So be it."

CHAPTER THIRTY-SIX

Lord Robert brought only five men with them so nothing could slow them down. They rode fast and changed horses at every inn along the way, so it was merely two hours later that they thundered into the entrance courtyard at Pyrgo. The two wings seemed to reach out to them as they drew close to that wide arched door, and their last arrival — to bright colours and children's voices — suddenly seemed a very long time ago.

They reined in and jumped off their horses, and Catrin's boots had no sooner touched the cobblestones than she was frozen in place by the sound of a long, keening scream.

Lord Robert let out a roar and drew his sword, and his men fell in behind them as he ran to the door and kicked it open. "Beware all! We will spare none of you; you will all fall this day if our queen is harmed!" he shouted, and plunged inside with his men close behind.

Catrin ran after them, dodging a flock of frightened servants bent on escape, and arrived in the Great Hall to find a strange tableau. Lord Robert and his men stood frozen in the doorway, facing a screaming Lady Mary in the centre of the room. Lord John Grey was cowering against the wall, and Anthony Grey loomed over him like an avenging angel, with a sword poised above his head.

"You humiliate the highborn!" he roared. "You kill the innocent! You are a vile, disgusting traitor who deserves to die!"

"No — Anthony, no!" Lady Mary sobbed. "He is your father — don't hurt him!"

"He is not worthy of life or breath," Anthony said through gritted teeth, and swung his arm downward. A chorus of shouts made the walls ring, and Catrin leapt out from the crowd, flinging her *stiletto* with all the speed and power she could muster. It flew the distance, flashing in the sunlight, and pinned Anthony's sleeve to the wall. The sword clattered to the ground, and Lord John collapsed in a gasping heap.

For a moment his panting breaths were the only sound. Then came a low, wry chuckle from Lord Robert. "Lady Catrin," he said. "You never cease to amaze me."

Catrin folded her hands before her. "Thank you."

Lady Mary scrambled over to her husband, pulling him further away from her furious son. "I told you not to — I told you it would end badly — oh, John, why did you not listen to me?"

"Tush, woman," he muttered, and pressed one hand to his heart. "I had no choice."

Catrin started forward at a steady pace, keeping her gaze firmly on the two of them. "No choice in what?"

"Murder!" Anthony cried, and pulled mightily on his sleeve in a desperate attempt to free himself. "He killed Alice, and the unborn baby within her!"

Catrin paused, turning on her heel to consider him. "Why would he do that?"

"Because the child is mine, and he thinks Alice is beneath me," Anthony spat. "That is why he sent her away from here when she was so near her time. We planned to meet, but were thwarted at every turn. And then, when I told Father I was going to leave —"

Lady Mary turned deeply red. "Don't, Anthony. Don't say it."

"He imprisoned me!" Anthony shouted the words to the skies. "He held me in the woods and ensured that no one could hear my cries for help. He even ensured that the queen's court would not come near my prison by keeping them here another day!"

Catrin remembered the cries she had heard and wished with all her heart that she had done more to find out what they meant. "So you kept your own son against his will, Lord John," she said thoughtfully. "That suggests you would do the same to someone else if you felt the need."

"Indeed," Lord Robert said grimly, and a moment later Lord John was looking at a sword hovering above his head for the second time that day. "Where is the queen?"

"Wh-what do you mean?" the man stammered. "I have not seen Her Majesty since she left my house three days ago. No, I have not seen her."

"My men and I will search every room, Grey," Lord Robert said. "If you are lying, I will cut your tongue from your mouth."

"I am not lying! Why would the queen be here? She is supposed to be at Ingatestone, and then progress to New Hall!"

Lord Robert nodded at his men to begin the search. "And so she shall," he said. "But first, you will explain to me why your wife's brooch was found at Ingatestone."

"Oh, it wasn't," Lady Mary said with her unnatural high-pitched giggle. "I secured it as Lady Catrin suggested — it is here, in my chamber."

"Is it? Would you be so kind as to fetch it?"

She nodded jerkily and skittered off, and Catrin crossed to Anthony. "Alice is not dead," she said, and pulled her knife from the wall, leaving a gash of raw wood in the panelling.

"Nor is the babe. Alice delivered a healthy son several days ago, and they are with my mother, Lady Angharad, in London."

Tears spilled from Anthony's eyes. "Truly?"

"I had a letter from her telling me so two days ago."

He swiped a tear from his cheek. "It is a matter of honour to marry her and raise my son," he said. "But it is a matter of love, too. I will not abandon my family."

"Then you are dead to us. You are *dead*," Lord John said harshly. "I will disinherit you, and you are no longer welcome here."

"I have not felt welcome here for some time," Anthony said. "But that does not matter. This very day I will go to London and find them."

"Give them my greetings," Catrin said, and watched the young man walk out of the room. He moved stiffly, as if his limbs were sore from his captivity, but even as she watched, his gait grew stronger and more determined. She was suddenly quite sure that Alice and Lufian, the new Viscount Heatherleigh, would be cherished throughout their lives.

Lady Mary crept back into the room, her face pale. "It is gone," she whispered, and held out a piece of paper. "This was in its place."

Lord Robert maintained his rigid stance over Lord John, so it was left to Catrin to take the letter and read it. "*You will suffer for betraying the queen. You are not worthy to serve her, and so you will die. I will offer up your body to my lady as a gift, and together we will watch your blood drain away.*"

Lord John choked. "We have never betrayed the queen! We fought for her in Wyatt's rebellion, remember? Why would anyone think —"

"He does not mean you," Catrin said. "He means the woman who betrayed Queen Anne Boleyn."

Lady Mary's hands flew to cover her mouth. "But that wasn't me — it was my aunt!"

Catrin carefully folded the paper. "I don't think he sees a difference."

Lord North was at supper with his family when Pierrick and Lucy burst in, with Thibaut and Symon close behind. He stared at them agape for a moment, grease from roasted pork running down his chin, but shock soon turned to fury. "How dare you!" he cried, and pushed his chair sharply backward when both Thibaut and Symon drew their swords. "By what right do you carry weapons in my house?"

"We are searching for a missing woman," Pierrick said calmly, as if it was all quite reasonable. "You have proven yourself less than a friend to her, so we come to see if you have anything to do with this."

"I know nothing of any missing woman," Lord North snapped. "Nor will I suffer being accused and threatened in my own house. Go, all of you, or I will set my men against you."

Pierrick set his jaw, and that made Lucy worry. She could see men all around the table picking up their daggers, each one as angry as Lord North himself. Pierrick, Thibaut and Symon had no chance against so many, but they would never admit it. So she walked into that echoing empty space between her beloved and their enemies and forced herself to smile. "Very well, my lord, we do apologise," she said, and curtsied before she took Pierrick's arm. "Prithee, enjoy your evening."

Pierrick muttered a protest, and both Thibaut and Symon looked seriously disgruntled, but she managed to pull them all from the room. "I am sure we could have persuaded them, my lady," Pierrick said. "There was no need for retreat."

"What if they guessed our true purpose?"

"I am more concerned that we will fail in our purpose," Pierrick said. "We cannot fall short today, my lady."

"No, you're right." She started walking away, sincerely hoping that they would follow. "So we need to find another way."

All three looked sceptical, but they followed her back into the entrance courtyard. Their horses were still there, held in place by a stableboy whose eyes were wide with fear. He was looking at something in the far corner of the yard, where a rickety wooden building leaned against the courtyard walls.

His gaze made Pierrick tense. "Hold, dearest; go no further," he murmured. "I believe someone is watching us."

"Who?" Lucy stiffened. "Do you think Lord North sent men after us?"

"That would be a cowardly thing to do." Pierrick pointed to Symon, who nodded once and then crouched low to take himself out of the lantern light. "But we will soon find out."

Thibaut did not like that idea. "My lord —"

"No time to protest," Pierrick said, and bent low next to Symon. They moved across the courtyard so quietly that they seemed to disappear; Lucy strained her ears but could not hear them. One of the horses whinnied, and Lucy stroked his nose, making soothing sounds even while her heart started to pound.

There was a cry behind them and Symon let out an oath, then the horrible silence returned, stretching Lucy's nerves to breaking point. She was about to cry her husband's name when a burst of laughter stopped her short. Pierrick emerged from the shadows, hauling a man along with him. "We found a pitiful puppy," he said, and pushed a man into the lantern-light. A young man, with round shoulders and a sulky expression that made him look even younger.

"Who is this?" Lucy asked.

The young man looked down his nose at her. "Godfrey Breen. I am the true Earl of Ashbourne."

Thibaut and Symon chuckled at this, and Pierrick rolled his eyes. Lucy just shook her head. "Not according to the queen," she said. "How did you come to be here?"

"Lord North made promises to me," he muttered. "I'm trying to make him fulfil them."

"How long have you been here?"

"Four days."

"Excellent. That means we have found another way," Lucy said. "He can answer our questions about all that Lord North has been doing."

Master Breen snorted. "Why should I?"

Symon shifted closer, his superior height and bulk casting the lad in shadow. "Because you will not like the alternative."

Breen shrank back, nearly falling over Pierrick, who abruptly pushed him in Thibaut's direction. "I suggest you protest no further. You are coming with us to Saintlow."

CHAPTER THIRTY-SEVEN

They had sent a messenger to warn the steward at Saintlow that they were coming, so when Catrin and Lord Robert arrived there were rooms ready for them and a meal on its way to the dining chamber. And Catrin, for one, was grateful to settle into a cushioned chair and take a moment to think.

"We now know Alice's story, and why she fought so hard to protect her child's father, who is Anthony Grey," she murmured. "She knew that Anthony's father would do all he could to prevent their marriage — including hurt Anthony himself."

Lord Robert sat down at the table and buried his head in his hands. "We also know that the brooch found at Ingatestone was stolen from Lady Mary Grey, and none of the Greys were at Ingatestone when the queen was taken."

"And we know that the person who took the queen intends harm on Lady Mary Grey, as revenge for Queen Anne's betrayal."

"A betrayal that happened twenty-five years ago, and yet seems fresh and raw to the person who wrote that note."

"That is strange, don't you think?"

Lord Robert let out a hollow, mirthless laugh. "It is all strange. The man stole a sovereign queen but did not kill her bedfellows. He stole diamonds enough to make him rich, then discarded them as if they were glass. And then he left behind a priceless brooch and stole a set of bedsheets instead."

Catrin lifted her chin. "I did not know that he stole any bedsheets. Was it from here at Saintlow?"

"No, from the queen's chamber at Ingatestone. One of the maids noticed that the sheets were missing from the linen chest."

Catrin rose and paced slowly over to the window, gazing out over the U-shaped entrance courtyard. "Alban Wyatt, our madman, attacker and thief, gave a set of sheets to Alice and said he would find another tie to bind. Those sheets had been sewn by my mother while she was Queen Anne's lady-in-waiting, and were used to wrap valuable objects, such as the golden ewer that was used at Queen Anne's coronation."

"That ewer has long been considered lost; some think that Queen Anne gave it to her servants to save it when she was arrested."

"And yet it was left for our queen to find just a few days ago. One of the reminders of Queen Anne." Catrin traced her finger over the lead that held the windowpanes together. "Do you know to whom it was given?"

Lord Robert shook his head. "I was a child of three when Queen Anne fell. Even my father barely knew her; he entertained her and the king when they were travelling in 1535, but his rise occurred mostly during the time when King Henry was married to Jane Seymour."

"No matter. I suspect they were not truly given, but smuggled out of the palace," Catrin said, and then straightened when several figures trotted past the gatehouse and headed for the main door. "Behold — Lord Pierrick and Lady Lucy are arriving, and they appear to have a prisoner."

"I would prefer it if they had a queen," Lord Robert said, and his voice cracked. He cleared his throat forcefully and called for wine, and a servant brought it in on a silver tray just as Lucy and Lord Pierrick joined them.

Lord Pierrick was escorting a reluctant Godfrey Breen, whose clothes clearly told the tale of how far he had fallen. His doublet was torn, dusty, stiff with dirt, and missing several of its gold buttons. Sold for food, Catrin guessed, and suddenly felt sorry for the poor misguided lad.

"Lord North would not speak, and his retinue was too extensive for us to engage," Lord Pierrick said, and pushed Breen forward. "Fortunately, he does not know that there was a spy in his midst who can tell us what we need to know."

"I am not a spy," Breen whined. "I had no intention of telling anyone what I saw. I was just there to —"

Lord Robert pushed himself to his feet with such force that the wooden legs of his chair screeched in protest. "Speak now, churl. Tell us everything you know, or I will remove your fingers one by one."

Breen gulped. "Lord North believes in the old religion and meets with others of that belief."

Lord Robert drew his dagger, testing the blade against his knuckle. "What else?"

"He — he entertains priests from the continent."

"That is not illegal, nor does it have anything to do with our current quest," Lord Pierrick said impatiently. "Did you see him bring a woman into his house today?"

"Or a boy," Lucy added, and bit her lip when Lord Robert sent her a curious look. "She could have been disguised."

Breen hunched his shoulders. "No one came to the house today."

"Not even men carrying supplies?" Catrin asked. "Merchants, perhaps? Carters? Woodsmen?"

"Only one man, carrying a string of fish," Breen said. "He walked to the kitchen door and the cook bought every one."

Lord Robert walked closer to the lad and stared into his eyes. Breen looked back until his eyes watered, and then he dropped his gaze and shuffled his feet. Lord Robert dropped into a chair, defeated. "I fear he may be telling the truth."

"Only part of it," Lucy said, and drew a small bundle of cloth from the purse at her belt. "These were hidden in his sleeve."

Catrin took the bundle and let the cloth fall open in her palm. It was full of jewels — a diamond ring made for a man, a diamond brooch, a trio of diamond roses set in gold. "All these jewels were once stolen from Lord North."

"I didn't steal them," Breen said hastily. "I found them."

Catrin picked up the ring, remembering that Lord North had claimed that it had been taken from his finger. A bold move, requiring a lightness and dexterity she did not believe Breen had. "But not at the Charterhouse, I wager."

"No … they were here." He pointed out toward the back of the house, where the unfinished kitchens still sat untouched. "By the scaffolding, on the grass."

"Why were you here?" Lucy asked.

"I wanted to ask Lord Heatherleigh for help, but I couldn't find him. The place was completely empty when I arrived — it looked like no one had been here for days. I wanted to eat some of the food lying around, but…" He shuddered. "There were flies everywhere."

Lord Pierrick frowned. "And you didn't raise the hue and cry?"

"I was going to, but then I saw someone going in there." He pointed, once again indicating the unfinished kitchen beyond the walls. "I followed him, but he couldn't tell me where Lord Heatherleigh was. He was a workman, about to dig into the floor."

"How do you know?" Lord Pierrick asked.

"He dropped the shovel when he saw me and jumped over the windowsill." Breen looked longingly at the jug of wine and licked his lips. "Strange man … he didn't blink."

"That sounds like Alban Wyatt," Lucy said. Lord Robert's eyes narrowed in silent doubt, but Lord Pierrick nodded.

"And where were the jewels?" Catrin asked.

"Just outside the doorway."

Lucy filled a cup of wine and gave it to Breen, a gesture of kindness only she would think to offer. "Like the diamonds in the queen's bed, Alban discarded them as if they were worthless."

"But he returned for the pearls from the queen's necklace — the ones that fell into Lord Heatherleigh's grave," Catrin murmured.

"Yes — that's why he was there with a shovel," Lord Pierrick said. "By then, Heatherleigh was dead and Master Ronald had buried him, and Alban would have had time to realise that the pearls from the 'B' necklace were gone. The only reason he would risk returning to Saintlow was to retrieve them."

Catrin turned back to Breen. "And what did you do when you found the jewels?"

"I left," Breen said. "I heard people arriving in the courtyard and thought I might be blamed for what happened, so I … I ran."

Lord Robert looked on him with scorn. "Nobility requires courage," he said. "Your actions are further proof that you are no more an earl than my horse."

Breen hid a scowl by raising his cup, a sneaky cover which gave further proof to Lord Robert's observation. Lord Pierrick waved Thibaut into the room. "Take him somewhere secure," he said.

"And make sure he is fed," Lucy added.

Thibaut smiled. "Yes, my lord — my lady," he said, and removed the empty cup from Breen's hand before he pulled the man out of the room.

Lord Robert gave a heavy sigh. "I fear I have wronged you, Lady Catrin. You were right; the way to find our queen is through the actions of the madman Alban, not through either Lord North or Lord John Grey. I have wasted most of the day."

"It is not wasted; we have learned much," Catrin said, just as several servants entered the room in procession, carrying platters of steaming meat and baskets of fresh bread. It looked like a simple meal, but well-seasoned and certainly well-timed. "And we can discuss our plans while we dine."

"What plans?" Lord Robert slumped into his chair. "There seems to be no clear path to take."

"I believe there is, but you will not like it."

"I like none of this, so that will not stop me."

"Then we must go back to the beginning, and force information from the person who first smuggled the treasures that Alban stole out of Greenwich Palace."

Lucy blinked. "Who is that?"

"A man whom I tried to persuade to speak the truth by staying silent," Catrin said. "Sir William Petre."

Lord Pierrick dropped into a chair, astonished. "You wish to go back to Ingatestone?"

"I think we must," Catrin said, just as someone knocked on the door. "Unless he has come to us."

"No, it cannot be Sir William Petre; his old frame would not survive the journey," Lord Pierrick said. "Come in, stranger, whoever you are."

A familiar bent figure opened the door, and Lord Pierrick sat bolt upright, amazed. "Sir William! It is you!" he cried. "What are you doing here?"

The old man made his way in, obviously in a great deal of pain. "I rode here as fast as I could," he said, and gratefully took a seat in a cushioned chair. "My conscience has been troubling me greatly, all this day."

Lord Robert took a long, weary drink from his cup. "We are neither priests nor confessors."

"Well, I know that. But still, you must hear what I have to say." Sir William Petre shifted the position of his cane so he could rest both hands on its head. "I know Joan Sandys — or Wyatt, as I knew her. It was I who arranged a home for her in High Wycombe, and gave her treasures that once belonged to Anne Boleyn."

The words fell into a shocked silence. For several seconds no one moved. Then Lucy turned to Catrin. "How did you know?"

"He asked about Joan when we spoke to the queen, the moment you mentioned High Wycombe," Catrin said. "And he was in power during Wyatt's rebellion."

Lord Pierrick blinked. "What does Wyatt's rebellion have to do with any of this?"

"Alban Wyatt is the son of Thomas Wyatt, who led the rebellion," Catrin said.

Sir William Petre nodded. "And Joan is his daughter. When their father was killed in such disgrace, it looked like the family would be lost to poverty. I could not let that happen."

"Why not?" Lord Pierrick asked. "What were they to you?"

"The grandchildren of a great statesman and poet," Sir William Petre said heavily. "I greatly admired the elder Thomas Wyatt, and I could not allow his name to be forever destroyed. At the same time, I could not allow Joan and her family to remain in London. While George, Thomas' youngest son, was quite respectable, Alban's madness was evident from a very young age. He had to be removed from society."

"Was Queen Mary complicit in this?" Lord Robert asked.

"No, I never told her. I simply made Joan her brother's keeper and gave her some of Queen Anne's wealth as recompense. I knew the queen would not notice when those treasures disappeared from the palace, and I knew that Joan could sell them if she had need, and support her whole family."

"She said they were meant to be her comfort in her old age," Lucy said sadly. "That was why she was so angry that Alban took them. She must have thought he was going to sell them and keep the money himself."

"But he didn't." Lord Pierrick slowly straightened in his seat. "He sold the ship brooch, which he stole from Lord Heatherleigh, but he never sold any of Queen Anne's treasures. I wonder why."

"To him, their value lay in the memories contained within them," Catrin said. "He cared only that they once belonged to Queen Anne."

Lord Robert let out a low growl. "I do not see what any of this has to do with the queen's abduction."

"It's the reason for it," Catrin said. "You hid the letters with the treasures, didn't you, Sir William Petre?"

Sir William Petre gave a heavy sigh. "I did, God forgive me. I thought they would be safe with the Wyatt family."

Lucy nodded. "They had the most to lose if the letters were revealed, for it would bring them further disgrace if the world knew that Sir Thomas Wyatt, the famous statesman and poet, was the man Anne Boleyn once loved and lost."

"Unfortunately, keeping them safe led to a different sort of danger. As Joan told me, Alban's madness takes a dangerous form. He creates fantasies in which he is a great man — be it a warrior, a man of God or a poet," Catrin said. "And when he found and read those letters, he decided to become his famous grandfather, Sir Thomas Wyatt."

Lucy gasped. "And then he cast our queen in the role of Anne Boleyn, Sir Thomas Wyatt's lost beloved."

Lord Robert buried his head in his hands. "So he thought that he was wooing a lost lover when he left those reminders of Anne Boleyn."

"Yes, he tried to bring Sir Thomas' famous poem to the queen's mind when he asked Alice to dress up as Queen Anne and wear a diamond necklace, wrapped tight like a noose. Then he tried again to remind the queen of it when he acted as a poet during the revels," Catrin said. "First he followed her, playing his lute and reciting Sir Thomas Wyatt's poetry. Then, after the attack on Saintlow, he came to the queen dressed as Ares, referring to the poem once again by claiming that he was a hunter who had sacrificed himself to win the greater victory and now intended to claim his prize."

"And claim her he has." Lord Robert gave a groan of despair. "Our queen has fallen into the hands of a madman and a killer. There is no hope at all."

Sir William Petre held up a warning hand. "Hold fast, my lord. This is encouraging," he said. "Alban does not plan to kill the queen; he thinks she will marry him and allow them to begin a new life together."

"And that gives us more time to find them," Catrin said, and went to the window for no other reason than that her muscles ached to move. It was late now; the sky was all but black, and the candles in the room behind her flickered so that she could see almost nothing beyond the thick leaded glass. "You knew Sir Thomas Wyatt, didn't you, Sir William?"

Sir William nodded a heavy head. "Lady Anne was one of my patrons, and through her I met Sir Thomas Wyatt at court. I was greatly impressed by his statesmanship, military skills, passion and poetry."

"Think for a moment, then. If Sir Thomas was alive today, escaping in the night with his Lady Anne, where would he go?"

Sir William seemed nonplussed by the question. "From what I remember … he was fond of Calais, and he once lived in Yorkshire…"

"Too far," Lord Robert said. "To travel so long would make him vulnerable to discovery."

"Yes, but I cannot think of anywhere else…" Sir William Petre gave a little jump. "Wait — when he left court after Queen Anne died, he lived in Allington Castle in Kent. He was very fond of the spot."

Lord Robert rose to his feet. "He could travel most of the way there by river. The Reding passes by this very place, and joins the Thames five miles downstream."

Catrin folded her hands. "Let us follow the hunter, then, and rescue his chosen prey."

CHAPTER THIRTY-EIGHT

Lord Heatherleigh's steward, Master Ronald, offered his master's wherry for the journey, a wide and shallow craft that at first seemed to ride too low in the water to take all of them. But he assured them it would be safe, and so Catrin, Lucy, Lord Pierrick and Lord Robert piled aboard. Master Ronald lit a lamp fore and aft, encasing them in a dome of light, and scrambled in after them.

"Watch carefully," Lord Robert ordered. "Search the banks for any signs of them."

It was good advice, and Catrin leaned over the side as far as she dared so that she could see more clearly. The River Reding was quite shallow and the banks thickly overlaid with lush grasses, sturdy reeds, and arrowhead plants blooming with small white flowers. A passing breeze ruffled them briefly, and then they went still.

For miles Catrin peered at the bank, searching for any sign of disturbance, and saw nothing. It was only when they were drawing close to a crude landing-place made of ragged scraps of wood that something caught her eye. She thought it was the eyes of an animal at first, for it glowed in the lantern light, but then she realised it was a single light, not a pair. And it was dangling from a white strip of cloth.

"Look!"

The others scrambled over to her, which in hindsight was not wise, but Master Ronald managed to keep the wherry afloat and drew it swiftly toward the landing-place. "It is a pearl," Lord Robert said, and quickly detached it from the post on which it was snagged. "Embedded into cloth."

"Perhaps it is from a nightgown," Lucy said.

"Perhaps, but it looks more like the edging of an embroidered sheet," Catrin said.

Lord Robert turned to Master Ronald. "Where are we?"

"Barking village, my lord."

"Is there an inn here? A tavern that rents rooms?"

"There's a tavern, but no rooms, and not much else but the church."

Lord Robert's gaze raked the dusky landscape in every direction. "So where would he go?" he murmured.

Catrin felt her heart racing. "When Alban was playing Ares, he said that he believed he had found his bride. Perhaps he's planning a wedding."

"Then he's in the church, damn him," Lord Robert said. "Tie up here, goodman, and stay with the boat. We may need to leave in a hurry."

"Yes, my lord," Master Ronald said, and wisely asked no questions. The four of them piled out of the boat and hurried up the rough path before them, pushing through a thin curtain of weeping willows that whispered to them in the breeze.

A cemetery spread out before them, long and wide. At the far end was a grey stone church with a square crenelated tower, surrounded by the broken ruins of an abbey. "He could be anywhere," Lord Robert said grimly. "Spread out, and look in every corner."

They formed a line without speaking, spreading out far enough that Catrin could hardly see Lucy on her right and Lord Robert on her left. And then they started to walk, footsteps muffled in the long grass, dodging tall gravestones and trying not to trip over deep-set memorial slabs. The first of the abbey buildings came up on Catrin's left; Lord Robert disappeared on its far side and Catrin stooped to peer through a small arched doorway. The moonlight showed her a simple square room with a fireplace, long dead, on the far side. It looked like no one had gone inside in years.

She ducked out and continued, jumping down into a shallow depression she suspected had once led to the abbey cellars, then climbing onto a shallow platform that led nowhere. Lord Robert appeared on her left and vanished again, the white lace around his collar the only thing she could see in the gloom. To her right, she could hear Lucy moving through the grass.

As they moved toward the church, the gravestones became older and more battered, many of the decorations worn away or broken off entirely. The grass grew rougher and more patchy, and finally faded away, leaving only dirt behind. The space gradually narrowed, drawing them closer and closer together, until they found themselves shoulder to shoulder at the edge of a small courtyard outside the main doors. Low stone walls marked its edge, and every one had been decorated with daisies, roses, violets and a wealth of greenery.

Lucy picked up a wilting rose. "A child, perhaps? Playing outside before the service began?"

"It would take hours to do all this," Catrin murmured. "I wager it was for a celebration of some kind."

Lord Robert drew his dagger. "Perhaps one that has not yet taken place," he said grimly, and pushed the door open. Candlelight trickled out, flickering cheerfully and scented with beeswax, and the two men led the way inside. Catrin and Lucy followed them into the chill of the stone vestibule, then through a set of beautifully carved doors that hung open as if welcoming all comers.

The nave was brightly lit, with many-branched candelabra set in the niche of each window so that the colours of the stained glass could be faintly seen. Chains of flowers were wrapped around each creamy white centre pillar, bar the one closest to the chancel. It was bare, but even as they watched, a pair of plump hands emerged on either side of it, a chain of daisies dangling from the fingers, and the air was filled with humming. It was a wedding song, if Catrin wasn't mistaken. A bawdy, bouncy tune called 'Away to Twither Away'.

Lord Pierrick and Lord Robert glanced at each other and melted away to the left and the right, where side aisles led to a tiny chapel or two. Catrin wrapped her fingers around the hilt of her *stiletto* and crept forward. "Hello? Is anyone here?"

A balding man with a square beard popped out from behind the pillar, beaming. He wore a clean shirt, but a large patch of dried blood marring the left shoulder of his doublet reminded Catrin of his injury at the hands of Lord Heatherleigh. "Good e'en, my lady, good e'en! You must be here for the wedding."

"Indeed I am," Catrin said, and held one hand out behind her to keep Lucy back. "Are you the priest?"

The man laughed heartily, but his eyes remained wide open and staring, as if they were entirely separate from the merriment on his face. "Nay, indeed! 'Tis I who takes a bride this night, my lady."

"Ah, I see. May God bless and keep you both," Catrin said. "Where is the bride?"

He waved an airy hand. "Preparing herself, I wager."

"May I go and help her?" Lucy asked bravely. "Every bride needs help to look her best."

"That is very kind," the man said. "She is in the sacristy; you may ask if she needs any assistance."

Lucy sent Catrin a single frightened look and rushed away. Catrin moved closer, raising her voice to mask any sound from Lord Robert or Lord Pierrick. "What is your name, my lord?"

"Thomas. Sir Thomas Wyatt, servant of the king." He gave an elaborate courtly bow and the daisy chain dropped unnoticed from his fingers. "And what is your name, fair maiden?"

Slowly Catrin drew her *stiletto*, hiding the movement with her sleeve. "Lady Catrin, Countess of Ashbourne."

His unblinking eyes locked with hers, and then he gave a sudden start of recognition. "You are the raven-haired maiden who nearly caught me, on the night I took the diamonds from the Charterhouse."

Catrin inclined her head. "And you are the man who smelled of the forest. The man Mistress Blanche said did not have a face."

"Yes, I hid it so I did not have to kill her." He clasped his plump hands together in a silent plea. "I did not want to have to kill any of you."

"Why not?"

"You have, all three, taken care of my bride," Alban said simply. "And she loves you."

Catrin could think of no response to that, and she did not have to. Three things happened in rapid succession: Lord Robert and Lord Pierrick leaped on Alban with a roar, a sword flashed into Alban's hand, and Lucy screamed Catrin's name.

Alban moved with the speed and ferocity of a man who knew no fear; it was all that Lord Pierrick and Lord Robert could do to engage him. In seconds they were standing back to back while Alban circled them, snarling like a dog at a bear baiting.

Lucy screamed again.

"Lady Catrin, go to her!" Lord Pierrick cried, and parried a blow that almost removed his ear. "Go and help Lucy!"

Catrin turned and ran, following Lucy's path. "Lucy!"

Lucy appeared in the doorway to the sacristy. "I'm here, I'm here," she gasped, and pulled Catrin inside. It was a square room with several large cupboards, a dozen shelves piled high with linens, and a massive carved chest shaped like a half-moon. Catrin recognized it as a cope chest, where the priests of the old religion used to store the highly decorated cloak-like garments they wore over their robes.

The queen hung above it, wrapped in sheets so tight it was like she was bound in a shroud, with only her head left free. Strips of fabric connected her cocoon to the ceiling and wrapped tightly around her neck, then snaked out in all directions. Some were attached to shelves, others to cupboards; one even slithered across the room and disappeared into a hole in the floor. All were weighted by slugs of lead or broken bits of stone and tied firmly to shelves or hooks.

He found it, Catrin thought numbly. A different set of sheets had become another tie to bind. "Your Majesty, can you move?"

"I can, but if I do, the noose tightens around my neck." The queen's voice was faint, but decidedly angry. "That venomous toad has wrapped me so tightly in my own bedsheets that I cannot help myself."

"Damn him for a blackguard and a traitor," Catrin muttered, and stepped up onto the chest to examine the wrappings. It was then that she noticed Queen Anne's necklace hanging crooked around the queen's neck, gaps in the gold chain showing where pearls had been lost, and the bottom stroke of the 'B' missing entirely. It seemed somehow obscene to see it there; Catrin wanted to tear it away nearly as badly as she wanted to destroy the shroud Alban Wyatt had created.

Lucy pressed her fingers to her lips. "What do you see, Catrin?"

"A clever trap created by a bleeding plague sore of a man," Catrin said. "Some of these strips of fabric will pull taut if I cut others. It is like a giant spider's web."

Lucy started to cry. "So we cannot save her?"

"We cannot fail to save her," Catrin said grimly. "Wrap your arms around the queen's waist, Lucy dearling. Take as much of her weight as you can."

Lucy stared at her in horror. "I am not allowed to touch the queen!"

"Inaction will bring the greater punishment, child," the queen snapped. "Do as she says."

Lucy climbed up and wrapped her arms around the queen, but tears started rolling down her cheeks. "What of Pierrick? Is he all right?"

Catrin traced several strips of fabric with her fingers. "They called Alban a demon in Saintlow, and he certainly fights like one, but I have no doubt those two men will prevail."

"Who knows of this, Catrin?" the queen asked.

"No one but the four of us, Sir William Petre and your two bedfellows." Some pieces of linen were bound around the queen's arms; others helped keep her attached to the ceiling. Some led to nothing at all. And all of them, it seemed, connected to the strip around her throat. The best course of action, then, was to cut the linen at its source point, so that none of the weighted fabric could tighten. The only trouble was that Catrin could not reach it.

"No one can ever know — even if I die here," the queen said. "I refuse to be known as the captured prince, carried away by her own subject and brought low like this."

"You would not be the first such prince, Your Majesty," Catrin said, and slid around to the right. "Can you straighten your head without pain?"

A pause, during which the sounds of clashing steel outside the room could be clearly heard. "I can straighten my head a little. That will have to do."

"Very good. Stay still for now; I will tell you when to move," Catrin said, and jumped down to search for something to raise her up higher. But there was nothing — not a stool, not a barrel, not a case of wine or a wooden box. She had only one option.

She opened the cope chest and started hauling out the vestments that lay within. They were made of strong, sturdy material, and so she started folding them in thirds and laying them one atop the other.

"Catrin! Those are sacred garments!"

Lucy's horrified cry made the queen giggle with mild hysteria. "I am the Supreme Governor of the Church, little Lucy. I will allow it."

Lucy surveyed the tottering pile as Catrin climbed up. "But —"

"You must trust me," Catrin said, and balanced carefully on top of the pile. It brought her face to face with the queen, who could easily see how precarious her perch truly was. Catrin smiled at her with a light-heartedness she did not feel. "You must both trust me."

"I trust you," the queen whispered, and then a dash of her old spirit strengthened her voice. "But if you give me a scar, my talisman, you will pay for it."

"Fair enough," Catrin said, and drew her *stiletto*. Lucy cried out when she slid the blade under the linen around the queen's neck, and the queen herself closed her eyes in dread. Catrin nearly did the same, but then she flicked the knife outward and the linen fell away.

The spider's web fell limp, but for the long strips that held the queen's cocoon in place. Catrin wrapped one arm around her, to help Lucy hold her up, and then slashed out with her blade.

They all fell, tumbling down over the vestments, over the chest, onto the floor. Strips of linen tangled around them and a faint shout could be heard from the church. "My bride! No! Fear not, my love, I will come to your rescue!"

The sounds of clashing steel did not stop, but the words unnerved them all. "Quickly, quickly," the queen said, her voice trembling. "I must be free afore that man returns."

"Fear not; I doubt he will ever return," Catrin said, and slashed at the linen around the queen until she could stand free, with shredded fabric pooled at her feet. All around them weights thumped uselessly to the ground, and fabric fell fluttering in eddies of air.

For a moment the queen stood there motionless, a tall, slim woman with skin nearly as white as her nightgown. Only her flame-red hair still had colour.

"Catrin, go and join the battle," she said at last. "And Lucy … find me something to wear."

Catrin ran out of the sacristy, knife in hand, and found Lord Robert and Lord Pierrick pressed against the centre column by the ferocity of Alban's attack. The position hindered them both from swinging freely at their enemy; they dared not raise their swords too high for fear of hurting each other.

Catrin leaped up onto the stairs that led to the sanctuary. "We have rescued your bride!" she shouted. "The bride you stole from the king!"

Alban let out a roar and spun in a half-circle, so his back was to the two men but he was out of range for attack. "You cannot take her back to him! He does not love her as I do — and he does not know her at all!"

Catrin advanced toward him down the centre aisle, trying to get close enough to throw her knife, but Alban kept retreating out of range. "He knows her well enough, I wager."

Alban spat on the floor. "He gave her diamonds — diamonds! She and I both know she prefers pearls. I could not stand it."

"So you took the diamonds."

"I did, and discarded them when it was safe."

"I understand." Catrin flipped the knife in her hand, holding the tip between her fingers. "Why would any man keep reminders of another suitor?"

"I kept the diamond she gave me – the one at the heart of an ouche made of sapphires and turquoise. She gave it to me because those stones would keep me safe. When I first resumed my wooing, I returned it to her."

Lord Pierrick moved into place at Catrin's side, sword at the ready, and Lord Robert slipped away to the side aisle in an attempt to circle behind Alban. Catrin kept Alban's gaze locked on hers, willing him not to notice. "In Lord North's coffer."

"Yes, it seemed an appropriate way to remind her that she was safe with me."

"Not everyone is safe with you. What of Wilkyn Burgh? What of Lord Heatherleigh?"

Alban shrugged. "Anyone who tries to stop me must be stopped."

"What of the clerk, Ursus? He did not try to stop you."

Alban swung his sword in sudden fury. "He would have tried to stop me, had I let him live, for he saw Wilkyn die. But he was useful at least — he told me where to find the necklace I gave my lady, with its pearls and golden 'B'."

"You killed Florie, too." Catrin raised her knife, her fingers tingling with anger. "An innocent young woman, unarmed but for a darning-needle."

"She was not innocent! She stopped me from talking to Alice; she sent me away." He raised his sword to defend himself, and for the first time his vacant, staring eyes blazed with real heat. "My lady, remember that you are but a maiden. Put that knife down now; I do not wish to hurt you."

"How very kind," Catrin said, and flung the *stiletto* at his weakest point: his injured left shoulder. She had hoped that it would make him weak, but instead it enraged him. He howled with pain and flung himself at Catrin; Lord Pierrick dived in front of her and for a horrible moment swords flashed in the candlelight, moving so quickly the blades were but a blur.

Then Alban slashed at Lord Pierrick with a strange twist of his blade, and Lord Pierrick's sword fell to the stone floor with a dull clang. A second later Alban had his sword against Lord Pierrick's chest, and a gleeful grimace distorted his face as he prepared for the death-blow.

He never delivered it. Another blade knocked his sword from his hand and spun him around, and then blood bloomed from his throat. He choked, gurgled, his lips working silently as blood gushed from his mouth. Then he slowly, slowly slid to the floor.

Lord Robert sheathed his sword. "It was too quick a death," he said grimly, and glanced at the white-faced Lord Pierrick. "But needs must, I suppose."

CHAPTER THIRTY-NINE

Master Ronald was understandably confused when they returned to the wherry with a clergyman wearing an alb and shoes that seemed far too big for him. He also probably wondered why the priest wore a thick and heavy black cloak on such a warm summer night, and kept the hood up for the entire journey back to Saintlow. Wisely, however, he did not ask.

They arrived back at Saintlow Hall just as false dawn was breaking, and Pierrick sent Thibaut and Symon to relieve Mistress Ashley and Mistress Blanche of their torment and bring back all that the queen would need. The queen herself retreated to the room prepared for Catrin, and watched while Lucy and Catrin found a large copper tub and carried many cauldrons of water heated at the kitchen fire to fill it. "That madman Alban called me 'Anne'," she said at last. "He called me 'Anne' and put my mother's necklace around my throat."

"In his fantasy, you *were* Anne," Catrin said. "When he read her letters to his grandfather Sir Thomas Wyatt, he came to believe that he was Sir Thomas, and the time had finally come for you to marry."

The queen shuddered. "I do not wish to see that necklace again. It has been tainted now, and nothing remains of my mother. Have Blanche send it to be dismantled."

Lucy bit her lip. "Yes, Your Majesty."

"Was he truly the poet outside my window, and the man who pretended to be Ares?"

"Yes, Your Majesty, and both times he recited his own versions of Sir Thomas Wyatt's poetry when he saw you, expecting you to understand the message," Catrin said, and poured the last cauldron of water into the tub. "I suspect that is also why he dared to touch you — to him, you are not a queen but a maiden waiting for a husband."

The queen's jaw firmed with anger. "What happened to him?"

"Lord Robert killed him," Catrin said simply.

"A shame, that," the queen said. "I would have enjoyed seeing that particular traitor hung, drawn and quartered."

"Lord Robert thought the same, but he had no choice. He did it to save Lord Pierrick."

"Is Lord Pierrick injured?"

"No, he is well," Lucy said, but even as she said it she shuddered in remembered fear. "Thank God and all the angels."

"Indeed," the queen murmured. "Where is Alban's body?"

"In another man's grave," Catrin said, and could not stop a smile. "Lord Pierrick and Lord Robert put him in an empty sarcophagus they found in the ruins of the abbey."

The queen laughed. "Let us hope that no one opens it."

"They placed several large stones on top, making it look like the walls around it are crumbling. Hopefully that will discourage the curious."

"A fine idea," the queen said, and sent Catrin a sidelong glance. "It sounds like something you would think of, my talisman."

Catrin smiled at her. "It seemed faster than digging a grave, Your Majesty."

The queen looked at her for a long moment. "*Quod in te est, prome.*"

Lucy poured the last cauldron of water into the tub. "What is in thee, draw forth," she translated. "That's beautiful, and it seems like the perfect motto for you, Catrin."

"Indeed it does," Catrin said. "Now I need only an emblem."

"What about the panther?" Lucy asked. "Tender and loving, but will leap to the defence of those she loves."

"No, the sphinx," the queen said thoughtfully. "Clever, all-knowing — and a great keeper of secrets."

Lucy chuckled. "Perfect."

The next morning, they returned to Ingatestone Hall through the tunnels to keep their adventure secret, and emerged safely in the queen's chamber to the great relief of Mistress Blanche and Mistress Ashley. With their joyful help, the queen could soon go out and face the court looking calm and carefully put together, wearing ropes of pearls and diamonds in her hair. She led her people outside for a walk in the gardens as if nothing had ever happened, chatting with her ladies and flirting outrageously with the courtiers. Meanwhile, Godfrey Breen was sent to the Tower under guard, and Sir William Cecil was dispatched to have a pointed discussion about loyalty and cooperation with Lord North.

Unusually, Catrin found herself too weary to walk. She and Lucy settled under the shade of a rustling oak tree instead and watched people chatter and laugh as they moved about the garden. "This is the longest time I have been still in weeks," Catrin said, and leaned back against the trunk. "And it will not last, for the queen is determined to progress to New Hall tomorrow."

Lucy sent her a sidelong glance. "So you intend to stay with the court?"

Catrin brushed her fingers over the soft petals of a forget-me-not. "Where else would I go?"

"You seemed to be longing for Ashbourne a few days ago."

"I was," Catrin said, and was surprised all over again. "For a few minutes, the troubles of running an estate seemed far less than the troubles of being a lady of the bedchamber. But common sense soon reasserted itself."

Lucy smiled. "And you realised they are much the same?"

"All troubles are troubles, be they great or small." Catrin tilted her head back so she could watch the dappled sunlight through the leaves. "And I am a countess, whether I am there or here. I will always have work to do."

"Yes, you will. As a lady of the bedchamber, the owner of an estate, a courtier —" Lucy suddenly turned bright pink — "and, perhaps, a wee baby's godmother."

Catrin sat bolt upright. "Lucy! Are you —"

"Tush! I do not want everyone to know; it is very early as yet." Lucy took Catrin's hand and squeezed. "But I hope so. I do hope so."

Catrin drew her friend into a fierce hug. "As do I."

A NOTE TO THE READER

First the facts, then the fiction. It is true that Queen Elizabeth went on long journeys every summer if she could, and it's also true that these progresses were not at all popular with her court. Sir William Cecil and Lord Robert Dudley tried to convince her not to go every year, but the queen felt that the connection she made with her people was worth the discomfort and confusion. And perhaps it was. A lot of the legends of 'Gloriana' that made Elizabeth so beloved took root during these progresses, such as the time she stood up in defence of some 'ferocious women' against the 'sour preachers' who wanted to cancel the Hock Tuesday play.

You can find out more about the progresses and their purpose in Mary Hill Cole's seminal work, delightfully entitled *The Portable Queen*. However, there isn't a lot of information on the 1561 progress, because there aren't very many records left. All we really have is an itinerary, which I followed as closely as possible. Lord North and Sir William Petre were actual hosts, and the queen did sometimes leave her host to have dinner with another courtier elsewhere, which in this case was Sir William Cecil, at the home he called the Strand.

Now the fiction. Much of the poetry attributed to Sir Thomas Wyatt in this book was actually written by him, including a poem about a woman called 'Brunet' which does seem to be about a hopeless love he had for a woman who rocked the entire kingdom, almost certainly Anne Boleyn. However, the letters between the two of them mentioned in this story never existed.

Speculation abounds that they had a relationship, but there is no proof of it (see the great study of Thomas Wyatt called *Graven with Diamonds* by Nicola Shulman for more information).

And speaking of letters, the letter from Anne Boleyn to King Henry mentioned in this story does exist, and does date to the right era. It was found amongst Thomas Cromwell's papers. However, no one knows if Anne really wrote it or if Henry ever saw it. Queen Elizabeth may have seen it, but that too is not certain.

Now let's address the elephant in the room: what happens to Queen Elizabeth I at the end of the book probably never happened. If it had, I'm sure there would be some record of it. However, it was while she was on progress that she was at her most vulnerable to this sort of event, especially since she had a tendency to change her itinerary on a whim and sometimes ended up in a home that hadn't been thoroughly prepared or checked. Also, she often chose hosts whose loyalty was questionable due to their political or religious beliefs, putting her in more danger still. It isn't outside the realm of possibility that someone would have come up with the scheme outlined here in the last few chapters.

And finally ... the background characters. I have reduced the number of people around the queen by at least one hundred, simply because it is too cumbersome to have so many characters in a story. There were maids of honour on the progress in 1561, all of whom I cut out of this story, and hundreds of courtiers and their servants. A lady of Catrin's status had the right to travel with up to seventeen servants, but I chose to have her travel with only the other ladies for company to make the plot move along more smoothly. It's all about the story for Catrin — like me, she just wants to know what happens next.

I hope you enjoyed reading this novel, and thank you for choosing it. If you enjoyed it, please tell all your friends, and post a review on **Amazon** and **Goodreads**. Reviews are really important for authors, so it would be much appreciated.

Readers can connect with me **on Facebook (Angela Ranson Author)** and through **my website (Angela Ranson Author)**, which includes not only updates on the Catrin Surovell series but humorous thoughts on writing, reading and Tudor history.

Angela Ranson

Sapere Books is an exciting new publisher of brilliant fiction and popular history.

To find out more about our latest releases and our monthly bargain books visit our website: **saperebooks.com**

www.ingramcontent.com/pod-product-compliance
Lightning Source LLC
Chambersburg PA
CBHW021532250626
47154CB00006BA/2081